Under the Blood Red Sky

By

Stephen Knight

Published by Stephen Knight.

First published in Great Britain in 2021 by
Stephen Knight
43 Emma Place
Plymouth
PL1 3QT

Printed and bound by Amazon PLC.

Disclaimer

About the Book

Detective Inspector Thorpe is due for retirement but takes on one last case before hanging up his gloves which turns out to be his hardest to date. There is a serial killer on the loose in Plymouth and the surrounding area which both he and Detective Sergeant Carter are finding hard to track down.

When an International author Byron Maddocks is murdered, the Sun newspaper send Investigative Reporter and personal friend of the author Jack Dempsey to try and make sense of the death and give the newspaper the story of a lifetime.

Set-in modern-day Plymouth, this explosive thriller takes us through the lives of both the Police Officers and the serial killer ending in a thrilling battle of cat and mouse resulting in a twist in the ending setting the question, *'Do you really know who your neighbour is?'*

About the Author

Thriller 'UNDER THE BLOOD RED SKY' is the third novel from Devon author Stephen Knight who lives in Britain's Ocean City of Plymouth, UK and has done for most of his life. As well as being an Author, he is a professional musician and singer/songwriter, playing percussion from the age of ten as well as keyboards and guitar.

Check out his Author Website where there are links to buy his books and eBooks.:

www.stephensamuelknight.co.uk

Dedicated to

My Son Gareth, for all his hard work and dedication in finding the right path to follow.

Chapter 1

Michael Carter felt oppressed. His dog Oreo, a rough and tough black Staffordshire Bull Terrier had looked at him and jumped for joy at the sight of her 'Daddy' as he came home from work. She then immediately indicated that she wanted to go for a walk, positioning herself beside the front door with her toy rope in her mouth. He looked at his canine friend with a smile and widened eyes, realising that he wasn't going to be able to eat his dinner prior to taking her down to Radford Park, where he knew she would run around the whole park enjoying her freedom.

"Is that you, Mike?"

"Yes, darling. But guess what?" He replied with humour in his voice to his wife who he could tell was in the lounge from the direction of her voice. She had jumped to her feet in order that she could see him before he disappeared with his dog.

Appearing in the doorway, she looked at her husband, who instantly walked over to kiss her on the cheek. "You love that dog more than me," she said with a smile.

"I know," Mike replied as he decided to agree with the love of his life. "If only she had been around all those years ago." He smiled at Emma, telling himself that he didn't know how she put up with him sometimes, what with the long working hours and, at times, the interruption of social and family events when he was needed urgently. The joys of being a detective, he told himself on many an occasion.

Emma returned the kiss and reached over to the coat hook, grabbing Oreo's lead that was hanging there with the coats. "I'll warm your curry up in the oven whilst you are gone."

"Thanks darling. What would I do without you?"

"Well, you wouldn't live on microwave meals," she replied. "You don't like microwaves." He didn't. Ever since the day he had heard from a Police Constable about a case of animal cruelty. An older woman had taken her dog out in the pouring rain. When she returned, the dog was wet and cold, so she decided to dry him off by putting him in the microwave oven that her son had bought her. The little Chihuahua had exploded after being on the turntable for five minutes. The animal lovers in the station wondered how stupid someone could be. But it was a talking point for months.

"Come on then," Mike said, looking at the doggie. "Let's go and wear you out!" He glanced quickly at his lovely wife and said, "I won't be long."

"Yes, you will," Emma replied, folding her arms as he opened the door and escaped back outside to the garden. She knew that when Mike went out with the dog he would think and reflect on the day. It usually calmed him and let him get some much-needed sleep without being disturbed by thoughts that would otherwise keep his mind active and preventing him from having a good night's sleep. She sometimes wondered how he got through the days what with all the stories he used to tell her and over the years she had become a good listener. Emma watched him walk down the driveway and head to the left to walk the 500m or so where the entrance to the park was.

Only a few minutes in as the pair were walking up to the top of the incline in Radford Park Road, Oreo started to whine, and even though it wasn't pitch black yet, Mike couldn't see very-far ahead of him, putting his vision down to tired eyes. The black princess continued to show concern at something. Suddenly, Mike noticed a young child stood on the pavement, looking around as though he was waiting for someone, but there didn't seem to be any adults around him. What was worse, the child was only wearing a pair of underpants. Had he gotten out of his house without his parents noticing? Mike approached him cautiously, and as he got closer to the boy, slowed, and then leaned down to be level height with him.

"Hi there. What are you doing out at this time of night?" He looked at the child who was nervously turning his head left and right as though he was looking for someone, whilst grasping his teddy bear in his hands. Mike took off his coat and wrapped it around the boy. He could tell something was wrong. "Is that warmer? My name is Mike. I am a Policeman," he said to the boy. "I bet a big lad like you can tell me your name?" The boy was upset, disturbed by the surroundings, scratching his left arm with his right hand whilst continuing to hold the teddy bear. "Where are your Mummy and Daddy?"

The boy looked at Oreo, who was as concerned as his master about the boy. Oreo nudged her head under the boys hand. In return he stopped looking around and started to smooth her. "Dog," he said.

"Yes, that's right," Mike replied. "She likes you! Her name is Oreo. Do you have a doggie?"

He shook his head in between briefly looking at what was a stranger in his eye, and the dog. Pointing at the dog he said as clearly as he could, "Oreo!" who in return heard her name and became even more alert to the needs of the boy, rubbing her head against him which was the attention that both of them needed.

"Oreo would love to know your name. Do you think you can tell her?"

He looked at the Detective, and then back to the dog, hesitating in his childhood state as he didn't know who to trust at that moment in time. "Max!" he said sharply.

"Well Max. Oreo here wants to go to your house to play! Would you like that?" The off-duty officer thought he would try everything in his negotiating skills to try and get the boy to trust him and find out where he lived. "Do you think you can show her the way?" He waited for a reply, but Max was too taken aback by something. That something, Mike told himself, was worrying for him, something big. Someone must know the boy. Right now, he could see the boy was freezing cold. "Max, I'm going to take you to Oreo's house, and she will help you to get warm. Is that okay?" The boy nodded in agreement and then raised his arms up as though he was expecting Mike to carry him, which he was going to do in any case. He picked little Max up, who cuddled into his shoulder, ensured the coat was wrapped tightly, and then started walking back the way he came. The dog lead the way and in no time they were back at the front door, Oreo barking for someone to let them in as Mike fumbled for his front door keys, finding it difficult to do so with one free hand which just happened to be on the opposite side to the one that the pocket containing the keys was on.

Emma peeked through the small window and then opened the door. "I thought I heard the dog barking," she said concerningly and then noticed that her husband had a visitor in his arms. "Who is this little fella?"

"We found him up at the top, no clothes on, just standing there. He is quite withdrawn. All I got out of him was his first name. Max."

"Max?" Emma asked as she reached up to take the lad down from her husband's shoulder. He had fallen asleep and was dead weight for the short distance, and as she took the responsibility of him, she could tell that her husband was glad to get the life back into his shoulder and arm. She took him inside and removed the coat that, although kept him warm, the boy appeared to be lost in. Mike appeared behind her and closed the door.

"Is he alright?" Mike asked, watching his wife check him over.

"Poor lad is knackered," she said in reply. "He is cold as well. I think we have some of Thomas' old clothes that he has grown out of up in a bag in the junk cupboard. They should be okay for now."

Mike disappeared upstairs to 'the junk cupboard' as it had been known by all the family, mainly because everyone threw their unwanted items in there in no specific order. On the way to the cupboard, he checked on Thomas, their six-year-old son who was fast asleep in his room. Mike realised the boy had worn himself out at school, came home and raided the refrigerator for orange juice and snacks and then waited for his Mother to shout at him for throwing his school clothes on the floor having to take his hand-held games console away from him to make sure he did it.

Downstairs, Emma wiped the dirty face of the young boy. She knew that she had seen him somewhere before, but she couldn't remember where. It wouldn't have been at the toddlers group that she used to take Thomas to at the Church hall because there was quite an age difference between the two. Suddenly it hit her. "Darling!" she shouted as her husband came into view at the top of the stairs with a carrier bag in hand.

He started walking back down the stairs. "Yes, babes. What's up?"

"I know whose boy Max is," she said. "It's Pete Horgan's boy. We met him at the Police children's Christmas party."

"Are you sure?"

"Definitely. They live just up the road. I remember his wife Jane saying that it was pretty convenient for them because all the facilities were close." Emma had that look on her face indicating that she was trying to remember more about their conversation, even though it was last December. "That's right. They live in that row of houses this side of the Drake's Drum! I remember her saying about the noise from the pub was the only downside."

The man was impressed at his wife's memory, thinking that sometimes he wishes his worked at the same rate, not giving himself any credit for the fact that he was tired at this moment in time. "I'm going to drive up there and make some enquiries with the neighbours darling. I need you to call it in for me about finding little Max."

"Okay," Emma replied. "Just be careful in case there is something wrong."

"I will. Don't worry." He shook Max's hand to make him aware of what he was about to say. "And you little man. I'm going to tell your Mummy and Daddy that you are safe." Instantly, Max began to cry with worry, as though he would be in big trouble with his parent's for going out of the house. He was frightened and began to shake and scream.

Emma found it hard to hold the boy as he started becoming hysterical, kicking, and waving his hands as he screamed as though he were having a childhood tantrum. "Max, calm down baby. Max, please!" Emma pulled him into her, holding him tight to give him the feeling of security. "You go, love," she said whilst looking briefly at her husband. "He will be okay."

Mike Carter frowned as he left juggling his car keys in his hand. He still had that feeling that something wasn't quite right. Driving at some speed to the left and up the incline that he had previously walked up, he saw no one. No worried parents, no one searching. No Police cars. He indicated and pulled over to the right exactly where his wife had told him, then looked at his watch. 2215 hrs. In his experience, some people weren't the most receptive at being woken up at this time of evening and most of the people around this area were either retired or thinking about retiring. He had his warrant card which he would show. Never off duty, he thought to himself as he stood looking at every one of the row of houses trying to pick out anything like an open door or window where Max could have escaped. Some of the houses still showed signs of life, with lights beaming through gaps in their curtains and blinds like sunlight echoing through the clouds during the day. He walked down the steps and headed to the nearest house with lights on, then banged the door knocker whilst getting his warrant card out ready.

"Who is it?" came the elderly voice from behind the door.

"Police," Mike replied, holding the card up to the arched windows at the top of the door for the occupant to see. The door rattled as it was unlocked and finally opened. "Hello, Sir. Detective Sergeant Carter. I was wondering if you could help me. I am looking for the residence of the Horgan's. Pete and Jane. I believe Pete is also a Police Officer."

"Who is it, dear?" asked a voice from the room to the left up the hallway.

"Police. They are trying to find out where the …." The old man had forgotten the name already.

"Horgan's."

"The Horgan's live," the older man continued. "Do you know, love? I don't know them."

"Yes," the female voice answered as the lady appeared from the doorway, immediately noticing the tall well-dressed man stood in the porch and brushing past her husband to get closer to the door. "Go to the right. It's the second house in. Lovely couple. Two great children."

"Thank you," Mike replied. "Do you know the children's names?" He looked at the woman as she frowned and put her forefinger to her lip as though it was going to help her remember. "Is one of them called Max?"

The old lady became alert again, thankful that she had been prompted. "Yes, Max. That's it. I saw them in the newsagents just yesterday. Is everything okay with them?"

He didn't want to give them any more information as he didn't exactly know just what the circumstances were at this moment in time. It could be quite innocent. Max could have just walked out of the door. But it was also most unusual. "Yes, I just need to speak to Pete." He smiled at both of them "Well thank you for the information. It was nice meeting you."

"You too," the man said, closing the door behind DS Carter.

Mike walked back up the path and turned to the right, arriving the top of the Horgan's path in no time at all. The first thing he noticed was that there were no lights on. They could have gone to bed, he told himself. Many an occasion when his child was younger, he and Emma had nodded off and then gone to bed early. He knew what it was like to have kids. He walked down towards the front door, on his way pulling out a pair of disposable gloves from his trouser pocket and quickly putting them on. The front door was locked. Good sign, he thought. But the side gate was open. It could have been where Max had escaped from. Something was telling him to call for back up, but he didn't want to look the fool if the situation turned out to be nothing more than a child wandering. He slowly walked around the side to the back garden, which struggled for light with only the moon shining in the distant, but Mike managed to see that the patio door was partially open, although the whole house was in total darkness. "Police! Hello. Is anybody in?"

No reply. No movement. They hadn't heard him. Some people are known to wear earmuffs to bed. He dismissed this theory immediately as the reminder that the Horgan's had two young children to contend with came back into his tired mind. "This is the Police. Come down with your hands where I can see them!" He reached over to the left and flicked the light switch on which lit up the dining room which adjoined the lounge through an archway. There was nothing out of place. No sign of a struggle. The kitchen entrance was to his right, and he quickly looked there. The same situation, no sign of struggle. Still, Mike didn't drop his guard, mainly because he had attended incidents like this before, a bit like the movie ending and suddenly the slasher comes alive at the last minute.

Another light switch. The lounge came alive this time. Mike Carter became worried. The flat screen television on the wall was damaged. The screen was smashed as though something had been thrown at it. He looked around for any objects that might have been used to do the damage, but nothing stood out. Then he stood still and listened for any sounds that may be coming from other parts of the house. Nothing, he couldn't hear a thing inside, only the sounds of the traffic from the busy road outside. He stepped through into the hallway, front door on his left and the passageway back to the kitchen on his right. The bottom of the stairs right in front of him. He moved forward cautiously and looked up the stairs, and putting his back to the wall, he slowly climbed each stair, looking upwards and then forwards as he reached the higher ones.   DS Carter reached for his mobile phone and used his speed dial to call the crime in as he noticed blood on the door of the main bedroom. The phone was answered quickly.

"DS Ayres," the voice on the other end responded.

"Jon, it's Mike."

"I thought you had gone home, Mike?" a surprised DS Ayres replied.

"I need back up at the home of PC Horgan, number 4 Radford Park Road. You had better bring CID as well." Mike continued slowly up the last few stairs as he spoke and was hoping that someone was still alive.

"Everything alright, Mike?"

"We have blood. Lots of it," Carter responded seriously.

"Right, we are on our way."

The telephone went silent, and Mike Carter replaced it into his pocket just in case he had to use both his hands to protect himself in any way. He was now at the top of the stairs, the bathroom directly in front of him and he quickly peeked in to check for bodies, or even someone hiding. There was no one or nothing suspicious there. The next door was ajar but not fully. Mike pushed it slowly and it creaked open as he stepped inside. He guessed that this must be Max's bedroom with the walls echoing pictures of Paw Patrol and a duvet cover with the same. He looked up to the wall dividing Max's room from the one next door. There were two holes in the wall which looked like bullet holes. He shifted his body over the cuddly toys that littered the floor and went back onto the landing, checking down the stairs by looking over the bannister. Then he looked at the blood stains on the door of the second bedroom, which he took to be the parents room. It had run down the door and stained the carpet underneath, the splatter pattern showing that at one point it had been opened inwards. Slowly pushing the door open to the right, he saw what he was hoping that he didn't want to see. On the floor there were two bodies lying face down with their heads in the direction away from the door. Blood was oozing out of wounds to the back of the head of each, and Mike could see that it was a man and a woman. He didn't go any further because he didn't want to contaminate the crime scene, but he put his hand over his mouth and made a near silent gasp whilst shaking his head. It was one of their own. This was a serving Police Officer. He went back downstairs to secure the crime scene.

Outside, Mike Carter took a deep breath and then grabbed his mobile phone from his pocket once more in order that he could let Emma know that he would be late.

"Hi darling," she responded. "What's happening?"

"Bad news, babes. The parents are both dead. It looks like they have been shot," her husband replied, his voice showing shock and concern which Emma heard in his tone.

"Are you sure that you are ok?"

"Yes, yes," he answered before hesitating. "Did you call the Police about Max?"

Emma looked at the boy from outside the spare room. She had managed to get him to sleep by letting him have one of Thomas' cuddly toys to cuddle after a drink of warm milk. Max sucked his thumb and was sleeping within minutes. "Yes, I called them. I guess they will bring Social Services. He is sleeping now. What do I do?"

"If they agree, let him sleep. They will have trouble finding a foster family at this time of night." Mike looked out for any Police Units that might be arriving, thinking that it shouldn't take the Uniformed guys long to arrive at least. "I'm going to be late. If the unit that comes to you is unaware of what I have told you, let them know."

"Okay," Emma replied. "Keep me informed."

"Will do, babes. Speak soon," he replied as he saw the flashing blue lights at the top of the steps leading up to the road. Several uniformed officers appeared and looked around to see which house it was, and the Sergeant noticed Mike standing outside the Horgan's front door.

"DS Carter?" the voice shouted as the officers descended the steps.

"Yes, that's me," Mike replied, warrant card ready to be inspected for confirmation even though some of the officers recognised him immediately. "It's not a pretty sight, Sergeant."

"SOCO are on their way from Charles Cross," PS Payton responded with some authority in his voice. "You have obviously been inside?"

"Yes, I have. Rear patio door was ajar, and the house was in the dark. My wife is looking after the little boy after I found him wandering around in the street." He watched the uniformed Sergeant wave over to one of his PC's.

"PC Rayborn, can you start securing the area for me please?"

"Yes Sergeant, will do," answered the young Constable.

"Sorry about that," Sergeant Payton continued and giving his attention once again to DS Carter. "Any dead?"

"Two that I saw, one male, one female. Gunshots to the head. You know the owner of this house is a Police Officer, don't you?"

Sergeant Payton shook his head. "No, I didn't. Is it anyone I might know?"

"PC Peter Horgan. I'm not sure but I think he is at Plymstock Police Station." Mike knew that the chances of their paths crossing whilst being at different stations were quite remote unless PC Horgan had done a training course or worked overtime at Charles Cross.

"I don't know the name," Sergeant Payton said whilst looking around to check that his Officers were following the protocol for a murder scene. He then saw a van appear and park up behind the Police vehicles. "Looks like SOCO are here," he said.

Mike Carter looked up and also saw his two colleagues DS Ayres and ADC Gibbons, who was a new recruit to CID coming from Uniform at Crownhill Police Station. "CID have arrived as well." He could see the CID Officers being held up by the two scene of crime officers who were dragging their kit down the steep steps, and as they all reached the bottom, both of his colleagues showed their warrant cards to the PC securing the taped area. Mike walked forward. "Hello Jon," he said, shaking his colleagues hand.

"ADC Gibbons, Sergeant," the young officer said introducing himself politely.

"In at the deep end then?" Mike replied.

"He certainly is," Jon Ayres replied, acknowledging both DS Carter and the younger trainee. "Did you look any further after seeing the blood you mentioned to me?"

"Yes. We have two bodies. To me it looks like a professional execution style killing. Both the male and the female looked like they had been made to get on their knees before being shot in the back of the head." DS Carter looked towards the front door as SOCO bundled their way in and started ascending the stairs.

"Are you okay to stay, Mike? I'm going to need a statement from you at some point."

"I'll stay for a while," DS Carter replied. "If that's alright with you?"

"Of course. We will have to wait for SOCO to finish before we get a peek at the scene."

"There's something else. This was all started by Pete Horgan's young lad Max who I found walking around our road with just his pants on. He is asleep at mine at the moment. Emma has put him in the spare room." The three started to stroll towards the front door.

DS Ayres held his hand to his chin, his normal thinking position. "So, he may have escaped the scene? He may have seen what happened, who knows? Why else would the boy be outside?"

"That's a possibility I suppose," DS Carter replied. "He may be our only witness."

They stopped and both overheard PS Layton giving instructions to his officers to conduct house to house enquiries. The two Detectives continued talking whilst DS Ayres' trainee listened, backs to the front door as they surveyed the action going on around them. Nosey neighbours started to gather at the barriers wondering just what was going on which was usually the case. Carter's boss used to call them 'Vampires' because they were hoping that the scene was bloodthirsty. All that was needed now were the usual white-lightning drinking teenagers who usually congregated outside the shops and the pub. That gave DS Carter an idea. They saw or heard something?

"Jon. Perhaps we need to keep an eye on the gathering crowd and see if anyone of them saw anything?" DS Carter was always one step ahead of everyone else in the force, which was why DI Thorpe liked to be paired with him. He also took criticism, whilst challenging situations no matter what rank suggested them.

"That's a good idea," replied DS Ayres. "If there were gunshots, they could have been misconstrued as the backfire from a motorcycle or something." DS Ayres waved his hand to try and get PS Layton's attention who was busy managing the tasks of his section. He must have seen Jon Ayres because he started to walk over towards the two detectives.

"Anything that needs doing, DS Ayres? We have the cordon up at a safe distance and house to house enquiries are in full swing. I am going to arrange a fingertip search for potential evidence as soon as."

DS Ayres nodded towards the gathering at the top of the steps. "In your opinion, is it worth talking to the crowd?"

PS Layton turned and looked. "Savages, the lot of them," he replied jokingly as he shook his head. "They gathered quickly. There was only one or two just now."

"Might be worth speaking to the teenagers as well," DS Carter said politely in a suggestive tone. He didn't want to teach a granny to suck eggs and, officially was not the scene commander.

"That's no problem," PS Layton agreed. "I'll will get on to that ASAP before they disperse." He walked off towards two of his uniformed officers who were returning their notes on the house-to-house enquiries that had given some potential information.

"Take ADC Gibbons with you. He can make a start," Jon Ayres said, nodding at his trainee. "Make sure you delve deep for any info," he said to ADC Gibbons.

"I will," the young detective replied.

Suddenly from behind the two Detective Sergeants, a white figure appeared, covered in the Forensic Service standard issue Tyvek suit. "You two gentlemen can come in now," SFO Watkins said, surprising the two with his stealth arrival behind them. "I have some bad news."

DS Carter guessed what that news could be, as he suddenly remembered his wife Emma saying that the Horgan's had two children. One was accounted for. "What is the bad news?" he asked in reply. "Don't tell me there is a third body?"

"I'm afraid so. It looks like whoever did this executed the parents and then went after the children. The whole family was the target." SFO Watkins led the two Detectives up the stairs whilst continuing to talk. "The gunman knew what they were doing. It was a very professional hit with two rounds in the torso and one in the head on each."

"What even the child?" DS Ayres enquired as they all reached the landing and SFO Watkins stood outside the third bedroom and directed the two detectives inside.

"Take a look for yourself," the forensic officer said. "It's not a pretty sight. Whoever did this must have no conscience whatsoever. Who in their right mind would kill a baby in such a way?" His eyes looked away. He didn't care what the two detectives would think of him for having a tear in his eye because at the end of the day he was only human, he thought to himself.

DS Ayres and DS Carter didn't spend long looking at the child. The head had exploded open on impact from the bullet hitting the small cranial forehead, and there was just blood and the discharge from the head everywhere. They both had children themselves and could put themselves in the role of parent if it were to happen to them. DS Carter looked at his colleague. "I had better get home, Jon. I'm thinking of that young lad who has just lost his family all in one go."

"Okay, Mike. I'll come around tomorrow and take a statement from you and Emma." He patted DS Carter on the shoulder as a show of support for the tragic circumstance as he walked back down the stairs. The death of the child had hit him hard, and he knew from experience that the vision of the baby in his cot would stay with him for a long time.

Mike Carter went up to his car and jumped in the driver's seat. But he didn't switch on the engine. He put both hands on the top of the steering wheel and rested his head on them closing his eyes. He could feel himself choking back the tears. He stayed there for a few minutes and then started the engine and headed home.

Chapter 2

The Waterstone's store in the Drake Circus Shopping Centre was close to breaking point and the Manager was thinking of putting a member of staff on the door to control the influx of people, the majority of them queueing for a book signing by international author Byron Maddocks. His crime thrillers had given him fame and fortune as a Devon based author with his latest, *'Where the wind blows east'* already having record advanced sales guaranteed to give him *'Bestseller'* status on this its launch day.

Byron looked down the queue. There were still a lot of fans waiting. Normally they wanted to chat about his books as well, which he never turned down the chat, but had the skill to move them on without it sounding pedantic. They were his bread and butter. Without them, he wouldn't get the royalties for the books and eBooks that were sold in their thousands. Many of the customers he had seen at the signing of previous books, and he never forgot a face which looked good to them. It also helped him know his audience.

"Mr Maddocks. What can I say? How are you going to follow up your last fantastic novel?" The fan stood in front of the table. "Can you sign it to Jeremy?"

"I can," Byron replied. "I remember you from the last time I was here. You must be a fan?"

"Well, I don't want to sound too *'Misery,'* but yes, I am a big fan," Jeremy replied, sounding quite infatuated in the tone of his voice. "I particularly like the way that you make the murders seem all so real."

The author briefly looked at him, pausing from writing inside the front cover because he felt there was something not right with his fan, a learning disability. Jeremy gave him the chills just being there, but then, with his wild imagination, most people like Jeremy made him feel that way in any case. Who knows, he would use his characterisation in a future novel. "Well thank you for buying my books, Jeremy. Have you signed up for the newsletter? It keeps you informed of everything including the release dates."

"Oh yes," Jeremy replied staring at Byron with wide piercing eyes. "I get that. Right, home to read this one. I hope it is good." He just walked off without saying any more, as though he knew that Byron was indirectly dismissing him.

"That was weird," he mentioned as the next customer came to the table. "It takes all sorts, I suppose." He watched Jeremy pay for the book and then leave the store. Then he diverted his attention back to the lady in front of him. "Right. Any message?"

"How about 'I love you Gloria. Byron' and lots of kisses?"

Byron wanted to shake his head, and inside his thoughts were giving him the impression that all the nutjobs were out in Plymouth today. But not to disappoint, he did as the lady requested. "There we go, Gloria. Enjoy!" As she walked away, he realised that this was going to be a long day. All he wanted was a quiet life which was one of the reasons he had locked himself away in a little village called Sheepstor on the edge of the Dartmoor National Park. He found that the serenity and peace gave him the inspiration for quite the opposite in his novels. The only problem with living in such as small community was that everyone knew your business. But no one had guessed that he was the author Byron Maddocks as yet, although

Byron was his middle name in reality, so if he ever did go to church or to the neighbourhood meetings, he would use his first name David. He tried wherever possible to keep himself to himself and escape the meetings. He remembered that at one meeting they decided to buy a new tea set for the church kitchen. They then spent 45 minutes discussing what colour the tea set should be and in the end decided on white. It drove him wild that evening.

He loved the area, though. Sheepstor was right above his place, and the grandeur of Burrator Reservoir a short walk away. Yes, in the summer it was plagued by tourists and day trippers, but on those days he stayed in and drafted his novels. He did laugh in the church coffee shop one day when he was there. There was a copy of his second novel '*Corrupt*' on the second-hand bookstand for sale at 50p. Still, no one had put two and two together to make four and seen that he was the author. Who knows? One day, he thought, although he often wondered what they thought he did for a living because most of the population of the village were either successful businessmen or retired. No one had ever asked him. Even in the winter, when the snow was heavy and most of the villagers complained about being snowed in. He appeared to be the only one who was glad to be snowed in because he never had any excuse for procrastination. Yes, living there was heaven in itself.

"Hey Mr. Maddocks. Is there going to be a sequel to your last masterpiece '*See you in Heaven*'? asked the young man in front of him. "It's bloody good, but you left it hanging at the end!"

Byron remembered this young man. Always one of the first to get his new books. He pointed his finger, looking slightly unsure when he tried to remember his name but hesitated and then became pleased with himself and he mentioned, "Callum?"

"You remembered!" Young Callum said joyfully.

"How could I forget my number one young reader?" Byron even knew what he would want written in his book but checked with him first. "Same as normal?"

"Yes please Mr. Maddocks. My family laugh because I have the same written in all your books. My brother reckons I sign them myself!"

Byron wrote whilst saying softly, "Enjoy the book Callum. Best wishes Byron." He also knew that it had to be in a specific place on the back of the front cover. He passed the book to the lad, and then commented, "In reply to your question, I'm going to keep you in suspense!"

"Nooooooo!" Callum said as he laughed, waved his hand, and walked off.

The afternoon went very quickly and thankfully one of the staff kept plying him with skinny lattes from the local coffee shop, which after all the talking, Byron was glad of. It had been a good sale day and he was pleased with the outcome and was glad when the Manageress lowered the shutter on the front door signalling that the store was now closed.

"I never want to sign my name ever again," he said as the Manageress come over to check how their guest was.

"Don't say that," she replied demandingly. "We always have a good day when you are here signing your books. Queue out the door, footfall triples, takings are extremely high. It's nice to see that people still read real books rather than eBooks."

"I'm glad for you in these difficult trading times," Byron replied as he started to clear the desk that he had been at for the past few hours. He stood up and stretched his weary legs, standing up on his tiptoes and reaching his arms above his head. "Time to go home!" Then something caught his eye outside the store as he peered out of the large display window. Jeremy was stood opposite the store, swaying from side to side on each leg and his eyes staring directly at Byron, who in return broke off the mutual eye contact knowing that it was too late to pretend that he hadn't seen him.

Jenny noticed him staring out of the window and then look down. She quickly looked behind her in the direction that he had been staring. "Everything alright, Byron?"

"Nothing I can't handle," he replied. "A fan." Byron nodded in the direction of the loner Jeremy who hadn't made any movement to conceal his obsessive stance. "Every time I have a book signing locally, he is there. He's a bit weird."

"We can ban him in future if you want?"

"It's not worth it," Byron said worryingly. "Although each time he seems to go that little further with the things he does."

The Manageress looked deeply concerned. "Like what? This is serious, Byron!"

He nodded. "Yes, I know. He has escorted me to my car before after a signing. Then on a different occasion I was going for a walk with a friend around Sutton Harbour, and he was there, of course he came over to me wanting to chat like he was my next-door neighbour."

"You really need to report this, Byron. It sounds like he is stalking you," Jenny mentioned as she continued to look back and forth towards Jeremy and Byron.

Byron nodded his head in agreement. "I know I should. The latest incident was in the Dunya Restaurant. My Publisher had come down to see me and discuss the marketing on the latest book. Suddenly, he was there having lunch at the same time. In the same restaurant. What made it worse, he ordered exactly the same as I did, even down to the coffee at the end of the meal." The author joined Jenny on looking back to see if the Stalker was still there. The thing was, at this moment in time, he wasn't actually doing anything wrong directly, even though stalking was an offense in itself. They would have to prove it was happening and considering that Jeremy had just purchased a signed copy of his book, the Police would just think he was an over-zealous fan.

"Do you want me to arrange for the shopping centre security staff to escort you to your car? You can use the staff entrance at the back of the shop."

Byron nodded, grasping his case tightly in his left hand. "That might be a clever idea. Thank you."

"Follow me," she said as she brushed past him and headed to the back office. "I wonder if that guy does this sort of thing to other visiting authors whom we have here for book signings."

"It may be quite innocent."

"Looks to me like its more than that, Byron. Infatuation comes to mind." Jenny opened the door to the manager's office. "I'll give security a call now. But you promise me you will call the Police when you get home?"

"I will. I promise."

Ten minutes later, two burley security officers arrived at the staff entrance. Jenny checked through to spyhole when they rang the bell before she let them in, and then they followed her back into her office in order that they could speak to Byron.

"You need escorting to your car, Sir?" asked the senior security officer, Marcus Powell. Ex-forces and well built, still in decent shape for his 40+ years and looked like he could handle himself.

"Yes, please," Byron replied.

"Jenny said something about a man stalking you?" Asked the second security man, Peter Morgan, who was slightly younger but had the agility that came with youth.

"Yes," Byron replied. "He is waiting outside the front entrance for me."

"Can we get him on the CCTV, Jenny?" Marcus asked importantly as though she needed to drop everything and do as she was asked immediately. Jenny took this just to be what he was used to doing in the army, so took no offense. She wheeled the office chair from one desk to another and started playing with the small pen like joystick that controlled the cameras in the store. She moved the front window camera around and tried to look for him in the position he was in ten minutes earlier outside the jewellers.

"He's moved," she said to Marcus. "He was stood there just now, staring at Byron."

"Okay," Marcus said confidently. "Let's get an archived history print up from about 15 minutes ago."

"Good idea," Jenny replied knowing exactly what he meant, searching the hard drive for a time minus fifteen minutes, and then pausing the camera. "There he is," she exclaimed, pointing at the screen. Marcus and Peter leaned over each shoulder and looked at his still.

"Okay," Marcus continued. "Can we screen shot that picture and email it up to me?"

"What are you planning to do?" Byron interrupted immediately. "Please don't ban him from the shopping centre. It could only make things worse if he thinks I have reported him. He follows me around enough now."

"How worse do you want it to get, Sir?" Marcus snapped. "This bloke. If he can't do it to you, he will do it to someone else. Experience tells me that they start at stalking, and it leads to something more sinister."

"I know that. Have you ever read any of my books?" Byron looked at the security guard. "This is just like a scene out of my last one, 'See you in heaven.'

Marcus shook his head. "Never read any of yours, Sir. I'm more of a James Herbert or Stephen King fan."

"If he has gone, Marcus, perhaps we can get the man up to his car," Peter mentioned calmly.

"You read my mind," Marcus replied intensely. Then turning to Byron, he asked, "Are you ready to go, Sir?"

Byron nodded, "Yes," he said before placing a hand on Jenny's shoulder and giving it a tap. "Thank you Jenny," he said sweetly.

Jenny spun around on the chair. "No problem, Byron. Anytime. And remember, call the Police!"

Byron nodded and followed Marcus out of the office towards the rear door where they had entered the store. Peter took up the rear as Jenny locked the door behind them. They scanned the area as they reached the car park level where he was parked which was still quite full. What they didn't see was the man sat in the blue Nissan Duke right at the end of the lane. Jeremy looked at them through his camera zoom and then clicked for pictures to be taken of what he was seeing.

"You are good to go," Marcus said through the open window, tapping the roof of Byron's car whilst continuing to look around the car park.

"Thank you for this," Byron said to Marcus and Peter before pushing the button to close the window. He followed the exit arrows towards the barriers, having been given a pass ticket by the security staff because he was working in Waterstones. The barrier opened as he inserted the ticket, and he drove through and down towards the main road.

He didn't see the car two behind him. Neither Marcus nor Peter clocked him even though he drove right past them. He had put a baseball cap on and taken his coat off showing a bright orange American football sports top. Jeremy Cornelius-Johnson. His mugshot would be on the wall of fame in the Drake Circus Shopping Centre control office now as banned from the Mall. But little did they know, he wasn't planning to return any time soon.

The traffic on the way home was busy and slow at times as Byron drove towards Yelverton. He was less worried now but knew that he would do as Jenny had asked and telephone the Police, although all he had to go on was a description and the man's first name. It was a long shot if anything which was making him question whether it was worth wasting the Police time. They would take the culprit in for questioning, give him a warning of some kind and he would be out to do it again the next time. At least the Security team at Drake Circus had a picture. Jeremy was known to Police, who knows?

Byron approached the Burrator Inn turning and headed right. It was quiet and the sun had disappeared below the horizon. He was being overly cautious. The incident with Jeremy had frightened him a little. He started watching some of the residents in Burrator Road wander out, putting the garbage out in their bins, some were feeding the local wildlife that regularly visited them as the birds, deer, foxes and even the hedgehogs knew that the people would feed them.

He took the turning for the Reservoir and was now feeling more relaxed, looking out over the valley as he drove. It was a partially cloudless sky which helped him see the beautiful view which was another of the reasons that he moved to this area. He could see the rocks of Sheepstor in the distance towering over the rest of the beauty. He didn't, however, take notice of the car behind him, although it was some distance behind, and slowing every so often trying not to be seen. Byron approached the viaduct at the Reservoir. It was a nice evening, so he decided to stop and take in the views from the edge of the water and the viaduct. He closed his car door and crossed the road, not even looking at the road because he listened for the sound of engines. There were none. Usually, this area was spoilt with tourists and people from the neighbouring towns and Cities, most of who just wanted to come and look at the water and then run around with their children up around Sheepstor or the Drakes Moat. He looked at the calmness of the reservoir with just a few ripples flirting with surface which appeared because of the ducks playing in the water on the other side. Byron took a deep breath of the freshened non-city air.

The car pulled up behind his as Byron was slowly strolling over to the middle of the viaduct and pushing himself up on his arms in order that he could look over the drop.

"Hello Byron. Fancy seeing you here!"

The author froze and turned around. It was Jeremy. "What are you doing here? You have to stop doing this, Jeremy."

"Doing what?" the fan asked quite calmly as though he was unaware of any wrongdoings of the way he was making Byron feel by being there. "I'm just out sightseeing."

"Following me around, what do you think?" Byron snapped in an upset and angry voice.

"I'm allowed to be here Byron. You don't own this part of the moors. Myfanwy's retreat is over in Sheepstor village."

Byron's eyes widened with fear. 'Myfanwy's Retreat' was the name of his house. How did this weirdo find that out? He was obviously following him, searching for him. Stalking him. He went to walk away back towards his car. "Right. This has gone far enough. I'm going home and I am going to call the Police."

"No, you're fucking not!" Jeremy snapped nastily.

Byron heard the click of a handgun being primed, and then stopped dead in his tracks, turning slowly to face the madman. He saw a handgun being pointed his way. "You need to put the gun down, Jeremy."

"You think I don't know what you have done, Byron? You went out of the back entrance to avoid me!" The anger was showing on his reddened face and his erratic behaviour became a huge cause for concern. "No doubt they will stop me going into your book signings from now on. They will probably stop me going into the mall full-stop!"

"Jeremy, this is not right. You are not like this," Byron mentioned calmly, trying to get him under control and willing to listen to reason.

"I am one of your biggest fans, Byron! You know that!" Jeremy screamed as he crunched up his eyes and face briefly whilst still aiming the revolver at his captive.

"Yes. Yes. You are right. And I do know that!" Byron said with fear in his voice. "But if you shoot me Jeremy, there will be no more signings. No more books."

"Don't patronise me!" the gunman snapped as he started to become more and more unstable in his characteristics. "Get down on your knees. NOW!"

"Jeremy, let's sort this out properly."

"Are you fucking deaf?" He snapped as he fired the gun, the bullet whisking past Byron's left ear. "Down on your knees!"

Byron was keeping an eye on the revolver. His head was telling him to make a run for it and was quickly weighing up the pros and cons of doing so. The stalker wouldn't listen to reason. He began to hope that one of the other residents of the area or even one of the tourists that he normally disliked would suddenly appear, but at the moment there was no such luck. "Jeremy, I'm sorry, okay? We can sort this."

The gunman turned his head slowly and stared at what he thought was a sorry state of a man who didn't want to know him. Then he aimed the revolver at Byron's head and pulled the trigger, He smiled as the back of his victim's head seemed to blow away, blood everywhere, and then the body flopped to the ground. He walked over and shot twice more in the torso, just to make sure that Byron Maddocks wouldn't be able to ridicule him again.

Jeremy Cornelius-Johnson stood over his prize and stared into the dead man's face. "Apology accepted," he snarled as he spat on the body. He put his revolver back in his pocket, ensuring that the safety catch was back on. Then he looked from side to side to ensure that no one had seen the execution. It was quiet. No one was around. He walked over, put one arm under Byron's dead-weighted legs and another under his shoulders, slightly struggling at first to lift his target. Once he had a secure grip, he walked slowly over to the wall of the reservoir where there was a high drop on the other side, and power-lifted the corpse onto the top of the wall, his voice letting out a sign of strength as the body rested on top of the wall. "Goodbye, Byron, he said psychotically as he gave the body a push and watched it disappear from sight. He steadily walked back to his car but stopped and walked back towards the wall to try and see where the body had landed. He couldn't see it anywhere, so walked back to his car, jumped in, and drove away.

The priest returned from his meeting at the Diocese offices in Exeter and headed back to his church in Sheepstor village. He had been there for three years now and felt the community spirit, increasing the number of people in his congregation ten-fold. He drove his car along the road to the dam, with his headlights showing the way now that it was getting dark. He saw the viaduct across the dam and turned right, ensuring first that there were no other vehicles about to cross from the other direction, which this time of evening was usually one of the villagers or a boy racer trying to beat the speed record for getting around the dam. Tonight, there was nothing.

As he moved forward, the light glared on something on the road, red in colour. He stopped his car and wound down his window, opening his door in order that more light would shine on the pattern. It looked like whatever had lost the blood had been dragged over towards the drop wall on the dam. He hoped it wasn't one of the moors animals. Quite often either a sheep or a pony was hit on the roads around the area, with the culprits either leaving the animal exactly where they had hit it, in some cases still barely alive and in pain. Sometimes they moved it off the road. Others they tried to dispose of the animal in a ditch or over a wall. He had never seen one thrown over the dam wall though but knew there was a first time for everything in life. He saw the blood splatter all over the road right along to the dam wall, up the wall and on top of it. Whatever it was that they disposed, it looked like it had been thrown over the drop side of the Burrator dam. He scanned the roadside. It didn't look like the impact of a car, he thought as he looked at the direction the blood was going. He saw other matter, what looked like hair, bone, and most of all, brain residue.

Grabbing his mobile telephone in panic, Father Reed dialled 999. "Police please!" he demanded as he looked in his rear-view mirror and saw the parked car at the edge of the road on the other side of the entrance to the viaduct. He turned his head to get a better view, then realised that he recognised the car. "Lord, no!"

Chapter 3

Father Reed tried wherever possible to secure the crime scene and was lucky that the area didn't attract many tourists that late in the evening. He didn't move his car, mainly because he had driven directly into the blood on the road, but he had telephoned his Church Wardens, James, and Michelle Buckley, to come and help him, explaining what he had found, and both brought their own cars to assist in stopping traffic. James drove the opposite way around the circumference of the reservoir so as not to disrupt the scene. Then he sealed the entrance with his car. His wife, accompanied by their teenage son Jordan, parked her car sideways in a prominent position where they could easily be seen by any oncoming traffic, and placed the warning signs from their European car kit on the road.

Father Reed walked over towards James Car as he got out of the driver's side. "Terrible, terrible business James," he said. "I'm not sure what has happened, but Byron's car is there, and on the crossing there is just so much blood."

"That is strange," James replied looking over at Byron's car. "Have you looked in his car?"

"No," the priest said shaking his head. "I have already driven into the crime scene. I want to leave anything else as pure as possible." He shook his head, and his eyes started to fill with tears. "This is such a shock."

"Well, it looks like the Police are on their way by the looks over it." James nodded towards the flashing blue lights appearing over the moorland from the direction of Burrator Road, which made it look like a scene from 'Close Encounters' if it were not for the sirens accompanying them.

"I called them nearly an hour ago."

"They have probably had to come from Plymouth. Most of the others are only part-time stations these days." He saw them coming closer and jumped back into his car. "I had better move for them."

Three marked Police cars screeched to a halt where James had moments before been parked, and the sirens were turned off, but the lights remained as an alert. Police Sergeant George Bickford stepped out of the passenger side of his vehicle which was driven by his long-term colleague Police Constable Brian Ferrell. The Sergeant was old school in the job, someone that the top brass thought was ready to retire in order that they could get the new, younger blood into the Sergeants position. At 54, Bickford had seen it all, and his old style of handling people produced an excellent success rate. He also worked with offenders to get them out of the vicious circle that they were in. He assisted in the set-up of training workshops in Car mechanics, which were usually attended by the young car thieves, and Painting/Decorating/Plastering workshops in conjunction with a local charity.

Bickford saw the priest and walked towards him. "Father Reed?"

"Yes, that's right. I guess the dog collar gave it away?" He replied calmly trying to make light of the situation.

"I am Sergeant Bickford from Crownhill Police Station. I believe that you have found blood?"

"I was driving home when my headlights reacted on the pool of blood. Shall we go and look?"

35

"Yes," the Officer said walking slowly over towards the Father's car. "I guess this is yours?"

"I didn't move it just in case. I drove right into the crime scene."

"Good call," PS Bickford answered, looking at the trail of blood. He turned his head slightly to speak to his colleague who was behind him. "Brian, we are going to need CID and SOCO down here immediately."

"Is that what I think it is, Serge?" PC Ferrell asked, looking at the splatter on the floor.

"It looks like it." Bickford didn't want to give much away, even though he knew that Father Reed had himself guessed what the remains actually were. He watched Brian Ferrell move back towards the Police car for some radio privacy. "Brian! Get the scene sealed off, both sides!"

"At first I thought it may have been one of the animals. Sheep or pony. But it looks like something was lifted up and over the wall," Father Reed said worriedly. "Then I saw one of my parishioners cars parked over there." He nodded over towards the four-by-four at the end of the viaduct.

Police Sergeant Bickford looked at the blood on top of the wall, but he didn't want to disturb the residue on top of the wall so didn't try and scamper a look over the top. "Is there a way of getting down to the bottom?" he asked as he pointed downwards.

"Yes. There are steps around the side. The gate has a padlock on it usually but is so small you can just hop over it." He pointed over to the area where the gate could be found. "Here, let me show you," Father Reed said as he started to walk over, prompting the Police Officer to do the same.

Reaching the top where access to the steps leading down to the base of the dam was, Sergeant Bickford stopped Father Reed going any further. "You had better stay here." Then he carefully started to walk the steep steps downwards. They were indeed steep, he told himself, and slippery as well thanks to the water spraying from the overflow on the dam. There was an area of grass to the left, about halfway down, and Bickford realised that he hadn't told anybody where he was, so he stopped for a rest and clicked his radio. "PC Farrell?"

"Yes, Serge?"

"I'm just going down to the base of the dam. Look for Father Reed and he will show you where I am if you need me."

"Okay, Serge. I think CID and SOCO have just arrived. Looks like DI Thorpe and DS Carter."

Bickford looked up as though he would be able to see anything happening at the top, but the trees and foliage surrounding the steps blocked the line of view. "I won't be long. Explain to them where I am. Is everything else alright?"

"Yes Serge. Cordon is in place at both sides of the dam. Units two and three are conducting a fingertip search and I am about to look at the car."

"Okay," Bickford responded. "Keep me updated!" He took a deep breath and continued his journey.

Up at the viaduct, DI Thorpe and DS Carter exited their pool car and both Officers immediately looked around the whole area to see that everything was being done to preserve the crime scene.

"We probably need to get some lighting hooked up so we can see what we are doing," DI Thorpe stated, looking at his colleague but then noticing a uniformed officer heading their way.

"PC Farrell, Sir. Just to let you know Sergeant Bickford is heading down to the base of the dam to try and see if there is a body there."

"Thank you PC Farrell. I will catch up with him when he returns. I guess this is the crime scene," Thorpe said, his hands both resting on his hips and brushing his jacket backwards as he noticed the SOCO team being shown under the cordon tape. "What happened?"

"The local vicar, Father Reed over there, was coming back home and noticed the pool of blood as he drove over it. Then he saw that it was all over the drop wall." PC Farrell pointed towards the Priest who was still hanging around the gate that Sergeant Bickford had disappeared over minutes earlier. "He also recognised the car over there."

"Okay, thank you young man." Thorpe looked around. "Mike," he said to DS Carter. "You go down and join Sergeant Bickford in the search for the body. I'll deal with SOCO."

DS Carter nodded as he turned and headed towards the priest that PC Farrell had mentioned.

DI Thorpe tried to grasp the attention of the two SOCO experts. "Okay to come closer?" He looked on and saw one of them nodded and waved his hand to indicate that he could, so he lifted the cordon tape and headed over towards them, although not too close. He immediately began to see what Father Reed had seen for the first time earlier that evening. "My God. Someone has lost a lot of blood," he commented.

"Looks like a gunshot victim, Inspector." SFO Armstrong stated as he picked up a shell casing using his equipment and placed it into an evidence bag. "Looks like a 9mm."

"I guess looking at the body pattern, the victim was shot in the head at some point?"

SFO Armstrong knew exactly what the Inspector was looking at. "Yes. Small pieces of brain residue all over the road. We will get to that later. Initially I would say that whoever is the victim was shot nearer the wall, body fell backwards and then was dragged back over to the wall, lifted upwards and thrown over."

"Surely there must be more than one culprit then?" DI Thorpe asked inquisitively, thinking of the strength that would be needed to lift a dead-weighted body to such a height.

"Possibly. Either that or that has got to be one strong person. Let's hope we can find the body and take some DNA from the clothing."

Sergeant Bickford reached the furthest point that he could get to on the steps. He grabbed his torch and flashed it over towards the dam wall trying to see if there was any blood trail which might indicate just where any potential body fell. He had slowly descended the steps, his age showing slightly through fear of slipping or falling, although he liked to think of it as a 'risk assessment' instead of admitting his age. He continued to shine the torch at the wall.

"Hello George," the voice said from behind him.

Sergeant Bickford turned around to check who it was even though he recognised the voice. "Mike! What brings you down here?"

"I had to check that you hadn't fallen asleep," DS Carter replied knowing that he had always had a good working relationship with George Bickford. He chuckled and then asked, "Any sign of a body?"

"I was looking for a blood trail, but the overflow is on. It has probably washed any sign of blood away."

DS Carter looked down to the water congregating at the base. "It could be in the water then?"

"If you look at the point that it may have been thrown off, I will say it may have landed on the rocks down there." George shone his torch down to where he thought. "Problem is, it is too goddam dark. We may have to wait until morning unless we get some lights out here."

DS Carter looked around, steadying himself by holding onto the metal fence post beside him, mainly because he was still stood on the steps. "Easier said than done. By the time they pack them up and transport them here, it will be light anyway."

"That's what I was thinking. What about if we go over the other side and try and get a look from there?" George pointed over to the woodland on the other side of the dam.

"Good idea. I'll let the DI know that we are on our way back up." He watched Sergeant Bickford make one last attempt to try and find a body, but with no such luck, or so it seemed.

"Hold on, Mike. What's that?"

"What?" DS Carter asked as he tried to focus on the same direction that the torch was being shone.

"There," Sergeant Bickford exclaimed, pointing with his other hand. "It looks like a leg hanging over the side of that small building."

"Can't we get any bloody closer?"

"I don't think so. It looks too dangerous to go any further." George Bickford continued to focus on what they thought was a leg. "Hold on, Mike. Let's try from over here." He walked towards the dam wall where there was a mud track, obviously made by workmen, heading up and down the edge of the dam, as though someone had used it instead of the steps.

DS Carter followed the older officer who walked up the mud bank and then turned around to reshine his torch. It was a much better view. "Anything? Carter asked inquisitively, hoping for some positivity in the answer.

"You had better let the DI know there is a body down here!"

Jeremy Cornelius-Johnson drove up onto his driveway. He had lived in Wembury ever since his parents had died and he was the sole beneficiary to their estate as their only son. He had given up his own house, selling for a huge profit having purchased it when property prices were at an all-time low. Moving into his parents old house had done him the world of good, or so he thought. He became a bit of a hermit, keeping himself to himself and outside of his work as a Court Clerk, had no direct friends. He wasn't married and needless to say had never produced any grandchildren for his parents. Not that he wanted any. He often described not having attachments as *'The ultimate heaven'* because he had no one to nag him, tell him what he could or couldn't do or hassle him on the telephone.

With a Father as a Crown Court Judge, the Rt. Hon. Rufus Cornelius-Johnson, it was easy for Jeremy to get a job in the Court, although he wasn't allowed to sit in on any cases that his Father was sitting on. He didn't have the best of relationships with his Father mainly because he was quite a delinquent as a child and his Father couldn't handle a child like that. Because he was picked on at school, he often didn't go and therefore didn't learn the subjects.

His Mother, Felicity, was one of those dotting housewives who did everything her husband told her to do, and also supported her husband in every decision he made. Inside, Jeremy could see that his Mother didn't want to support him, like the day that his Father had thrown him out for being lazy and told him it was time for him to get a place of his own.

Jeremy's parents had died in suspicious circumstances. The Police could only put it down to a burglary that went wrong, as both were stabbed several times ending their lives and there was extraordinarily little evidence for them to go on. Jeremy only heard when he turned up to work and one of his Father's colleagues who had already been given the news that Rufus wouldn't be there, sat Jeremy down and told him. Jeremy broke down, but for his Mother. But deep inside Jeremy had a dark secret.

He was now the king of his castle, limiting contact with anyone, even the neighbours whose greetings he kept to a 'Good Morning,' 'Good Afternoon' or 'Good Evening' depending on the time of day. But there was another reason that Jeremy didn't like anyone in the house. The spare bedroom. He had moved all the furniture from the bedroom and put it in the back garden where there was a large shed about twice the size of a garage space.

There was a lock on the spare bedroom and the curtains were always drawn. Inside on the wall there were details of persons that had ridiculed him at some point. There were also plans as to how he was going to dispose of their bodies once he had killed them. He used to follow any potential victims taking photographs of their homes whilst they slept or keep an eye on their standard routines such as leaving and returning home from work or going shopping.

Sometimes he didn't have a plan. Someone would get him so angry that it would just be a random act of violence. Once they were dead, Jeremy would add a photo of the victim in a dead state next to the live photo. He also kept copies as his trophies and indexed them in folders on the hard drive of his laptop and looked at them quite regularly to admire his handywork.

He slammed his car door shut and then walked the short distance to the front door. Once inside, he poked his head into the living room door on the right and shouted, "Hiya Mum!" He knew that she wouldn't answer. She was dead. But he still liked to speak to his parents and would often do so, even down as far as holding full scale conversations with them, something that he wouldn't have had the chance to do when they were alive. Jeremy walked up the stairs and into his spare room. He removed his mobile and opened his laptop lid, plugging the phone into the adapter that was already plugged into one of the USB ports on the laptop. Then he created a new folder, entitling it 'Maddocks,' which fitted in alphabetically with the rest of the victim folders. Then he cut and paste the photos to the laptop. Job done, he thought to himself.

"Who is next, Mum?" he asked to the empty room. The answers appeared to come in his head like silent thoughts instructing him who to target. He knew that he just couldn't stop because he didn't want to be a disappointment any longer to either his Mother or Father. He received the answer even though there was no one there to tell him vocally. Then he went on the laptop once more and searched on Google for a picture that he could print and put on his wall. The printer burst into life and Jeremy jumped up off his chair and waited patiently for the finished product, pulling it out of the tray and pining it to his 'Wall of Fame.' He took a step back and looked at the photograph, tilting his head to the left slightly and staring at the pose.

"Oh no, no, no." He said psychotically. "You think it is right to abuse me in a place of justice, do you?" Jeremy looked at the photograph of known Plymouth criminal Neil Marsh, who had so far managed to get away with burglary several times and ABH. The worst thing at all was that the recipient of the bodily harm was an old lady in her 'eighties who disturbed him whilst he was trying to burgle her. The witnesses for the prosecution seemed to want to change their minds at the last moment, or even not turn up to the court at all. The old lady had died. All Neil Marsh had received in the past three years was a suspended sentence for racial aggravation. He had also indicated that he wanted to headbutt Jeremy when he went to leave the court. Now he had to pay for his crimes. He was a nasty piece of work, and the City wouldn't lose any sleep if he were gone. "Your time is coming."

The thing was Jeremy had no conscience. He never did. Ever since the day he left school and the child like bullying ended. Now he just had to put up with the adult bullying. That is why he enjoyed his job. He enjoyed seeing people getting punished for what they had done. Not for one minute did it cross his mind that he could be there in the dock one day. His head wiped out any wrongdoing and only focussed on what he had to do in the future, not what he had done in the past. People deserved punishment.

Back at the murder scene, DI Thorpe and DS Carter were patiently waiting for SOCO to finish their investigation at the scene. They had tried to get to the body via the same means as Sergeant Bickford and DS Carter, but to no avail. It was as dangerous for the younger SOCO officers as it was for the two Sergeants and with extraordinarily pinpoint light on the scene, they didn't even attempt it.

DI Thorpe got annoyed. "We need to get those bloody spotlights here before the rain washes away any chance of some evidence!" He looked around at some of the Constables each with their own responsibilities and noticed PC Farrell. "Has anyone chased them for us?" He asked, grabbing the young lads attention.

"I ordered them, Sir. But I haven't chased them up."

"Can you radio through and see where they are for me?" DI Thorpe was a good judge of character and PC Farrell gave the impression that he was on the ball and very much a career cop.

"I'll do that now, Sir," he replied, immediately grabbing his radio.

DI Thorpe noticed the priest coming towards him and walked over towards him in order that he didn't come too close. "Hello Father."

"Hello Inspector. I was wondering if I could go back to the vicarage as you haven't finished with my car. One of my parishioners who helped me has offered to give me a lift back."

DI Thorpe started to think if he needed the witnesses for anything more here at the scene and realised that they could be more of a hindrance than help, and any statements could be taken at their homes tomorrow. "I tell you what, Father. Do you go, and I will get one of the PC's to drive your car back to you at the Vicarage when SOCO give us the green light? How's that?"

"That would be perfect," Father Reed replied. "And the statement?"

"We will do that tomorrow. Go home and try and get some sleep, Father, and thank you for your help."

The Priest looked at the senior officer and smiled. "No problem, Inspector. Glad I could help." He walked off towards James Buckley who was patiently waiting to leave. He had already spoken to his wife to confirm that she and his son had gone back home some time ago when the Police had arrived to take over the roadblock. Father Reed jumped in the passenger side of the car. He was shaking with fright as the shock of the situation got to him.

James noticed the nervousness in his passenger. "Everything alright, Father?"

"No. Not really. Scary stuff. I've never experienced anything like that before."

"You aren't the only one, Father. It never happens here in the village or surrounding area," James replied calmly, sharing the Priest's shock immensely. "The most that we get is boy racers around the dam."

"What sort of person would do such a thing?"

James shook his head as he continued driving around the dam on what his son called 'The long way.' "I don't know, Father. I really don't know. But it looks like that evil has come to us tonight."

Chapter 4

The Crown Court was bustling for a Monday morning with defendants, Solicitors and Barristers all clogging up the waiting areas after reporting in to the receptionist in order that the court knew they had arrived. Nothing was confidential once all the side rooms that the Solicitors used to talk to their clients were taken. They would just discuss their cases either by just sitting beside their client in the waiting area or at one of the tables. Anyone could listen in. Some did. Some liked the gossip and there were often overheard conversations such as *'You wouldn't believe what I've just heard'* between related parties.

The court staff were busy preparing the cases to be heard in the three operational courts, with papers being carried from one to another. They had been under pressure recently with an increase in cases but the delay in others through things like Jury's not being able to conclude, or missing witnesses had ensured cancellations at the last moment of some important court cases.

Today, Jeremy was assigned to Court three, and one of the Judges he hated. His Honour Judge Kang Lim Koh. Of Malaysian Chinese descent, he had done the same in his home country before moving to the UK in 2001. Jeremy found him arrogant. The judge never said 'please' or 'thank you' and was never lenient towards any of the defendants if they were found guilty, always handing out the maximum sentence that he could which was the only thing that Jeremy liked him for. Solicitors and Barristers hated being in his court room because of the strictness of his demeanour. But Jeremy didn't care about it.

He had already come into work early and looked at the information for Neil Marsh. Surprisingly, Marsh lived in quite an upper-class area although how he got the money to live there was another story, Jeremy thought to himself. He looked at the court listing on his sheet whilst waiting for the defendant to be brought up from the cells underneath the court. But his mind was on his plan for Neil Marsh. He knew he had to concentrate on the court proceedings, especially with the nominated judge who would soon express concern if Jeremy was flagging in anyway.

The Security Officers brought the defendant Stuart Newell up from the custody suite and ensured he was sat in the chair. Jeremy looked at the sheet. He was charged with battery on a woman, namely his wife. Jeremy heard movement from the door behind the bench and announced, "All rise!," as the Judge came out and took his position on the red leather-clad chair embossed in oak wood, something that looked decades old.

"Please be seated," the Judge said sternly, looking at the occupants of his courtroom through the top of his glasses. The defendant was made to remain stood by the security officer behind him.

Jeremy stood once again and said, "Stuart Newell, you are charged with Grievous Bodily Harm in that on 4th October 2019 you did viciously attack Rachel Newell inflicting serious injuries. You are also charged with Assaulting a Police Officer whilst in the course of his duty when he was trying to arrest you. How do you plead?"

Newell smiled, the sort of smile that made everyone want to hit him in the face at the same time, and then said, "Not guilty!"

The Judge looked at the two Barristers who were both ready and eager to go with their opening statements and nodded his head at the prosecutor, Oakley Barratt who was quite an old hand at prosecuting in Plymouth for the CPS having been with them now for the past fifteen years. He looked threatening because of his height, all of six feet and five inches and because of that he was quite toned, liked to keep himself fit and work out to de-stress. The defendant's Barrister, Theo Nicholson from the Brady Law Firm was quite the opposite and gave the impression that he used to unwind at the end of the day by gorging himself on decent food and wine. Judge Kang Lim Koh had never experienced Theo Nicholson in his court room before today. Now he would.

Five hours later, the Court Clerk was glad that the day's proceedings had ended. Opening statements. Points of law. Jury retired to their back room several times. They had progressed no further than they had when Jeremy had read out the charges at the beginning of the session. Now for the real work. Neil Marsh. He lived in the houses down behind Mainstone woods, the only access being from Marsh Mills passing the caravan park. Jeremy also knew that some of Plymouth's worst criminals lived there. He remembered one case where a car dealer's house had been raided and they had found an arsenal of weapons and a large stash of both drugs and money. The Police had somehow deduced that a backstreet car dealer who never sold any of the old bangers on his forecourt should never be living in a house valued at £500k. Luckily on the morning of the raid which began at 0500 hrs, the Copeland gang were all sleeping and never had the chance to use any of the guns that they could have used if they had wanted to.

He turned into Leigham Manor Drive and admired the scenic route as he drove slowly along, the river with dogs playing in the water, the fields and tall trees and the calmness of the woodland with its paths that led up to Leigham and Mainstone. Jeremy knew he would have to be careful. There would be a stranger in the midst of a very upper-class area and if he were to sit in his car he would look overly suspicious, so he decided he would park his Nissan Duke in Parkfield Drive to the left of the fork in the road facing downwards just in case he had to make an escape for any reason. Neil Marsh lived in Woodlands Lane which was on the right fork. Tonight, Jeremy just wanted to get a feel of the area. Look for any hazards such as CCTV, nosey neighbours, guard dogs or private security firms. It was early evening, so if anything did rear its ugly head, he would say that he was looking to buy in the area and was just looking to see how good the neighbourhood was. Jeremy wouldn't be lying. He had been thinking about moving out of his parents' house for some time to escape the memories of their deaths. He knew that he still felt their presence there and that alone would try to keep him in the house.

As he walked down the road, he looked into the wilderness of the woodlands somehow knowing that one day it would be spoilt, and they would build more houses there. There were already a couple of 'for sale' signs propping up at the end of front gardens. The residents suspected the same.

There it was. The Marsh's home. Neil was a taxi driver in the evenings although Jeremy knew that this was just a cover. The Police whom Jeremy had spoken to in the Court suspected that as Marsh picked up passengers he would chat to them as taxi drivers did, and find out what they were doing, going away on business or holiday, whether the wife, husband or children were going to be home. Then he would make his move, only on the last occasion that the Police had tracked him down, he didn't expect the old lady to be there, and she had put up a fight, but Marsh was too strong for her and realised that he would have to beat her off if he were going to escape. One neighbour saw him and gave a good description, and another managed a partial index on the number plate of his hired Mercedes Taxi. Both witnesses later contacted the Police and gave further statements that they weren't sure that what they had seen was right because it was dark outside. Both feared for their lives.

Jeremy stopped momentarily outside on the pavement on the other side of the road, pulled out his mobile phone and activated the camera. Then he started taking shots from all around, but mostly of the Marsh's house. He noticed that it had a side gate running down the left-hand side of the town house. To ease any suspicion just in case anyone had seen him, he continued walking down the street, showing interest in the two places that were for sale. They were similar to the Marsh's place. He would book an appointment for a viewing with the estate agents, and with his camera took two photos of the estate agents telephone numbers on the board.

"Can I help you?" the male voice asked from behind him, sounding as though it were approaching quickly.

"Oh hello. I'm just looking at places that might be ideal to buy in the area," Jeremy replied calmly. "I quite like the area. Seems peaceful."

The man eased his suspicion. "It's very peaceful. Untouched by the outside world here. Where do you currently live?"

Jeremy could tell that the guy was lying about the area. He knew about all the cases and information about the area. Drug suppliers, illegal arms dealers, suspected people traffickers. All those that needed to keep their heads down at times. "My parents have recently died so I am living in their place on the coast. Too many memories for me to stay there. How much do these go for?" Jeremy nodded at the two whose signs he had just photographed.

"You will need between £375k to £425k to buy one of these."

"That's okay. I sold mine to move into my folks place, and theirs is worth over that." Jeremy replied, continuing to look interested by talking whilst looking at the houses. "Neighbours okay around here?"

The man smirked. "Some are better than others. But they do tend to take their lives away from here."

"Oh, right," Jeremy replied cautiously, even though he already knew the answer to his own question.

"Don't be put off by that," the man said. "We have a bit of a community here and look after each other."

"I like that," Jeremy said, nodding his head. "Well, thank you. I am going to go home and tomorrow call for viewings."

"That's ok. Good luck with it. Bye." The man walked on, and Jeremy let him pass and gave him some distance before he started to walk back up towards his car. What he did notice was that every house had either CCTV outside or alarms. Some had the Ring door video system. At the moment, it didn't matter. He was going to go ahead with stage two. Arrange the viewings, do the research, and then start to follow Neil Marsh to make him paranoid. The latter could start now, he thought to himself as he watched a taxi driven by Marsh heading down towards his home. Jeremy started his car and then turned left down to follow him. He drove past the Marsh's home to the turning bay of the dead-end Woodlands Lane. Then he turned the car and drove slowly up towards Marsh who had parked his taxi on his driveway and was just getting something out of the boot. Pulling his baseball cap over his eyes, Jeremy started to stare at Marsh as his car continued slowly, and then he raced the car away back towards Leigham Manor Drive and home. He knew that Marsh wouldn't report any such matters to the Police and risk having them come around his home. He thought that it was the Police who were following him and as long as he didn't recognise Jeremy from his court appearance then it would be okay.

When he arrived home, Jeremy grabbed the remote control for the television and flicked the switch to turn it on. He then toyed with it to get the correct channel for the news. The death at Burrator had reached the National News on the BBC, with Jeremy only assuming it would be on the local 'Spotlight' programme. He could feel the rush going through his body as his ego was taking a step further to notoriety. He increased the volume on the TV.

"There is increased Police presence at Burrator Reservoir in Devon today due to the suspicious death of a man named by Police as top author Byron Maddocks, whose body was found at the bottom of the dam on Saturday evening. A Police spokesman told BBC News that Mr Maddocks had received three fatal bullet wounds prior to his body being thrown over the wall."

Jeremy watched the report and became aroused as the camera zoomed in on the body being removed from the landing site, and the spotlight on the human debris on the wall at the top of the dam. He stood in front of the television and closed his eyes, tilting his head back and then from side to side until his neck clicked. In the background, the news reports continued, but he had heard enough. He turned the television off and then lifted the lid of his laptop, clicked a few buttons, and pulled up the music app. In seconds there were echoes of Dangerous Moonlight and the Warsaw Concerto sounding around the room, its haunting piano filling Jeremy with energy as he devoured the beauty of his classical choice. He loved this piece of music. His eyes still closed, he stood straight, his body rigid and began waving his arms as though he were conducting the orchestra, his mind engrossed in the charade.

It relaxed his mind. Took away the feelings of destruction from those who scolded him in whatever way. It made him forget real life. With music you could be whatever you wanted to be, the conductor of an orchestra, the Rockstar, the dancer, the musician. Tonight, he was someone, if only for a while.

As the Warsaw Concerto came to a dramatic end, Jeremy stood completely still, his eyes still closed, his arms stretched out to the sides, but as still as the night, his breathing slow, taking in every breath of air from around him.

It was midnight. Jeremy told himself that he was getting tired and would soon need his head to hit the pillow because he had to be in work early in the morning. He went upstairs and into his special room.

"What do you think, Dad?" Jeremy asked the ghost of his Father wanting his opinion on how to execute the plan. He stood staring at his photo-wall. "I know I need to follow him. I want to put fear in his heart just as he did to the lady. Let him know how it feels." He looked at his watch and confirmed the time on the wall clock with that on his timepiece, sighed loudly, and then went next door to his bedroom. Within minutes, he was sleeping.

Tuesday morning and the CID Office at Charles Cross Police Station was bustling as though they had too much work for the team. Every Officer seemed to be juggling many cases, trying to prioritise their work by putting some on the backburner, although not totally forgetting any case.

DI Thorpe burst through the doors with an unhappy face having just been in a meeting with his boss, DCI Tomlinson, who was concerned that there had been several high-profile murders on his turf and his team didn't seem to be any closer to making a break through. DI Thorpe knew he was under pressure from up above and that the ball-breaking would be passed down the ranks, although he found it demoralising to pass it any further in such a negative way. He felt he had some of the best Detectives on his team, especially with two very experienced Sergeants in Mike Carter and Jonathan Ayres and the addition of two trainees with ADC's Ben Hardy, who had received the chance after his bravery at a previous case, and Martin Gibbons.

"Everything alright, Guv?" DS Carter asked calmly, knowing that his meetings with the DCI usually meant getting more out of his team with less overtime.

"You don't fancy riding a bicycle to the scene of a crime do you, Mike?"

"That bad, eh?" DS Carter chuckled. "I guess the department is spending too much?"

"It's the public. I wish they would stop committing crime." DI Thorpe shuffled the notes he had made on the paper in his hands. "We have been told to up our game. We need results on the Horgan and Maddocks cases. What have you got so far?"

"Forensics is due back this morning on the Maddocks case. We already have the results from the scene at the Horgan's house. We are hoping that we may be able to get something out of the little boy Max."

DI Thorpe looked at his junior. "Oh yes. He is staying with you at the moment, isn't he?"

Carter nodded. "He is very withdrawn, Thomas has tried his hardest to get him to play, but he wants his Mum. He cuddles Emma non-stop."

"You have a good one there in Emma," DI Thorpe said praising Carter's wife immensely. "Keep hold of her, Mike."

"Don't tell her that. I'll have to buy her more shoes otherwise," he replied jokingly as he remembered that most of his side of the wardrobe contained her shoes. She just loved shoes and had to be colour coordinated with her outfits for the day.

"I won't," the DI replied with a smile on his face. "I think we need to call in the whole team in 30 minutes. "My office. Can you see to that?"

"No problem, Guv. I'll chase the forensics for the Maddocks case as well to see if we can get them for the meeting."

"Good Idea," DI Thorpe replied as the two went their separate ways, the DI heading over to his office and DS Carter heading over to summon the team to the meeting.

Thirty minutes later, the DI's office was filled with some of his finest Officers and the noise of the various conversations filled the room. DI Thorpe could hear them as he walked across towards his office from the stairwell. He had just been down to buy a sandwich at the staff canteen for his lunch and it had taken him longer than he thought because he had landed up talking to some of the hierarchy who had questioned him on his progress. Finally, he reached his team.

"Good Morning, gentlemen," he announced as he walked in, to which there were various replies of 'Guv,' 'Sir' and 'Morning,' all though he could not tell whom had replied with which gesture. "Are we missing anyone DS Carter?"

"Yes, Guv. DC Bolton and ADC Hardy are attending Waterstones in the Mall to interview the manager about the Maddocks case."

"Hopefully, we will get a lead from there," DI Thorpe replied as he looked at DS Carter out of the top of his glasses.

"They are just about to finish there, so shouldn't be long, Guv," Carter continued, checking his watch to see just how long they had been since he had spoken to DC Bolton. Ten minutes, he thought to himself.

DI Thorpe placed the papers he had in his hand down on the table in front of him. "Right team, thank you for dropping whatever you were doing to come to the meeting. I'll get right to the point. The DCI is concerned that we aren't making specific progress."

"We are stretched as it is, Sir," DC Johnson stated, rubbing his eyes whilst he talked, having been in the office until 0100 hrs the previous night, and then back at 0600 hrs this morning.

DS Ayres was stood beside him. "We have all had some long days recently, Guv. There has been a spate of serious crime in the past weeks. Is the DCI concerned about overtime or something?"

"That was one of the comments," DI Thorpe answered. "I told him it can't be helped. But leave that argument between me and him for another day." He rested his backside on the corner of the table. "He wants results to justify the overtime. You all know that PC Horgan and his family were murdered recently, and then on Saturday Byron Maddocks was found at the bottom of the Burrator Dam having been murdered."

There was a tap on the door and without invitation SFO Todd Armstrong came into the room. "Hello."

"Just the man we want," DS Carter said as he acknowledged the arrival of the SFO that he had been chasing for results on the phone.

SFO Armstrong walked over to the DI and presented a report with his findings. "There are the results of the Maddocks autopsy."

DI Thorpe looked at the newcomer. "In short, Todd?"

He turned to face the majority. "In short, the same gun was used both on the Horgan's and Mr Maddocks. They were even executed in the same way, with one bullet centre forehead and two in the torso close to the heart. There was no physical contact between any of the Horgan's and the attacker, no residue under any fingernails, although we are still matching blood, hair and fibre samples to see if any do not match the victims or their family, as in the case of the Horgan's."

"My God. So, the same person shoots an entire family and then a civilian. There must be some kind of link surely," DI Thorpe commented intensely.

SFO Armstrong looked at the DI and said, "Potentially. There was physical contact between the killer and Byron Maddocks. We know that because someone had to lift him over the dam wall."

DS Carter piped up suddenly. "We are just about to go through PC Horgan's outstanding and recent cases, Guv. See if there's anything that will flag up there."

"I will have to go, Sir," SFO Armstrong said confidently. "I am working non-stop on the results at the moment and will update DS Carter as and when we find something."

"Yes, thank you for your arduous work, Todd." DI Thorpe commented as he watched the Forensics Officer head towards the door.

"Cheers Todd," DS Carter added, patting him on the back as he walk past. As he exited, he exchanged places with the arrival of DC Bolton and ADC Hardy.

"Good evening, DC Bolton!" DI Thorpe said much to the delight of the others in his office, although DC Bolton knew his Guvnor's sense of humour. ADC Hardy on the other hand was a little bit naïve as he looked at his watch and frowned as he noted that it was still morning.

DS Carter watched his expressions and then whispered, "Plonker. He was joking!"

"Ahh," Ben replied.

"Sorry we were late, Sir," Bolton said. "We had to wait for the Security boys to give us a copy of the CCTV from Saturday."

The DI's face lit up. CCTV. Was there something that they needed to see? Something that he could report back to the DCI. "Did you get anything of relevance?"

Bolton looked at the younger officer who was going through his notebook. "Yes, Sir," ADC Hardy replied, suddenly realising that there were many sets of prying eyes staring at him from various parts of the room.

"Let's have it then son," DS Carter exclaimed humorously.

"Well, the Manageress of the Waterstone's store, a Jenny Baker, had reason to call the Police on Sunday when she heard about the death of Byron Maddocks. He had been in the store book-signing his new novel on Saturday. She mentioned a suspicious character who Byron said was stalking him and goes by the name of 'Jeremy.' It appears that this character was also waiting outside the store when the book-signing finished, so Jenny arranged for Security to escort Mr Maddocks to his car." Ben flicked the page over in his notes. "DC Bolton went to get the CCTV."

"Anything on it?" DI Thorpe asked excitingly.

DC Bolton smirked. "There sure is. It's not a clear picture, but I'm certain the tech boys can clear it up a bit."

"Did we get a surname to this 'Jeremy'?" DS Ayres shouted over the room.

"Unfortunately, no," DC Bolton replied whilst shaking his head.

"That's a shame," DS Carter added. "Not that he would be giving the correct surname. Who knows if 'Jeremy' is his real name?"

"But it is a lead," DI Thorpe intervened. We need to know why PC Horgan and his family and Byron Maddocks were murdered, and if there is a link between them."

DS Carter exchanged eye contact with his DI. "You said that these two cases have to take priority, Guv?"

"The DCI wants these two cases to be investigated above anything else. We have to find the killer and soon. Use every trick in the book. Contact your snouts. Where did he get the pistol? We need to know."

They all started to leave the room and head back towards their desks, some picking up their telephones whilst others grabbed their keys to their vehicles.

Chapter 5

Judge Kang Lim Koh liked to relax when he had finished with the psychologically mind-bending courtroom dramas that even though he enjoyed because it gave him a sense of power, he liked to forget once home. He knew that he took his job very seriously, in fact too seriously at times he thought. Everyone used to laugh that he always gave out the maximum sentence if the defendant was found guilty, but that is what he believed in. If he had his way it would be hard labour, cutting slates or making post bags as they used to. But these days, it was about the Human Rights of prisoners, with the criminals suing if the prison pool table was out of action, or the X-Box wasn't working. Like most law-abiding citizens, he hated that the criminals always had more rights than the victims, and that is why he always went for the maximum sentence, even if they had showed remorse.

He opened the door to his bungalow situated on the outskirts of Plymouth at Yelverton. They had all heard about the Byron Maddocks murder at Burrator which was just over three miles away in a close-knit community where everyone looked after everyone, and reaffirmed Father Reed's comment that things like that just didn't happen up here. It was a peaceful community, frequented by friendly tourists and locals who just wanted to have a good day out by letting their children climb the rock situated across the road, something that generations had done for decades.

So far he hadn't put any lights on in the bungalow. He loved the dark. His wife had died one year previous. He had created a situation back in Malaysia when he married her. He was Malaysian Chinese and therefore a Buddhist, whereas his wife Wong Xin was Malaysian and therefore a Muslim. So, they came to England to escape the hardship of one of them having to convert religions if they wanted to be together. Wong Xin didn't know it, but she was riddled with Cancer and her life in England was cut short after two years.

He stopped in the loneliness and tranquillity of the silence, the only light that was shining was the moon forcing it's fullness through the trees at the bottom of his back garden. But suddenly he froze. There was a silhouette stood in front of the patio door. Someone was there. In the house. A burglar? "Who's there?" he shouted commandingly whilst at the same time reaching over towards the light switch. The lounge light reacted, but he could still not see who it was.

"Do not put any more lights on Judge," the stranger said.

"Who are you?" Kang Lim questioned, worried that someone was in his house. He had heard of Judge's getting murdered whilst sitting on cases. He was questioning in his mind just how did he get in?

"That doesn't matter. You will listen and I will make this quick."

"Okay," the judge replied nervously. "What do you want? Money? Jewellery?"

The Stranger stayed still in the moonlight shadow. "Neither. In fact, quite the opposite. I'm going to give you money."

"What for? What do you want?" Kang Lim was now the most nervous and frightened as he could be. Guns weren't legal in the UK, but he somehow wished they were at this moment in time.

Under the Blood Red Sky

"You are overseeing the case for Stuart Newell at the moment."

"Yes," Kang Lim snapped.

"Let's just say, things are going to happen that will make you abandon the trial."

"I can't do that," the Judge replied. "You know I can't do that."

"Tonight, there will be £20k paid into your bank account. If you don't want to join your wife six feet under, then you will find a way. Now turn around."

Cautiously, Kang Lim turned around very slowly, his hands held up slightly towards his chest. He was wondering how this man knew about his wife being deceased. How he got into his property in the first place as the bungalow was heavily alarmed. How they got his bank account details.

"No Police. Make the wrong moves and you die. Make the right ones, we will let you live." The stranger slid the patio door open. "Don't forget, Mr Koh!"

The room went silent, but Kang Lim wasn't sure if he had actually gone, or whether he should turn around. He couldn't feel any presence as he did before, just the chill of the moorland wind blowing into his bungalow through the doors. Suddenly his mobile phone pinged. He reached into his pocket and pulled It out to read. It was now or never. Would he get shot or beaten up for moving? The answer was no. The stranger had gone, but still he cautiously turned, still hearing the man's London accent in his head, *'No Police.'* He looked at his mobile screen and saw the notification from his bank. £20k had been deposited into his account just as the stranger had said. Kang Lim tried to think of his next move. He didn't want to die. He looked at his phone screen once again, and then back at the tabletop before falling back into the sofa to think. "This could be an integrity test," he said out loudly to himself. He knew that the Court Service and the Police did them for just that reason, to draw out the ones who loved to be bribed. But then, if it wasn't, he valued his life. But then again, if he did call the Police, he would be protected.

His mobile rang, the comical 'Ride of the Valkyries' tune which everyone found quite funny for a person in a high-ranking position to be using. He didn't know who could be calling him. The screen showed a withheld number. "Hello?"

"Are your cogs turning in your brain? I know you want to call the Police. Try it. Go on, I dare you."

The line went dead, but Kang Lim became more apprehensive about the situation. Surely if it were an integrity test, they would not use these sort of tactics? Should he take the risk? He went to bed to sleep on the decision, not that he needed the £20k, but he knew that if he did what the stranger requested once, there would be another request, and another, soon after. Plus, it would make him as bad as the criminals he was putting away. That was against both his own morals and those of his family and race culture. Still, later that evening he went to bed and slept on the idea. Everyone has a price.

Jeremy ensured that everything was set up in court number three ready for the Judge, prosecutors and defending barristers. He checked that all the computer screens were working just in case he had to call IT prior to the start. The last thing he wanted was to have a request for something in the middle of the trial. As soon as he was happy, he set up his own desk ensuring everything was straight and that he had reserves of pens and paper just in case he needed them. He was yet to receive the documentation for the day but kept a space on the desk for the paperwork. He then walked around the bench and tapped on the door that led through to the Judge's chambers.

"Come in," was the reply, barely heard through the thick oak that the door had been made from.

The Court Clerk obliged and opened the heavy object. "Hello, Sir," Jeremy said. "I was just wondering if there was anything that you needed before the commencement?" He watched the Judge slowly edge his way around his desk and slump back in his leather chair. His demeanour seemed different to Jeremy this morning. Kang Lim Koh was normally efficiently commanding, ensuring and double checking that all documentation was where it should be.

"No. I'm sure everything will be fine, Jeremy. I'm just going to have a drink. Would you like to join me?"

Jeremy knew the rules on drinking alcohol before or during a trial, although he also knew that the Judges and QC's regularly flouted the rules, especially if they went out for lunch when the wine was free flowing in some cases. "I'll just have some orange, Sir. Here, I'll get it," he walked over to the drinks trolley in order that the Judge didn't have to get up again. "What can I get you?"

"I would like to say a brandy. But you know me. A stickler for the rules." He knew that he really wanted something stronger. He hadn't slept very well in the night, tossing, and turning all night, frightened with worry. Today, he would have to make a decision that could change his life forever. "I'll have the same as you, please."

Jeremy seemed relieved that the Judge chose correctly. Officially, if he were seen to be drinking alcohol it would be the Court Clerk's responsibility to bring it to his manager's attention, which would result in a delay in the trial because the Judge would be removed from the trial. He poured the fresh orange from the bottle into two small glasses and then passed them over to Kang Lim. "There we go," he commented softly as he ensured that there was a strong receiving hold on the Judge's glass. He noticed the Judge wasn't really with it, still distant and slightly withdrawn from the real world around him. That was the last thing that they needed in the Courtroom today. "Is everything alright, Judge?"

Kang Lim was still thinking about the previous evenings event, and still wondering how he was going to abandon the trial or even if he was. He drank his orange straight down as though it were that brandy that his body so demanded at the moment. Then, rubbing his eyes, he looked at Jeremy and replied, "Yes. Thank you. I didn't sleep very well last night. I'll be okay. Let's get started."

Jeremy gulped down the last of his orange and then walked back to the Courtroom. As he went through the door, he noticed that the gallery was filling up with those members of the public who just wanted to observe the case. He looked at them all, wondering which side they were on, the husband or the wife. Next through the doors were the prosecutor and his assistant who seemed to be arguing over something serious as the came in, sat down at their desks, and dropped their heavy files containing all their information for the trial.

Oakley Barratt raised his voice. "Get on the phone and see where they are," he was overheard saying. "I'll ask if I can have time with the Judge before the trial starts." His assistant, June Hornett, stood up and walked towards the door to go out into the hall, not that it was any more private than the Courtroom, but it was less enclosed and there were more people than her making calls.

Jeremy noticed some of the crowd in the observation smiling cockily, as though they knew exactly what Oakley Barratt was talking about to his assistant. He noted this on the paper in front of him, just as he saw the Barrister approaching his desk. Jeremy stood up. "Yes, Mr Barratt. How can I help?"

"Is it possible that I could see the Judge immediately, please?" He asked abruptly, being one of those Barristers who took his job and his self-importance very seriously.

"I will ask if he is available," Jeremy replied, knowing the answer to Barratt's question as Judge Kang Lim Koh always refused to see anyone apart from himself before any trial. Anyone else had to make an appointment. "Could I ask what the problem is?"

Oakley Barratt cleared his throat and lowered the volume of his voice before leaning forward and whispering, "I need an adjournment."

Inside, Jeremy was laughing, because he also knew that this Judge hated requests such as this without a good reason. "Could I ask why?"

"All of our witnesses have disappeared."

He picked up the telephone and raised it to his ear. "That is a bit of a problem, Mr Barratt. Hold on, I will see if he is free."

"Thank you," replied the legal man.

Jeremy waited for the Judge to answer his call and surmised that he must be putting on his gown and wig ready for the trial because he was not answering the call. The court clerk replaced the receiver. "He is not answering at the moment so probably doesn't want to be disturbed. Perhaps this is something to bring up once today's proceedings get underway?"

"I guess so," Oakley replied although he was feeling a little angry that Jeremy had only tried to contact Judge Kang Lim Koh by telephone and hadn't physically tried to contact him. "Can you keep on trying if you have time before the proceedings start?"

"Of course, Mr Barratt." Jeremy watched as Oakley Barratt returned to his desk, sat down, and started reading the papers that he had brought with him. Then he looked to the back of the court where the door was opening and Theo Nicholson, who had just returned from the cells after speaking to his client, arrived with a sense of calamity. Jeremy looked at his watch and noted that Theo was pushing it a bit because he only had two minutes before the case restarted.

Next came security who stomped up the stairs leading into the dock with Stuart Newell close behind him. The two guards pushed him down into the chair and then one of them sat beside him whilst the other returned back down the stairs.

Once again, Jeremy heard movement, and the jury were led into their area, with seven men and five women making up what seemed like a fully structured jury, with young and old members who looked like a mixture of business people, factory workers, retailers, and students. Quite a collective, Jeremy thought to himself as they all shuffled into their perspective rows. Jeremy signalled to the court usher to be ready as the Judge was ready to appear.

"All rise," Jeremy announced as the handle on the chambers door rattled, the door opened, and Judge Kang Lim Koh presented himself to quite a packed courtroom. He sat down and looked at the congregation out of the top of his glasses, as they all replaced their posteriors back into their seats. He looked at the public gallery. One man was staring directly at him, but Kang Lim didn't know if this was the stranger who had apprehended him the night before.

June Hornett entered the court, replacing her mobile telephone into her handbag and as she reached the prosecutors bench, she shook her head at Oakley Barratt. He stood up before the Judge could open the proceedings for the day. "Your honour, before you start, I would like to request an adjournment for reasons that appear to be out of my control."

"And what are those reasons, Mr Barratt?"

"Well, your honour, we need to locate all of our witnesses who seem to be waylaid at this moment in time."

"All of them?" Kang Lim asked gruffly. "Every single one?"

"That is correct, your honour. None of them have turned up for court this morning."

"Your honour," exclaimed Theo Nicholson as he stood up. "This is most irregular. If the prosecution have no witnesses I must ask for the case to be abandoned and my client to be freed. This trial has already been delayed twice and the psychological effect is taking its toll on him. Now another delay?"

"Thank you Mr Nicholson," Kang Lim said as he briefly looked at both Solicitors in turn. He remembered what the stranger had said to him last evening.

'Let's just say, things are going to happen that will make you abandon the trial.'

He could do it now. Not allow the adjournment and abandon the trial immediately. But the prosecution would appeal, and the case would be heard with a different judge and a different jury on a different day. Or he could show a little mercy and adjourn until the afternoon.

"Mr Barratt. You know I do not like delays in my courtroom. This case has already been delayed twice previously as pointed out by the defence."

"Yes, your honour. I am sorry This is most unusual, I know, but a bit of a coincidence that they have all failed to show up this morning." Barratt was just feeling angry and was riling up inside. He went to whisper to his assistant. "Did no one answer?"

She shook her head. "Not one," she replied concerningly.

"I will grant you an adjournment until after lunch today after which if your witnesses still haven't arrived at court I will have no option to abandon the proceedings and let Mr Newell go free.

"Thank you your honour. I'm sure that they will be here by then."

The stranger in the public gallery winked at the judge who was now in the pockets of crime and his integrity as a Judge went out of the window. "Court is adjourned until 1400 hrs." He banged his gavel on the bench as he continued to stare at the man who had winked at him. The occupants of the court began to stand prior to

Jeremy instructing them to do so, and Judge Kang Lim Koh acted as though he couldn't wait to get back to his chamber.

Jeremy watched the court empty except for the two lawyers, who started mumbling about Oakley's request for an adjournment. Theo Nicholson was surprised about the whole situation. Oakley knew that Theo was straight down the line, if his client had mentioned about anything funny going on with the intimidation of witnesses, he would approach the Judge immediately.

"June, did anyone answer on that list?" Oakley asked his assistant.

"No, not at all. In most of the cases it went straight through to voicemail."

Oakley knew that he could trust her even if she was in her more mature years and ready for retirement. He shook his head at her reply. "Sorry, Theo, I will have to go. See you later."

"I hope you contact them, Oakley. It seems strange that all the witnesses are not available." He started to pick up his box files and then headed towards the door. Oakley and June watched him leave.

"So, what do you really think?" June asked worriedly, still concerned as to why she was earlier unable to contact the witnesses.

Oakley shook his head as his thoughts looked at the worst-case scenario. "I think we could have a big problem. There could have been some witness intimidation and they have all decided not to give evidence. Even his own wife hasn't turned up and she is the one that was beaten senseless."

"Let's go out for some fresh air and try those numbers again," June exclaimed. "You never know, we may get lucky."

"Let's hope so. We have under three hours to find four witnesses."

The time went quickly, and Oakley returned with June in tow to the Courtroom. Both he and his assistant had failed to contact the witnesses. He had videos of Rachel Newell and her injuries but knew that there would be objections about using them if the victim wasn't present. He could also read out the statements of what the witnesses had told the Police but the same might apply and the defence may disagree with the hearsay application. But if you didn't ask, you didn't get, Oakley thought briefly to the saying that his Mother used to say to him. They took their positions at the prosecutors bench once more and both he and June sat down at the same time.

Theo Nicholson entered the courtroom whilst talking on his telephone. It sounded quite serious whatever it was. For the second time that day, he clumsily dropped his box files on the desktop which silenced the room momentarily with its unannounced 'Thud!.' He looked at Oakley whilst still speaking on the phone and mouthed 'Sorry' at his learned friend who in return just waved his hand indicating that it didn't bother him.

Jeremy looked at his watch and noted it was one minute to go. Judge Kang Lim Koh was a stickler for time, so Jeremy announced, 'All Rise' as the door opened dead on 1400 hrs.

"Thank you," the Judge said as he took his seat on the bench for the second time that day. He noticed Oakley Barratt standing as if to address the bench once more. "Mr Barratt."

"Yes, your honour. Thank you for the adjournment this morning. We still haven't been able to contact any of the four witnesses, your honour. Even the victim, Mrs Rachel Newell who is the wife of the defendant." He looked at June once more because she had messaged the numbers hoping that a text would reach the recipients better than a voicemail. She shook her head as he saw her check her phone. "I would ask you honour for a further adjournment to allow the prosecution to locate the said witnesses."

Judge Kang Lim Koh read his notes in front of him as Theo Nicholson stood up as well but was interrupted by the Judge who looked at the prosecution lawyer and said, "Sorry, Mr Barratt. In light of the fact that this case has been delayed on two occasions prior to today make it hard for me to consider that. Quite frankly, I do not like delays in my courtroom."

"I realise that, your honour. But this situation looks like it could have potential Police intervention if there has been witness intimidation."

Theo intervened quickly. "The emphasis being on the words 'could have,' your honour.

Kang Lim looked at his notes again. "So, you do not have any witnesses at all present this afternoon?"

"No, your honour."

"Well," the Judge prompted. "It's a mess. A complete mess. It is up to the relevant Solicitor to ensure that there is excellent communication to enable witnesses to arrive on the correct day and at the correct time."

"We did, your honour. Each one was contacted last evening," Oakley pleaded, but he could see in the Judge's face that he was having none of it.

"I'm sorry, but the Crown does not have a case in its present form. I therefore have no alternative but to abandon the proceedings. Mr Barratt, you have the usual time to decide if you are going to demand a retrial. Members of the Jury. Thank you for your time today. I will release you because of the discontinuance of today's trial."

Oakley Barratt couldn't believe what he was hearing and stood with a look of astonishment on his face, as Judge Kang Lim Koh turned around to face the defendant.

"Mr Newell. The prosecution have not come up with the necessary evidence or witnesses in order to proceed with a trial. It has therefore been discontinued. The prosecutor must now decide if they want a retrial. But until that decision is made, I am releasing you from custody on bail. You are a free man for now.

"Thank you, your honour," Stuart Newell said politely.

Jeremy was just as flabbergasted as Oakley Barratt, and stood silent and confused, but quickly realised he had to announce. "All rise!"

Kang Lim Koh exited once more through the oak door and out of sight, rested his back up against the door, removed his wig and wiped his frightened, sweaty brow with the arm of his gown. All the time he was in the court, the same man had been staring at him in a threatening manner. He was sure that he was the stranger from last night, just by the manner in which he was psychologically killing him with the stare.

The Court Clerk walked in without knocking first as he normally did, and this startled the Judge because it took him with surprise as he thought it might be the stranger. "What the hell was that all about?" Jeremy snapped, knowing that the decision just wasn't the right one, especially by this Judge. "I knew there was something wrong this morning. Are you feeling unwell?"

Kang Lim had to think on his feet. The dirty deed had been done and to prevent himself being arrested and charged for perverting the course of justice the situation needed a cover story. "Not too good. I have a feverish temperature which is making me sweat. I think this morning I was just getting the symptoms."

"You know that Oakley Barratt is going to ask for a retrial don't you?"

"It's his right to do so on behalf of the CPS. It's whether they will let him do so because of cost reasons. It's gone nowhere the first time. Unless it is crystal cut guilty verdict at the end of it, they will just throw it aside."

Jeremy was fuming with the Judge's view. It was totally unlike him to think that way. He was Mr. Maximum. "So, he walks free?"

"The prosecution never had a case without witnesses. They couldn't provide them, so I had no other option."

Jeremy shook his head. "Well, I and many others would like to know how four witnesses could just disappear."

"You know it happens, Jeremy. The persecution of witnesses. Who knows, they may even be dead. We don't know and it is not up to us to make a decision on the outcome based on people who fail to turn up to court to give testimony."

"You tell that to the victim. If she is ever found!"

Chapter 6

The evening soon came around and Jeremy left the Court after completing all the paperwork for the day. His mind was working overtime on the day's events. His first instinct was that Judge Kang Lim Koh was on the take and grasped the opportunity to throw the case. But he knew Kang Lim was usually better than that, a man who followed the rule book to a T. But today was out of character for him.

Jeremy cleared his mind as he drove the short distance from the Court in Armada Way to the car park situated just to the right of the turning for the train station. He fronted his car into the space, so it was overlooking the taxi office on the other side of the station road. Then he sat there and waited for the arrival of Neil Marsh. It was time to put the fear of God in him and make him feel vulnerable just like the old lady he had burgled and indirectly killed.

Whilst he was waiting for Marsh, Jeremy poured himself a cup of coffee from his thermos flask and took sips from the metal cup which topped the flask when it wasn't being used. He sat quietly, not even having the radio on through fear it may distract him. It was early days for Neil Marsh. It was a game for Jeremy, something that gave him power and control over someone, which was something that he had never had before he had started the game. He heard the voices of his parents shouting at him and making him feel at times worthless, when his homework scores were bad, if he was caught fighting at school even if it was through no fault of his own but to protect himself against the bullies.

'You are a waste of space.'

He heard from the back seat of the car, but he shrugged it off. The memories were still in his head, but he knew that his parents were dead. He knew it because he had killed them. He had made sure that he had got one thing right and had a good alibi because he was in the Court all day. He let someone else find them, repeatedly calling and leaving pleasant messages on their voicemail when trying to contact them. So, he had power over his parents for the first time in his life. The legal world in Plymouth was rocked and incredibly supportive to Jeremy.

As car after car pulled into the taxi car park, Jeremy looked closely at each of the drivers trying to catch a glimpse of Neil Marsh. It was getting dark, although there was what seemed like a mini football spotlight overlooking the premises which made it easier for him to see across the road. Suddenly he felt like luck was on his side as a taxi pulled into the car park and a familiar face stepped out of the driver's side door. Marsh started talking to a couple of the other drivers whilst waiting for his next fare.

Jeremy put his baseball cap back on and pulled it slightly down over his eyes. He then stepped out of his car and leaned on the door that he had just opened. He looked across the road as he rested his chin on his right hand whilst his left was holding the door. His eyes staring, his smile now gone, his anger building, his breathing heavy. The voices were all around him.

'Teach him a lesson!' 'He is the scum of the Earth!' 'Kill him, Son!' 'How would you like it if he had done that to your Mother?.'

They were right, Jeremy told himself as he stared psychotically at Marsh, hoping that there would be a return of limited eye contact before Jeremy drove home. But Marsh wasn't that observant and was more interested in maintaining a good rapport with his fellow drivers. Always have a Plan B, Jeremy told himself. He would sound the horn to get attention if Marsh didn't notice him soon. He watched Marsh talking, not letting any of the others get a word in edgeways, wanting to impress with his self-confidence.

Jeremy reached in and sounded the horn several times. Finally, two of the taxi driver's looked over to see who was trying to get their attention thinking it may have been another private hire driver. They saw Jeremy, although could not see his face very well.

"That guy is looking over here," one of the driver's said. "Anybody recognise him?"

They all shook their heads. "He's not a taxi driver I don't think. Not in that car," one of the others said before taking a sip of his coffee.

Jeremy sounded the horn once again whilst staring at Marsh.

"Looks like he is trying to get your attention, Neil," the first taxi driver continued.

Marsh looked over and tried to focus on the overcoming evening darkness. "I have no idea who that is," he said, shaking his head."

"Well, he is staring you out," the second driver said with a laugh. "You been a naughty boy with someone else's Mrs?"

"Not for a long time," Neil chuckled loudly as he looked over towards Jeremy. "I'll go over in a minute and see what he wants." He began to suspect that it was a relative of the old lady whom he had burgled. Would they let his employers know the extent of his crime? He appeared a lot larger than the guy who was staring at him, so it wasn't as if he couldn't put up a fight if her were attacked by the stranger. He scrunched up his plastic coffee cup that he had got from the vending machine. "I won't be long," he said as he started to walk over towards the junction.

Jeremy quickly got back in his car, started the engine, and reversed out of the parking spot. He noticed Marsh just crossing the road as he drove out of the car park and turned left to go up towards North Hill.

Marsh stopped dead in his tracks and raised his hands as he shouted, "What the fuck?" before shaking his head.

He looked at the car in the distance, and then turned around to walk back towards the taxi parking area. "God knows what that was all about," he exclaimed to his two co-workers.

"That was pretty weird," said the first driver.

"Totally," said the second. "Did you get his registration number?"

"No," Marsh replied. "I was too interested in him." He wasn't frightened, just inquisitive as to why someone would be following him in this way. Could it be a cop? He didn't recognise him and with his record he knew all the Plymouth CID Officers because he had given taped interviews to most of them under caution. Suddenly, Neil Marsh's notification system beeped inside his car indicating that he had a fare to pick up. "I'll catch you guys later." He drove away, still thinking of the incident at the taxi office.

The next day, Neil was at home in Woodlands Lane. He hadn't arrived home too early the previous night because he had a long fare right at the end of his shift from Plymouth to Tavistock, so he didn't have the chance to tell his wife about the incident the previous evening. She was home for lunch, which was the time that Neil got up after a late shift. He came down in his red t-shirt and shorts which showed off a pair of knees that looked like they had been both been hit with a hammer at some point in his life.

"Everything alright, Neil?" she asked as she watched him yawn as though he were still tired.

"I didn't sleep well. Darling have you noticed any strange cars around or anything? Or even worse anyone following us?"

"His wife stopped stirring the baked beans and looked at him. "Why do you ask?"

He yawned once more and stretched his arms up in the air. "I think someone was watching me at work last night. He was staring at me from the other side of the road. When I tried to approach him, he jumped in his car and raced off."

"Police?"

Neil shook his head. "I don't know. I thought that at first."

"What sort of car was it?"

"It was dark blue. Nissan I think," her husband replied as he tried to picture it in his mind from the night before. "That's why I don't think it was the Police."

"Did you get the registration number?" Lydia asked as she passed his plate of food over to him.

"No, I didn't. If it happens again I'll make sure that I go for that first." He looked at her as he started tucking into his sausages. "Just be vigilant when you are out and about, love."

"I will. Don't worry." She passed him a mug of tea, white with two sugars and watched as he gulped it down. She had often commented that he must have a stomach lined with lead to drink hot tea or coffee like he does. "Right, I'm going to eat my sandwich and then get back to work."

"Was there any post this morning?" He already knew the answer to his own question because he could see letters protruding from behind the knife block which is where Lydia usually shoved them.

"Yes. Bills, bills and a letter for you." She reached over and grabbed the large letter for him, placing it down on the work surface close to him.

Neil finished his mouthful of food and brushed his hands together just in case there were any bits of food or grease on his fingers. He wiped his hands with the tea towel to his right, and then picked up the letter, ripping open one end of it. Then he peered inside before putting his hand in and pulling out some photographs and a note which was folded in half. He unfolded it.

"Who is that from?" His wife asked calmly. "What are the photos of?"

He hesitated as he read the brief note silently and felt cold, his body covered in goose bumps, his face going white as a sheet. Then without speaking he passed the note to Lydia. She read it aloud.

'There are four kinds of Murder: felonious, excusable, justifiable, and praiseworthy. Yours will consist of all four.'

Neil started flicking through the photos, placing the ones that he had looked at the back of the pile. In all there were about twenty photos of their house and their garden, including several of Lydia on her mobile telephone walking around the back garden and the children playing on their own. "Shit," he exclaimed as he lightly threw the pile of photos across to her on the work top. Lydia dropped the letter and picked the photos up.

"We are going to have to call the Police," Lydia snapped as she instantly began to feel threatened and scared. "The kids! The kids!"

"They are safe. They are at school! I'll pick them up as normal." Neil took the pile of photos from her in order that he could look at them once more. "You know we can't call the Police darling."

"Neil, this is serious! Someone is threatening to kill you and has managed to take photo's around the outside of our house!"

"They are not the first and they certainly won't be the last." Neil stared in front of him trying to think who could be responsible for this. Then he banged his hand on the work surface. "It must be something to do with that old lady who died. What was her name?" He clicked his fingers many times hoping that it would help him.

"Brenda Hargreaves." Lydia remembered the name every day. She also remembered the Police clambering all over the house looking for evidence, searching for Neil's clothes that he had worn on the night of the burglary that had gone wrong and impounding both of their vehicles.

"That's it!" Neil exclaimed as though he had remembered it himself. "She had a son and a Grandson who both had a go at me when the case was dismissed."

Lydia shook her head as she realised that Neil was about to do something that would get him in more trouble. "But what if it isn't them, Neil? If you made a list of the people that had a grudge against you, well, you wouldn't have time to see them all!"

"Thanks for the vote of confidence darling," Neil replied.

"What I am saying is, it is about time that we used the Police to work for us for a change. If we are being threatened, let them investigate it." Lydia looked at her watch. "Look at the time. I had better get back to work. I'll see you just after 5pm." She pecked him on the cheek and then headed to the front door.

Neil didn't know what to do for the best. Usually, he sorted things out himself or with the help of a few of his hardcore mates which was something that he hadn't ruled out as yet. Something was wrong with the whole situation, and he hated it when he didn't have a clue what it was. Lydia wanted to go to the Police. He knew deep in his heart that this would normally be the correct move for them to make, especially because he had the children to think about. He looked once more at the pile of photographs trying to work out just where they were taken from. The side of the house. They were taken from the side of the house. Whoever took them must have been on his property and have the nerve to be so close to his wife and children. Now, he started to panic.

ADC Ben Hardy walked into the CID office as though he were on a mission carrying some paperwork which he had retrieved from the Plymstock Police Station. His mentor, DC Bolton, had instructed him to go on as he needed to relief himself quite urgently.

"Everything alright, young man," DS Ayres asked as Ben passed his desk.

He stopped momentarily. "Yes, Serge. We have just come back from Plymstock Station with some copies of PC Horgan's active caseload."

"Did you find anything?"

"Possibly, Serge. I think I should explain it to DI Thorpe as well. It's quite a critical piece of information."

DS Ayres got up from his desk. "Okay, we had better find out what it is then. Let's go." He led the way towards the DI's office and tapped on the door, louder than he had anticipated, but it didn't matter because if anything it alerted the DI who was in conversation with DS Carter.

"Jon!" DI Thorpe exclaimed. "You had better come in. We can catch up on the information we have." Thorpe turned and looked at the whiteboard behind him, and started writing with his markers, firstly ensuring that they were whiteboard markers because he had made the mistake of using permanent markers on a previous occasion. There was a black faded line at the top of the board to remind him of his mishap which just wouldn't wipe away.

"Well ADC Hardy has some valuable information. He's just come back from Plymstock Police Station."

Both DI Thorpe and DS Carter alerted to the junior officer. "Great!" Thorpe said. "Let's have it then, Ben."

The young man moved forward and presented the photocopies that he had to the DI. "This is a list of his open cases. His Inspector said that the most important case he was working on was that of two complaints of stalking by a suspicious looking man."

"How is this linked to the murder of Byron Maddocks?" The DI asked, knowing the answer because he had read the Waterstone's Manageress' statement which read that Byron had told her that 'Jeremy' had been stalking him, turning up at various places unannounced.

Ben Hardy was quite bright and guessed that it was a test of his detective skills. "Well, Sir, if you remember, DC Bolton and I took statements from Jenny Baker, the Manageress at Waterstone's in the Mall. Byron Maddocks was book signing there on the afternoon of his murder. They both clocked Jeremy waiting outside the store at closing time, and Mr Maddocks then told her that he thought he was being stalked by this Jeremy."

"Good work, young man," DS Carter added to the conversation as he removed himself from the table and stood up.

"There were various scribbled notes on post it's on his unfinished reports. They are a bit cryptic, but I took photocopies of them all the same."

DS Ayres chuckled. "He will be taking over your job soon, Guv."

"It wouldn't surprise me," DI Thorpe replied whilst looking at ADC Hardy. "No, exceptionally decent work. Don't stop there." Suddenly DC Bolton tapped on the door.

"Come in!" DS Carter shouted over at the door as it opened prior to the invitation.

"Your ADC has been telling us about what you have found," DI Thorpe said. "Quite a lead, I would say."

"Yes," DC Bolton said. "Ben, sorry ADC Hardy picked up on it whilst I was talking to PC Horgan's colleagues to see if there was anything that he had spoken to them about that was on his mind."

"And was there? Anything important?" DS Carter asked inquisitively, folding his arms in the process as he waited for a reply.

"Sergeant Murray, who was PC Horgan's shift Sergeant normally, mentioned that he had spoken to someone down at Plymstock Broadway on the day before his murder. But neither of us could find any record of it. We think he just hadn't completed his paperwork."

"Do we know the approximate time?" DI Thorpe asked DC Bolton, but before he could answer, continued, "Would there be any CCTV that we could pull from the Broadway?"

DS Bolton nodded. "I sent ADC Hardy over to find out."

"There is CCTV, both the monitored Council cameras and other store CCTV from Iceland, Boots and a couple of the banks." Ben Hardy was now looking at his notes in his book. He was glad that he had written everything down and knew that this was a learning point for future reference. "We haven't seized any CCTV as yet, Sir."

DS Carter looked at the pair. "Can you both chase this up? Get the private CCTV before they erase it and check to see if chummy is clearly visible on there. At the moment, we do not have an unobstructed vision of his face."

"Yes, Serge," DC Bolton replied importantly, noting ADC Hardy nodding in agreement.

DS Ayres held his upper arm up. "I'll get on to the Council to request access to the CCTV."

"Good idea, Jon," DI Thorpe said.

DS Carter looked at them all. "It might be a promising idea to pass all CCTV to PC Murphy if he is on duty. He has the eyes of a hawk when it comes to CCTV."

"Oh yes," Thorpe replied. "I remember his input on the Tyrrell case. That's a clever idea." DI Thorpe was deep in thought, hand on his hip and the other on his forehead. "DS Carter, I think we need to take over the stalking complaints made to PC Horgan. I will clear it with Plymstock. Can you interview the two complainants?"

"Yes, Guv. I'll get onto that." Mike Carter looked out into the office to see who was available to accompany him. "I'll take DC Johnson with me. He looks like he needs a bit of excitement."

"Right, let's get going!" DI Thorpe ordered, waving his hands as if to schuh a herd of animals from his office. "We need results boys!"

Back at the Marsh household, Neil was still considering what to do. The Police would laugh at him if he called them because they knew that he normally sorted things like this himself. Someone was bad-mouthing him in the pub just over a year previous. The bartender was a friend of his and let him know. Neil instantly drove to the 'Red Lion,' walked in, grabbed the person responsible and dragged him outside. At the time, he heard the pub go quiet and felt a thousand eyes on him, but as soon as he exited with the screaming trouble maker being pulled by the hair, it returned to general conversation. Not one of the punters was bothered with what was about to happen. David 'bright' Sparks wasn't so 'bright' after being kneecapped in both knees with a sledgehammer. Neil Marsh had just walked off casually, as though he had just purchased a packet of cigarettes at the newsagents.

Neil remembered the incident. He could sort the matter himself but at this moment in time he had no idea who to chase. Who was causing him the worry? He banged the worktop with the lower side of his fist. "Fuck!" Then he walked up to the front door and ensured it was locked, then over to the rear patio door leading to the back garden and did the same before returning to the kitchen to finish off his drink. He decided to get some protection in for Lydia and the kids whilst he was at work. Grabbing his mobile, he flicked down his contacts and pressed on the name of Paul France.

The phone was ringing for a while until Paul himself answered. "Hello?"

"Paul, it's Neil."

"Marshy! How you doin' me old mucker?" He replied joyously expecting a similar reply from the normally equally excited fellow rugby player. He didn't get one and acted on the momentary silence from his old friend. "Something wrong, bud?"

"You could say that." Neil placed his mobile to his other ear. "I've got a slight problem."

"What's up mate. Tell me."

"I've got a death threat through the post and last night, someone was staring at me whilst I was in the car park at work."

"Listen mate, I'm on my way around. You can tell me then. Won't be long." Paul grabbed his car keys from the key hook in his hallway and then left in his Range Rover.

It wasn't long before he pulled up in front of Neil's house, stepped out of the four-by-four and locked it with his remote key whilst continuing up towards the front door. He saw Neil looking out front behind the curtain and then waited for him to unlock the door. "You are looking white, pal," Paul said as the door swung open.

"Come in," Neil replied as he closed and locked the door whilst Paul headed for the kitchen. Neil followed him and noticed that he picked up the death threat letter as soon as he walked in. Then mumbling along, he read the note out beneath his breath.

"That is some shit there, Neil."

"God, I know. It could be anyone, and I'm at a loss as to who."

Paul looked at the letter once more and shook his head. "You want me to try and find out?"

"No. Not at the moment. I am going to work tonight, mainly to see if the guy in the blue car returns for round two." He shook his head and looked down towards the floor, hesitating with silence.

"Are you sure that is wise, Neil?" Paul asked, knowing that if he were in the same situation he would do the same anyway.

"I need you to stay and keep Lydia and the kids under watch. Please."

"That's no problem, bud. I can do that."

Neil was still slightly flustered, not with fear but with frustration that someone was doing this, and he didn't know who. "Thanks. I'll owe you one."

"So, what are you going to do if he shows again?" Paul asked, hoping his mate wasn't going to get himself into any more trouble for Lydia's sake.

"I need to get his car registration. I missed it last night."

"Ideally, try and get a photo of him on your phone," Paul said suggestively. "You have the iPhone. You can zoom in and out and it's a decent quality picture on it."

Neil nodded in reply. "I didn't think of that. I couldn't even see his face because he was wearing a baseball cap pulled down, so the visor was blocking his image."

"Why don't I get a couple of the boys up there? One in the car park that the guy was in and another in the road opposite. Then if he does turn up and try to escape, we could block him in?" Paul was trying to come up with the best ideas to help his mate in every way. He looked at it that if you could catch a mouse in a trap, then you could catch a rat as well.

"I can't think straight. I really can't. What you are suggesting might be an idea actually." Neil looked at his watch and realised that he was grasping for time. "I have to pick the kids up from school."

"I'll come with you. Just in case, like."

"Thanks mate," Neil said with gratitude in his voice which was felt deeply by what was edging out to be his bodyguard at that moment in time. "Come on. Don't want to be late. Bloody kids will kill me."

Half an hour later, Neil had returned home with his two children, Peter, aged eight, and Bella, aged six who were both happy to see 'Uncle Paul' for the first time since Peter's birthday party a few months previous. Paul remembered seeing a disgruntled face at the party because he thought that Peter supported Tottenham FC. How wrong could he get. Peter liked Chelsea FC. In fact, he had been to London with his Dad many times to see them play, and Paul remembered being told that they were off to London to see a team play and swore blind it was Tottenham. So, on his eighth birthday, little Peter received two football shirts.

Neil gave the children a snack to eat prior to their Mother coming home and cooking dinner for them. Both children sat down in the living room and started playing with their toys whilst the two adults sat at the dining room table deep in conversation. Then at about 1650 hrs, Neil checked his watch. "Lydia will be home soon. I have to get my bag packed for work," he said as he jumped up from the dining chair and headed towards the kitchen.

Paul watched him make his flask of coffee and sandwiches and then place them in his rucksack together with his jumper, ready to leave as soon as Lydia returned. "Have you told Lydia I will be here for her safety?"

"No, I haven't yet," Neil replied calmly. "I'm sure she will be thankful for your company. If you need to stay, there is the guest bedroom that you normally have."

"Thanks Neil. See how tired I am!" Paul replied, looking at the kitchen clock. "Where does Lydia work these days?"

"Just over at Curry's PC World. Not far. I have told her that she doesn't need to work, but she says it is for her sanity. I don't mind. At least we get discount off electrical products!" Neil looked at his watch. "She is pushing it a bit tonight." Neil didn't think of the situation that was overhanging them. He just thought Lydia was later than normal. He didn't know that he wouldn't be going to work that evening.

Chapter 7

He sat in his car near the junction of Leigham Manor Drive and Longbridge Road waiting for Lydia Marsh to drive through the lonely lane to get home. Jeremy Cornelius-Johnson decided that the easiest way of getting to someone like Neil Marsh, a man with no conscience for his actions, was through his family. His wife. He was patient, like a lion waiting to ambush its prey when hungry. The bright LED light on his dashboard showed the time as 1706. It wouldn't be long. He chuckled as he read the sign on the verge opposite where he had parked reading, 'Do not park on the grass.' There was no grass there, just mud, and if you parked in the mud, you wouldn't be able to get the car out in any case.

Sure enough, Lydia Marsh turned into the road that she thought would take her home as usual. It was pitch black and so she flicked the light switch onto full beam because there were no other vehicles coming towards her at the moment and therefore she wouldn't blur their vision. What she didn't see was the stinger on the road that had been extended out by Jeremy just in front of his car, so partly obscured by the fact that she had to overtake him. She began to pick up speed after turning into Leigham Park Drive, not bothering to indicate as she pulled around Jeremy's car. There was a 'bump' twice in quick succession, and it suddenly felt as though she had driven over something. Immediately her steering started to become heavy and uncontrollable. Lydia held on to the steering wheel for dear life, but the darkness was just as bad because she could just see where she was going but couldn't control where she was heading. She tried to brake, and the car pulled to one side where the damage was more prominent on the tyres.

Jeremy got out of his car and quickly collected the stinger. Then he jumped back into the driver's seat, started the car, and quickly raced behind her in a menacing way, flashing his lights and sounding his horn at the same time to try and scare her. His initial plan was to just put the fear of god into her and wait for her to stop before just driving away. But looking at her swerving he could tell that she didn't know what to do in such situations. There was no one around. He checked for lights, pedestrians. Nothing. So, he put his foot on the accelerator and headed for the rear end of her car, nudging the passenger side rear, once, twice, three times with the front drivers side of his own. Finally, the car skidded out of control, changing direction so the front of the car was facing the other way. As well as the screeching tyres on the road from the skid, Jeremy could hear the woman screaming inside the car, and a quick glance at her showed the fear on her face. The car continued to turn, the passenger front wheel heading down the bank towards the river making a loud bang as it hot a sharp stone and burst. The car continued to slide sideways towards the water, the angle of the bank just too steep for the car to hold and it started to roll. There was thud and a sound of breaking glass as the car landed in the river upside down with its roof under water in what was one of the deepest parts of the river.

Jeremy turned the car around and then stopped. He looked down towards Lydia Marsh. There was no movement. Stepping out of his car but holding onto the door just as he had done on the evening before when he scared her husband, he grabbed his torch and pointed the light beam down towards the driver. He could see her, motionless, her head under water, and the blood from an impact wound on her skull making the water slightly discoloured. He was happy, so returned inside his car and headed home as though nothing had happened. He was calm, smiling and his pulse never once went higher than his normal resting pulse of sixty-six.

Neil Marsh looked at his watch. Lydia was now fifteen minutes later than normal. Where was she? She had been caught up at work. Difficult customer? He decided to call her, but her phone went straight to voicemail. "I've got a very bad feeling about this, Paul." He tried calling her again, but it still went direct to voicemail. "She is never late. Not like this."

"Ring the store and see if she has left yet. There might be quite an innocent explanation," Paul suggested trying to put a positive note on something that may never be.

"I hope you are right," Neil said unconvincingly as he searched for the number of Lydia's workplace in his contacts list. He had it listed but had never had the need to call it until now. It rang and rang. Finally, it was answered after what seemed like ages to an impatient Neil.

"Curry's PC World. How can I help?"

"Hello. This is Neil Marsh. Lydia's husband who works on customer services."

"Oh hello, Mr Marsh. This is Lydia's workmate Matthew."

"Can you tell me if Lydia has left work yet? She hasn't arrived home, and it is nearly 5.30pm now."

Matthew looked at the clock on the desk in front of him. "Well, she went out the back ten minutes before five like she normally does. I'll just pop out and check if her car is gone," he continued without even waiting for a reply and walked out around the counter to the car park where he knew she had been parked. No car. She had gone, so he walked back into the store. "Her car has gone, Mr Marsh.

Do you think she has popped into Sainsbury's to do some shopping or something?"

"She would normally tell me, and in any case, her mobile is going straight to voicemail. It's okay. I will wait for her. Thanks for looking." He ended the call.

"Any luck?" Paul asked worryingly, now becoming as concerned as his mate.

Neil shook his head and bit his lip. "No. She left on time. Her car is gone." Neil's mind was now working overtime, trying every scenario that he could think of except the one that come to mind, but he had placed it at the back of the mental list that was in his head. But it suddenly came to the front on his mind and top of his list as he tried Lydia's mobile one last time and reached her voicemail again. "Paul. Stay with the kids for me, will you? I'm going to drive down that way. See if she has had a breakdown or something. Her phone battery might be dead."

"Yes, that's no problem, mate," Paul replied watching Neil already disappear after grabbing his car keys from the key hook in the hallway. At this moment in time, he was just as anxious as his friend, especially after what Neil had told him about the previous night at the Taxi office.

Paul reversed his car out of the driveway and then sped off down Leigham Park Drive at some speed. On the way, he checked every layby and entrance to the football pitches and lastly the caravan park. Nothing. No sign that she had broken down. But then his headlights picked up something on the road surface, as what looked like fresh skid marks. On the edge of the river bank the grass had all been turned up. Neil skidded to a halt, turning his car as he did so in order that his headlights shone on the disturbed grass. But he found something else. "Fuck! Lydia!" he shouted as he got out of the car and slid down the steep riverbank on his rear, his feet and legs disappearing into the water to just above his knees.

Neil reached the driver's side door and tried to open it, but the driver auto-lock prevented him from doing so. He pulled the door, trying his hardest to get it open. He also noticed that the overturned car was partly underwater and could see Lydia's head was also underwater. She was not moving. With all his strength, he punched at the side window on the Driver's side door and after three attempts, the heavy-duty security glass shattered. He punched the shattered glass to clear it and then reached in to the door handle, fumbling for the position as he did so, and unlocked the door. He pulled it with all his might until it was partially open. It wouldn't go any further as the top of the door had wedged itself in the stones on the bottom of the riverbed. But he reached inside the car and managed to undo the seatbelt. Lydia's lifeless body dropped towards the water even more, but Neil caught her and instantly went about getting the unconscious lady out of the car. The deadweight of a wet body made her heavy, but he got her top half out of the door and then locked his hands around her chest to complete the last pull.

Lydia wasn't out of danger yet as he pulled her to dry land. Neil checked her breathing but there was no sign of life. "Fuck! No! Lydia!" He started pumping on her chest to perform CPR, alternating with mouth- to-mouth breaths as he did so, but also becoming frantic when she failed to respond immediately. "No! Come on!" he shouted impatiently. "Lydia!"

Suddenly he was joined by a barking dog who thought that Neil was playing with it in some way. Neil thought that where there is a dog there is usually an owner. He started to shout, "HELP! HELP ME!" with a hope that the dog owner would hear his voice and come to look for his dog. The dog continued barking as Neil saw a man coming towards him.

"What's happened?"

"It's my wife," Neil snapped. "She rolled the car into the water. She's not breathing." Neil started to sob whilst he continued the compressions on her chest.

"Have you called an ambulance?" The man asked, watching Neil shake his head. "I'll call one."

"Tell them to be quick! She's not breathing!" Neil carried on with all his strength forced into the compressions on his wife's chest. But there was no sign of life. None at all. Lydia had drowned in the attack.

The ambulance arrived fifteen minutes later with their lights reverberating across the darkened early evening sky. The ambulance staff and paramedic were waved down by the man who had called them whilst Neil tried to resuscitate her. As they approached him, all they could see was him holding his wife in his arms, already grief stricken.

"Hello. My name is Jordan. I am a paramedic. Can I take a look at the lady?"

Neil's eyes were red with tears as he looked up at the medical staff. "She's gone. I can't get her to breath," he cried painfully.

"Can I see her, Sir?" Jordan said, moving forward cautiously because he didn't know the man's state of mind or demeanour. Many medical staff had been assaulted in recent months just for trying to help those who were injured. He edged slowly towards the body. "Can you put her down for me?"

Neil looked at the younger man. "It's my wife. I tried to save her. Her car was in the water."

"Can I take your name? And the name of your wife?"

"Neil. Neil Marsh," he replied solemnly as he placed his wife's body gently on the ground in front of him. "This is Lydia."

Jordan edged forward a bit more and checked for a pulse, and then checked her eyes, and then he knew that he was too late to do anything for Neil's wife. "I'm so sorry,

Neil. Lydia has been taken from you tonight." Jordan nodded to the support staff behind him who passed over a silver foil blanket to cover the body and wrapped her up as though she were just cold.

There were more flashing lights in the distance, but not from another ambulance, this time from the Police cars. Neil pushed himself up and brushed his clothes down. He still couldn't believe or come to terms with what had happened to her. How was he going to explain this to Peter and Bella? They had lost their Mother and Neil had lost his wife and best friend. He looked around and saw the Police cordoning off the area as a crime scene with 'Police – Do Not Cross' tape. The ambulance staff had told them it was a suspicious death, and the officers had to preserve what evidence they could in order that the Road Policing Investigators could try and ascertain just what had happened. They had been called, along with CID.

Neil Marsh sat on the riverbank staring at his wife's car in the water. He knew that something wasn't right.

The day shift in the CID office were just thinking about clocking off when DS Carter's desk phone rattled into life. "DS Carter."

"Hello Sergeant. It's PS Bickford here."

"How can I help you tonight then George?" DS Carter replied, remembering the Officer from their meeting at Burrator. "We met at Burrator. DS Mike Carter."

"Ah yes. I remember. Well Mike, sorry to bother you, but we have a suspicious death down here at Leigham Park Drive." George Bickford checked the activity going on behind him. "The victim is a Lydia Marsh."

DS Carter knew the name. "Is her husband called Neil by any chance?"

"Yes. How did you know that?" George asked inquisitively, not liking the fact that the victim's husband was known to Police.

"I arrested him for burglary and manslaughter some months back. He got off because all of the witnesses withdrew their statements."

"Well, you had better get down here then, before he disappears," George Bickford said jokingly.

"I'll grab the Inspector now. See you soon." He walked over to DI Thorpe's office and tapped on the open door.

"Yes, Mike. What can I do for you?"

"You weren't planning on going home early tonight were you, Guv?" DS Carter said with a serious tone.

"Why? What have you got?" DI Thorpe saw the glint in his Sergeant's eye that usually meant that something serious had come up.

"Suspicious death. I wouldn't normally ask you, but the victim is Lydia Marsh, wife of no other than .."

DI Thorpe intercepted what Mike Carter was going to say. "Neil Marsh? THE Neil Marsh?"

"Yes, it seems so," DS Carter replied. "George Bickford has just called to say it was suspicious how she died so I told him someone would be with him soon."

"So where did it take place?" DI Thorpe asked as though he were wondering if it was anywhere near any reported burglary on the same evening.

"On the same road that leads down to where the Marsh's live," Carter replied. "I can handle it if you wish. I just know that you had a personal interest in catching Marsh."

DI Thorpe grabbed his jacket from the back of his desk chair. He had a coat stand in his office right by the door, but always chose to put his own coat on his chair. Laziness, he used to tell himself, because if he ever needed to get anything out of his jacket, he wouldn't have to get up and walk across the room. "Come on then," he said, closing his office door behind him and then following DS Carter over towards the entrance to the stairs which would take them right down to the car park.

"So, what is your interest in Marsh?" DS Carter asked his boss, knowing that he had been after him for years.

"He burgled my Mother years ago. His wife gave him an alibi when we went to question him as one of the known and active burglars in the area."

"No DNA or other evidence?" DS Carter asked worriedly.

"He was very clever. Wore the full protective suit. CCTV picked someone up, but it was a stolen car and he had goggles on so what evidence we did have with the CCTV was inadmissible under PACE.

DS Carter looked serious as he opened the fire door at the bottom of the stairs. "The thing is, he is not even particularly good at it. Old fashioned if anything." They reached the vehicle and jumped in either side with DS Carter instantly taking the driving seat.

"Well, we think he was taught the trade by his Father Tony, who was taught by his Father."

"So, it's a trade that has been passed down through the generations then?" Carter asked as he headed down towards Cattedown roundabout.

"These days he tends to get caught because of the CCTV and other alarm systems. He has never moved on. Always doing it his Dad's ancient way, who always did it his Dad's way." DI Thorpe paused for thought and seemed a little sad for a moment as he stared out of the window. "His last time he did the full suit thing, gloves. But he was disturbed by the occupant who was an elderly lady who lived on her own. We knew it was Marsh but again couldn't pin the crime down to him. He even turned up at the old ladies funeral. Why would he do that? He didn't know her."

DS Carter shook his head in disbelief. "I hate cocky little shits like that."

"Tell me about it. Things like that just make this job worthwhile because you are even more set on nabbing them."

"Not far now," DS Carter exclaimed as he slowed at the traffic lights at Marsh Mills roundabout.

"Good. Mike I'm going to tell you something but it's for your ears only."

"Sounds ominous," Carter replied thinking that the DI had some unwelcome news that he couldn't tell anyone else.

"I am." He hesitated before the next word. "Retiring. I'm taking early retirement."

DS Carter seemed shocked at his statement. The DI and him had worked together for years now on and off, except when he had gone undercover for GMP for several months in 2017. "I can understand. You are not ill or anything?"

"No. No," the DI replied shaking his head. "There is so much red tape now trying to get a conviction that I've decided to spend time with the family. When I first started, you didn't sit behind a desk worrying about how much it was going to cost to catch a thief and what percentage of murders you had convictions for. I'm getting out while I'm sane!"

Still shocked, DS Carter started to accept what he had been told. "Well. Thanks for confiding in me. That means a lot. When is this going to happen?"

"Let's just say, this will probably be my last case."

"Wow. That quick?"

"You know me. I will see it through until the end. But then I will just disappear. I don't want it going public. It's between me and the DCI at the moment."

"Hey, Guv. Your secret is behind sealed lips with me, you know that."

Thorpe nodded in agreement. "I know that. You are one of the best Sergeants I have worked with which is why I had to let you know. That, and I was asked by the DCI who I thought could take my place and I told him you were the best candidate if it was internal."

DS Carter started slowing the car as they approached the cordon where an officer stood holding the blue and white tape. "You are going to make me cry in a minute," he stated as he shook his head. "But thank you for your friendship, mentoring and the recommendation."

"Ah, we are here," DI Thorpe commented getting out of the car and closing the door shut. He produced his warrant card as he approached the cordon. DS Carter was right behind him as the tape was lifted for the both of them and they walked through heading towards the voices in the darkness at the edge of the riverbank in front of them.

Sergeant Bickford had seen them both arrive in the unmarked vehicle and started to walk over to meet them. "Hello, Guv," he said as DI Thorpe approached. He nodded to DS Carter whom he could see in the shadows.

"What have we got here, Sergeant?" DI Thorpe asked in his official voice in order that any press gathering in the darkness behind the cordon would report that he was on the scene and investigating. "I've been told it is Neil Marsh's wife, Lydia."

"Yes, that's right. We have the RPLI down looking at the car at the moment."

"Okay," DI Thorpe replied authoritatively before turning around to DS Carter. "Can you go down and see if he has any idea how it happened, Mike?"

"Yes, Guv," DS Carter said as he stepped around them both on the thin pathway which was a mixture of mud and grass and headed down towards the upturned vehicle. He pulled his torch out of his pocket and turned it on to add to the lighting around covering the scene and to assist in him in not slipping on the way down and going head over heels. As he reached the bottom near what was left of the beach because of the high-water level, he flashed his warrant card at the investigator. "DS Carter."

The older man stopped and smiled. "How are you doing? I'm Mark Robinson, Lead Investigator. Somewhere

over there is my Assistant Investigator, Alistair Mackenzie."
He pointed over to the other side of the car.

"I know it's early days, but do you have anything?"
DS Carter asked politely. "Do you think it was it an
accident?"

"I can tell immediately that this is going to be a CAT
A. Looking at the skid and tyre marks on the road, it looks
like this car was forced off the road. I confirmed this as
there is damage to the rear of this vehicle which is not
cohesive with the damage caused by the roll into the river."

DS Carter looked in horror. "Was there just the one
victim in the car?"

"It looks that way. She had her head under water
for some time and I guess if she was conscious at any
point, she was stopped escaping by the seatbelt and the
water pressure on the door." Mark Robinson stood up and
stretched his back and legs after being leaned over for a
while looking at the damage. "Once we get the car back to
the yard, I will be able to tell you more and not speculate."

"Yes, thanks for the info. Just to put us in the
picture as you can understand." DS Carter turned and
carefully went up the riverbank back towards his DI who
was still speaking to the Police Sergeant. He didn't say
anything to interrupt their conversation as he appeared in
the shadows of the pair.

DI Thorpe saw him there and started to end the
conversation with a "Thanks Sergeant," as he turned to his
own Sergeant. "Anything, Mike?"

"Bad news. The RPLI reckons that it wasn't an
accident, she was forced off the road by another vehicle
which appears to have rammed her car."

DI Thorpe shook his head. "Well, I hate to say it,
but what goes around comes around." He looked over
towards Neil Marsh who was still sat overlooking the crash
site and the body of his wife. "So, what do we think?"

DS Carter was deep in thought, hand on his lower
lip. "Let's face it. It could be anyone."

"That's why we need to get him in to speak to as soon as possible. He may be able to provide us with some information about who, where and why." He looked over towards the sitting figure who looked a shadow of a man he usually was at that moment in time. "I'm not sure if he will be glad to see me, but he is going to."

DS Carter watched as his boss started walking over towards Neil Marsh, and it looked like DI Thorpe wasn't in the sympathetic mood. Was he ending his last case on a good note? That was yet to be seen, Carter thought to himself.

DI Thorpe towered over the criminal who was in so much shock that he didn't notice the man who had arrested him on several occasions before stood behind him. "Neil?"

The widower turned his head. "Mr Thorpe. You know, I was thinking, if there is one Detective I need to find out what happened, it would be Detective Inspector Thorpe."

"I'm sorry about your wife, Neil. Past incidents put to one side I wouldn't wish this on anyone." DI Thorpe looked around and down to the car. "Listen, Neil. The Investigator has indicated that it wasn't an accident."

"That doesn't surprise me," Neil answered.

"No? Is there something that I need to know?" DI Thorpe caught on to what Neil had just said. It doesn't surprise him. Why doesn't it surprise him? "We are going to need to talk about this at some point."

"My kids are at home with my friend. I need to get home to them." Neil was picking up blades of grass and twisting them nervously, appearing not to have any motivation. "Can you drive me there? It's only at the end of the road here. I don't think that I should drive."

DI Thorpe waved over to DS Carter who started walking towards them both. "We are going to take Mr Marsh home and hopefully have a chat with him about what has happened tonight." He looked into DS Carter's eyes with a stare, as though he were trying to tell him something without words.

DS Carter had seen it before, like a morse code with the eyes. "Whenever you are ready, Mr Marsh, the car is just over at the cordon." Mike Carter was surprised that the DI had been so nice to Marsh after what he had said, but then he reminded himself that the night was young.

"No time like the present," Marsh said, pushing himself upwards using his hands and then brushing the mud and the grass that he had been twisting earlier from his clothes. He followed the two detectives across the road, watching as DS Carter directed any civilian or press member away who tried to get close. Minutes later, he was in the car, and being driven though the array of emergency vehicles that had attended the scene towards his home.

Chapter 8

Wembury was just a small locale on the outskirts of Plymouth. It was quite a close-knit community, with a resident's association that regularly organised events for the community. Everyone knew everybody in the vicinity who lived there, and someone always made it their business to welcome newcomers.

They had heard about the death of Jeremy's parents, and many had been around to offer their condolences much to the resentment of Jeremy himself who just wanted to be left alone. The deaths of both Rufus and Felicity Cornelius-Johnson had come as much as a shock to the community as it had their son, except Jeremy was only putting on a front for the sake of getting away with murder. In a total frenzied attack, he just stabbed the both of them in their beds over and over again. The Police had never seen anything like the scene in the area, with the bloodstained sheets, splatter all over the walls and floor, and throats cut after the attack to make sure that they were actually dead. He had then stolen many items of value and smashed the pane of glass in the kitchen to make it look like a burglary.

Yes, Jeremy had gotten away with murder after being able to provide an alibi supported by a logon to his X-Box account. He was also very convincing about his parents death to the Police.

He arrived home, driving his car onto the driveway whilst watching the next-door neighbour who was out on his porch having a cigarette. The neighbour waved, a gesture that was returned by Jeremy as he stopped the car. Jeremy knew that the neighbour would just try and strike up a conversation of some kind. He was a 'nosey neighbour' in more than one sense of the word, regularly letting Jeremy know that he should water his lawn during the summer but either first thing in the morning or last thing at night. All because Jeremy chose to do it at any time he was free. When he had explained this, and his job, the retired neighbour started watering the lawn and flower beds for him.

"Evening," Ken shouted over as Jeremy stood up at the side of the car. "You are later than normal tonight."

"Yes, I went for dinner with work colleagues after we had finished," Jeremy replied, hoping that the explanation would be accepted quickly.

"Saves you cooking," Ken Meadows continued happily. "Especially as you sometimes work long days." Ken then tried to focus within the dim light on his porch at Jeremy's car. "You've had a bit of a bump, young man. On the front there."

Jeremy had taken the car to the power wash on the way home to clean the debris from the damage and the mud from the wheels. But the damage would be there until he managed to get to the garage. "Yes, I know," he replied. "Someone backed into me at work," Jeremy said as he moved around to convey the damage again and shook his head as though he were concerned and frustrated. "Right, Ken. Have a good night. I'm going to have a drink and rest."

"Yes, goodnight."

Jeremy went inside but kept the living room lights off as he checked outside looking from behind the curtains. He had a feeling that Ken Meadows would come over and check the damage on his car and then make it his business to recommend a good repairer whom he had *'Used before and done a decent job'* as he normally did. He placed his briefcase on the chair beside him and watched through the side of the partially open blinds. Thankfully, on this occasion, Ken had stubbed his cigarette out on his manufactured extinguisher, and then disappeared inside his own house. Jeremy felt relief and so walked over to flick the light switch on his upright lamp. Then he sat down on the sofa, grabbed the remote control, and turned on the television.

There were no reports yet on any of the channels either nationally or locally. The BBC local bulletin was normally on after the 10 o'clock news, so he had time to kill if he wanted to watch it. But he left the television on just in case there was a breaking news broadcast, which he doubted because they didn't normally give prime time to such incidents. In the kitchen, he opened the refrigerator and took out his attempt at a farmhouse salad, placing the plate on the side before opening the bread bin to take out two bread rolls. Then he returned to sit on the sofa, grabbing a knife and fork on the way.

Jeremy munched away on the cheese and ham, dipping it into the pickle before ripping open the bread roll and thrusting the meat inside. All the time, he was thinking of his next move on Neil Marsh. He needed an appointment to view the houses for sale in order that he could park just down from Neil's house at a time when he knew Neil may be mobile, coming in and out of the house. He would recognise the car and become aggressively frightened. In reality, Jeremy could not predict how Marsh would react. But he would leave it a few days to let the dust settle because no doubt Neil Marsh would tell the Police about the dark blue Nissan that had appeared at his works on the night before his wife died. He also had the note and the photos.

The Spotlight news came on and instantly zoomed in on the Leigham Park Drive incident. It didn't shock

Jeremy when the newscaster announced that the fatality was being treated as suspicious and would be investigated as a murder. Jeremy shook his head and made a noise by blowing his nose briefly. It was only a news headline, and soon the story changed. Jeremy turned the television off and sat in silence in the dimmed lit room. He pictured Neil Marsh on the day when he was in court and had tried to headbutt him when he was acquitted. "That has really fucked up your life," he said out loudly with the picture on his mind. He didn't try to actually kill Marsh's wife. In fact, just the opposite. But it had happened, and he had no conscience.

He heard the voices of his parents again in the background.

'*Well done. Criminals, the lot of them.*'

The voice of his Father spoke clearly, whilst his Mother was more concerned for his welfare commenting something sensible.

'*Make sure you cover your tracks, son.*'

Jeremy looked behind him as though he were going to see the both of them standing in the archway between the living room and the dining room, but they weren't there. They had never been there, not even when they were alive. As he concentrated that little bit more, their voices dispersed just like they were on surround sound around the room. He clicked the remote and turned the TV off, then grabbed his plate and took it out to the kitchen placing it in the sink. He would deal with that in the morning, he thought to himself. He was tired. It was time for bed.

DI Thorpe and DS Carter stood in the Marsh's kitchen. Neil's friend Paul Francis had put the children to bed before they arrived and then checked to see if the Police wanted him to leave or whether he could stay to support his friend. They were happy for him to stay.

"You will get whoever has done this, Inspector, won't you?" Neil said with a strained voice and tears in his eyes. "I know we have never seen eye to eye, but you are the best detective in this county."

DI Thorpe looked at DS Carter and then back to Neil. "Thank you for your confidence, Neil. I will do my utmost best, believe me. Now you know the drill. I need to get some background."

Neil knew that he hadn't wanted to involve the Police and wouldn't have done if Lydia hadn't have been run off the road. "Some bloke in a blue Nissan Duke was watching me last night at work."

"Where do you work?" DS Carter asked taking note of everything that Marsh fed to them.

"Class Car Taxi's up at the top of the railway station," Neil replied before focusing back on the DI. "As I went to see what his problem was, he got up and sped off."

"Did you get his registration number?" DI Thorpe added.

Neil shook his head whilst walking across to the kettle and filling it up with water. "Sorry, I need a drink."

"Let me make it," Paul said, joining him over by the sink.

"Thanks," Neil said to him solemnly, looking as though he were about to collapse with the shock of what had happened tonight. "Anyway, today the Postman delivered this," he slid the note over to the DI via the work surface and then did the same with the pack of photographs.

DI Thorpe took out a pair of protective gloves from his pocket and quickly put them on. The he read the note out in order that DS Carter would also know what it contained.

'There are four kinds of Murder: felonious, excusable, justifiable, and praiseworthy. Yours will consist of all four.'

"Wow, Neil. That really is a death threat. Have you upset anyone recently who might think of taking revenge of any kind?"

Marsh shook his head as he watched the Inspector pass the letter to his DS and then start to flick through the photographs. "He was that close."

DS Carter was passed the photographs to look at and copied the Inspector by flicking through them before taking an evidence bag out of his pocket and placing them in there, repeating the task with the threatening note. "We will have to take these, Neil."

He nodded in agreement, his normal angry temperament towards the Police now lying dormant as his heart was telling him that he needed their help.

"I suggest that you do not stay here, Neil. I don't think it is safe," DI Thorpe said to him importantly whilst looking at him eye to eye. "Who knows what this man is capable of next. Have you got friends or family that would take you in for a few nights?"

"We can drop you wherever," DS Carter added. "Make sure that you get their safe and sound and that you are not followed."

"Or if you want to take your car, we can follow you. It's up to you."

"I'm going to call my Mum and Dad, tell them what has happened and see if they can have the children."

"Why don't you come over to me, Neil," asked his friend Paul. "You've slept in the spare room on many an occasion. It may also be a good thing to separate you and the children to reduce the threat on them."

"That might be a clever idea," DS Carter exclaimed. "If it is you that he is after, it is best to reduce the level of risk."

"Okay," Marsh said softly. At this moment in time, he was looking for someone to make all the decisions for him because he just couldn't think straight. There were so many questions going around and around in his brain that he was glad to be going over to Paul's house if he were honest. He would have asked Lydia's parents to look after the children, but they were God-bearing people and would have given him a sermon on how this was God's way of telling him to stop his criminal activity. But he would have to speak to them at some point quite soon. It was their daughter. "Let me make some phone calls."

"You go ahead," DI Thorpe snapped. "Take your time," he replied watching Marsh grab his mobile phone and walk into the dining room to gain what little privacy he could at this moment in time. Thorpe placed his hands on his hips and brushed back his suit jacket. Then he looked at DS Carter and raised his eyebrows before asking, "Well, what do you think?"

"There is something not quite right," DS Carter responded inquisitively. "Someone obviously has a grudge against him. That note. That has come from a very learned person."

"That's what I was thinking. Four descriptions of death all in one-word expressions." Thorpe scanned around the room, not actually looking for anything in particular, but knowing that Marsh was usually in possession of stolen goods, he knew it was worth a look even if at this moment in time he wouldn't do anything about it. But the possession of some object that had been reported as stolen in a burglary usually gave them the culprit or a link to the culprit. He shook his head and then thought of something that his wife had once said to him, 'Always on duty.' "It sounds like a quote from something."

DS Carter was closer to the dining room and could overhear the conversation that Neil Marsh was having with his parents which was making him even more emotional. He listened so carefully, trying to notice anything that might be said he could be a suspect until he was proved otherwise. Many cases had seen the husbands killing their wives in a jealous rage because they had been having affairs. But his gut instinct told him that this wasn't one of those cases, or if it was, Neil Marsh was playing a very convincing part.

Paul France came back into the living room, to investigate the conversation between the two officers. He knew that something was being said that they didn't want anyone to hear because as soon as he walked in, the two detectives went quiet. "He is frantic," Paul said calmly. "Lydia was his everything."

"Paul we need a bit of background information," DI Thorpe said to him. "Is that ok?"

He nodded. "I guess from an outsiders point of view?"

"Yes. You could say that. Do you know of any problems that the two of them were having in the family?" DI Thorpe asked quietly, hoping that Neil himself wouldn't hear because of his conversation on the phone. He also knew that there were somethings that criminals wouldn't say about their friends or 'Grass' about as it would be seen as.

Paul shook his head. "You would be barking up the wrong tree there, Inspector," he said imminently. "Neil did as he was told and worshipped the ground that Lydia walked on. Likewise, he would do anything for his children."

"You realise we have to ask these sort of questions just to try and get a picture in our minds and rule out anyone we might think to be suspected of foul play," Thorpe explained to him.

"Yes I understand. But If Lydia said jump, Neil was the one who had to ask, 'How High' in that marriage. Despite all of our wrongdoings, they loved their family and friends."

"Thanks for that," DI Thorpe said to him as Paul had backed up the lack of suspicion that he had that Neil had been responsible and wiped out any concerns that one of them might have been playing away from home.

"What about the photos and the letter?" Paul asked concerningly.

DS Carter held both packages up in his hand. "We will get them analysed. I doubt there will be any fingerprints of them apart from Neil, Lydia, and yourself, but there are other avenues that we can investigate such as the paper used, who sells it, or if the photos were printed by a company."

Paul France nodded. "I know you will do your best, Detectives," he said as Neil suddenly came back into the living room. "Everything alright, bud?"

Neil's eyes were reddened with tears as he nodded. "My parents are on their way over to take the children. Paul can you keep an eye out for them?"

"Course I can mate. I'll stand outside and wait for them." He walked over toward the front door and stepped out into the chilly night, looking up to the full moon that was providing the additional light to the street beaming down like a giant spotlight at a sports game.

Back inside, Neil looked at the two detectives. "Could you please arrange for someone to escort my parents back home. I'm just worried that someone might follow them."

"Mike, can you get onto that?" DI Thorpe asked DS Carter, who instantly got on his radio in the background to request uniform assistance.

"Thanks, Inspector. I had better call Lydia's parents. This won't be so easy."

"Good luck," DI Thorpe said as Neil went back into the dining room to make the second of his calls. He watched as Neil waited for someone to answer the telephone, and then looked at DS Carter to see how he was getting on organising uniform assistance. His junior officer gave him the thumbs up before saying his goodbyes and returning his mobile to his pocket.

"George Bickford is sending a unit straight over, Guv."

"That's good. More of a deterrent that anything, but if it helps put their minds to rest, so be it." DI Thorpe looked back at Neil Marsh who appeared to be having a tough time of it on the telephone with his in-laws.

"I guess that is the victim's parents he is speaking to?" DS Carter said hearing the raised voice and at one point the shouting down the telephone before a threat that Neil was going to end the call, which he did and then threw his mobile done on the dining table. "I hate them. I humour them most of the time just for the sake of my kids," he said angrily and shaking his head. "I told them there is nothing that they can do by coming here, but they are adamant they are on their way. Probably want to do a prayer meeting or something."

"We can turn them away if that is what you want," DS Carter said calmingly. You will have a Family Liaison Officer attending soon to oversee things once myself and the DI leave." He waited for a reply but noticed that Neil Marsh had just come to his senses and realised that Lydia had gone. He broke down crying, his body falling back into the waiting chair behind him. He did not reply to DS Carter.

Fifteen minutes later, a car pulled up just outside the house having managed to get through the blockade back along the road at the scene of the crime.

"Didn't think we were going to make it," the big burly man said as he got out of the driver's seat. He recognised Paul France having seen him many times in the past both at his son's house and when they had both turned up at the parent's house.

Paul France nodded to them both and then hugged Henry and his wife Carla as they approached the door. "You managed to get through the cordon, then?"

"Yes. Had to give ID." Henry went to go inside the house but stopped and asked quietly, "How is he?"

"Frantic," Paul replied. "This has devastated him." He let the pair walk in and then followed them, accepting that he had been standing out in the cold for a while now and his hands were suffering as he was beginning not to feel the life in his fingers.

Neil saw his parents and stood up. "Hi Mum. Dad," he said as they both welcomed him with open arms. "Lydia is dead, Mum!"

"I know, love. I know," Carla replied pulling her son into her as tightly as can be. He was always a mummy's boy when he was young, and she knew that. He would never cry as a child in front of his Dad if he fell over or got into a fight. Neil always seemed to want to have a hardman image even as a young child and follow in his Father's footsteps. Henry had put him to boxing classes in Devonport and Neil had toughened up as a child which helped as it prevented him being bullied at school.

"Hello, Mr & Mrs Marsh. I am DI Thorpe from Devon and Cornwall Police. This is DS Carter."

Henry acknowledged the two officers with a nod of his head. "Do you know what happened?"

"It's early days," DI Thorpe replied solemnly. "The traffic investigation officers are at the scene now trying to work things out. As you can understand, these things take time."

"Neil tells me that it wasn't an accident," Henry continued maintaining a serious look on his face as though he expected results as soon as possible.

"That is the preliminary findings. It is suggested that her car was forced from behind and needless to say she lost control and plunged into the river." DI Thorpe knew that there was a sign of hostility coming from Henry. Whether or not he had dealings with the Police before or was known to them wasn't known at this particular moment in time. "I will keep you informed of any updates through your Family Liaison Officer."

"Darling," Carla interrupted. "We had better get the children ready. Get them out as soon as possible so as not to disturb them too much."

Henry nodded to his wife. "Yes, okay love. What about you, Son?"

Neil lightly pushed away from his Mother's embrace, wiped his tearful eyes, and then said, "I'm going to stay with Paul."

"Only if you are sure, love," Carla said reassuringly, indicating that she would prefer him to come home with them.

"Why don't you come home with your Mum and me?" his Father suggested nicely, hoping that Neil would change his mind because it was his Father that had suggested it.

"I need some space. It's much appreciated. But Paul only lives half a mile away, and it will be easier for me."

"As long as you're sure?" Henry asked, not bothering to pursue the subject anymore. If there is one thing that he had learned about his son, it was that once he had made up his mind about something, he never changed it.

Neil nodded. "I'll be okay."

"Right, let's go and get the kids," Henry said to his wife.

DS Carter looked at the pair heading towards the bottom of the stairs. "We have arranged for a Police Car to escort you home and ensure you are safe."

"Thank you," Carla replied politely. "That is much appreciated." She didn't know much; only what Neil had told her on the telephone about the note and photographs. So, she felt that a Police escort would be beneficial in a big way.

As the parents disappeared upstairs, there was a tap on the open front door. Two uniformed officers walked into the house and through the door to the living room. "PC's Longbrook and Markham, Sir. We have been assigned to you for protection duty."

"Yes, thank you. We need you to escort a family back home and make sure they are not compromised in any way," DI Thorpe said to the two. "Be aware of any traffic following you, and act accordingly if you are suspicious."

"No problem, Sir," PC Longbrook replied. "Where are we going?"

Neil pulled himself together and announced, "Just up to Derriford. Dunraven Drive."

DI Thorpe looked at Neil and decided to change the subject a little. "Neil, I know you are going to Paul's house, but we will need a statement from you at some point." He looked at Paul. "And also, you, Paul. Now I find that it is best to go over things whilst things are fresh in your mind. I realise how traumatic this has been for you tonight, so is it okay if we pop around in the morning?"

Neil looked at Paul who nodded back to him. "Yes, that is fine." He heard movement on the stairs as his Father carried the two children down, both sleepy and unaware of the surroundings. Bella was still dead to the world and cuddling into her Grandad whilst Peter was rubbing his eyes.

"We will leave you to it, Neil," his Mother commented concerningly. "They can stay will us for as long as you want them to."

"Yes," Henry said. "I have packed them some clothes, but we may need some more."

"I'll get them to you," Neil said following them out of the front door. He moved sideways so that the two PC's could get past him and walk over to their unmarked Police car.

"We will be following you," PC Markham commented as he walked by the car where Henry was putting one of the children in the child safety seat.

"Ok, thanks." Henry said, and then he looked over to check that Carla had strapped in Peter to the other child safety seat. They got in the front of the car and drove off.

Neil waved to them, and then walked back inside, his eyes still red from the upset of the evening. He looked at his friend. "Can we get out of here, Paul?"

"Anytime you want, mate," Paul replied, showing concern for his friend's welfare, and holding his upper arm as though to steady him. "That is alright with you, Inspector?"

"Yes," DI Thorpe replied. "We will come and see the pair of you in the morning."

Chapter 9

It was Friday. Investigative reporter Jack Dempsey from the National newspaper 'The Sun' was watching what was happening in Plymouth, having been born there and still with family living close to the city. He told himself that it wasn't the same place these days. Crime was on the increase and there seemed to be more major crimes such as murder, drug-related crime, and even sexual assaults in what used to be the self-proclaimed 'Ocean City' of the UK.

Jack had covered the Tyrrell/Bresland case some months earlier and had also put his feelers out for the escaped Steven Jefferies, thinking what a scoop that would be if he could find him whilst the Police had failed to do so. Devon and Cornwall Police had tried everything to stop the newspaper printing the story but hadn't succeeded.

But now there was another story in the making in his hometown and Jack was about to stir things up with an investigation that would prelude his article. He knew that it would step on a few toes, and that his Editor would receive a reprimand which would be escalated down, but headlines like this sold newspapers, so the Editor would print a one-inch apology on page 7 where no one would see it, and it would all be forgotten and in the archives in no time at all.

He sat on the train, first class, with his laptop open and was just finalising the first story as he headed to 'The Crime Capital of the South West' as the headline would point out. Many had said the same about Torquay and even Bristol. But the recent events had proved fatal for Plymouth when it came to the press. The announcement came over the speaker that the train was now approaching Plymouth, so Jack quickly packed up his rucksack made especially for laptop use, and then grabbed his small suitcase from the luggage rack.

Minutes later, the train pulled into the station and Jack disembarked rolling his case on its wheels over towards the exit. He was hoping that his Sister would be there ready and waiting for him as they had previously arranged. Then he saw a familiar face waiting for him on the other side of the ticket barrier.

"Hello, you," his sister Beth said with a big smile across her face. "Welcome home!" She gave him a hug.

"Hello, Sis," Jack replied with excitement. "It's good to be back."

"Alex is outside in the car park waiting in the car, so he doesn't have to pay anything. You know him. He hates paying for parking. Here, let me grab your case." She led the way out of the main entrance and to the right, as though Jack wouldn't remember the way himself.

"How is he?" Jack asked, remembering that the last time he saw Beth's husband he was just changing jobs.

"He is great. Much happier in his new job. It's made my life easier as well."

"Being happy in a job certainly helps," Jack replied as they approached the white Mercedes parked up in the short-term car park outside the Transport Police office.

Alex watched them approach from the side window and opened the boot electronically so Jack could put his luggage in there. "Hi Jack." It was always Alex's little joke that Jack had heard over and over again ever since he was at primary school.

"I haven't heard that one before," Jack replied with a laugh. "I'm fine Alex. How are you?" Both Brother and

Sister got into the car and Alex pulled away towards the main road.

"Brilliant! I feel like a new man these days."

"So does my Sister, no doubt, with those jokes." He saw Alex look at him through the mirror and both of them smiled. They had always got on and the man banter was something that made them friends.

"You two, behave!" Beth said, joining in the light-heartedness.

"So, what do we owe the pleasure?" Alex asked inquisitively, knowing that they didn't see Jack very often mainly because he was always working so hard.

"It's business. I'm doing a story on my hometown." He hesitated, waiting for a reply that wasn't coming at that moment. "But I will still have time to spend with everybody."

Alex smirked and looked quickly at his wife. "Working for your comic, it can't be a story on how wonderful a place Plymouth is to live."

"Far from it," Jack responded in an upbeat tone. "It's all about the death rate in the city from the increase in crime. I'm here to find out why and hopefully, who."

Beth turned her head. "There have been a lot of murders in the past year. We had a shoot-out between two drug gangs a few months ago."

"There is sense to my madness. An author friend of mine was murdered up at Burrator Reservoir." Jack realigned his seatbelt as it was digging into his shoulder.

"Byron Maddocks," Alex snapped. "Yes, I have read a couple of his books."

"Of course," Beth added. "Jack, didn't you start out by reviewing books before getting promoted?"

Jack nodded but then realised the pair of them probably couldn't see his action, so added, "Yes that's right. I met Byron several times and we stayed in touch after I left."

"So, what's the plan for tomorrow?" Beth asked her brother.

"Well, first thing, I need to get a hire car to ride around in. Are there any local to you?"

"Not far," Beth replied. "I'll show you in the morning.

"I need to see Mum and Dad as well. You didn't tell them I was coming, did you? I want it to be a surprise." Jack remembered that he had asked his Sister not to mention the fact that he was coming down. He wanted to stand on their doorstep and ring the doorbell.

"No. Although you had better make sure that you don't give Mum a heart attack, you turning up there."

"Well, I thought about that," Jack replied. "I was just going to ring their doorbell, but then I thought I might call her and then tell her to open the front door."

"You never change, Jack," Alex said chuckling away at his Brother-In-Laws plan.

"You know me," Jack replied.

Neil Marsh hadn't slept very well. He was up and down all night and getting very emotional at times. Finally, he dozed off on Paul's sofa after a couple of glasses of scotch but was woken the next morning by the squawking of a bird. A very loud bird, he thought to himself as he remembered that Paul had an African Grey Parrot that he himself had taught to say 'Referee' when watching the football. The bird was vicious to anyone except Paul though, and he had one hell of a bite on him that had previously drawn blood on Neil's fingers.

Neil sat up and rubbed his eyes before stretching his arms upwards and then jumping up on his feet and stretching his legs. He heard movement upstairs and could tell that his friend Paul and the Mrs were up and about. Suddenly Paul appeared on the stairs.

"How are you, mate?" Paul asked still concerned for Neil's welfare after the incident.

"I haven't slept well," Neil replied. "So much going through my head."

"That's understandable. Joanne is just having a shower. She has to go to work. Do you want some breakfast?"

Neil shook his head. He couldn't concentrate at all at the moment. His face filled with sadness and anger and his mind was full of thoughts of different things, everything from Lydia, the crash, the children right through to how he was going to handle it. He knew what he wanted to do to the person responsible for his wife's death.

"Did the Police say what time they were coming around?" Paul asked, hoping that it wasn't too early because he wanted a shower prior to them arriving and also he wanted Joanne out of the way, knowing that she was a right gossip queen. At times he used to call her 'Dot' after Dot Cotton in the soap Eastenders, whose tagline was '*I ain't one to gossip, but ..*' and at the moment he knew that Neil didn't need it.

"They just said first thing. I suppose by the time they get into the station and collect their things it will be nine or ten."

"Good. I want to have a shower and I'm sure you do," Paul said to him realising that he would have to put things to his friend in a way that would remind him over the next few weeks because his head was elsewhere.

"Listen bud. I don't want to be a burden on you and Jo. I just had to get away last night." Neil just didn't know where to put himself. He knew his mate would always help him and vice-versa, but he also didn't want there to be any friction between them by him being there.

"You are staying here until we sort this," Paul commanded and showing that he wasn't going to take a 'No' for an answer. "Now let's get moving."

It wasn't long before Joanne came downstairs, all spruced up and ready for her job as Assistant Manager of a ladies clothing store in the Drake Circus Shopping Centre. "Hello, Neil. Come here, babes." She pulled him in for a supportive cuddle. "I'm so sorry."

"You are going to have him in tears again in a minute," Paul said as he poked his head around from the kitchen.

"It's okay," Neil said. "Thanks, Jo. Guess I need a hug!"

"You make sure you take care. Paul has told me about what happened." She shook her head, and a tear came to her eye. "Lydia and I were pals."

"Yes, I know."

"Paul, I'm going to have to get to work, but if you need me for anything, give me a call on the mobile." She kissed Neil on the cheek and then waited for her husband to take a break from cooking the breakfast in order that he could bid her farewell, which he soon did, and she left.

"I'm sorry about that, Neil. She can be a bit full on sometimes."

"Yes. She means well, though. I'm going for that shower," Neil replied calmly. "After the Police, I need to arrange things with the undertakers."

Paul looked at him, not knowing what to say because he had never been in that situation, so he just nodded as he watched Neil head upstairs.

It was coming up for 10:30 am and a car arrived outside. Neil was anxious and worried that they hadn't turned up as early as he thought they would and had to be calmed down by Paul several times. The two officers walked in as Neil opened the door to them. Neil knew it was time to think.

"Hello, Neil. Apologies for the delay. We have had to arrange a few things and get officers looking at the CCTV on the main road down to the retail park. There is no

CCTV on Leigham Park Drive unfortunately." DI Thorpe followed him through to the dining room.

Neil looked at him and was thankful that the investigation was showing promise even in the initial stages. They all sat around the table. "You will have to excuse me. I haven't slept very much."

"That's fine," the DI commented. "Take your time. DS Carter will be doing the writing. Just go through everything since your visit from the mystery man at your place of work the night before last."

"Are you going to do an appeal for witnesses or anything?" Neil asked.

DI Thorpe looked briefly at his junior officer and then shook his head. "We have discussed that, Neil. Not at this moment in time. We will have everyone phoning in every time they spot a blue Nissan otherwise and each sighting would have to be investigated. That would take labour time away from actually finding your wife's killer."

"But he must have damage to his car. There was quite a lot of impact damage to Lydia's car where she had been hit."

"Yes, I know," DI Thorpe replied apologetically.

"My team will be putting out alerts to many garages this morning just in case he gets it repaired. Mobile units will also be looking for blue Nissan's with front end damage," DS Carter added.

DI Thorpe looked at DS Carter and continued, "These things aren't solved overnight, Neil." He started opening the book in front of him where he kept all of his notes. "We are trying to get identification of the vehicle. Even from CCTV around the area of the Taxi Office the other night. He must have got there somehow."

"Just make sure you get him before I do," an angry Neil replied with a raised voice.

The morning had dawned over the coast, the sun appearing on the horizon with its brilliant light reflecting on the calm waters. Jeremy told himself that this would be the only thing that he would miss if he were to decide to sell his parents place and move to another house. He could move to one with the same horizon beside the coastal waters again, he thought.

He had made the appointment to view the two houses in the same street that Neil Marsh lived in, Woodlands Lane. His plan was to try and spook the criminal by parking his blue Nissan Duke, which he knew that his target had seen two nights earlier, in view of his house. He would get his car fixed first and then view them on the weekend.

Jeremy looked out of his bedroom window for a bit longer. But then he saw something that he didn't like. His neighbour. Ken Meadows was out early attending his garden but had slipped across and was looking at the damage to Jeremy's car. "Fucker!"

He now had to decide what he wanted to do about the neighbourhood busy body. If the Police put out a description of the car, no doubt Ken would report it.

'*You know what you have to do,*'

His Father's voice was once again behind him.

'*He has to be taken care of.*'

Jeremy nodded as he adjusted the blinds in his room which had moved as he looked at the neighbour. He would obey his Father and be looked on as a failure. He rushed downstairs and out through the back door into the rear garden. Then he went into his garage workshop through the side door and started to look around, spotting his mechanic-style overalls that he used when using the electric lawnmower because he didn't like getting cut grass on his clothes. Quickly he put them on, struggling with pulling the last arm, his right, onto his shoulder, but managing it finally after quite a bit of cursing to himself. He clipped up the poppers on the front of the suit, stopping and silently listening to the quiet within the workshop. Grabbing his gardening gloves, he went back outside through the side door and put the gloves on whilst walking down towards his neighbour who was still looking at the damage to the car. "Hello Ken. You are up early."

"You know what they say. The early bird catches the worm. I was just looking at your damage again. It's going to cost a pretty penny." Ken continued to touch the bumper, prodding it as though it was going to fall off at any moment.

"Ken I was wondering if you could give me a hand for a moment. I can't get the lawnmower down." Jeremy tried to show him the way to the workshop entrance even though the old man had a similar building in his back garden, so would know where to enter.

"Well, I will try, young man. I'm not as nimble as I used to be," the old man replied as he started to follow Jeremy to the workshop.

"Thank you Ken," Jeremy said, turning in order that he could still talk to the neighbour. "It's quite simple usually. I think it is caught on something." He opened the door as though he were a gentleman for his elder. "After you, sir," he said.

Ken walked in and looked around. "I thought you said you were going to sort this out," he said as he surveyed the clutter of old tools and broken household items that his Father had kept there for years.

Jeremy was behind his old neighbour. He picked up an old rustic vintage garden tool from the worktop beside him, raised it above his head and said, "There is something else I have to sort out first!" before bringing down the sharp bladed tool onto the top of Ken's head, who screamed out in pain. Jeremy didn't give him any chance to try and fight back as he continued to hack time after time, across his neck, on his head, and even managed in all the commotion to chop off one of Ken's ears.

Ken was trying his hardest to fight back, raising his arms to protect his face, but losing the battle as he lost consciousness and his limp body fell to the floor.

Jeremy didn't stop as he stood over the body and continued to hack away, ensuring the old man was dead. Then, after checking his kill, he turned around and calmly pulled down one of his Father's tarpaulins from the shelf behind him. "All you had to do was stay away from my car," he said as though he were having a conversation with Ken just as he had in the garden. He laid the tarpaulin out on the ground in the space where the car normally parked. Jeremy never parked the car in the garage, mainly because he wasn't particularly good at reversing and was afraid of damaging one of his prized possessions.

He wasn't finished. The body was too big. He looked around the workshop and saw a chainsaw over on the racking where his Father had kept all of his power tools and equipment. He walked over to pick it up. He didn't even know how it worked but had seen it on the television. Somewhere there had to be something that you pull. He looked and saw what looked like a large duffle coat toggle. That must be it, he thought to himself. He put the chainsaw on the ground. "Here goes," he said to himself loudly as he pulled the starter chord handle once and it chugged like an old motorcycle trying to start. He tried again and the same happened. Three, four, five times. No luck. He grabbed the starter chord handle tight and pulled it forcefully. Luck was at last on his side as the machine burst into life.

Jeremy picked up the chainsaw. He noticed a black trigger type catch under the main handle and took it to be the throttle. He tested it, depressing the throttle and the blade started to spin. Then he went over to the corpse laying on his floor, pressed the throttle again and brought it down on one of Ken's wrists. The blood started oozing quickly out of the clean wound and the hand just detached. An arm. He would try the arm.

After cutting the limbs off the torso, he went for the head, slicing the neck. The blood splattered everywhere as he did so, until the body was headless. Jeremy looked at the expression on the face of the decapitated Ken and smirked psychotically, thinking that the old man wasn't going to annoy any more neighbours now. His nosiness and busy body days were over.

The killer pressed the cut-out switch and the blade on the chain saw ceased working finally coming to a thundering halt. Jeremy began laughing. He looked at his handiwork before taking the chainsaw back to its prominent position on the rack. He saw some large plastic bags that his Father had used for putting the cut grass in and grabbed a handful of them before returning to his kill. He picked up the pieces bit by bit, the arms and hands first and placed them in one of the bags before taking the bag over to the tarpaulin. Then he went back for the legs, carrying one in each hand and into a separate bag. The head, it seemed heavy. Jeremy stopped and slapped it across the face with his free hand, and then started laughing again. He put it into a third bag and then grabbed the second and third bags one in each hand and threw them in the middle of the tarpaulin. Finally, the torso. He struggled lifting it, so placed the refuse bag on the floor and slid it up and over the bloodied body part. Then he dragged it over to the tarpaulin. There, he thought. Extra protection for any blood spill.

Grabbing the edges of the large blue covering, he folded it in until there was just a bump of body parts in the middle. Then from the other end, he started to roll the tarpaulin, finding it harder as the corpse reached the rolling process. He had to lift and roll. What could he tie it with? He saw a number of bungees hanging up on the wall above the workbench, so walked over and grabbed two of them. Then he tied them around each end of the parcel and looked at the elasticity of them as the pressure of the tarpaulin seemed to be at maximum. It would hold.

Now for the difficult bit. How was he going to get rid of the package? The refuse collection was today. But how would he get it into the back of the lorry by himself? He knew how. He always spoke to the refuse collector if he saw him, and always gave him a Christmas tip. There would be no issues. He just had to make sure that he caught them arriving to empty his bins.

Jeremy opened the garage door. He then put his shoulder into rolling the heavy object out onto the top of the driveway next to the bins. At first he struggled but then finally gained momentum as though he were a contestant on 'Britain's Strongest Man' moving a bus. To him, the hidden body just as well had been a bus, because it was heavy. He managed to get it where he wanted it, and then ran back to close the garage door.

He looked down at his Overalls, still bloodstained, knowing he would have to destroy them and then have a shower. He had time because the bin lorry used to come around 11.15 normally. But first he would hose down the bloodied murder scene, knowing he would have to be careful as chances were that the blood would exit under the garage door to the water chute on the outside which emptied into the drain. His Father had installed it because when the heavy rains occurred, the garage would sometimes get flooded, and he found himself having to sweep out the rain water several times a day. He remembered his Father constantly moaning about it for years before actually doing something about it.

Jeremy walked back into the side door, grabbed the hose, and checked that it was attached to the water system via the garden tap. He turned the tap to 'on' and the strong burst of water started firing out of the adapter on the other end. For ten minutes he washed everywhere he could see blood and other small bits like skin or ligament ensuring that any sign that Ken had been in his garage workshop was washed away. Reopening the garage door, he flushed away the reddened water into the flume and down to the drain.

After locking the garage door and the side door to the workshop, he removed his overalls and headed down to the bottom of his garden. He dumped them in the burner, which was already half filled with paper and leaves from the oak tree overhanging the garden. He took a lighter out of his trouser pocket and lit the fire, and then placed the funnel lid on the burner. It soon began to burn, and the large flames dispersed though the funnel trying desperately to get to the oxygen in the air.

Jeremy was happy that they would be burnt to smithereens within minutes, so left the burner glowing and went back inside to shower. Once inside, he scrubbed himself meaninglessly, getting any trace and smell of his victim away from his body. Twenty minutes later, he was wiping himself down and then getting dressed in clean clothes, making sure his dirty ones were ready to go into the wash immediately.

He looked at the time on the clock in his bedroom. It had gone quicker than he had thought. He remembered that he had to catch the refuse collection but hoped that they hadn't arrived early as they sometimes did. So, he ran downstairs, put his shoes on and went outside. The sun was still beaming on this glorious day, he thought to himself as he stepped outside the front door. He listened out and could hear the lorry approaching from further up the road. He hadn't missed it. Looks like he was just in time. He told himself to keep calm. He would ask.

'If you don't ask, you don't get.'

He heard his Mother's voice say from behind him.

It was there. The lorry appeared at the bottom of his drive. "Hello Mr Johnson," the young man said to him.

He was nervous as he replied, "Hello. I was hoping to catch you. Would you be able to take this old tarpaulin for me? I'm cleaning out the garage, and this one is ripped and damaged."

"Anything for you, Mr Johnson."

"Oh, thank you. I'll give you a hand as it is very heavy." Between the two, they managed to roll the item down towards the back of the refuse truck.

The young youth shouted across to his colleague. "Mikey? Come give me a hand with this?"

"Is that industrial waste, Jamie?" asked the older operative. "You know we can't take it if it is?"

"No. Just a tarpaulin. Not really household rubbish, but Mr Johnson is a precious customer. Always gives us cold drinks in the summer and lets us fill our flasks if we need to," young Jamie replied to his older work colleague, trying his hardest to paint a good picture of Jeremy.

Mikey walked over and started to survey the rolled-up item. "Okay. On three. One, two, three." On first try the old tarpaulin was in the back of the lorry. "Bloody hell, what was in that thing?"

"Nothing I don't think," Jeremy replied calmly.

"Well, it is gone now," Jamie added as the three of them watched it disappear into the crusher. "Just the bins now Mr Johnson?"

"Yes. Just the one today." He pulled two £20 notes out of his pocket once he was satisfied that the item had disappeared. "Here, Jamie, is it?"

"Yes, that's right. Anytime. But you didn't need to do that, Mr Johnson."

"There's one for you as well," Jeremy added, passing the other £20 note to Mikey." Mikey was beginning to wish that he hadn't questioned the job now.

"Thank you Mr Johnson," Mikey added.

"No thanks to the both of you. I would have struggled to get it into my car to take it down to Chelson Meadow. Then I would have struggled there as well."

Jeremy knew he would have struggled there because someone may have tried to stop him putting it in the waste and try to recycle it meaning the body would be discovered. At least now it would be compacted and hard to find. He could relax. For the moment anyway.

Chapter 10

Jack Dempsey had hired a car and gone up to Burrator Reservoir to try and delve deeper on whether anybody had seen anything. He parked in the same spot that Byron Maddocks had that fatal early evening on the Saturday in question. Then he walked over to the reservoir wall. It was quite obvious where it happened because of all the flowers and stems from the older flowers that had been placed. There were also remnants of the Police Forensic team markings on both the road and the walls.

He looked at the photo's that had been sent his way by a fellow reporter from the local newspaper the day after the murder. Then on digital recorder, Jack commented, *'Must be strong.'* Byron Maddocks wasn't the lightest guy in the world. He was fit, but very toned with some muscle. He would have taken some lifting over the wall, especially at dead weight.

Jack had arranged to meet the man who found the remains on the evening, Father Reed. He asked if he could meet him over by the scene of the crime, although jack was ten minutes early which in some ways was beneficial so he could get a feel for the murder scene in his own way. He tried to picture the evening in his mind. The car, Byron looking at the water. It was usually only kids that wanted to look over the wall down to the bottom of the dam. He knew that Byron would have stood there at the water's edge, closed his eyes, and tried to come up with a theme for a new book. *'It was someone he knew,'* he said into his recorder. It had to be. He kept himself to himself and wouldn't have been there with anyone because he liked his own company. But he knew them in some way. *'A fan, or staff at one of the outlets.'*

Now the Police hadn't given much away, mainly because they had no leads themselves. They would have the same thought processes as he did but were juggling other caseloads as well. So, he had the upper hand. He had received information that Byron was at a book signing prior to travelling home that day which was something that he had yet to follow up on. He would have to be careful because these big companies restricted their staff from talking to anyone except the Police, and especially the press.

Jack saw a car arriving on the tourist side of the viaduct and looked over to see if it were his appointment guest, although he would have thought that Father Reed would have come the quickest way from the village. His dress gave it away as the priest got out of the parked car, his white dog collar showing out amongst his black attire. He walked over towards the priest to show courtesy for giving his time. "Father Reed?"

"Hello," he replied holding out his hand. "Jack, wasn't it?"

"Yes. Jack Dempsey. Thank you for meeting me." Jack started walking back towards the actual crime scene hoping that the Father would take his lead and follow him, which he did. "So, you were the one that came across the scene of the crime?"

"That's right," he replied calmly as he strolled beside the reporter. "Quite a shock. Blood everywhere. They concluded that he had been shot three times and then his body thrown over the wall on the drop side."

"That must have been terrible for you. Did you know Byron very well?"

Father Reed shook his head. "He mainly kept himself to himself. No one in the village even knew he was a top-selling author, not even the one villager who actually read his books."

"So, he wasn't a church goer then?"

"Now and again," the Father added. "I think he only ever attended one resident's meeting."

"Well, he appeared to be well liked," Jack said nodding towards all the flower tributes that were at the base of the wall. He walked over and started reading some of the 'with sympathy' cards that were attached. "His fans are literally obsessive. He always said they were."

"You knew him then?"

"I did. I used to review his books a couple of years ago before I got promotion. Nice guy." Jack continued to read the cards.

"He was. Very polite. Not a bad bone in his body." Father Reed stepped forward and knelt down before starting to tidy the flowers. Jack got back up and removed his mobile from his pocket. Then he started to take some photo's on the phone, including a few of the priests kneeling before the shrine. He looked at the road and noticed that despite efforts to remove the blood stains, it was still there partially. So, he zoomed in and took some more photos.

Father Reed finished sorting the dead flowers from the live ones and put them in relevant order, neatly standing on their stems. Then he backed up beside Jack. "Would you like to see where the Police found the body?"

"Can we get down there?" Jack questioned, not realising it could be done that easily and thinking he would have to trespass over ground through the valley to descent to bottom of the dam.

"Yes," Father Reed replied as he grabbed Jack's arm as though he were relying on him to help the older man walk. He wasn't, it was just something he always did when talking and walking. "There is a gate and then steep steps. The Police tape is still there I think. Unfortunately, it is too steep for me. My balance isn't as good as it was when I was your age." They reached the top of the decline. Luckily, it was only the size of a small garden gate because it had since been padlocked because of the murder. Father Reed pointed downwards. "The body was found on top of that workshop building."

"Here goes then," Jack said as he hopped over the gate. "I won't be long." He descended the steep steps which dropped quite viciously. He should write a piece on Health and Safety instead, he thought to himself. Finally, he reached the open space that the forensic team had based itself on with Sergeant George Bickford when the Police attended the scene. Like Father Reed had said, the Police 'Do Not Cross' tape was still around the area. But Jack was used to breaking the rules to get the story he wanted. He needed to get up on the flat roof of the workshop. He jumped up and grabbed the roof edge, puling himself up with his strength, then flipped his left leg onto the roof and rolled the rest of the way. Still on his back, he looked around the roof whilst catching his breath. Then he sat up and pushed himself up to a standing position. He got his camera out again and started to take random shots of where the body fell and the height at which it fell. He snapped the complete drop, aiming to report just how high the drop was. But he knew that Byron was dead before the drop in any case. He shook his head, then closed his eyes and tried to imagine the scene. Did the culprit look down the dam to check on his kill after pushing the body over the wall? He could just imagine it. The killer had to be a psychopath to do this in the first place.

He grabbed his digital recorder once more. *"This guy is intelligent. Doesn't get on with people very much. We know he reads books. Murder books. Is he getting his ideas from them?"* Jack then looked around for anything that the Police may have not found and looked over the far edge of the roof down to the very bottom of the dam which was partially waterlogged. The height made him feel like he had butterflies in his stomach from the fear of falling. He had done so as a young boy when he climbed a tree with his friends but slipped and hit the ground with some force, breaking his collarbone. Luckily, he didn't hit his head and the grass below the tree was long and softened the blow. It didn't make him afraid of heights but just more cautious around them.

Chances are there might be something down there, but the risk outweighed the need, he told himself. Or did it? He would decide later and return if necessary. So, he returned to the other side of the roof and jumped down, straightening his jacket as he stood upright. Then he headed back up towards the waiting priest.

"I'm glad you came back," Father Reed said worryingly. "I've just had this funny feeling that we are being watched."

Jack jumped over the gate, not showing any concern just in case the priest was right. "Where from?"

Father Reed didn't look up at the rocks where he thought someone was peering at them. "It may just be an inquisitive tourist. But the rocks about halfway up behind me on my left."

"Okay Father. Can I meet you back at the Church? There is something I need to ask you."

"Yes, that's fine. But you are going to follow me?" Father Reed asked inquisitively with a worried frown on his forehead.

"Soon. I'm going rock-climbing first."

"Please be careful," the Father said as he started walking over to his car.

"I will. Don't worry." With that, Jack looked out of the corner of his eye towards the direction that Father Reed had given him. There was definitely movement up there. Looks like whoever was up there also had a camera. It was another reporter? Or a Police Officer waiting to see if the culprit returned to the scene of the crime as sometimes they did. Suddenly jack started running up the grassy mud bank until he reached the start of the rocky interface. The baseball-capped man saw him coming, stood up and started going in the other direction at some pace. Jack was certain that the stranger knew the terrain which he personally never had a clue of and therefore had to watch his step, especially on the rocks. As he was thinking that his foot slipped into a small crevice between two of the rocks which slowed him up fractionally as he pushed himself back up and tried to recapture his balance. He started jumping over the large rocks hoping that they were stable as he landed on each one, his balance being tested on many a try.

He finally reached the spot where the man had been photographing from and looked around for him. All he could see was a distant figure heading towards a waiting parked car on the road that led to the Drake's Moat. Jack didn't get a look at his face, but the speed he ran indicated he was fit, and in his late twenties or early thirties. He tried to see what type of car the stranger was driving but it was too far away for him to make a good judgement.

Jack Dempsey caught his breath and then surveyed the area where the man had set up. A piece of paper. He reached down and opened it. It was the guarantee slip for a camera, a Canon 450 ED. Unfortunately, it wasn't filled in with any details and Jack flipped it over to check. Nothing. He would go home and find out just how old that model of camera was. Someone must have sold it to him. Canon may be able to give him the batch number and area it was sold by matching it to a retailer. If not him, he would pass it to the Police.

Slowly he descended the rock surface that he had just rushed up at speed, and then walked with his feet sideways in order that he wouldn't slip down the muddy grass bank near the road. As he started walking towards his car, he realised that his ankle was hurting, from when he slipped, and he started to limp slightly to his car.

Ten minutes later, Jack parked outside the Church at Sheepstor village. Father Reed was waiting for him in the doorway of the church. Jack smirked as he thought that the priest was going to make him pray for his sins of working for his newspaper. Jack got out of the hire car and walked in through the gate towards the priest.

"Did you manage to catch up with him?"

"No," Jack replied shaking his head in defeat. "He was too fast. He was showing signs of suspicion though. Why run? He was taking photographs, I guess of us. I would say he knows the area."

"That is worrying," Father Reed said as a million thoughts ran through his head. He then told himself that he would make sure that his doors and windows were all secure from now on. "So, what else do you need from me?"

"Is there any chance that I could see the house that Byron was renting?" Jack knew it was asking too much.

"Well, the outside. That's all I can show you. No one has keys to get in, apart from the Police or the Landlord."

"That's fine," Jack replied. "Outside is fine." He really wanted to see if there was anywhere that the killer could have been watching Byron at home. How did he know that Byron would be in the area of Burrator on the evening of his murder? He might have had prior knowledge or even followed the author home before.

"Well, it's not far. Two minutes away. We can walk it."

"Perfect," Jack said as he watched the priest lock the front door of the church and then join him walking side by side back towards the Church gate. "So how long have you been here, Father?"

137

"Too long!" he laughed. "I tell you what it is so laid back here that you just lose track of time some days. I even forget it's Sunday sometimes. He saw Jack look at him seriously as though he were thinking 'how can a priest forget a Sunday?.'

"You are joking, Father, aren't you?"

"Of course, I am," laughed the priest. "Didn't think I would ever catch a reporter out." He stopped outside a gate. "Here we are."

"You weren't joking when you said two minutes away!" He stood looking at the place trying to see how accessible it was for anyone remembering what the priest had said to him about the village being so laid back. He then asked himself the question, *could it be one of the villagers?* Although he would not record the thought until the Father had gone as he didn't want to appear judgemental. "I won't be long." With that he disappeared through the front gate and walked down to the bay window which he took to be the living room overlooking the front garden. Raising his hand beside his eyes to block out any light or reflection, Jack tried to see inside but with little success. The blinds were tightly closed. There were just glimmers of light strands pushing through the minimal gaps.

"Can you see anything, young man?" The Father shouted from the gateway.

"No, nothing. I'm going to pop around the back." He walked around the side, looking around for anything that might signal something suspicious, especially after the photographer in the rocks earlier. There were huge patio doors to his left, and he went to look in them but then guessed someone had shut them for privacy, but because of the size he could see just a bit more through the slats. He hoped that someone had forgotten to lock them as he tried to slide them apart, but no such luck. He stood there, back to the patio doors, and looked around the huge garden. It had been well kept, the lawn had been mowed recently, the flowers attended to, the trees cut back so as not to block out the light.

Down at the end of the garden there was a bolted gate which led into what he could see was a woodland area, quite dense and green. He thought back to his earlier inspiration. Did the killer know where he lived? If he did, was he watching Byron before killing him? There would be more than a chance of that happening if it were an infatuated fan. He looked at the large trees outside Byron's gate. How many were accessible and overlooked Byron's place directly so the culprit could easily look into the patio doors or the bedroom? Two. He could see two.

Jack walked down to the gate and pulled the bolt aside. The gate swung open which surprised him as it didn't seem at all maintained unlike the garden. The two trees in question were situated on each side of the entrance. Left first, he thought. He looked at the base of the tree to see if there was any of the bark that had fallen off where someone had tried to climb it. Then he surveyed the trunk. Nothing. There was even evidence of fungi still intact. In any case, the branches were so high that whoever wanted to try this one would have needed a ladder or rope. He looked up. There were no ladder marks on the top of the trunk and no rope marks on the branches. Time to look at the other tree.

The old oak was a completely different scene. It was apparent that someone had scaled this tree immediately. There were holes in the bark on the trunk of the tree which Jack touched. He then pulled out his mobile and started to take photographs of the tree and the area around it. Further over where the ground was damp, there were still footprints in the mud. He took more photos. He had a hunch. Just what did the killer do whilst up a tree? He had to get up there. It didn't look like the Police had checked this out as the scene was too clean. Jack noticed a low branch so ran and jumped, his hands wrapping around on first try. He hated trees after his accident as a child, but this was important, and he had no intentions of a repeat performance. He had amazing upper body strength, pulling himself up on the branch just as he had done on the workshop roof at the bottom of the dam earlier. Then he put his leg over the branch for support. He was up.

Jack Dempsey rested to catch his breath, a mixture of anxiety at having to climb a tree for the first time in years, and the jump itself. His Father had taught him how to edge himself along a rope and he used the same method to edge himself along the branch, with one of his legs pointing downwards and the other on the tree. He still held on for dear life and was relieved when he finally reached the trunk of the tree which was at least thicker than the branch he had chosen. Pulling himself up, he held on tight and sat in the middle of the three upright branches springing straight from the trunk. Jack wiped his brow. He was sweating so he took a handkerchief out of his pocket, wiping his hand first and then his brow. He composed himself and then got back to the objective of why he was there. He needed to see Byron's house from where he was sat. He did. Perfectly. Out came the mobile switched to camera mode. He took photographs of the view, the tree and was about to replace it in his pocket when he saw something more important. Someone had carved out a 'J' in the bark of the trunk in front of him. It was quite recent because it hadn't yet tried to heal and go a dark colour. This was still cream coloured and near fresh. He took photos of the find, betting that the Police had not even suspected this sort of behaviour by a potential killer.

Ten minutes later, Jack was on safe ground having hung by his arms from the same branch that he had climbed up on and just dropped to his feet. He immediately went back to Father Reed at the front of the house.

"I was beginning to wonder where you had gone," the priest said concerningly.

"Yes, sorry Father. I had a tree to climb."

"Did you find anything of importance?" Father Reed asked, hoping that the reporter would share the information with him. He would love to be able to tell his parishioners that they had caught the culprit who had killed one of their flock.

"Yes, possibly. I will have to check it out before I let anyone know if it is of value."

"But you will let me know," Father Reed pleaded with Jack. "We are praying every day that someone is caught for the murder and brought to justice."

"I promise, Father. I will let you know."

"I can see that you are a good man, Jack." He started to make a move back towards the Church and Jack this time followed his lead.

It was an hour before Jack arrived at Plymouth City Centre. He parked above the Drake Circus shopping centre, knowing that he could claim the parking charges back from his employers, otherwise he would have found somewhere cheaper and walked in to the centre. He took his parking ticket with him and put it in his jacket pocket, and then headed down the stairs to the ground floor. He had no intentions of waiting for the escalator because previous experience had told him that on a busy day like today he would be waiting for ages and wanted to avoid the scuffles of someone jumping the queue by brushing past.

He looked up and down the length of the ground floor to see how many units had changed hands since the last time he was here. Then he headed down towards Waterstones, stopping to look at their window displays first just in case there was anything new out in print that he might want. Not that he had the time to read very much. But there was an alternative motive for standing outside. He was also observing the activity in the store, trying to pick out who was the one in charge directing the other staff because that would be the person he headed for, especially if it were a female. The local newspaper reports had indicated that it was a Manageress, and her name was Jenny Baker. He peered through the gap in the display and saw what he wanted, a lady showing some authority in directing customers and stopping her staff to give directions as to what needed attention in the store. Time to move, he thought.

He walked in through the entrance and saw the lady that he wanted filling a new display with this week's best sellers. Jack stood beside the display and picked up one of the books. "Jenny Baker?"

The woman stopped. "Yes, that's me," she replied. "Can I help you?"

Jack moved closer to her and held out his hand for a handshake which nervously was met. "Jack Dempsey."

"Hold on," she said, taking her hand away. "Are you from the press?"

"I'm an investigative reporter," Jack said firmly.

"What's the difference?" She asked, wondering whether or not to get him removed from the store. "Reporter. Investigative Reporter. You are all after the same. I have told the Police everything I know."

"Well, there is quite a difference. I investigate a story quite deeply and stay on it until I have the facts, not the fiction." He started to read the back of the book he had picked up. "I am also a friend of Byron Maddocks. Known him for years ever since I used to review his books, and I want to help the Police catch his killer." He looked at her confused face and could tell that she was trying to work out whether to speak to him or not as the case may be. "Is there somewhere private that we could talk?"

Jenny decided to give him the benefit of the doubt and waved over towards her Assistant Manager who put the books down that she had in her hand and walked over to her colleague. "Emma, I have a meeting with Jack here. I'll be in the back office."

"No problem, Jenny," Emma replied before returning to her display.

Jenny then turned back to Jack. He was actually quite good looking for a reporter, she thought to herself, although she had a typeset view of reporters all being old and chubby like the ones on the television. "This way." She headed to a door that had a sign on it indicating that it was *'Staff only allowed beyond this point'* and then clicked the code on the keypad that secured it. Then she ensured Jack was inside before making sure the door was secure, then led him into the back office where all the store CCTV was set up and her desk sat in the corner cluttered up with paperwork and books. "Please grab a seat," she said to him pointing to the chair opposite. Jack looked behind him to check that there was nothing on the chair that he might sit on and then sat down. "Now whatever I say must not be quoted to me. I will deny anything if it is."

Jack nodded in agreement. "That's no problem. I'm not here for a terrible story. I leave that to the comedians they have working for them."

"I haven't got long," Jenny said looking at her watch. "The area manager is due down this afternoon."

"That's ok. Can you just outline why Byron was here on that fateful Saturday? I guess he was here for a book signing?" Unknowingly to Jenny, Jack had clicked on his digital recorder to save him the task of writing whatever she told him down on paper.

"That's right," she replied. "There was a long queue. At the end of the session Byron became concerned about one of the people who had asked for a book to be signed. He said that the bloke had been stalking him a few times, turning up at other places where he was going like restaurants."

"Did you tell the Police this?"

"Yes. Unfortunately, neither the store or shopping centre CCTV picked up a clear image because he had a thick anorak and a baseball cap on." She shook her head and looked at the store CCTV indicating to Jack just how poor the picture was. "You can see from here that we have little chance of catching shoplifters, let alone weirdo's."

"What about a name? Did he have his book signed?"

"Yes. He has been in for previous book signings. The name that he always gives to Byron was 'Jeremy.'"

"Jeremy?" he replied with a frown on his forehead as he remembered the 'J' that he had earlier found carved into the tree.

"Yes. Jeremy," she said nervously. "Security escorted Byron to his car through the back of the store because it was obvious that this Jeremy was waiting for him at the front."

"And I don't suppose you have a description?"

Jenny shook her head. "I only saw him at a distance. Average body size for a man of about 30 to 35. Green anorak style jacket and a green NYC baseball cap."

"Right, thank you Jenny. I won't keep you any longer. Let you get back to your books."

"That's ok," she replied as they both got up. "Oh, hold on," she continued. "These might be beneficial to you." She reached up for a file above her computer on the shelf and took out two photographs. "These are copies of the shopping centre CCTV image." She pointed to what she called her 'wall of fame' behind her. "As you can see, he is on our wanted list."

Jack looked at the blurred image. "Thank you, Jenny. This is most helpful."

Chapter 11

Neil Marsh was frustrated. He knew it had only been a few days, but in his world when someone wronged you or your family, you took matters into your own hands. He was sat moping on his friend Paul's sofa, not saying a word to his friend or Paul's wife. The plans in his head were just going around and around and not making any sense at the moment. But where would he start on this one? Some complete stranger had murdered his wife and the Police were no closer to solving it than they were when it had happened. He told himself that he was just being too impatient, but all he had to go on, and all the Police had to go on was some guy in a dark coloured car antagonising him at work, and he didn't even know if that incident was related to Lydia's death. He suspected it was.

"Paul, I've got to get out of here. I feel so useless just hiding away like this."

"Mate, you are a moving target if you go out." Paul looked at his wife who just didn't know what to say although she would be happier if he wasn't staying with them because whilst he was there, he was putting them in danger as well. "What can you do? You don't know who you are looking for."

"I need to go back home," Neil snapped.

"Okay, I'll drop you back. What have you got to pick up?" Paul asked inquisitively, knowing that Neil had brought clothes with him.

"Nothing. I am going home to stay, mate. If I can draw the culprit out then he would be just as vulnerable as me." Neil knew what he was thinking. If it were the guy that had appeared at his work the other night, he would stand no chance against Neil himself, what with his muscly body and heavy frame.

"Think about it mate, because at the moment you are not thinking logically. You are safer here." Paul felt he had a responsibility for his friend as much as he did his wife. But he also knew that once Neil had something on his mind, there was no stopping him.

Neil jumped up off the sofa. "There is no time like the present," he snapped as though he had made up his mind. "I am putting Joanne and yourself at risk by being here. I wouldn't want anything to happen to either of you."

There was no argument, Paul thought to himself. "Okay. We had better get your stuff together then. Make sure this is what you want, Neil. You are welcome here anytime, so if you change your mind."

"I know, and I appreciate everything you both have done. But the time is now."

Half an hour passed, and Paul was helping Neil back into his front door. "Do you want me to stay, Neil?"

"No. I need to get my head around Lydia's death and get this whole thing sorted. You go home and give Joanne a big hug."

"Okay. You know where I am. Don't suffer alone my friend. I'll be calling you regularly and if I think you need help, I'll be around here quickly." Paul tapped Neil's shoulder and hesitated whilst he looked at him. "Don't do anything stupid, Neil."

Neil shook his head. "I won't. Don't worry." He watched Paul get back in his car and drive back up the road. Then Neil said to himself, "Right you bastard. Bring it on!" He was sure that he wouldn't bring his children home yet but leave them with their grandparents who appeared quite happy to have them stay. It was always a case of *'If Daddy says no, ask Grandad'* anyway. They spoilt the kids rotten. It was too dangerous for them to be here as well whilst this was going on. He would see them at the funeral and always made sure that he telephoned them several times a day.

So, did he just sit and wait? Would the person responsible come back for him, or did they just target Lydia to teach him a lesson? He didn't know the answer. He only guessed that someone was after him because of the stranger at his workplace. But they were there just to follow him. Could Lydia have been the target anyway? He shook his head and then thought about the note. It didn't actually say it was him that was going to die in the four ways mentioned. The letter was addressed to him though. He then began to try and think logically. These things might not happen, he told himself.

Keep busy, he thought. He went out to the hallway and picked up the pile of letters that were on the floor, checking through to try and guess what each one was. Bills, bills, and more bills. One letter then caught his eye. The writing was the same as the threatening letter or so he thought. He couldn't directly remember. He should give DI Thorpe a call and not open the letter, although he doubted very much that they would get any finger prints off of it. But all the same he had to make it look like he was doing things the right way especially as he would now have the sole responsibility for two children.

Getting the business card out of his wallet that DI Thorpe had given him, he dialled the number, but it went straight to voice mail. "Hello, DI Thorpe. This is Neil Marsh. I think I have received another letter. I am at home. I haven't opened it but left it for you. Please get back to me." He really wanted to open the suspect letter just to see what it said and looked at it as though it were a child looking at a birthday card. But he wouldn't although his will power was making him impatient in every way. Of course, it could just be a 'With Sympathy' card from one of his friends or family. It certainly felt like a card of some kind.

He decided to go upstairs and unpack his bag that he had brought back from Paul's house, although he would want to wash most of his clothes that he had taken there because even though Paul's wife had washed them, he didn't like the smell of her washing powder very much. He firstly walked over to the washing machine, bag in hand, unzipped the bag and then transferred the contents into the machine. He hadn't done washing before because Lydia had always handled such chores, so he just put everything in, filled the drawer up with powder without even measuring the correct amount of washing powder, and did the same with the comfort softener. He looked at all the programmes on the control panel, not knowing which one to choose, but as he pressed the on/off button, the programme defaulted to the one Lydia had used before her death, so Neil let it be and hit the start button. He watched the machine as it filled with water and frothed up the soap. He didn't know if it were supposed to do that or not so just in case he walked away and ascended the stairs. He needed to lie down because his eyes were heavy, and he was feeling absolutely drained because of the events of the last few days. He fell on his bed and was sleeping in no time at all.

DI Thorpe arrived back to his office after another long meeting with DCI Tomlinson. He sometimes wished that the DCI wouldn't spend so much time calling meetings because it took the necessary time away from real Police work and as he was a hands-on DI, time was precious. DS Carter saw that his boss was back and headed over to his office just as the DI was picking up his voicemails.

"How did the ..." DS Carter was cut off mid-sentence as the DI held up his finger to indicate that he was listening to his messages. Then he put the receiver back down.

"Neil Marsh thinks he has had another letter."

"Well, I have some other news that may surprise you. Forensics came back with the results of the ballistic tests on the ammunition," DS Carter exclaimed seriously. He saw the DI stand alert to what he was about to be told. "It looks like the gun used to kill PC Horgan and his family was also the gun that was used on Byron Maddocks."

"My God. We may have a serial killer on the loose." DI Thorpe didn't know which way to look. He stared at the crime information board and then back at Carter. Then he shook his head. "Is there any connection between Horgan and Maddocks?"

"DC Bolton and ADC Hardy are just going through PC Horgan's open caseload notes now, so we should hopefully find out something from that." DS Carter waited for the DI to reply. It was like he didn't know what to do next, either that or his mind was working overtime. "ADC Hardy has also found out that the photo's which were sent to Neil Marsh were printed in Boot's, but we don't know which one at the moment. Ben is waiting for a telephone call back from the Boot's head office to find out which branches have photographic facilities."

"I know that the one in the Drake Circus Shopping Centre has print facilities. Plus, it is right next door to Waterstones. The suspect could have done them on the same day as the book signing. We need to get out and see Neil Marsh and take a look at this suspicious letter. He also said on his message that he has gone home."

DS Carter looked at the DI. "We could do that now and then Bolton and Hardy should have finished looking at PC Horgan's notes."

"You are a stickler for making effective use of time, aren't you? You will have to mention that at the interview if you go for my job." DI Thorpe threw some papers down on his desk. "Come on then, let's go."

Twenty minutes later they were stood outside the Marsh's house banging on the door. They didn't think that he would have gone anywhere especially because of the threats against him. DS Carter moved over to the front window and tried to peak in.

"There's no one there I don't think. I can't see any movement." Suddenly the window above them opened and Neil Marsh poked out his sleepy head rubbing his eyes and stretching his arms.

"Hello Neil!" the DI said, looking up to the window. "You called and I've just picked up your message."

Neil Marsh was still 'In the land of nod' as his Mother would say to him, where he was not putting his brain to work. "Two minutes," he said, closing and locking the window whilst still stretching and yawning. He certainly needed what little sleep he had. It was okay sleeping in a strange bed or on the sofa as the case may be, but nothing beats your own bed. He could also smell Lydia on the duvet cover and pillowcases which relaxed him a little. He imagined that she was there beside him, and he was cuddling her, his arms around her pulling her close.

He suddenly remembered that the two Detectives were still waiting for him at the front door. He quickly ran down the stairs and opened the door. "Sorry about that. I must have fallen asleep," he said as the two Detectives welcomed themselves inside.

"So, we got your voice message about the letter," DI Thorpe said to him.

"It's in the kitchen on the worktop," Neil replied showing signs of recovery after his sleep. He tried to focus his eyes that little bit more as he really felt like he had been out on the town the night before. He then felt like he had been ripped off because he hadn't been out on the town but was feeling the effects.

DS Carter went into the kitchen and saw the pile of letters, so put his surgical gloves on and then picked them up.

"It's the handwritten one," Neil shouted down the hallway. "All the rest are bills. You are quite welcome to pay them for me."

"I don't even pay my own bills," DS Carter replied as he passed the suspicious letter to his senior.

"You can open it. Carefully!" DI Thorpe said to him. "Try to make as minor damage as possible just in case we can get a reading on any saliva used to stick it down." He watched DS Carter return to the kitchen and carefully pull the envelope flap upwards until it was loose and take out the contents. It was a single page but there was a photograph loose inside. He let the item fall out of the envelope onto the kitchen work surface and then opened the folded letter out.

"You had better see this, Guv," DS Carter said whilst looking at the writing. "My God." He shook his head as the DI joined him in the kitchen.

DI Thorpe looked at the clear writing on the piece of paper and read it loudly so all could hear.

"Suffer the children. I have no conscience so that does not worry me. Women are just the collateral damage for the justice not served on man."

Both Detectives then looked at the photograph. It was of Lydia Marsh in the overturned car, the water from the river gushing into the car over her face. "We have to catch this guy soon!" DI Thorpe was just angry with the way that Lydia's killer had just thrown the responsibility for her death into the river as well.

Neil hadn't heard the letter being read as he was in the living room looking outside through the window. He then joined the two officers in the kitchen.

"You don't want to see this," DS Carter said authoritatively.

"Oh yes I do," Neil replied, his face staring at Carter as if to say, *'Get out of my way.'*

"Don't touch them, Neil!" DI Thorpe demanded forcefully. "We need them analysed by forensics." He watched as Neil bowed his head and read the note, and then looked at the photograph.

"He has got to be crazy," Neil said as he read it again. "What sort of man would take a photo of a woman who was drowning when he could have redeemed himself and saved her? It wasn't Lydia's fault that she was married to me."

"Unfortunately, they are around. These types of people are ill, yet they walk amongst us," DS Carter said to the widower.

"Yes but read it. I think it is saying because I got away with supposedly killing that old lady, my children are going to suffer by not having a Mother."

"We don't know that Neil," DI Thorpe said to him trying to make him think positive because at first he appeared to be wanting to get the killer before the killer got him.

DS Carter took two evidence bags out of his pocket. "I'm going to have to take these, Neil. We will get them analysed. Hopefully, there will be a fingerprint or some other DNA on them somewhere." He put the letter in one bag and the photograph in another and sealed each one. "Please Neil, don't do anything stupid."

Neil shook his head. "I won't. I'm too heartbroken to even think about doing anything. Don't worry."

DI Thorpe looked at him. "Are you sure it is an innovative idea for you to be here by yourself? Why didn't you stay at Paul's house?"

"I don't want to put them in danger," Neil replied thoughtfully. "Especially as this guy doesn't have any issues with killing members of the opposite sex."

"Okay. We will be in contact. Let me know if anything else becomes known." DI Thorpe knew that in a way, Neil Marsh was able to take care of himself and had done so since he was a teenager. He had been a right tearaway from day one. "Right DS Carter. Let's get back to the station."

They left, getting back into the unmarked vehicle, and driving off in the direction of the City Centre. "So, what do you think?" DS Carter asked his boss hoping that his answer would coincide with what he was thinking, even though they regularly had differences in opinions on subjects that were accepted by the DI as long as he put up a good argument backed by facts. He always did. The DI used to say to him *'Don't bullshit a bullshiter'* if he thought Carter was wrong.

"I think there is more to this than meets the eye. Do we have two cases on the go, or can we link 'Jeremy' to all three?"

"Surely," DS Carter continued, "The Marsh's crime is a totally different MO?"

DI Thorpe looked out of the passenger side window. "Is it though? Those two notes that Neil Marsh has received. I would say that they have been written by a highly intelligent man, a scholar, well-educated. Someone who reads books. That would provide a link with the Byron Maddocks case."

"What about the Horgan's?" DS Carter asked, not seeing the link, and disagreeing with the theory so far.

"Well, whoever was responsible killed the wife and children. He has no conscience, just like Neil's note said. Suffer the children."

"But the other two cases never received letters," DS Carter said back to him.

"Byron Maddocks murder was opportunistic. I don't think the killer woke up on that fateful day with any intention of killing his favourite author."

"Let's hope Bolton and Hardy have managed to dig something up," Carter said with a sense of hope that the two junior officers could get some recognition.

DI Thorpe started to chuckle. "Laurel and Hardy," he said through his little laugh.

Carter was confused and frowned. "Who?"

Back at the station, DC Bolton and ADC Hardy were busy trying to pick out faces on the two external CCTV discs that they had been given by two different retailers. They decided to firstly look for someone that resembled 'Jeremy' from the incident with Byron Maddocks at the Drake Circus Shopping Centre. They knew that DS Carter and DC Johnson had been to speak to the two ladies that had reported the suspicious character.

"What about this one?" ADC Hardy pointed out a man standing with his shoulder against the wall in the entrance to the tunnel that led to the car park behind the Broadway.

"It's possible. Let's watch and find out," DC Bolton replied. They were disappointed as a female gave him a hug and they both walked off together. Bolton shook his head. "Obviously under the thumb," he said jokingly. "You've got that to come!"

"Hold on," ADC Hardy interrupted suddenly. "This one." He pointed to the screen as DC Bolton put it on slow motion. "There are two ladies just coming out of the coffee shop, and he appears to be taking an interest in them." They watched further as the two moved slowly looking in shop windows and so did the suspect who always stood one shop away and pretended to do the same. They then disappeared into Poundland. DC Bolton froze the image of the suspect at the entrance to the store just as the stranger followed them in.

"He resembles the guy from the Mall. Even down to the anorak and the baseball cap," DC Bolton said as he stared at the image. "Let's try and get a close-up image."

154

He started pressing some buttons on the control console and the image zoomed in, but the CCTV was such a substandard quality that the image just blurred. "Damn!"

"I guess that PC Horgan never had the chance to look at these," ADC Hardy said to him. "He managed to get them but that was as far as he got."

DC Bolton then pointed to the screen again. "Hold on. Is that PC Horgan there?"

"Well, it is a Police Officer. He just appears to be talking to members of the public." ADC Hardy got closer to the screen and watched the movements. "He just looks like he is on patrol. Perhaps he was just street walking that day."

Without the pair noticing, DI Thorpe and DS Carter walked in through the swing doors and headed over towards Thorpe's office. DS Carter stopped. "All Officer's working on the Horgan/Maddocks/Marsh cases, please come into the DI's office."

Within minutes, DI Thorpe's office was busy with an array of different ranks. What DI Thorpe didn't expect was for DCI Tomlinson to suddenly appear and join the meeting. DI Thorpe was wondering whether he would stay for the whole thing.

"Okay, quieten down," DS Carter said whilst trying to bring some order in the room for his boss.

DI Thorpe seemed thankful that Carter had taken the plunge to shut the team up. When the level was acceptable he cleared his throat. "Thank you for dropping whatever you were doing. We need to see where we are and share any information on the three open cases, the murders of PC Horgan and his family, the author Byron Maddocks and most recently Lydia Marsh." He looked at DS Carter to start the ball rolling.

"Okay. We have a link between the Horgan and the Maddock's murders. Forensics have come back and indicated on a 96% probability that the gun used was the same gun."

DC Bolton perked up. "Do we know what calibre the ammunition is, Serge?"

Carter nodded his head. "19mm which makes it almost certain that the weapon is a Baretta 9000 which is probably the easiest weapon to get hold of illegally at the moment."

"The link is there, gentlemen." DI Thorpe was looking to see who he would ask to speak next. "The question is why? The Horgan's and Byron Maddocks had no connection. DC Bolton. How is the CCTV analysis going?"

"ADC Hardy and I have been concentrating on PC Horgan and his open cases prior to his death. Now we found out that he had collected CCTV from a few of the local shops in Plymstock Broadway after speaking to a man about stalking two days prior." DC Bolton noticed a hand raised and nodded his head in the direction of DC Johnson.

"DS Carter and I interviewed the two women who had reported that they thought they were being followed. They did so whilst they were shopping in Poundland." DC Johnson looked at his notebook quickly. "Apparently it was passed to PC Horgan who was in the Broadway at the time. He gave the man some friendly advice and moved him on."

"Did we get a name, Guv?" DS Ayres asked quickly.

"He gave a false name and false address it appears. Very comical. David Jones, which just happens to be the real name of singer David Bowie. His address he gave as 22A George Place, Plymouth, which just happens to be a hostel. He is not known there at all," DC Johnson stated.

"It must be said that the adult victims received similar gunshot wounds, two in the chest and one centre forehead, apart from Lydia Marsh of course," DI Thorpe mentioned.

"We have a visual image of our suspect in the Broadway, but it is very grainy," ADC Hardy commented. But DC Bolton and I both think it is likely that it is the 'Jeremy' from the Byron Maddock's murder."

"So," DI Thorpe said authoritatively, "We need to find this man known as 'Jeremy' and find out if he is guilty or whether he has an alibi when the murders happened and therefore take him off the list of suspects."

DS Carter interrupted again. "Now DI Thorpe and I have been investigating the death of Lydia Marsh. Some of you may know her as the wife of our favourite burglar Neil Marsh." There was some unrest in the troops within the office.

"The RPLI at the scene has indicated that it wasn't an accident. She was forced off the road by another vehicle and tragically landed upside down in deep water," DI Thorpe said sorrowfully. "A terrible way to die."

"So did the other driver not stop to see how she was?" ADC Hardy asked with a frown on his forehead.

"Well, he didn't save her, but we know he stopped to admire his handywork, ADC Hardy," the DI replied accordingly. "But there is more to this. The night before, Neil was stalked at his workplace, and the next morning this was delivered to them along with some pretty damning photographs." He clicked the control for the visual board, and the first note received by the Marsh's popped up on screen.

'There are four kinds of Murder: felonious, excusable, justifiable, and praiseworthy. Yours will consist of all four.'

"This morning, Neil Marsh contacted me on my direct number and informed us that he had received another note." The DI clicked the remote for the second visual.

"Suffer the children. I have no conscience so that does not worry me. Women are just the collateral damage for the justice not served on man."

"There was also a photograph of Lydia Marsh dying in the overturned water-logged car with the second letter," Thorpe concluded.

"Now we know from the postmarks on the letters that both were posted in Plymouth," DS Carter added importantly whilst looking at each and every officer in the room.

Suddenly DCI Tomlinson perked up. "You all have my full support team, but I'm sure you know that although we cannot give it the status of 'serial killer' at the moment, the press and the public are going to pick up on it pretty soon."

"So, we need action!" DI Thorpe demanded, the urgency showing in his request. "Put your feelers out. We need Jeremy."

DS Carter looked at his DI. "The two ladies who were followed at Broadway are currently in the station doing identifits, so we should have better ideas of what he looks like. We know that all the CCTV images are no good and would not stand up in a court of law because of PACE."

"Someone must know him," DS Ayres commented. "We need those Identifits."

"I will get you all copies out as soon as they are finished," DS Carter said, nodding his head.

"Now the last thing, I have heard that investigative reporter Jack Dempsey from the Sun newspaper is in town and making noises as he was a friend of Byron Maddocks. I must stress, no information must be given to him. If he asks, direct him to me!"

"Right team," the DCI said with a view to closing the meeting, "Let's get going."

Chapter 12

Jeremy Cornelius-Johnson had picked up his car and checked the repairs to the front of his vehicle before he left the forecourt. He was very particular about the service he received from retailers and services like car repairs. But upon inspection it appeared that they had done a decent job, so he drove away after paying the £380 for the replacement parts and fitting. He just didn't want it going through his insurance in case the insurance company questioned the damage.

He arrived home and noticed a Police car outside Ken's house. He parked his car on his driveway and chose not to take any notice of the officer standing at Ken's front door. The young man was banging on the door at first and then decided to look down the side of the house and into the back garden before returning to the front door. After a while, he gave up, but saw Jeremy about to go inside.

"Excuse me, Sir," the Officer shouted across. "Have you seen your neighbour Mr Meadows recently?"

"Oh," Jeremy replied putting his hand over his mouth and staring to make it look like he was thinking. "I think it was a few days ago. I came home from work, and he was doing his garden. Why do you ask?"

"One of the neighbours opposite has said that they haven't seen him, and they are concerned for him. They said it's not a usual practice for Mr Meadows to leave his gardening tools out when he has finished with them," the PC said as he started to walk over to Jeremy.

"Looking at it that way, no it's not usual. He's always so particular. I don't really see him that much. I'm a Clerk of the Court and sometimes don't get home until late as you can understand." Yes, Jeremy thought, use your professional standing to help you get out of this!

"Okay, Mr?"

"Cornelius-Johnson."

"Well thank you, Mr Johnson. I think I will just see if I can see anything through his back window. He might have fallen or something."

"I hope not," Jeremy replied as he suddenly realised that the PC had thought his surname was Johnson, so probably thought Cornelius was his forename. He watched the uniformed officer go into the side path and around the back of the house. Jeremy knew that he wouldn't find anything. An open door, but no sign of Ken Meadows. He went inside and looked out of his front bay window for the officer, just as he had done with Ken who was looking at his car. It was a few minutes before the young man headed back towards his Police car whilst speaking into his radio. He drove away, and u-turned at the mini roundabout to go back to the station.

Time for the next part of his plan to piss Neil Marsh off, he retorted to himself. He changed his clothes and looked at the time, having arranged to meet the Estate Agent at 17:30 hrs at the house in Woodlands Lane and had plans to view two of them that evening more or less side by side.

He put on his black hoodie and baseball cap and changed his smart trousers for jeans. Picking up his keys and his wallet, he locked the front door but then went to the side of the house and down to the workshop entrance at the side. He opened the door and instantly smelt the dried blood that hadn't managed to be washed away. He told himself that he would give it a second wash, this time with bleach, at the weekend. Jeremy looked to the worktop and picked up two registration plates that were lying there. He took them to his car and reversed out, heading in the direction of Plymstock and then Laira Bridge. It wasn't long before he was on Embankment Road heading towards Marsh Mills, and then into Leigham Park Drive. He could see the Police tape still visible where Lydia's car had entered the water.

Jeremy stopped his car and picked up the false number plates that he had dropped on his passenger seat beside him. He looked down at the river. The car had gone after being picked up by the recovery vehicle to be taken to the Forensic Science Lab. He placed one false plate over the front plate on his vehicle. It stuck with a Velcro type effect. This wasn't the first time he had done this, and it helped him not to get caught. He repeated the process with the rear plate. Then he got back into his car and headed towards Woodlands Lane deep within the jungle of evergreen trees and rivers.

Jeremy drove right down the bottom of the Lane, turned around and parked up behind the waiting Estate Agent just down from the Marsh's house but on the other side of the road. He saw the young lady approaching him. "Hello. You are from Fox's I guess," he said brightly and with politeness.

"That's right. Jane Ackland," she replied holding out her hand for him to shake.

"David Jones," he replied nicely. "Right, shall we get on with the viewings?" He wasn't really interested as he crossed the road and looked over at the Marsh's house.

"Your house. Is it in a chain or ready to sell?" She asked, knowing that if it were free from chain there would be a quicker sale if he liked it.

"My parents died recently and left me the house. Too many memories for me to stay there. But it's free from chain and all paid for." Jeremy still looked around as he stepped onto the pavement and watched Jane go up the path of the first house and knock on the door.

The door opened and a young man showed his face, aged about twenty-five. "Hiya," he said to Jane as he shook her hand not seeing Jeremy hiding in the shadows at first but then realising that his potential buyer was stood behind her. "Oh, so sorry! Welcome. Do come in."

Jeremy and the estate agent spent about ten to fifteen minutes looking around the property. He had no intention on buying it but just wanted to know the layout, what the standard locks were that had been installed by the builders because chances are these were the ones that were still installed in the Marsh's house. He smirked as they went to view the upstairs and on the way he noticed a standard Yale lock on the front door with a chain. That was it, he thought to himself. That was their security, and he wondered whether the Marsh's shared the incompetence.

Jeremy thought that he should show interest. "It's genuinely nice. You have done well with the décor. Nice big rooms. How much was it on the market for?"

Jane looked at her paperwork. "This one is £374,950.

Jeremy pouted and lifted his eyebrows high. "That's not bad for a four bedroom with both a garage and a workshop in a nice quiet area. Office downstairs."

"There is plenty of storage space," Jane commented trying her hardest to sell it to him.

"What about the garden? Does it lead out to the woodland?"

The owner shook his head. "No. There is a back lane that goes all the way down to the woodland. We have a gate for access. It's just quicker if you want to go for a walk. There is also a quick way to get to the local superstore."

Jeremy turned and started walking back down the stairs. "Well thank you for showing me around. I have got a lot of thinking to do!" He looked at Jane. "I'm not sure if it is worth looking at the one next door."

Jane smiled, thinking that she was going to get a sale here because he liked the place. "That's fine. We can cancel the appointment." She then turned to the owner and said, "Thank you. I'll be in touch."

"No, thank you. I'll wait to hear from you and then discuss things with my partner," he replied nicely as he watched the two walk down the driveway.

Jane reached the other side of the road with Jeremy just in front of her. "What did you think?"

Before he could answer, he noticed a man stood in the porch over at the Marsh's and smiled as he realised it was no other than Neil Marsh himself, who had recognised the make and colour of Jeremy's car and put two and two together. "It's you! Bastard!"

Jeremy pulled Jane around between the two cars as Neil stormed over. Jane screamed and Jeremy looked at him. "What the hell are you doing? Who are you?" he demanded to know, indicating that he didn't know Neil Marsh.

"Why did you do it? You killed my wife and you have been stalking me!" Neil shouted not realising that Jane was on the phone calling the Police.

Jeremy unlocked his car. "You are loopy man. What are you on? I've been here with the Estate agent viewing a house." He looked at Jane who had managed to get into her car and lock the doors. Deep inside he was slightly frightened, but he had hoped for this minute, if not just to scare the living daylights out of Neil Marsh.

"You are fucking dead!" the angry widower snapped whilst pointing at him and making an angry face as though at any moment, Jeremy was going to be attacked. He slowly backed up and got close to the driver's door. With minor delay, Jeremy opened the door and jumped in, and Neil realised he was too slow as he tried to open the locked passenger door. Neil started the car and drove off at speed, so Neil ran back over to his house and grabbed the keys to his car from the key hook, and then jumped into his car, reversing back out onto the road at speed and narrowly missing Jane's car which was parked slightly down the hill from his driveway entrance. Neil then sped after the man he thought had killed Lydia.

Jeremy had the lead on him of about one minute and had managed to speed down Leigham Park Drive with no traffic heading against him. He reached the junction but turned left and headed up the wrong way going through the road that was marked as a 'No Entry.' He hoped that he wouldn't meet any traffic, especially any busses as he knew that the number 50 came that way. Luck was on his side.

Neil Marsh meanwhile had reached the same junction but turned right and headed towards the roundabout. He couldn't see the suspect car in front. What would he do to get away? He asked himself. Go into the retail park? That would be too relevantly obvious. What about turn right and head into the small industrial estate? He would try that. His car went around the roundabout with him nearly losing control of the vehicle, but he didn't care. He looked into each unit's car park, but there was nothing. Saturday. Most were empty as only the very few were open. He put his foot down and headed around to the main drag. He stopped at the junction and looked up and down the road, and then banged his steering wheel with the palms of his hands using some force.

Flashing lights came his way from the Parkway roundabout as the Police answered Jane's call. The car zoomed past him heading towards his street. He decided to follow them. He would need to explain things to the frightened Estate Agent and apologise. But he was sure that the man was the same man he had seen parked opposite the taxi office. But he knew that he had some explaining to do. The guy definitely had something to hide, otherwise why would he have driven away at top speed? Or he was just feeling threatened by him? He might have been completely innocent. Time to face the music.

Jeremy had driven home via the Plympton and Coypool routes which he never had seen himself using that often at all. He got home and there were several cars parked outside on the road. He thought for a while as this usually happened either in the hot weather when people used to park there and walk down to the beach in order to save parking fees, or if there was an event on in the village like the Winter Fair. Someone had parked right outside his house blocking him getting in on his driveway. He sounded the horn on his car a few times, and after the third attempt to get someone's attention, a man in a suit appeared from behind the trees in Ken Meadow's garden and waved to him, jumped in the driver's seat, and pulled out of the way for Jeremy to turn and get in to his drive. Then the man reversed the car back to its original position.

The stranger got out of his car and walked up the driveway to greet Jeremy, flashing a warrant card as he did so. "Detective Inspector Chandler," he said as he introduced himself. "You don't mind if I park there, so you? Parking is a nightmare around here."

Jeremy shook his head whilst staring at the Police Officer with thoughts going through his mind about just what he wanted. "No problem," he replied. "I don't think that I need to go out again, but if I do I'll search you out."

"I think we may be here for hours," DI Chandler said whilst noticing Jeremy's body language which appeared uneasy.

"Is Ken alright? I see there is some activity over there."

"Well, we don't actually know," the DI said sharply. "The neighbour across the road reported him missing because he hadn't seen him for a few days and had left all his gardening tools outside."

Jeremy nodded. "Yes, the Police Officer said when he came around and asked about him."

"Well Mr Maxwell had Ken Meadow's son's telephone number in case of an emergency so telephoned him to see if Ken had gone there, but he hadn't. So, he called the Police again and it was passed to CID."

"Yes I know Dave and Ken share the same love of gardening, unlike me."

DI Chandler was still identifying the nervousness in Jeremy. "PC Hartley states in his report that you saw him a few days prior to Mr Maxwell calling the Police."

"That's right. I explained to the young man that it was very unusual for Ken to leave his tools out, and that I had seen him when I returned from work late one evening. That's all I know really." Jeremy shrugged his shoulders. "I don't know what else I can tell you."

"Did you hear any noises or shouting or anything that evening?" DI Chandler asked inquisitively as he watched Jeremy shake his head slowly with a look of amazement on his face.

"Like I said, I came home late and then had something to eat for supper and went to bed."

"That's fine, Mr Johnson. I may need to speak to you again. But thanks for your help," The DI said turning to walk back to Ken's house.

"I do hope the old guy is alright," Jeremy shouted after him.

"Me too. It looks like you may have been the last one to see him."

Jeremy went indoors and did his usual ritual of looking out the front bay window through the blinds to see if anything was happening. There was a lot of comings and goings at the front door, and they were obviously looking for something because they were putting assorted items of Ken's in plastic evidence bags and taking them down to one of the vehicles parked outside Ken's house. He then began panicking a little as he realised that he hadn't managed to give the garage/workshop a deep clean as he planned to do. It wasn't worth worrying about now, he told

166

himself. They could only look in there if they had a reasonable suspicion that he had done something to Ken Meadows and right now they didn't.

All sorts of thoughts were going through Jeremy's head. Should he get away? Go on holiday? He was owed a great deal of leave by his work as every time he tried to take some they came up with an excuse that there was a big case due, and they needed him because Judge Kang Lim Koh had personally asked for him. What it really was, he thought, was that the staffing budget was too excessive, and they couldn't get a replacement so if he went, the case would be abandoned.

Over at Ken Meadow's house, DI Chandler knew that he had suspicions about Mr Johnson. When he got back to the station he would check him out on the PNC. But then, PC Hartley had been told he was a Clerk of the Court, so he should have top clearance and be whiter than white.

"Everything alright, Guv?" DS Kent asked as he watched the DI's cogs turning in his head. "Only you are looking bewildered."

"I have just got a feeling," DI Chandler replied suspiciously. "There's something not right with the neighbour next door."

"Do you think he knows where Ken Meadows is?"

Chandler shook his head. "I think Ken Meadows is dead. Our Mr Johnson next door was the last to see him."

"Can't we get a search warrant?" DS Kent asked as he questioned in his own head the sense of the DI's madness.

"On what grounds? A hunch?" Chandler retorted. "We don't even know if the old man is dead. There are no signs of any struggle in his house and no blood stains. It's clean from top to bottom."

"Don't you think that in itself is unusual?" DS Kent queried as he thought of his studies into serial killers who cleaned up after themselves and removed most signs of evidence.

"The evidence in Mr Meadows house does not show any signs of foul play. In fact, there is no evidence," DI Chandler said as though he were disappointed. He looked at it from a Detective's point of view, where if there were a dead body, he would prefer that there was some indication that there was a reason for the death. "Let's face it. He could have gone for a walk down at Wembury beach or over to Wembury Point and slipped or fallen. Chances are if that happened, an old man still unseen would have probably died from hypothermia by now or been washed out by the tide."

"That doesn't explain your hunch," DS Kent exclaimed as he tried to give reason to his senior officer. "His wardrobe looks untouched so I think we can rule him out of going on holiday. Well, we know he is not at his son's."

"Unless we can prove otherwise, Ken Meadows will go down as a MISPER," was the response from the DI whilst looking over at the house of Jeremy Cornelius-Johnson. "But just to try and ease my suspicion, I think the both of us will go and see if we can take a statement from Ken's neighbour."

"Okay," DS Kent. "I guess that won't be the real reason why we are going?" Kent responded with a smile on his face. He knew exactly what his boss wanted. The standard 'Could I use your toilet' act or looking at photographs on the wall and commenting on them, looking at his body language and mannerisms.

"I may be wrong," DI Chandler answered. "But it doesn't hurt for us to rule him out and two heads are better than one."

DS Kent looked over towards Dave Maxwell's house, the neighbour who had reported Ken as missing. "We may have another suspect. It is known on many cases for the person reporting the crime to be the culprit."

"I don't get the same feeling with Mr Maxwell as I do with this guy next door," Chandler said. "But I have been known to be wrong, so perhaps we will do the same there. He has already given the plods a statement, so we will further question him. Let's go!"

Back at Woodland's Lane, Jane Ackland was still locked in her car as the flashing lights and sirens of the Police vehicle sounded the arrival of the help she needed. She was slightly hysterical as she got out of her car and waved them down, and the Officer skidded to a halt at the side of the road.

"Hello, we have a 999 call from you saying you were being threatened. Are you alright?" PC Longbrook asked, knowing that she wasn't because she was nervous and choking up with tears so much that she couldn't seem to speak very clearly.

"N...n...n. It was the man from that house," she exclaimed, pointing over towards the Marsh's house."

PC Markham appeared from behind is colleague. "Weren't we there the other day?"

His colleague nodded. "How did he threaten you?" Longbrook asked softly showing some compassion in his voice in order to try and calm the situation down.

"There he is!" she started screaming again as Neil Marsh's car arrived at speed and pulled up on his drive. She saw him get out and immediately head over towards them.

PC Markham withdrew is baton and extended the protective weapon shouting, "Stay where you are! Get down on your knees!"

"What?" Neil Marsh replied, astonished by the commands of the younger man.

"I said, down on your knees! Hands behind your head!" PC Markham shouted authoritatively whilst remaining distant from the suspect.

Neil did as he was ordered, knowing that his earlier actions made him look like a violent mad man and that was why the woman was currently in a state of hysterical screaming. PC Markham approached him cautiously with his baton ready to strike and then withdrew his handcuffs from his belt and slapped them on Neil's wrist.

"Hands behind you back!" he shouted as he realised that Neil was slightly resisting. "I said hands behind your back!"

"Look, there is no need for this!" Marsh reacted. "There is a perfectly good explanation!"

"What's your name?" PC Markham asked as he ensured the cuffs were locked on.

"Fuck off! I don't believe this," Marsh retorted angrily. "I see the man who killed my wife, and you fucking arrest me?"

"NAME?"

"Marsh. Neil Marsh. Get me DS Carter!"

PC Markham looked at the offender and then nodded towards his colleague to signify that he was secure. "All in good time. Neil Marsh, I am arresting you on suspicion of threatening behaviour. You do not have to say anything, but it may harm your defence if you do not mention when questioned, something that you later rely on in Court. Anything you do say may be given in evidence. Do you understand?"

"Fuck off!" Marsh responded as the Officer forced him over towards the van, opened the doors and shoved him in the back in a secure containment. Marsh started kicking the cage. "Fucking get me DS Carter!"

Markham walked back over to his colleague. "One in custody," he laughed, pretending to catch his breath because of the struggle.

"Miss Ackland here was just telling me that he attacked her client, a Mr David Jones after they left a property that they had just viewed across the road. She is an Estate Agent."

"So where is he now?" PC Markham asked, looking around as though he was going to see a man hiding in the bushes.

"He got in his car and drove off at high speed," the lady interjected. "Left me here by myself with that idiot banging on my car bonnet and kicking my door!"

"Okay Miss Ackland," PC Longbrook said calmly as he still tried to comfort the lady. "We are going to need you to come down the station and give a statement. Can you do that?"

She nodded in agreement. "Yes. What do you want me to do? Follow you?"

"As long as you are alright to drive?" asked PC Markham. "We know what incidents like this can do to people."

"I'm just angry now," she replied. "I was frightened. Now just angry."

PC Markham nodded at his colleague. "I think I should drive you to the station in your car to help you calm down a little more. Especially after one of our canteen cups of tea!"

"You certainly know how to woo a girl, don't you Constable? Cup of tea." She looked at him and knew that he was right. She was too angry to drive and felt that it would only take one of the bad drivers to pull in front of her for the wrath to show itself in road rage. "Okay, I'll let you drive," she said as she handed over her keys.

Chapter 13

Charles Cross Police Station was bustling with life at the enquiries office although many couldn't get past the tripods with camera's fixed to them which were all set up directly outside. The tabloids had heard about the serial killer in Plymouth who had killed an international author and a Police Officer together with his family. They had all set up waiting for an official statement from someone in authority who was dealing with the case. Two uniformed Officers had been deployed to the front to stop the press getting any closer than they should.

DCI Tomlinson loved getting the limelight in such opportunities and having heard about the gathering downstairs had started preparing his statement ready to read to the crowd. He called DI Thorpe and DS Carter into his office just to make sure that what he was going to say was gospel. "Just to clarify," he said to the pair, "We have confirmation that the Horgan's and Byron Maddocks were killed by the same gun."

"That's right," DI Thorpe responded. "It is going to be up to you if you mention the suspects name 'Jeremy.' We just don't think that it would be beneficial at this stage because the switchboard would be called at every minute of the day with people telling us that their neighbour or pet cat is called Jeremy, and we don't even know if that is his real name as yet."

"I think you are right," the DCI said calmly. "It would just constitute a lot of unnecessary leg work on wild goose chases. He stood up and put his jacket on and then ensured his tie was straight before heading to the door. "Wish me luck!"

Thorpe and Carter thought they would go down with him for support so jumped in the lift with him as the doors opened for the DCI. "Thought we would come and cheer you on, Guv," DS Carter commented jokingly.

"I'll need every bit of support I can get no doubt," the DCI responded politely as he looked in the mirrored glass on the inside of the lift and straightened his tie for the fourth time since leaving the office.

DI Thorpe looked at DS Carter and smiled. Thorpe really wanted to ask his boss if he had his make-up done prior to the unofficial news conference but knew that this wasn't the time to be funny. Luckily, the sun was shining outside and for once looked like it had made plans to be around for a few hours yet. DI Thorpe opened the front doors for the DCI, and he stepped out into the limelight amid a forest of flashing lights from the photographers.

Questions were instantly being thrown at him in no order by the majority of the reporters each of whom were hoping that he would hear theirs and reply, but the DCI held both hands up and then said, "I have a statement here that I will read." The noise quietened down as they all wanted to make sure that they heard the information. DCI Tomlinson looked at the paper and then cleared his throat before starting to talk.

'There has been an increase in violent crime over the recent weeks resulting in the deaths of a local Police Officer and his family and also international author, Byron Maddocks. I can now say that the Police are looking into these murders because forensic information has linked them through ballistic testing showing that the same weapon was used in both incidents. Current enquiries are being made into the whereabouts of a suspect seen on CCTV. The Investigation is ongoing. Thank you.'

DI Thorpe stepped forward. "We will aim to answer as many questions as our time allows."

"Does Plymouth have a serial killer?" someone shouted, although DI Thorpe didn't see the origin of the question.

"We have no evidence at this moment in time that there is a serial killer in the area," DCI Tomlinson commented authoritatively before acting like a chairperson and pointing to a reporter who had his hand up.

"Have there been any further reports of violence not yet linked to the serial killer?" Daily Mail reporter Jeff Hollis shouted.

"There has been one other death, but the MO was different and has yet to be linked to the others," the DCI replied to Hollis looking seriously at him. "Please do not refer to the linked murders as a serial killer at large."

Jack Dempsey caught DI Thorpe's eye who in return tried his hardest not to look at the reporter. "There are rumours DCI Tomlinson about the name of the wanted suspect's first name. Are you able to release this to us?" Jack knew the name but didn't want the Police knowing where he had got the information.

"The name is not confirmed at the moment so won't be released to prevent every person with the same name being targeted."

Jack Dempsey intervened again. "How efficient was the investigation into Byron Maddock's death?"

DCI Tomlinson instantly began to wonder if this was a question that was going to trip him up, but then knew that Jack Dempsey wouldn't release any potential information that he didn't think the Police had. "It received the same level of investigation as all murders receive." He saw Jack Dempsey smile and raise his eyebrows in defiance. Why did he ask that and why was he looking so smug? His facial expressions told both the DCI and DI that he had information and even though they usually didn't meet with individual members of the gutter press, both officers knew Dempsey was a little bit different. You scratch his back, and he will scratch yours thought the DCI.

DI Thorpe looked at Dempsey with a serious face before saying, "That's all for today, people. You will know more when we have more to tell you." He then led the DCI back into the foyer whilst DS Carter took the rear ensuring that no one was following.

Outside, Jack Dempsey hung around resting his back on the fence and somehow knowing that he was about to be invited in to speak to CID. He watched the others all packing up and discussing what they had or hadn't been told as the case may be. Many spoke into their digital recorders. Many spoke their exaggerated assumptions and Jack could overhear their potential morning headline's being spoken in the form of lies into their devices. Finally, they all dispersed, and Jack watched the silhouettes exiting down the steps or down the disabled ramp used for wheelchair access.

DCI Tomlinson, DI Thorpe, and DS Carter waited for the escalator. "Do you want me to get Dempsey in, Guv?" Thorpe asked. "You heard his questions and saw the look on his face."

"He could be bluffing," replied the DCI cautiously.

"This is one guy that has never bluffed," DI Thorpe said back to him knowing that it was certainly worth the risk, even if the information he had was the same as that of the CID Team. Thorpe knew that the DCI didn't like to be pressurised into doing something that he would normally disagree with and was about to back off when the DCI perked up.

"DS Carter. Go and see if Mr Dempsey is still around and ask him if he would like to come and have a cup of tea."

"Yes, Guv," DS Carter replied as he turned back the way he had walked minutes previous to look for Jack Dempsey.

"There," the DCI said to Thorpe. "Happy now?"

"Yes, Guv. Good decision."

"On your head be it," the DCI replied jokingly as they both welcomed the lift arriving and got into the empty compartment.

DS Carter meanwhile walked out of the front door towards the waiting Jack Dempsey, thinking that the guy was cockily assuming that they would come back for him. "Jack," he said having met the reporter several times before. "What do we owe the pleasure of you down in sunny Plymouth?"

Dempsey looked up to the blue sky. "Yes, it is quite sunny," he replied, holding out his hand to welcome the Detective, who both had a mutual respect for each other. "I sort of knew that you would be back for me. Mind you I would have looked like a complete prune if you hadn't."

"So, have you got something for us, Jack?"

"Possibly, Mike. Possibly." He watched Mike Carter press the call button for the lift. "I've been to Burrator Reservoir, to the scene of the crime."

"Not a pretty sight, is it?"

Dempsey shook his head. "Not at all. If the gunshots hadn't have killed him, then the fall would have." The elevator arrived and the two walked in. "I met Father Reed and he took me over to Byron's house. I mean, I didn't go inside, but I had to get a feel for the outside."

"Yeh?" Carter said as though he were not surprised by the reporter's actions. "Did you find anything?"

"Let's wait until we see the DI. It will save me explaining it twice. But listen. Don't bullshit me. I know his name. The suspect. Jeremy."

"I thought you might, Jack," Carter exclaimed, smiling at the younger guy. "When have I ever bullshit you? Cheeky bastard." He let Jack exit the lift first and then walked behind him. "Far corner, Jack."

"Mr Dempsey," DI Thorpe exclaimed as he tapped on the DI's door. "Thank you for coming."

"How are you DI Thorpe?" Jack asked him politely before any officialities progressed.

"I'm good, thanks. Now. What was all that at the news conference?" he asked coming straight to the point with the reporter. "Do you know something that we don't? You know withholding evidence is a criminal offense."

"Did the search team find anything outside the grounds of Byron Maddock's house?" Dempsey asked.

"You know I'm not allowed to tell you that, Jack," the DI responded. "But why? You tell me what you have found and if I insist on you leaving empty handed you'll know we don't have a clue what you are talking about." He looked at Jack's folder that the reporter was holding tightly in his left hand and assumed it contained information received from whatever investigations he had been making.

Dempsey opened up the folder and pulled out a copy of the photo he had taken of the carving he had found up in the tree and slid it across the DI's desk for him to see. "Just wondering if you have seen this before?"

"Where did you get this from?" Thorpe asked with confusion because he hadn't seen the carving at all before.

"Up a tree. A tree that overlooks Byron Maddock's house and garden."

"Fucking hell Mike," DI Thorpe stormed at DS Carter. "Who was in charge of the house search?"

Carter knew the answer instantly. "Uniform handled the preliminary search, but I think they only arranged to do the house and surrounding garden."

"Not that it tells you anything, Inspector," Dempsey said, trying to defend DS Carter in some way. "It is just the letter 'J.' For Jeremy, I guess."

Thorpe stared at Jack with piercing eyes. "You have been busy, haven't you?"

"Not only that, Inspector. Whilst I met Father Reed at Burrator, someone was taking photos of us. Someone who didn't want to hang around for exceptionally long."

"Did you see him?"

"No. Only the back of him running towards his car," Dempsey said cautiously. "I'm sure if it were a reporter he would have hung around. But whoever it was ran faster than a lion chasing its prey. I couldn't catch him."

Thorpe's telephone rang loudly. DS Carter used to think that his boss was going deaf in his old age because of how loud the ringtone was, or if they were watching something on the screen, he would always ask for the volume to be increased. "DI Thorpe," he answered snappily, not wanting anything to defer his meeting with Jack Dempsey.

"There is an important call for DS Carter," DC Johnson said from outside the room.

"Okay, thank you," the DI responded before looking at Mike Carter and exclaiming, "It's for you." He passed the handset over and watched as DS Carter disappeared into the corner of the room.

"Carter," he said forcefully.

"Hello DS Carter. It's PC Markham."

"What can I do for you, Constable? I'm pretty busy at the moment," Carter exclaimed to him, hoping that it was nothing trivial because he had so much on his workload at the moment that there weren't enough hours in the day.

"Neil Marsh is in custody. He will only speak to you or DI Thorpe, sergeant." PC Markham waited patiently for a reply.

"What was he taken in for? DS Carter enquired as though he were expecting something like drunk whilst driving.

"Threatening behaviour," PC Markham responded. "He was threatening an estate agent and her customer and

178

saying that the male had killed his wife. The male drove away it appears whilst the Estate Agent stayed in her car and called us."

"Okay. I'm in an important meeting at the moment, but please tell Marsh I will be down to see him as soon as."

"That's fine, DS Carter. I'll go and tell him."

"What was that about Neil Marsh?" DI Thorpe asked after listening in to the call whilst also listening to Jack. He called it multi-tasking, but DS Carter called it being nosey.

"He's been arrested."

"What the hell for? I thought he was locked up tight in his house?" DI Thorpe snapped, realising that it must have been something that had upset him.

"Threatening behaviour. He has asked to see me and won't talk to anyone else. What do you want me to do, Guv?" DS Carter knew what he would do under the circumstances of him losing his wife. They had done it before for others, but he thought he should wait for his guvnors go ahead in the case of Marsh.

DI Thorpe took the thinking stance, looking at the floor, hand brushing his jacket back and his other hand on his chin slightly covering his mouth. "Who arrested him?"

"PC Markham."

"Speak to him and see if we can get the arrest voided. It has to be his decision as the arresting officer, but he surely knows of the circumstances. He escorted Marsh's parents the other day."

Jack Dempsey was also listening to the conversation. "Neil Marsh. That name rings a bell. Is there something I should know?"

"Well, it's common knowledge so I don't see why not," Thorpe said to him. "He has been receiving threatening notes and then the other day, his wife was run off the road on her way home from work and her car landed up the wrong way in the river. She drowned."

"So intentionally run off the road?" Jack asked inquisitively, already preparing to take notes on his digital recorder. "Do you think it is anything to do with the other deaths at all?"

"Off the record, I do. But nothing is confirmed yet." Thorpe looked at DS Carter and then ordered, "Mike, you go down and see to Marsh. See what he has to tell you about why he blew his top."

"Okay, Guv." He looked at Jack. "In case you are gone when I get back, nice to see you again."

"I'm staying put," Jack commented jokingly, much to the dismay of the DI whose body alerted when he said it. DS Carter took the stairs down to the custody suite, mainly because he didn't want to spend the time waiting for the lift again. He arrived at the bottom of the stairs and headed over towards the custody Sergeant. "Hello Nick."

"Mike. How's tricks?" Sergeant Nick Garrett responded calmly although he was looking like he had been subject to a bad day so far.

"Not bad. You have a Neil Marsh in custody?"

"Yes. He has asked for you personally. Something about him being innocent," Garrett replied with a little chuckle. "I wonder which burglary he wants to admit to this time."

"He has just lost his wife in suspicious circumstances. That's why he wants me," DS Carter responded.

"Okay, I'll let you in. You know you are not supposed to speak to him without his solicitor present?" PS Garrett exclaimed, worried about any aftermath that may occur on his watch.

"It will be okay, Nick. I promise," Carter said as he watched the Sergeant grab his bunch of cell keys and then lead him to Neil Marsh's cell on the left of the detention block.

"There we go," Nick said as he left the door ajar for DS Carter. "Don't be too long."

"I won't," Carter replied as he disappeared into the cell.

"DS Carter. I saw him! I saw him!" Neil Marsh appeared frantic both with worry and anger as he remained seated on the edge of his bed.

"You saw who, Neil?"

"The guy in the Nissan who eyed me up at work. He was parked right outside my house," Marsh replied as though he were begging for Carter to believe him.

"But the report says it was a woman who was threatened," Carter replied looking at the detention notes.

"She was an Estate Agent showing him around the house down the road from me." Neil raised both hands to aid his begging to the DS. "You have to believe me. It was him. If it wasn't, why did he drive off and leave that poor lady all alone?"

"Did you get the registration by any chance?"

"Yes. DA20 YPW. I wrote it here on my hand." Marsh pointed to the pen marking on the back of his left hand.

"Okay Neil, let me go and check this out. It was a blue Nissan Duke. Is that right?" He watched as Neil nodded in agreement. I'm aiming to get you out of here, but I will have to speak to PC Markham first." He left the cell slamming the door shut behind him as the auto-lock took effect securing the cell door instantly. DS Carter then went into the enquiry room and acknowledge the controller with a nod of his head.

"How can we help you, DS Carter?"

"Could you do a vehicle check for me to save me going back upstairs?" DS Carter asked knowing that he was just being lazy really but also trying to save time, so told himself that one outweighed the other.

"What's the registration plate?" asked the controller, knowing that CID only asked when they wanted something done for them and there was no other reason.

"Thanks Bob. It's DA20 YPW. It should be a Nissan." DS Carter waited patiently for the reply.

Bob had a confused look on his face as he tapped the system keyboard. "Are you sure that you have the correct number? It's just that plate belongs to a Peugeot 305. The last owner lived in Cardiff, South Wales."

"Well, that is the one that I was given. I guess we have some stolen or duplicated plates, which, to be honest, I expected. Okay thanks Bob," he said as he left the enquiry room. Then he began to wonder whether his prisoner had written down the number correctly, so thought he would try and see if the witness who was currently having her statement taken by PC Markham, had also taken down the number. He looked to see which of the soft interview rooms was currently being used and tapped on the door to the first one he came upon, opening the door to see that it wasn't the people he was expecting. "Oh, I'm so sorry," he said politely as he closed the door again before continuing to look at the 'engaged' slides on each door. He found another, so tapped on the door and again opened it slightly. This time he was successful as he recognised PC Markham sat opposite Jane Ackland.

"Oh, hello Serge. I'm just taking Mrs Ackland's statement. Do you need me for something?" The young PC asked whilst looking at the DS.

"Sorry to bother. I was just wondering," he said, stepping into the room and closing the door quietly behind him and leaning on the door with his hand still on the handle. "Hello. I'm DS Carter. Sorry I should have introduced myself."

"This is Jane Ackland," PC Markham said, introducing the witness and watching as she got up and shook the Sergeant's hand.

"I was wondering Mrs Ackland did you get a name and the registration number of the car that the man who was with you?"

She grabbed her large shoulder bag and started looking inside. "It is standard practice to text the registration number to the office before you meet the client. Let me just look for my phone."

DS Carter smiled slightly as the lady continued to look and something in his mind was telling him, 'everything except the kitchen sink' as she searched. "That would be very helpful."

"Here it is." She started finger clicking the buttons on the mobile's keyboard to bring up the texts. "Blue Nissan Duke. DA20 YPW. The man's name was David Jones." She looked at the Detective and noticed the disappointment in his face. "Is that helpful?"

"Yes, yes. Sorry. The plates were false. I guess your client's name that he gave you will be false as well." DS Carter thought for a few moments whilst keeping still and searching for inspiration from staring at the ceiling.

"But why would he do that?" asked the lady, confused as to why this had happened. "He seemed quite genuine. I even have his mobile number and I have spoken to him on it to confirm he was attending."

The last statement she made alerted DS Carter. "What? You actually called him?" She nodded whilst still wondering what was going on. "Could you let me have that number please, Mrs Ackland?"

"Yes. Sure." She clicked down the list of contacts. "Here it is. David Jones. 07772897950," she replied whilst wondering what was going on. "Is there something I should know?"

DS Carter thought that now was the time to try and get Neil Marsh pardoned by the young lady. "We suspect that your client wasn't really there to look at the house. He is harassing the man who you thought was being aggressive to you both. Your client is suspected of murdering his wife recently."

She looked shocked. "Oh my God," she snapped. "That poor man. No wonder he was shouting at Mr Jones initially."

"Mr Marsh would like the opportunity of apologising to you, whether or not you choose to go forward with the complaint." DS Carter looked into the eye of PC Markham, the look telling the Constable that he could really do with having this complaint knocked on the head, or at the most for Neil Marsh to receive a caution and be let out as soon as possible.

"He did scare the living daylights out of me," she responded.

"Yes," PC Markham added. "He was very uptight and threatening, even towards the Police."

"I will leave it up to you," DS Carter exclaimed as he went to leave the room. "If you would like to tell PC Markham here what you would like to do and then we can proceed either way." He walked out and headed back to the custody suite, knowing that he would have to see Neil Marsh again if Nick Garrett would let him. Twice in one day was normally a no-no. It only took for the defendant to say something to his solicitor, and the case would be thrown out and Carter knew that, and at the end of the day he wouldn't want that to happen no matter what decision was made by Marsh's complainant.

Sergeant Garrett saw Mike Carter come through the doors again. "Tell me you do not want an off the record conversation with Marsh again?"

"I just need to clarify the number plate that he gave me. It's not showing up." Carter knew he wasn't telling lies but just bending the truth a little.

"Last time!" Garrett snapped again grabbing the cell keys and leading the way. He opened the door and left it ajar once more, watching DS Carter go inside.

"Neil. Can you just confirm that registration for me?"

Neil looked at his hand. "DA20 YPW," he replied. "I'm quite sure. It was right in front of me. Why do you ask?"

"False plates," Carter answered shaking his head. "Don't worry yourself about that because I have another lead. But listen. There may be a way of you getting off the charge. I'm not sure yet. But you may have the chance to apologise to the female victim. How do you feel about swallowing your pride?"

"You know me Mr Carter. I am sorry she got in the middle of it."

"I will try and arrange it," Carter replied. "So, sit tight as I have things I have to check."

"Thank you DS Carter."

"Don't thank me yet," Carter said as he left the cell once more and ensured the door was closed tight. He walked past Nick Garrett and said, "Thanks Nick. I owe you one!"

"You owe me more than one! Any more and you will be setting up a tab!" Both men laughed as Carter walked through the swing doors and headed up the stairs back in the direction of CID, as fast as his legs would take him.

He reached the floor that he wanted and walked over towards the DI's office. As he approached, he was surprised to still see Jack Dempsey who was in a heated conversation with Thorpe.

"Ah, DS Carter. We were just talking about you," DI Thorpe commented as though the subject had been him for some time, but it hadn't been. "Just wondering where you were."

"It turned out to be a bigger task than I thought, Guv," Carter responded importantly. "Do we want Jack listening to this?"

The DI smiled knowing that whilst DS Carter had been downstairs, he and Jack Dempsey had come to an agreement. "We have agreed to share information on the case. In return, Jack here gets the exclusive story concentrating on the hard work of our team. So, carry on."

"Well, I spoke to Neil Marsh and got the registration plate of the vehicle of the man who was parked outside his house in a blue Nissan Duke. I confirmed the number plate with the Estate Agent, Jane Ackland. The vehicle had false plates and we guess he gave a false name and address to the estate agents."

"What name did he give?" DI Thorpe asked inquisitively."

Carter checked his notes. "David Jones, I think," he said flicking the pages in his pocket book. "Yes, here it is. David Jones."

Jack started smiling. "Typical false name. I used to give that name as a teenager, so I didn't have to see a girl for the second time."

"Why is it a common name?" Carter asked inquisitively as a frown appeared on his forehead full of misunderstanding.

"It is pop star David Bowie's real name. Davy Jones."

"That I didn't know," Carter responded in an astonished way.

"Me neither," the DI commented in a way that made him as surprised as his Sergeant. "But it could tell us something about the suspect."

"If he knows about the Davy Jones thing, there is a good chance he was born in that era," Jack Dempsey commented, noticing what the DI was getting at. "Or was brought up with one or both parent's liking David Bowie."

"Mike, because of the false plates situation, I want random stops of all blue Nissan Dukes in the City," DI Thorpe exclaimed. "Try and arrange that with the duty uniform Inspector. Secondly, can you get both Jane Ackland and Neil Marsh to do Identifits. We might get a better picture of what chummy looks like then."

"Will do, Guv," DS Carter said instantly turning around and leaving the room again.

"What about you, Jack?" DI Thorpe asked politely.

"I'll continue doing what I do best. Don't forget, share information. You have my number," Jack replied seriously. "I think there could be more to the carving."

"I'll get someone to see you out."

Jack Dempsey left the station and headed back over to collect the hire car from the car park. Time for a rest, he thought to himself. He still had to see his Mum and Dad, so headed back out towards Sparkwell village on the outskirts of Plympton. They had retired there in the dainty little village and his Father spent his time volunteering at the local Dartmoor Zoo. Jack had often joked with his sister on the telephone about what would happen if his Father fell into one of the animal cages. Jack had exclaimed that Dad would start talking to the animal about the tennis and bore the bloody arse off the poor thing. But his Dad enjoyed it and it kept him active.

He parked in the village hall car park and then walked across the road. Three doors down from the pub, Jack remembered from the first time he visited. He banged on the door and at first thought that no one was home, but then saw the silhouette of a dainty lady behind the frosted glass panels She opened the door. "Hello Mum!" Jack said as he leaned forward and hugged her so much so that he lifted her off her feet.

"Jack!" his Mother replied with tears of joy in her eyes. "My Jack!"

Chapter 14

Jeremy Cornelius-Johnson continued to check on the activity outside of his house, again by peering out of the side of his curtain on the front bay window but in such a way that he couldn't be seen. He was also thinking about the next stage of his harassment of Neil Marsh, getting into his house and moving things around to worry him even more. He knew the layout. He knew that the locks on the doors were insufficient and would only probably take a kick or a jimmy to get open. Should he ask DI Chandler to move his car in order that he could go back there? Chances are, the Police would still be around Woodlands lane after the escapades earlier. He decided to stay put, just as he noticed two officers coming in the direction of his house.

DS Kent banged on the door and waited. He became impatient and banged once more just as Jeremy opened the door. "Hello, Sir. DS Kent and I believe you have met DI Chandler. Just like to ask you some questions about your neighbour, Ken Meadows."

Jeremy knew that he couldn't act suspiciously by refusing them access, so decided to welcome them in. The house was clean, well as clean as it can be, he thought to himself. There was nothing left around that could incriminate him in any way. The door was locked on his special room and the garage and workshop were all locked. He knew how nosey Police Officers could be, having dealt with them in the courts. "Would you both like a cup of tea? I've just put the kettle on."

"Not for me thank you," DI Chandler replied looking at his Sergeant slyly as if to say, *'Don't you dare.'* "We shouldn't be awfully long. We just need to clear up a few things and get a bigger picture on where Mr Meadows has gone."

"Well, there's not a lot more I can tell you, Inspector," Jeremy replied as he finished pouring the water from the kettle into his cup. "I didn't really know him or have any friendly contact with him. I've been to his front door a couple of times, but never been inside."

DS Kent started moving around the living room and looked out the front window. "Beautiful view you have here," he said nicely, trying to ease Jeremy into a false sense of security.

"Did you not suspect anything when his garden tools were left outside on the lawn?" DI Chandler asked, knowing that any normal neighbour would have questioned it and knocked on the door at least.

"I didn't really take any notice. It's dark when I go to work and dark when I return at the moment." Jeremy knew at this point that they were on a fishing trip and trying to get him to slip up. He had seen it all before with the lawyers in the court room and experienced the good cop – bad cop routine when entering the interview rooms to call witnesses. "I think your best point of call is Mr Maxwell. He knew Ken better than me."

The DI Hesitated as he looked around the room, thinking that he had better make some friendly gesture in order that he didn't look guilty for scanning for any clue that Jeremy had something to do with it. "You have a huge back garden. Lovely flowers as well."

"This was my parent's house before they died and left it to me."

"Oh, I'm sorry," Chandler said as he nodded to DS Kent indicating that it was time to leave. "We may need to speak to everyone again, Mr ..." He looked at his notes. "Johnson is it?"

"Cornelius-Johnson. Hyphenated. My Mother kept her birth name attached to her married name." Jeremy was going to give the name of David Jones again but then realised that he had already confirmed his name with the PC who had called earlier in the week. He knew that in the next few days at least he would have to remain whiter than white and not bring any attention to himself.

"You are the clerk at Plymouth County Court aren't you?" Jeremy nodded in agreement. "Yes the PC has indicated that he spoke to you. Okay, sir, we will leave you alone. Thank you for your time."

Jeremy watched them both leave through the curtain. They also stood outside for a while talking and using hand gestures to point around, both at his property and one across the road. Suddenly they both headed towards Dave Maxwell's house, firstly ensuring it was safe to cross the road before completing their short walk and struggling with the gate.

The psychopath then ensured his front and rear doors were secured before walking upstairs to his 'special room,' unlocking the door, and then closing it securely behind him. He had another target. He had dealt with Neil Marsh for the time being, now it was time for Stuart Newell to feel the wrath of the injustice of being set free.

Jeremy looked at his board. He pinned up a photo cutting that he had extracted from the local newspaper who had been covering the story and reported heavily on the fact that case had been abandoned, and the witnesses, including the victim, had all disappeared. What made it worse was that Stuart Newell had not even reported his wife, the victim of his assault, as missing and was going around telling everyone that she had left him, and he couldn't care less about her. The husbands of the other three witnesses had reported their wives and partners as missing to the Police, but no progress had been made as to their whereabouts. No bodies, no evidence of abduction, no witnesses. All four had simply disappeared off the face of the earth.

He knew it was something to do with Stuart Jewell even if the culprit was in custody at the time. He had friends who would do anything for him. Kill for him, intimidate witnesses, or even bribe a Judge. The latter thought suddenly crossed his mind and led him back to the day of Stuart Newell's court case. The Judge was on edge. Nervous. He couldn't wait to abandon the trial. Was he in the pocket of Newell? It was a possibility. He should confront Judge Kang Lim Koh when he saw him in work this week.

'Be a man for once in your life. Kill them both. Rid the world of this rubbish!'

He heard his Father's voice going around and around in his head. Jeremy would have to do as he were told in order to prove himself to his Father.

'Don't listen to him, love.'

This time it was his Mother. Her voice calm and collective as though she were worrying about her son.

Jeremy began to think about how he would go about ending Newell's reign. He would find Newell's details in work just as he had done with Neil Marsh. But this death would have to be quicker just in case the Police were watching him for whatever reason. He had the suspicion that they would be after DI Chandler's visit that evening. He knew a quick and easy way to rid Plymouth of this evil man.

Monday soon came around and Jeremy jumped up out of bed at his normal time, showered and had breakfast before heading to the County Court for work. No one appeared to be following him from Wembury. There was hardly any traffic around. He headed down through Staddiscombe and into Plymstock, stopping at the newsagents just to see if he was being followed as he became more paranoid with the situation. He parked up and headed into the shop, purchasing the Guardian and a sandwich for lunch together with a small bottle of fresh orange. Then he continued his journey to work using a route he wouldn't normally take and backtracking on himself a few times using tactical diversion tactics. The thing is, he thought to himself, they know where I work, so is there any need for them to follow him at this moment in time?

At last, he arrived at work and headed straight for the staff room to see what he was assigned for the day. Judge Kang Lim Koh again. The start of a murder trial involving the parents of an eight-month-old baby whose death had hit the headlines recently. Both had been held in custody pending trial. Jeremy knew that this was going to be a harrowing case that would last for weeks. He had time before he started to get some information from the system on Stuart Newell. He went into the office. There was just one member of staff there at the moment, so he logged on to a free terminal using Judge Koh's log on details which he found inside the Judge's drawer in Chambers some time ago and knew that he would find it useful as the Judge had a higher access than he did. He typed in the details for Newell, writing down his address and work information as they come up. Quickly he logged out of the system. Now if there was any query, the Judge would be in the firing line, and the member of staff at the other end of the office hadn't taken any notice of him or even seen that he was there. Now he just had to wait until the end of the day to put his plan into action.

Stuart Newell was a violent man. At 6'6" tall and eighteen stone of muscle, most of Plymouth knew that you didn't mess with him. He had made his name in extreme sports; Kickboxing, MMA, Tai Kwando where he fought in Thailand when he was younger and then headed over to Japan. He gave up because he fell in love whilst back in Britain visiting his Mother and Father. His Father wanted him to take over the family business because Stuart's Father was old and could no longer handle things, and he couldn't rely on Stuart's brother Craig because he was unreliable. So, Stuart made the decision to stop his professional fighting in which he had earned his money, and to justify his decision he told himself that it was getting tougher and tougher to take the blows. His Father always used to say to him, *'When it begins to hurt, it's time to stop it hurting,'* and Stuart knew he wasn't getting any younger, but the opponents were.

To beat the pain of any injuries he did sustain during his time fighting abroad, he dosed up on cannabis, regularly smoking and feeling at ease, but also getting the withdrawal symptoms which made him angry, and the paranoia which came with the after effects. So paranoid that one day he accused his darling wife of having an affair and beat her black and blue in front of three of her best friends. One of them managed to call the Police, but whilst being arrested his hit out at the officer as well. His wife and the three witnesses had since disappeared. No trace. Stuart Newell had walked free from court.

He arrived at one of the gyms he owned, this one in the back lanes of Stonehouse, aptly named 'Newell's Dojo.' With a big following from all the young fighters who wanted to be just like him when he was in his prime, he ran several classes there a few nights a week and on other nights they were run by his second in command, the man who had managed to get Judge Kang Lim Koh on his side, Mick Walters. Both Stuart and Mick had met whilst serving time when they were both teenagers. They had been stood in a queue outside the Caspian Fish Bar in Union Street when one of the sailors made a snide remark about Mick's shirt. Mick hit him hard, and the sailor's mates all joined in. Stuart hated fights where it was more than one on one, so decided to help Mick out on this occasion.

It was just before 6pm. Opposite the Dojo, a blue Nissan with false number plates attached drove into the car park of the bed and furniture retailers. The driver put on his baseball cap and then walked to the gate to check if anyone had followed him. No one. Jeremy couldn't see anyone behind him. He was just being paranoid he was sure of it. What he had seen was Stuart Newell going into the Dojo just before he had gone into the car park. He looked up and down the street. The only CCTV was on Edward's Carpet and Furniture Store overlooking the front door. There was none in Rendle Street itself. Underneath the Dojo was a car workshop which was just closing.

Jeremy decided to go into the Carpet and Furniture store and look around for a while. He went upstairs and looked at the beds, thinking that he could do with a new one at some point, so asked the salesperson what the delivery schedules were like. Indecisive, he said he would be back, went back downstairs and left the shop empty handed apart from a handful of brochures. He got in his car and drove out of the car park onto the street parking just up from the Dojo. The buildings were centuries old, and Jeremy knew that they only had one way in and no fire escapes. That added to the plan.

He plucked up the courage, and opened the boot of his car, took out a petrol can and walked over towards the entrance. He poured some of the petrol into the letterbox of the downstairs car workshop and then the rest into the entrance doorway and onto the stairs that led up to the reception of Newell's Dojo. The can was empty, but he made sure by tapping the can on the floor. Then he searched into his trouser pocket for a box of matches that he had purchased at the newsagents that morning. He struck the match and threw it onto the ground, grabbed the petrol can and quickly walked back to his car. In his rear-view mirror, he could see flames coming out of the Dojo entrance and going under the shutter door of the workshop. The fire caught quickly. These older buildings didn't take much to get the fire set quickly. Jeremy calmly drove away into the darkness.

He was headed over Eldad hill when he heard a massive explosion come from behind him and the night sky filled with light that he could see in his mirror. Screams filled the air as everyone around became panic stricken. Everyone except Jeremy Cornelius-Johnson, whose face filled with a psychotic smile as he looked in the mirror and said, "Cunt!" He wanted to drive back to admire his handywork but knew that it would be too much of a risk. Although he would mingle in with any onlookers that would gather. Jeremy also knew that the Police filmed the crowd just in case they recognised anyone. So, he wouldn't go back. Not today. He would head home.

'You did well son. Justice has been served.'

Jeremy's Father's voice was in his head once again. Sometimes he wished that it would go away. It was one part of his life that he had tried to forget repeatedly, but his parents were always there in the background watching over him and still ordering him about. He knew that at the end of all this, it wouldn't be his Father who would be punished for the justice that he was serving. But he had to show his Father that he was a real man.

He headed back towards Wembury through his normal route, still checking that no one was following him. It was 19:30 hours when he drove his car up onto his driveway. There were no Police around, not even in Ken Meadow's place. It was in total darkness. But he knew that the Police would be back. They didn't trust him; he could tell it in their demeanour. Or did they just not trust anyone?

He went indoors and realised what had happened, so slid down onto the floor with his back against the front door. Chances are he had killed a lot more people than Stuart Newell this evening. But he didn't care. He had no conscience. He was just worried about getting caught before he could finish his mission.

'Get up boy! Be a man for once in your life!'

"I am a man! I've done what you have asked! Now leave me alone!" But he did as his Father's voice requested and got up from the floor and to take his mind away from the voice, went into the sitting room and turned the TV on via the remote control, flicking through the channels to see if there was anything worth watching but then deciding that he didn't care what was on just as long as there was somebody else's voice in the house. It wasn't as if he had any friends to call upon because he just hated people. He found them repulsive, angry, and self-centred. So, he didn't trust anyone to be a friend. The people that he worked with were just that, work colleagues, and nothing more to him. Most of them would stab you in the back in order to further their careers and he knew that when he took the job. It was every man, or woman for himself/herself. Even neighbours, like Ken Matthews and Dave Maxwell had tried to be friendly, inviting him in for coffee and trying to suggest he get into gardening. But neighbours were just that, he told himself. Neighbours.

He switched the TV channel over to BBC in order that when the local Spotlight news came on, he would hopefully hear it. He wanted to know the outcome of the fire at Newell's Dojo. Most of all he wanted to know if justice had been served on Stuart Newell. He looked at his watch. 20:05 hours. He had some time for a nap, so laid down on the sofa with the television on in the background and closed his eyes.

Something woke him, a bad dream, or was it a dream he wondered as he tried to sit up and get his wits about him. He had forgotten to remove the false plates on the car, so he jumped up and ran to the front window to check that no one was around that could have seen them like the Police. The neighbours wouldn't know in any case. Jeremy composed himself and then stepped outside and walked towards his car, firstly removing the front plate, which was closest to him, and then the rear. He quickly opened the boot of the car and threw them in before closing the boot and heading back inside.

Jeremy began thinking once inside his house. His special room. What if the Police searched the house for whatever reason? He thought that they were acting suspiciously the last time when they had knocked on the door, with the Sergeant seeming to look around whilst the Inspector kept him occupied with questions. But surely if they had anything on him, they would have been by now with a warrant and would therefore have the power to break the door down to his special room. It's what they would find that would worry him. Or would it? His victims had all deserved their plight. Horrible people all of them for whatever reason. He sighed. He didn't need to worry.

Beth Mackenzie had spent a few hours preparing and cooking her speciality, lamb hotpot, for the two men in her life, being her husband Alex and her brother Jack. Both loved it and always asked for 'seconds' as Jack would say. She was waiting for her husband to return home from work whilst Jack had spread his paperwork all over the dining room table which he knew that Beth would need at any moment now.

She walked over towards him whilst wiping her hands in a tea towel. "Anything interesting?"

Jack shook his head. "The Police are no further to catching this guy as I am. I have plenty of theories going around and around in my head, but nothing concrete." He picked up various bits of paper individually, quickly scanning each one before putting it back on the table.

"Perhaps dinner will refreshen your brain," Beth said. "I need the table babes."

"I thought you might," Jack replied looking at his sister and smiling, a kind of smile that told her that he was glad to be there. "Let's gather up all my stuff then," he continued, getting all the A4 sheets together into some order and then taping the pile on the table to get them in line.

"This is nice," Beth said as she picked up a picture of the carving that Jack had found in the tree behind Byron's house. "Is this part of the investigation?"

Jack nodded. "Yes, but all it tells me is that the killer's name begins with a 'J' which we already knew. Jeremy."

Beth twisted the picture clockwise and then anti-clockwise and started at the contents. "Must just be me, then."

"What do you see then, dude?" Jack said laughing at his sister, knowing that she was always the same when they were growing up. Their parents took them whilst on holiday to an art gallery in New York and one of the ushers asked the pair of them what they saw in a painting which was 'The Starry Night' painted by Vincent Van Gogh. Jack asked if it was the village featured in the film 'American Werewolf in London,' whereas Beth stated that it reminded her of someone dying in a peaceful place because of the black figure and the church, and the bright night sky. Needless to say, Jack always listened to his Sister afterwards about such things after she was congratulated by the usher. He did look at Jack as he walked away and shook his head. Whether it was in disgust, Jack never knew.

"Well, look at it a different way. The way he has crossed the 'J.' What are those things on the end?" Beth continued to turn the picture whilst her forehead obtained a frown before passing the picture to Jack.

"Oh yes. I see what you mean. Looks like umbrellas or something hanging upside down," he said, still not able to make it out. Then jokingly he said, "It could be the village in 'American Werewolf'," laughing as she grabbed the piece of paper back and smiled and shook her head.

"That, brother, is a set of scales on top of a 'J.' Look how it is heavier on one side tilting what you thought was the top of the 'J.'"

"My God, I think you are right," Jack snapped back at her, jointly looking at the picture as he edged his way over to her side of the dining table. "But what does it mean?"

Beth stared at it again just as Jack was going to say something. She held her finger up as if to silence him, so he didn't speak. "I don't think that the 'J' is for Jeremy as you thought. Or it might have a double meaning. I think the 'J' is for justice."

"So, the suspect is someone who wants justice done?" Jack asked inquisitively.

"I think your suspect," Beth said before being cut off by her brother.

"Is something to do with the law!" Jack smiled. "You are a genius, dude!"

"I know that, and you know that as well," Beth replied like she had just won at Trivial Pursuit. "I think you should be looking at Police, Lawyers, Barristers."

"This will open up a can of worms," Jack said as though he had just won the jackpot on the lottery. "A noticeably big complex issue. If you are right, it could be anyone who has something to do with the law."

"And if I were you," Beth said as she passed him the picture for him to hold, "I would see how many are called Jeremy." She smiled as the pair stared at each other and smiled. "Now, can I have my table back?"

"Of course, you can," Jack replied happily. "I'm going to call DI Thorpe and give him my theory on the carving."

"Your theory?"

"Definitely," Jack said funnily, pulling up his contacts list on his mobile at the same time. He clicked Thorpe's number and waited for him to answer as he listened to the ring. It went to voicemail. Jack didn't like leaving voicemails, mainly because in his experience not everyone listened to them. The same with answering calls that withheld the number. Some people hated that. "Hello DI Thorpe. Jack Dempsey here. Can you get back to me at some point? I have some new information for you. I think we need to meet up again. Thanks."

"Voicemail?" Beth asked inquisitively, looking at her brother because he looked like he was talking to himself.

Jack nodded in agreement. "I think tomorrow will be a long day!"

The killer sat in front of the television as the nightly news came on and then the local news programme afterwards. The Spotlight local reporter was stood at the end of Rendle Street behind a Police cordon, trying her hardest to get her camera operator to see any action that was happening behind her.

"We are at the scene of a major fire here in Rendle Street, Plymouth where earlier tonight just after 6pm an explosion occurred setting several commercial properties alight. So far there are four fire crews in attendance being hampered by explosive materials in some of the units. The Police have indicated that they have not yet been allowed into the buildings although they suspect that anyone caught in the blaze has not made it out alive. Back to the studio."

Jeremy smirked whilst drinking his bottle of beer. No one alive. How many were dead? He didn't care. Anyone who knew and supported Stuart Newell wasn't worth their life in any case. It was a Dojo, and he knew that there could have been children or teenagers being taught in the burning building. He still didn't care. Quickly he switched channels to see if it had made the national news yet. Nothing. He told himself that it was a bit early for the transition. Perhaps when they know the death count, Sky News will pick it up. He clicked the remote control for the TV to shut down, and then walked up the stairs. It was bedtime.

Chapter 15

Jack Dempsey stood in the foyer of Charles Cross Police Station waiting for someone to come and sign him in and take him to see DI Thorpe and the CID team. DS Carter's face appeared through the glass on the other side of the door and the reporter could see him talking to someone in the enquiry office before the secure door was clicked open for the officer.

"Jack, my man! How's things?" DS Carter exclaimed and held out his hand for a courteous handshake.

Jack responded to the gesture. "Fine as normal, Mike. What about you?"

"I can't complain. Well, I could but I don't know how far it would get me," he replied jokingly. "DI Thorpe says you have something new for us to look at?"

"Yes, thanks to my sister's eagle eye. I swear she should be one of yours. She looks at things from different ways." Jack knew that the reason he and his sister had always got on was the help and support that they always gave each other in any way. The two men got in the lift and remained slightly silent for the momentary journey. As the doors opened at their floor, Jack exclaimed, "Well here I am, back again!"

"Hey, it's when you are here from early morning to late evening every day that you can call yourself a part of the furniture," DS Carter said back to him sharply but with humour in the tone.

As they approached the DI's office, Jack smiled at the DS and said, "You want some violins?" Carter poked his tongue out.

"Jack, come in," DI Thorpe said, offering him a chair with the show of his hand. "Grab a seat."

"Thank you, Inspector," Jack replied as he took him up on the offer."

"So, I got your message. Sorry I didn't reply. I had to take the wife to the cinema as a treat last night."

"That's ok."

"Jack has said that he has some vital information for us, Guv," DS Carter said as he impatiently wanted to hear what the reporter had to say, a bit like a child waiting to open his Christmas presents on Christmas morning.

"I have," Jack said, opening his jacket and pulling out the picture he had discussed with his sister the previous evening. "I think we have missed something, Inspector."

"What do you mean?" DI Thorpe asked inquisitively.

"This carving in the tree I found. My sister saw this picture of it last night and pointed out a few things. She exclaimed that it looks like a set of scales. The scales of justice. We just thought it was a 'J' for Jeremy."

The DI got up and walked over to the incident board, where a larger version of Jack's picture had been pinned up. "I think that she could be right, Jack. There is definitely something there."

We also thought that perhaps the 'J' either might be for justice or have a dual meaning of both 'justice' and 'Jeremy'."

"Yes, I can see it now. What do you think Mike?"

DS Carter joined his boss over at the larger image. "Well, it gives us another take on the case. But there is definitely something we haven't seen."

"I think, gentlemen, that the reason that the suspect has evaded you so far is that his profession is closer to home than you think," Jack exclaimed although not wanting to indicate that every Police Officer called Jeremy was the wanted man.

"You mean a Police Officer?" DS Carter asked with widened eyes and a gasp at the possibility.

"Possibly, Mike," Jack replied. "But anyone who has something to do with executing justice on criminals."

"So, you are thinking, Police, Solicitors etc?" DI Thorpe asked as Jacks theory rattled around his brain and put him in true Detective mode.

"Well, I will leave that for you to work out, gentlemen. But I think that is where you should be looking, and then perhaps consider releasing this picture and the name 'Jeremy' to the press." Jack didn't want to say the next statement, but he knew that it would start to rub his relationship with the two officers up the wrong way. "My Editor wants results as well. He is on my back about a story of some kind on the death of Byron Maddocks."

"You can't let this get out, Jack. We need time." DS Carter said calmly as though he were speaking to his best friend and not a tabloid reporter.

"I've stalled him by letting him know that I am onto something bigger than the death of an international author." There was silence as Jack looked at both of the officers.

DI Thorpe looked at DS Carter. "How is the random stop and search going of blue Nissan drivers?"

"At last count, Uniform had stopped seventeen. All negative. ADC Hardy suggested contacting the dealerships for a list of persons who have bought such a vehicle, so I have sent him on the task of doing that."

"He's a bright lad, Hardy." DI Thorpe thought a bit more. "Okay. We will now search records for a Jeremy within all departments of the Police. DS Carter get onto the SRA and the BRB about Solicitors and Barristers in the area whose name contains 'Jeremy,' although we may need a warrant to get the information due to GDPR."

"I think that you also need to look deeper," Jack intervened quickly.

"Deeper?" DI Thorpe questioned.

"Yes. Who deals out the justice? Judges. Perhaps even their staff at the courts."

The DI nodded. "Good point," he replied before silently thinking once more. "Well thanks for your input, Jack," the DI said. "As per our agreement, as soon as we have anything, one of us will be in touch."

Jack knew that the Police would always limit the amount of information given to outsiders, agreement or not. But then, so could he. "Thank you Inspector," he replied just to be courteous as DS Carter walked him to the stairs.

"Well. That was a good lead that you gave us today," Carter said nicely and in some ways happy that they actually had something to go on, even if it led to a dead end. "The DI will be happy. Something to report back to the DCI."

"Glad I could be of assistance," Jack replied as they both descended the stairs and quickly reached the ground floor.

Carter opened the secure door and then smiled. "Thanks again, Jack."

"No worries," the reporter replied cautiously. "I'm sure you will remember; I scratch your back and you scratch mine."

"I know. We will be in touch." Carter watched Jack nod indecisively, knowing that the reporter didn't trust the DI one bit and that meant that there could be some type of story appearing in his newspaper soon. So, they had to act quickly. He rushed back up the stairs to the DI's office to find out what he really thought about Dempsey's information. Carter knew that Jack Dempsey was switched on when it came to investigating and this latest information was crucial. The investigator would follow his nose to smell out the trouble, and therefore, so should the Police.

Jack wondered what the Police would be concentrating on first and recalled the DI telling DS Carter to contact the Solicitors and Barristers governing bodies. Uniform were trying to find the car and DI Thorpe had one of his team investigating the damage on the car. No one was targeting the courts, he thought to himself. That was a good start then. He headed down towards the Plymouth Magistrates Court, moving his car into the Drake Circus Shopping Centre car park. He looked at the prices. £12 for the day. His Editor would moan about him reclaiming that, telling him that he should have found somewhere cheaper. The fact was that parking in London would have cost him more like £70 for the day, plus the congestion charge. The chances of getting into the office car park were minute. In fact, he would have had to turn up for work at about 3am to get a space and considering that sometimes around deadline he was still in the office at midnight he chose to pass on an early start.

It wasn't extremely far from the mall to the Magistrates Court, but he had to battle the shoppers first by stepping from side to side trying to avoid those who were on their mobile telephones whilst looking down at the floor or the Mothers with prams that were pushing with one hand and holding their device in the other. Both situations annoyed a normally timid Jack Dempsey. He also thought of his boss who used to answer the telephone without warning whilst he was in deep conversation with him. Now he found that rude, but partially essential, so he used to ignore it.

There was a small queue at the entrance to the court as the security officers enforced the scanning process to ensure no illegal objects such as knives or even explosive devices were taken in, or drugs. Each person had to remove everything from their pockets and put them into a tray and then walk through the scanner. It was his turn, and there were no problems, so he collected his things and moved on towards the notice board that indicated which cases were in which court on that day. Unfortunately, the board did not include information about court staff. He could be cheeky and ask one of the security officers but was unsure if they would tell him and might even question why he was asking. It would make him look suspicious, he thought to himself, so he didn't bother.

Four courts in session. He would visit each one and try to find out. He walked into court one and headed to the immediate right and a vacant chair. Then he listened, although names were never announced, but they were printed on wooden slide displays that could be changed when the staff changed. The problem was, he was right at the back of the court and couldn't see the names very clearly. He would have to wait until he could get that little bit closer, at recess or at the end of each session. Then he had an idea. It might still get him thrown out or arrested, but it was worth the try rather than him waste time in each court.

Jack waited for the court usher to go outside into the corridor and then got up and followed him. Jack watched as the usher started talking to two men in the waiting area who looked like Solicitors, so acted casually until he had finished talking and walked his way. It was now or never, he thought to himself. "Excuse me, can you help me?"

"Quickly," the usher said, looking at his watch as if to indicate that he didn't have a lot of time.

"Thank you. I was told to meet Jeremy here at the court. He is one of the court staff. I can't find him." Jack knew that he was due in hell when he died in any case just for being a reporter for the Sun, so a little white lie wasn't going to change anything.

"Jeremy? What Jeremy Cornelius-Johnson?"

"Yes, that's right. I have a meeting with him about bringing some school children in to watch the court."

"Typical teacher," the usher replied, shaking his head as though Jack was over the time he was allowed. "You are at the wrong court. Jeremy is the court clerk at the Crown Court. This is the Magistrates."

"Ah, that would explain why I can't find him. Thank you very much," Jack said as the usher shook his head and went back into the court. "Bingo!" he said aloud as he turned towards the exit. Time to go to the Crown Court. It wasn't far, he knew that. There were no security checks on the exit from the magistrates court and so he just walked out onto the street and turned immediately left. Then he took a short cut across the church car park and from there could see the rear of the Crown Court building. He quickly rushed around to the front and walked up the steps. It was quite the same with security frisking you before going through an electronic scanner to check for weapons. The courts themselves were up the stairs with the offices downstairs. He headed to the right and up the stairs and went straight to the notice board which didn't provide any information that was useful. There were monitor screens displaying court information as well. He looked around and saw many tables and chairs which seemed to be all occupied by lawyers and their clients. He took out his 'Press' ID and put the lanyard over his head and then tried to find somewhere where he could sit and observe the goings on. Staff would walk around talking to each other, most on first name terms, so in the first instance he would sit near the reception desk and listen out for 'Jeremy.' He sat on the end of a row of cushioned seats and could hear freely the conversations around him, who was in front of a judge and for what reason, what was going to happen, how the solicitor would plead on their behalf.

Jack looked up at the information monitor. There looked to be three courts in session this morning. He listened in every time someone went up to the receptionist, who, in her own right was very authoritative and didn't take any prisoners. He walked over to the vending machine on the other side of the reception desk and put £1.50 in for a small bottle of fizzy drink whilst still listening in to conversations around him. One side the receptionist ordering someone who didn't have their court reference paperwork, and on the other side what appeared to be a Mother and Father talking about their son and his partner who were up for murder of their baby. Jack overheard them protecting their son and putting all the blame on the Mother. Jack also knew that it would be a good case to give to his Editor as a sweetener for the article he was going to write.

He quickly placed his press badge inside the front of his jumper and then turned to the two parents of the murder suspect. "Sorry, excuse me, which court are you in?"

"Two, mate," said the Father. "Our lad is up on a murder charge."

"Good that you are here to support him," Jack replied.

"He is innocent. It was his wife," the Mother snapped defensively. "He has been in nothing but trouble since he has been with her."

Jack nodded. "It happens that way sometimes," he said as he tried to look interested when in fact if they were guilty, he would have volunteered to put the noose around both of their necks if hanging were still legal. "Well good luck," he said as he turned back to listen into the receptionist conversation who seemed to be juggling several tasks at the same time.

Suddenly a member of court staff in a black gown approached the desk and placed a pile of folders on the raised desk. "Vanessa, can you ensure that these get to Mr Ogley, the defence Barrister for the Crown V Stevenson case? It's just I haven't seen him yet."

"Yes, no problem," Vanessa replied busily as the Court Clerk went to walk away. "Oh, oh. Jeremy, I have something for Kang Lim," she said as she put a pile of papers on the other end of the raised desk.

Jeremy looked at the cover sheet in order to ascertain whether he needed them urgently or not. "Thank you Vanessa."

Jack Dempsey's ears pricked up as he heard the name Jeremy, and with his eagle eyes he watched his every move from then on, as he moved quickly and entered court two. It looked like he was on the same case that he had been speaking to the Mother and Father about. He would have to find out if there were any other Jeremy's who worked there, in the offices downstairs, but then he thought the chances of getting two 'Jeremy's working for the same organisation in the same building were very remote compared to say, a 'John' or a 'David.'

It was nearing 10am, and people were walking into the courtroom. The case itself would attract lots of attention because nobody liked a child killer in any circumstance. The public gallery would fill up fast, so Jack walked over towards the entrance doors to Court two and open the door to walk in. He saw 'Jeremy' talking to another member of court staff, and then decided to ask, "Where do members of the public sit please?"

Jeremy let the court usher answer as he walked off towards the Judge's chambers. "Just there to your right, sir," the usher said.

"Thank you. Most kind." So far there was nothing to suggest that Jeremy was any murdering psychopath. But he was in a position of power which was one of the traits. Well, two, he thought to himself. Power equals control. Manipulation and the lack of a conscience came from power and control. Jack sat himself down and decided to stare out the man identified as Jeremy, not knowing if he had the right guy, but by giving him the feeling that he was being watched, he could get a step closer. If he were right, it would also put his life in danger. He was used to that having infiltrated London gangs and reported on knife crime with a promise to the gang members that they would not be identified but known as A, B, C, etc. Any photographs would be blurred out on the faces. He put it to them that it was a chance for them to give their side of things what with the dramatic increase in knife crime and stabbings in the capital. The outcome of the article was that he could walk down the street in places like Hackney and Lewisham and if there were one of the gang members that he interviewed, they would stop and speak to him and usually bang fists as a sign of respect. He was an unofficial member of the Sabatiers.

Jack was thinking of his next move after the court session finished. He could approach Jeremy outside and introduce himself as a reporter, but chances are court staff were not allowed to talk to members of the press individually. What he did need was more information on him. He needed to know where he lived, who he was, what he did in his spare time, who his friends were.

Meanwhile Jack was deciding whether or not to report his find to DI Thorpe and DS Carter but then thought at this moment in time he didn't know if this 'Jeremy' was their suspect. He certainly looked the part, same build as the man in the CCTV at Drake Circus Shopping Centre who was waiting for Byron Maddocks. But that was a pretty average build that described a third of the men in the UK. He decided to go back to his plan and stare the guy out in the first instance.

The jury arrived and positioned themselves in the two rows assigned for them. Next were the defendants In the Crown V Stevenson case who were shown the place that they had to stand and sit for the duration. Then the Court Clerk stood and shouted, "All rise," as Judge Kang Lim Koh came from his chambers, sat at his desk, and nodded to Jeremy as the people in the court all sat down again.

"Michael Stevenson you are charged with murder in that on October 26th, 2020, you did murder one Kieron Stevenson aged eight months causing him severe injuries prior to his death. How do you plead?"

The defendant smirked as he stood upright in his borrowed black suit, trying to give the impression that nothing was worrying him because he was 'hard' and said cockily, "Not guilty!"

His wife meanwhile was shaking with a look like she had never been in this situation before and had obviously been getting stick whilst on remand from the other inmates, evidenced by a black eye and cuts around her head. Jack thought about what the man's parents had said to him outside and thought for a moment that it looked like it was the other way around. But you can never be too sure.

"Kayleigh Stevenson you are charged with murder in that on October 26th, 2020, you did murder one Kieron Stevenson aged eight months causing him severe injuries prior to his death. How do you plead?"

She was still shaking as though she didn't know what to do or say and looking like she was in shock.

"You must answer, Ms Stevenson," the Judge reminded her.

She looked at him, then looked at her husband. "Guilty!" she replied as the court filled with gasps and her defending Barrister stood up quickly.

The legal team were expecting a 'Not guilty' please from her as was the Judge. "Mr Carwardine. Would you like to enlighten me further?" asked Kang Lim.

Her plea had the Barrister in a bit of a pickle and at first he didn't know what to say. "Your Honour, this is a bit irregular. As you know, my client was insisting she was not guilty until now. Could I ask for a recess in order that I may speak to her?"

"Please come into my chambers. Both Barristers. Members of the Jury I must ask you to step back into the

Jury room for the time being," Judge Kang Lim Koh exclaimed as he now knew that this case wasn't going to be as straightforward as what it could have been.

"All rise," commanded the Court Clerk once more, noticing the stare coming directly from the direction of the public gallery. The man hadn't taken his eyes away from him since he noticed, and it was making him slightly paranoid again. Jeremy pretended not to notice as he grabbed a few important files from his desk that shouldn't be left when the court was adjourned. Then he headed towards the door. The man was still watching him with piercing eyes. "Can I help you?" he asked as he stopped beside the row Jack had seated himself in.

"I beg your pardon?" Jack replied cautiously, still looking into evil eyes.

"You have been staring at me for some time now."

Jack had already thought of a good answer. "Oh, I'm sorry. I'm just trying to think of where I have seen you before. I didn't want to appear rude."

"That's okay," Jeremy replied, still appearing suspicious of the stranger. "It's just in our position, sometimes we get death threats or someone staring at us for the wrong reasons to intimidate."

"I understand," Jack said, knowing now was the time to put his plan in motion to see if he had the right person. "Weren't you at the book signing in Waterstone's the other day? I think that is where I might have seen you."

The question made Jeremy even more suspicious of Jack Dempsey and he decided to exit left quickly. "No. You have the wrong person there." He went silent as the two of them stared at each other. Jeremy was wondering just who he was. He didn't look like a Policeman. A private investigator or a reporter.

"Oh, I must be wrong, I'm sorry," Jack replied. "I could have sworn it was you at the event for Byron Maddocks new book. I'm a big fan of his. Terrible news about his death I must say." Jack had lit the fuse. He had a habit of doing that and usually his instinct was right. In this case, he knew this was his man. The question was, what was he going to do next?

"Can I ask what business you have in this court?" Jeremy asked sternly whilst still looking at his nemesis.

Jack pulled out his press badge from inside his jumper. "Press," he said importantly flicking it up for Jeremy to see. "The people of Britain like a good child murder case."

Jeremy nodded. "Thank you. I bid you goodbye."

"You too," Jack added as he watched the suspect finish walking towards the door. "Nice talking to you." Jack paused and then continued, "Jeremy!"

The court clerk froze momentarily. The stranger knew his name. He could have overheard it, but why use it in such a context as though he were talking down to him? He continued to go out into the corridor and headed right towards the staff room, suddenly turning his head to look behind him as he felt the knife of staring eyes in his back. The stranger had followed him out of the court room and was staring at him still. Did he know something? Was the story of the child murder just a cover? One thing he had noticed when shown the badge was the stranger's name. Jack Dempsey.

The reporter watched his suspect disappear into a door on the right at the end of the corridor. Did he need to tell DS Carter or DI Thorpe? He didn't feel that either of them were taking his sister's theory seriously, so to get the best story, he had to take the case to the limit and then involve them. It was time to follow Jeremy. Firstly, he had to double check if there was a blue Nissan Duke in the court car park. This would confirm his suspicions about the Court Clerk. He walked out of the main door, turned left and then left again in the direction that he had taken from the Magistrates Court earlier. There was an automatic barrier at the entrance to the car park and what looked like a security patrol guarding the cars.

Jack tried to act inconspicuously by just making it look like he was hanging around waiting for someone to pick him up. Every now and then he would look over to the car park and try to see if there was the reported car there. Nothing. It was around the corner in the part of the car park that was hidden by the court buildings. He would never know.

Quickly he walked back towards the Mall and picked his hire car up, driving it down in the direction of the Crown Court. He looked for a road parking space where he could see the automatic barrier, but anyone who was exiting would have trouble seeing him. He managed to get one outside the Methodist Church, then looked at the clock on the dashboard of the car. He guessed that Jeremy would not finish until around 17:00 hrs, so he had a bit of a wait. He put 4 hours on the ticket that he purchased, and then walked back towards the coffee shack opposite the entrance to the Crown Court. Time for refreshment, he thought as he purchased a skinny latte and a BLT sandwich and then sat on the fixed seating made of concrete which overlooked Armada Way. In one direction the City Centre, and in the other the historic Plymouth Hoe. He sat there thinking how glad he was that it was a dry day, and what he could do for the next four hours, realising that he should go back to his car just in case Jeremy decided to leave work earlier than Jack thought, especially as the suspect was now spooked.

Inside the Court, Jeremy had gone into the security office and asked one of the guards if they could pick up the CCTV images for about 10:30 outside court two giving the excuse that he thought someone looked suspicious, that someone of course being Jack Dempsey. They managed to do so and printed off the best still image that they could in order that Jeremy could show the rest of the staff. He had no intention of doing so of course because he just wanted to get more information on who was showing interest in him and why.

Chapter 16

ADC Hardy came back into the CID Office and went over to his mentor DC Bolton, who was himself busy collating evidence after DS Carter had given him the task of contacting the SRA about Solicitors in the area called 'Jeremy.' Bolton thought it was a 'shift blame' task, as he was hitting a brick wall and being passed from pillar to post, whilst being told different things about why he could or couldn't have the information. One would say that he needed a warrant because of Data Protection whilst another Manager understood that because it was in relation to a crime or a series of crimes that it was important and could be released. In any case, Bolton was going to see the DI and get a warrant just to cover his back.

"Hi Ben, how is it going?" DC Bolton asked as he put the phone receiver down after a call.

Ben Hardy had a pile of notes in his hands, copies of receipts with addresses on from the Nissan dealerships that had sold a blue Nissan Duke. Ben had asked for details of any one with the forename 'Jeremy' but also remembered that he was using the alias of 'David Jones,' so requested the search on that as well.

"I think I've found a match," ADC Hardy responded, excited with the find which, to him, was important.

"Have you told the DI?"

"Not yet. I thought we could both go in." Ben looked at the DC and could see that he was busy, but this lead might let him off the current task. "It will save me telling everyone about the find twice then."

"Okay," said Bolton as he locked his computer to prevent anyone looking at his files or using his logon. "I'm coming." He watched ADC Hardy walk on towards the DI's office but look back to check that he was following him.

Ben tapped on the DI's door. "Sir? Are you free?"

"Tell me you have some good news, Ben?" The DI responded, looking at the youngster holding a pile of information.

Ben Hardy nodded whilst he noticed that DC Bolton was just behind him. "One blue Nissan Duke has been sold by the Nissan dealer at Marsh Mills in the past year."

"To Jeremy?" the DI Asked inquisitively, hoping for a positive answer but looking at the young man he could tell it wasn't.

"No, Sir. To David Jones."

"There is that name again!" DI Thorpe said slowly, momentarily hesitating.

"Well, I know we were looking for Jeremy, but then I thought that he might be using the alias that he gave the estate agent to cover himself for more than we originally thought. Including buying a car."

DC Bolton tapped Ben on the shoulder as a compliment for using his initiative. "Well done, Ben."

"Yes, very well done," DI Thorpe said. The good thing about the DI is that he always gave his team credit where credit was due and in return he was given the respect of his officers, most of whom looked up to him and weren't afraid to knock on his door if they had a problem. He knew that, and also knew that it was the way it should be. "Do you have this David Jones address?"

Ben shuffled the invoice copies and pulled up the one that he had been given. "I do, Sir. Do you want DC Bolton and myself to check it out?"

"What do you think, DC Bolton?" the DI asked, hoping that he would get the answer from his junior officer that he would expect.

"I think if it is our man, we need to tail him for the time being." DC Bolton thought for a while. "I wouldn't necessarily knock on the suspect's door but find out from the neighbours in the first instance if he still lived at the address."

DI Thorpe ˙smiled. "Perfect. Lesson to be learned there, ADC Hardy! Time! Never go in all guns blazing until you are 110% sure." He watched young Ben nod in agreement.

"Is that a go then Guv?" DC Bolton asked.

"Get right on it, you two. Be discrete." He watched the two leave the office and head back to their desks, pick up some things and then out of the CID office via the stairs.

"What was that address, Ben?" DC Bolton asked. Is it local?"

Ben nodded. "Yes," he replied. "Plymstock."

"Big place, Plymstock," Bolton replied jokingly. "Which part? The address. I need the address! I'm going to have to speak to your Mum about you!"

Ben Hardy loved his Mum and had even taken DC Bolton around for a quick coffee for him to meet her because Ben needed to change his shirt after searching some bins as part of a case they were working on. "Oh yeh!" He looked at the paper to make sure he got his answer correct. "Lands Park."

"I know where that is. What number?"

"Thirty-two," Ben said in reply. "Do you need the postcode for the Sat Nav?"

"No, I know the street. I can get there without the GPS." Tony Bolton headed up Billacombe Road and took the third exit at the roundabout heading up towards the school. "Nearly there," he said calmly. Bolton turned the car into Lands Park and headed down towards the end of the cul-de-sac, attempting to turn the car around in the turning bay which somebody had parked in, making it difficult for him to do so. "You know now why I never had the chance to drive Sierra One," he said.

"I wonder why?" ADC Hardy responded with a smile filling his face. "Number thirty-two. Just up there on the left."

"Okay. We will park up here, so we don't alert the suspect if he is home. We will observe for a while, get a feel of the area and then approach the neighbours."

"Which neighbours do we target? Those closest to him or further afield?" ADC Hardy didn't know the answer because in his short time in CID he had never been on an operation like this, so he was relying on the expertise of his experienced mentor, who used to joke with him that Ben was being puppy walked.

"Well, start directly next door to him. I'll go the far side, and you the side closest, and you always come tooled up," DC Bolton laughed as he reached into the back seat of the car and grabbed two clipboards. "If the suspect sees you, to him you look like a salesman."

"I guess we don't knock on every door because he is more likely to know the close neighbours than those up the other end of the road?" Ben asked inquisitively, but then thought a bit deeper into the situation. "Unless he knows someone from the other end."

"You are answering your own questions now. That's what makes a CID Officer!" Bolton looked at some of the neighbours in the street, busily out gardening, retired most likely. Some stood talking, pointing to their gardens. He chuckled as he imagined competition in this area on who can grow the best dahlia's or daffodils. He then realised that dahlia's and daffodils were the only two types of flower he knew, so it would be funny if that's what they were growing. "Okay. Let's go. Just say you are looking for Mr David Jones or his friend Jeremy. We can then decipher which name he was using in the neighbourhood."

"Good idea," Ben replied, ready and eager to go as he stepped out of the car. They both walked side by side until they got to the first house, number 34, that ADC Hardy was going to door knock on. His senior nodded to him and walked on to number 30.

DC Bolton was going to walk down the pathway but remembered the gardeners who were on the opposite side of the road, so turned and crossed over. He pulled out his warrant card. "Hello gentlemen. DC Bolton, Devon and Cornwall Police. I was wondering if you could help me out a bit?"

If there was one thing that the public liked to do, especially the older generation, was to help the Police and feel so important that they would tell their partners about the situation. "Yes, officer. How can we help?"

"Well, we need to contact a Mr David Jones, but we are unsure which house he lives in," Bolton said, trying his hardest not to give much away.

Retired Royal Marine Captain Bert Farlow felt that he should speak as he had seniority over his retired Naval Chief Petty Officer, William Youngman. "I have never heard that name, have you Bill?"

He thought for a minute and then shook his head. "No, I don't think anyone with that name lives here, and I have been here about twenty years."

DC Bolton wondered about the other name. "What about a Jeremy? That's all I have. No surname."

"There was a Jeremy at number 32. But he moved out some time ago," Bill said instantly. "Kept himself to himself. Didn't even come to the residents group."

"Can either of you remember his surname?" DC Bolton asked them both hoping that they could confirm things for him, but both men stood shaking their heads and staring at the ground as they tried to remember albeit unsuccessfully.

Bert broke the silence. "Never really had much to do with him. I only found out that he was called Jeremy because I went around and invited him to the meeting and that's how he introduced himself."

"I don't suppose you know where he moved to?" DC Bolton continued questioning. Again, both men shook their heads. Bolton decided that the old guys couldn't give him any more information so decided to exit right. "Thank you. That's been extremely helpful. Bye." He walked in the direction of ADC Hardy to see how things were going with him and if he had any success with his enquiries. "Anything, Ben?"

Ben nodded and looked at his notes. "Jeremy Cornelius-Johnson. One of those hyphenated names. He used to live there up until about a year ago and then suddenly packed up all his belongings and left without even saying boo to a goose. House went on the market and was sold within days."

"Yes, I got that, except the surname, from our friendly neighbourhood gardeners. So, we are getting there gradually." DC Bolton also printed the name in his notes to make sure he didn't forget. "Did he use a removal company?"

"The neighbour in number 36 seemed to think so because she remembers the lorry parked partially on the pavement blocking access for her pram."

"You know what I am going to ask you now, young man?" DC Bolton stated seriously.

"The name of the removal company?" he asked as he watched DC Bolton nod. "No such luck. She remembers that it was a big lorry and was dark blue. That's about it!"

"Okay," DC Bolton said, deciding about what to do next. "Let's continue our enquiries. As much info as possible."

"Will do," Ben replied as Bolton walked away. He then headed towards his next point of call.

Back at the Police Station, DI Thorpe was waiting for DS Carter to return to update him on the current progress. He decided to call DC Bolton to get an update in order that at the end of the day, he could give the DCI some positive feedback for the first time since the investigation began.

"Tony. How's the enquiries going?" DI Thorpe asked authoritatively. "Have you found anything worth following up on?"

"Jeremy Cornelius-Johnson is the full name. He moved out some time ago. It appears he was an unsociable person and never had much time for the neighbours. That's about all so far!"

"That's a start," DI Thorpe said pleasingly. "How's Ben doing?"

"Great. It was him that sourced the surname," Bolton replied hoping that the DI would take him on after this case.

"That's good. Keep him on his toes and keep me informed if you get anything else please."

"Will do, Guv," Bolton replied as the line cut off.

The end of the day soon came around. Jeremy had a full-on day with legal challenges, new pleas and the jury going in and out of their room on several occasions. He needed to rest because the events of both today and the previous few weeks had begun to take its toll on him and interrupt his normally good sleeping pattern. He left on time for once and went out the back staff entrance directly into the staff car park. Placing his case in the boot of his car and then opening his door, he was happy to sit down and look forward to going home. But it wasn't going to happen. His Father was speaking to him.

'Marsh. Finish the job you good for nothing.'

"I'm not listening, Father," he replied to the voice. "Not tonight because I am too tired."

'The press are on to you. The Police will be soon.'

Jeremy turned up the music in his car with Tchaikovsky's Swan Lake echoing in his speakers and blocking out the voices. Then he drove up to the exit barrier which lifted for him to exit. He looked both ways and then headed over to the main road that would take him towards home. Notte Street was jammed with rush hour traffic and not moving amazingly fast. "Traffic lights! Traffic lights! Everywhere!" He banged his steering wheel with both hands. All he wanted to do was get home because today was a day that he had experienced enough of people. What he didn't see was the car following him, not directly, but two cars behind him.

Jack Dempsey had watched him exit and started his car trying his hardest to stay in sight, which was hard trying to get out onto Notte Street from the side road. He had also noted the traffic signals but for a different reason and that being that he had to tail the suspect. Not that he could go far in this traffic, he thought to himself. He battled the traffic lights that allowed him to go out onto Exeter Street only just making them before they turned red. In fact, he thought, he may have gone through just as they went from amber to red. Hopefully he wasn't caught by the traffic camera that overlooked the junction. He knew that in London the cameras were so sensitive, picking offences up easily even if your tyre went just over the bus lane line. He wasn't sure about them in Plymouth, and he doubted whether his Editor would pick up the bill for any traffic violation that occurred.

Jeremy went ahead at the Cattedown roundabout and headed down towards Plymstock taking the inside lane of the two because the outer lane always attracted queues for the Morrison's store on the other side of the roundabout. Usually, the inner lane moved consistently due to a through lane whilst the other lane stop/started.

The reporter was behind him keeping his distance. Luckily, there was too much traffic on the road at that moment in time for him to be clocked. But jack knew that if he went off onto the side roads, then the killer would realise he was being followed. In his mind, Jack had already labelled him as the guilty party mainly because there were too many coincidence's for it to be anyone else. But what if he wasn't working alone? Most psychopaths worked on their own and Jack knew that having studied them in some detail.

Jeremy looked into his rear-view mirror as he took the last turning which led to Wembury Road and would take him directly home, although there were a few lanes that used to cause congestion due to the width of them. There was a car behind him keeping its distance. Most people were impatient bastards who tailgated you for any reason, he thought to himself, but he would try a diversion tactic just in case, stopping at the petrol station at the top of the hill to get some bread and milk. He soon turned into the forecourt and parked up with his car facing the opposite exit to which he would take. The car he thought was following him drove right past the petrol station, but Jeremy was still alerted. Other people knew diversion tactics as well. He was waiting for him in the layby up the road thinking that because his car was pointing that way towards Staddiscombe, then that's the way he would go. How wrong he was, Jeremy thought. Then it couldn't be the Police because they knew where he lived. Jeremy then suspected that it was the reporter from earlier. No one else would follow him. The question was, why was the reporter following him? Did he know more about Jeremy than he had let on?

Jack waited for a while in the layby and then did a U-turn to head back to the petrol station. The car had gone. There was only one way he could have gone. Towards Wembury. But there were several turn offs on that road, Bovisand, Fort Stamford, Jennicliff. But if Jeremy had only sussed him near the petrol station, why would he come this way? It had to be Wembury or one of the villages along the way. He drove at some speed out of the forecourt and turned right at the exit towards Wembury, still speeding as though he wanted to catch Jeremy up but knew that he had a good head start on him. Each set of houses or bungalows he came to, he slowed and looked for the car, the blue Nissan Duke.

Meanwhile Jeremy had arrived home and turned onto his driveway quite angrily, without indicating although there was nothing behind him and practically taking the turn on two wheels because of his speed. He drove right up beside his bungalow with the nose of his car nearly touching the garage door which was the first time he had done so for ages. Quickly, he exited the car, opened his garage door, and pulled out a blue tarpaulin similar to the one he had wrapped Ken Meadow's body in. He unfolded the tarpaulin as fast as he could as though his life depended on it and pulled it up and over the car making sure that every bit was covered. Then he went into his home and closed the door tightly realising at this moment in time that he was going to have to sort that garage out to make room for the car. He didn't switch any lights on in the house through fear of it being made to look as though someone were home. The he curtain twitched out of the front bay window to check if he could recognise the car that he had seen earlier that appeared to be following him. Or was he just being paranoid again?

Jack kept looking for any signs of life, any cars that might still be active with lights on or drivers exiting, but he didn't see anything. Wembury was bigger than he remembered. There was a pub, the Odd Wheel. It might be worth asking in there if they knew him. He parked the car on the other side of the road and then walked over to the pub. As he went in it was like a stranger entering somewhere he shouldn't be, a typical yokel atmosphere where there was plenty of conversation prior to him walking in, and then silence when he did. He walked over to the bar. "Half a pint of Doom Bar, please."

"Coming up," the bartender replied. "Are you sure you don't want a pint?"

"No thanks," Jack said realising that he couldn't really drink and drive. "I'm driving. Just needed a little light refreshment."

"Bad day?"

"Just a little." Jack knew it was time for the reporter side to come out now. "I'm here to visit a friend."

"So, you are not from around here then," the bartender continued. "Stranger in the midst!"

"I am originally from Plymouth, but I now live and work in London." Jack took a sip of his beer as the bartender put it in front of him.

"£2.25 when you are ready, Sir."

Handing him a £5 note, Jack sipped the drink a bit more and appreciated it. "Mmmmm. That is nice."

"So, who is it you know out here in the sticks?"

"His name is Jeremy," Jack said whilst pretending to cut off his conversation mid-way by having another sip of the beer.

"What Jeremy Cornelius-Johnson? I didn't realise he had any friends. He lives like a hermit that one." The bartender started wiping down the bar area with a cloth where his regulars had all spilt their beer when picking it up.

Jack knew he was there. Finding out just where he lived. "Jeremy is alright once you get to know him. I haven't been to his house yet. Is it close?" "He hasn't long moved into his parents old place on Mewstone Avenue," the bartender replied. "Nice place. Bungalow with four bedrooms, so there will be plenty of room for you to sleep. It's not far."

Time to make it look as though he really knew the suspect. "I should have met him at the court where he works. I wouldn't have got lost then."

"Well, it was quite a tragic situation his parents going like that. Shot the way they were because it doesn't happen out here. The Police put it down to someone who old Rufus had put away. He was a judge at the same court." The bartender started changing the empty optics and replacing the bottles with new ones. "And now his neighbour has disappeared. So, if you need any help finding the house, just look for the Police cars."

Jack downed the last of his half. Hopefully, this little break had also let Jeremy think that he wasn't following him anymore, who knows. "Thanks for your help," he said as he left. He thought of what the bartender had told him. Both parents shot. Next door neighbour missing. Surely he wouldn't do something that close to home? He got in his car and drove up turning left into Mewstone Avenue but didn't see any Police cars. He didn't even see Jeremy's car as he looked up and down the driveways on either side. This could mean that Jeremy had something to hide, but Jack already knew that. He drove up and down the residential area but saw no blue Nissan. The something caught his attention. Who puts a tarpaulin over a car? They weren't expecting a freeze overnight and the sand from the beach wouldn't blow up this far if it were high winds in the area. He suddenly had a hunch, well more of a suspicion really. To be sure, he would have to check physically, or he could just go to one of the neighbours and ask where Jeremy lived. Again, would they tell him? He could just park the car at a visual distance again and look to see if Jeremy made an appearance. The only issue with that was it was evening. Some people didn't even surface after getting home, and if Jeremy was the hermit that the landlord of the Odd Wheel had indicated then the chances were that he was one of them. He would try parking his car for a while.

He did a turn in the road in order that he was facing the way that it was easier to escape out of Wembury. Then he parked up the street just enough so he could see the front of the Bungalow that he suspected was Jeremy's. Then he waited, looking over at one moment and then checking his mobile to see if he had any messages or missed calls. Nothing. He looked over towards the bungalow again. There weren't any lights on. He had got it wrong. The car was covered because they were on holiday. There was only one way to find out.

Jack got out of the car and looked around to see if there was any activity in the neighbourhood thinking to himself that this must be one exciting place to live. Or not as the case might be. It was dead. Not a soul. He crossed the road and walked along the pavement keeping his wits around him as he continued to look around him. He ran up the inclined driveway, looking to see if there was any movement inside yet, but he still couldn't see anything, so he edged closer to the car and as he got to the rear, he lifted the edge of the tarpaulin upwards in order to satisfy his suspicions. He was right.

"Can I help you?"

The voice came from the direction of the back garden to the right of the garage. Jack looked up and focussed his eyes on Jeremy Cornelius-Johnson. "Oh, hello again."

"Can I ask what you are doing on my property?" Jeremy asked seriously, the tone in his voice showing anger even though he was calm. "You know you are trespassing and what is your interest in my car?"

Jack had to think of something to say quite quickly. "I was wondering where you lived. I told you, I am a reporter."

"Yes, you did," Jeremy replied, his haunting blackened eyes staring at Jack although he hadn't moved from the position that he was originally in. "That doesn't give you the permission to follow me and come onto my property. Just what is your problem with me?"

Jack thought he would plant the seed a little more. "I'm just investigating the death of Byron Maddocks. I told you."

"And what do you think that has got to do with me?" Jeremy asked this time raising his voice with more anger as though he were going to run and attack Jack at any moment.

"You want the truth?"

"Enlighten me," Jeremy snapped back whilst expecting the answer and staring psychotically at the reporter.

"Okay. I think you did it, in fact, I know you did it," Jack exclaimed, knowing that if he were wrong several things could happen including a lawsuit on defamation grounds. "I just need more evidence."

Jeremy smiled at him with his eyes piercing Jack with an indication that the reporter was in danger. "I'm afraid you are wrong, Mr Dempsey, and you have no proof that I was there. I have an alibi."

"Absence of proof is in no way proof of absence, believe me. I will get to the truth." Jack started backing away, returning the stare that he was receiving in a defensive mode. He then walked quickly down the driveway and crossed the road towards his car, looking back to see that Jeremy had moved and followed him but stopped at the top of the incline. But he was still staring. Jack locked the doors on his car. Nothing usually shook him, but this guy was frightening. He decided just to hang around for a while to see if there was any movement. He was sure that Jeremy was looking out from behind the curtains because of the small movement of them every now and then.

There was a bang on the window which startled Jack as he instantly looked out to see who it was. The man on the other side flashed his warrant card at the window.

Jack opened the window just part way, so he was able to speak. "Can I help you?"

The warrant card stayed this time. "Detective Inspector Tom Chandler," the officer said sternly. "DS Kent is in the car a bit further back. Would you like to accompany me?"

Jack closed his window, unlocked the doors, and stepped outside the car, closed the door, and locked it. "What's this all about?"

"Quickly, sir. I will explain in the car." DI Chandler led the way back to the unmarked Police vehicle and opened the back door for Jack to get in, and then got in the front seat. He turned his body sideways in order that he could see a confused Jack Dempsey. "Can I ask about your business with Mr Cornelius-Johnson?"

"Has he called the Police on me?" Jack demanded to know, shaking his head, and chuckling as though he thought that Jeremy had a nerve for doing so. Jack reached into his jumper and pulled out his press badge. "Jack Dempsey. I'm an investigative reporter for the Sun. I believe Jeremy Cornelius-Johnson is responsible for the death of my friend, the international author Byron Maddocks."

"Well, that wouldn't surprise me one bit," DS Kent said as he still watched Jeremy's place in case there was any movement. They didn't know that he had already disposed of Ken Meadow's body and expected him to do something that they could intersect, like put the body into the boot of his car.

"So, what have you got on him?" Jack asked inquisitively as he leaned forward in order that he could see both officers. "I mean you guys wouldn't be sat here if he wasn't suspected of doing something."

"His next-door neighbour has disappeared," DI Chandler exclaimed. "We suspect that the man may have had something on the suspect and has been killed."

"Are you guys working with DI Thorpe and DS Carter at Charles Cross?"

"No, not at all. Unfortunately, this is a MISPER at the moment and up until a concerned neighbour telephoned for the second time, it was being treated as such." DI Chandler picked up his folder from the floor in front of him.

"You guys really need to learn to communicate with one another," Jack exclaimed, shocked that two different teams were investigating Jeremy. Then he thought, DI Thorpe's enquiries hadn't substantiated Jeremy's complete name yet so wouldn't have made the cross reference to this potential crime. He should call it in to DS Carter and let him know what he had found.

"This guy is whiter than white," DI Chandler replied. "We know he works for the courts and know his Father was high court judge Rufus Cornelius-Johnson until his death. But Jeremy hasn't even had as much as a parking ticket. But I will contact DI Thorpe."

Jack shook his head. "I bet you don't even know that he has an alias. David Jones?" Jack didn't need a reply because the look of astonishment on the DI's face said it all. "Listen, here's my card," he said reaching into his pocket and then handing his business card to the DI. "I'm going now. I will leave you to it."

"Okay," the DI said, not wanting to keep the reporter any longer than he had to. "Be careful! This guy is dangerous."

"Yes, I know."

Chapter 17

Morning was never a problem for Jack even when he had a late finish the night before. Chances are he would have to be working late to get the headlines on the paper and then be in early for a pick of the stories to investigate. Most of the leads were from members of the public but he had to be careful which ones to investigate as some of the suspicious stories were just jilted lovers trying to get their own back on their partners. He had seen them all. One wife who claimed her husband was planning to blow up the Houses of Parliament. When Jack asked his name, the reply was 'Guy Fawkes.' Then he had another story where someone was planning to kill the President of the United States, Donald Trump, on his visit to Britain. Apart from thinking that this would do the world a favour, he passed over to his contact in Scotland Yard.

There was a bang on the bedroom door. His Sister's visitor's room had a bed in it, but it was a single bed, and the mattress was hard. Jack told himself that it was lucky that he didn't sleep very much, but it wasn't doing his back much justice.

"Hello?" Jack shouted, responding to the noise.

"Bruv, it's nearly eight. Breakfast is on the table," Beth shouted through the closed door.

"Okay," Jack responded. "I'll be down soon." He put his legs sideways out of the bed but still laid vertical for a while whilst he rubbed his eyes to wake up properly. Then he was up. He put his dressing gown on and went down to Beth's beckoning call. He knew that she wouldn't mind him wearing a dressing gown, but if his Mother were here on the other hand, he would be told to get showered and dressed first as a sign of respect to the others at the table.

"You were up quite late," Beth said as she saw him come down the stairs. "Busy night?"

"Keep this to yourselves, but I came face to face with who I think killed Byron last night!" He picked up a slice of buttered toast.

Alex alerted as his eyes widened. "You are joking?"

Jack smiled whilst biting off the corner of the bread. "No joke. I found him."

"How on earth did you manage to do that?" Beth asked as she carried the plates with the cooked breakfasts over to the two men in her life. "The Police haven't found anyone yet. Well, there has been nothing in the newspaper."

"I'm an investigator. I investigate," Jack said humorously. "Well, most of the time. Other times I just ask you!"

Alex still had a serious look on his face. "Did they arrest him? I mean you did call the Police?"

"I'm off to see DI Thorpe and DS Carter after breakfast to tell them what I have found. I doubt they have found anything worth mentioning because they are looking in the wrong places." Jack dipped his toast in his egg and then in his beans and then put the small piece right in his mouth.

"Well, you just make sure that you take care my little brother," Beth said, sitting down beside her husband with her own plate in her hand. "I know what you are like. You would always be the first to jump off the highest diving board."

"Plymouth Hoe!" Jack responded as he pointed his forefinger at his sister and started chuckling.

"The fun we used to have," Beth replied happily remembering the times that they used to have there. "The diving boards have been removed now. Health and safety reasons!"

"No way!"

"Yes way. Plymouth City Council. Bunch of loonies operating the asylum," Alex added. "They are frightened that they might get sued by some kids parents for allowing them to climb past the barriers and hurt themselves."

There was a momentarily silence and then Jack cleared his throat. "Listen, you two. Whilst I am here, I just need you to both keep vigilant. I'm not saying this nutter would do anything, but then he did follow Byron."

"You think that will happen?" Alex asked with a sense of worry in his strained voice.

"Probably not," Jack said whilst trying his best to indicate to them that they just had to be aware of the things around them. "Just stay alert and if you are worried dial 999."

"But there is a possibility?" Beth asked, pausing her eating as she forked her sausage.

"If you are worried, Beth, I will get a hotel. I don't want to put either of you in danger."

"Don't you dare. I don't want my Brother in a hotel all alone," Beth snapped back at him, slightly annoyed that he would even suggest such a thing.

"The option is there," Jack said to her, slightly preferring if she had just said 'yes' because he didn't want trouble to come their way.

"Yes, thanks for thinking of us, Jack," Alex commented as he thought different to his wife but would discuss it with her later when Jack had gone to the Police station.

Beth thought she would break the ice as she realised just what Alex was thinking but also knew that it would cause an argument between them if he said anything. Which she knew he would. "Coffee anyone?"

"Tea please, darling," Alex replied.

"I know!" Beth said back to him. "Jack?"

Her brother looked at her and smiled. "Yes please, Sis. Not any of that cheap stuff either! What was it?"

"Mellow Birds," she laughed back.

"Bitter birds more like," Jack said in reply whilst finishing off the last item on his plate. The beans. He always saved the beans until last, mainly because if you moved them they would get their sauce all over the other things like hash brown and make them mushy. He hated that.

Beth poured the water into the kettle. "I get the message. Douwe Egberts it is." She held up the jar for him to see.

"That's a Douwe Egberts jar filled with Mellow Birds knowing you."

Two hours later, Jack Dempsey was stood in DI Thorpe's office together with DS Carter, DS Ayres, DC Bolton, DC Johnson, ADC Gibbons and ADC Hardy. He had told DS Carter on the telephone that he had some vital information, and that this wasn't the time for either the Police or him to withhold anything from each other.

As DI Thorpe was about to open the meeting, there was a knock at the door and two men stood awaiting an invitation into Thorpe's office. DI Thorpe had never met either of them but looked at their ID badges around their necks and realised that he had heard of them from Crownhill Police Station. "Can I help you, gentlemen?" DI Thorpe asked, wondering what they wanted as this meeting was important.

"DI Chandler and DS Kent," the more senior man responded importantly as though he were introducing himself to a civilian under investigation. He saw Jack Dempsey out of the corner of his eye and nodded towards him, adding, "Hello Mr Dempsey. Nice to see you again."

"Is it me that you wanted to see?" DI Thorpe asked politely. "We are a bit busy at the moment."

"Yes I know. Mr Dempsey here told me last night." Chandler nodded Jack's way as he mentioned his name. "We have a common denominator I believe, and I think we need to share information and then maybe link the two investigations together."

DS Carter looked at Jack with an element of distrust. "Have you two met then?"

Jack nodded. "I found our possible suspect yesterday."

DI Thorpe banged his fist on his desk. "I thought we had an agreement, Mr Dempsey!"

"Believe me, it all happened so fast, and I wasn't sure if my hunch was right until just before I met the two officers here." Jack knew he wasn't making excuses although did now realise the danger he was in and on hindsight knew that he should have contacted DS Carter. "I have found Jeremy."

There were gasps in the room from the CID Officers and DI Thorpe's eyes widened. "So was your hunch right?"

"When I left here yesterday I went for a scour of the courts in the area. Jeremy Cornelius-Johnson is a Court Clerk at the County Court." Jack felt pleased with himself as he realised that he had done something that the Police had so far failed to do, but he wasn't the sort of man who played the 'I told you so' card.

"Cornelius-Johnson? I know that name."

"You should do, Guv," DS Carter interrupted. "It's the same surname of that Judge we used to call hangman! He was found dead along with his wife a few years ago."

"What old Rufus?"

DS Carter nodded with widened eyes to give the DI some indication that there was more to the death of the victims than met the eye. Then he looked at Jack. "So, did you manage to speak to this Jeremy?"

"Better than that. I found out where he lives and can confirm that he drives a blue Nissan Duke," Jack exclaimed.

DI Thorpe looked at his equal ranking officer DI Chandler. "Did you not pick up that we were looking for someone called Jeremy on the PNC?"

"Well, it works both ways," Chandler responded with some concern that blame was being proportioned his way. "I think the problem is that we had registered our crime as just a MISPER whereas you are obviously looking for something more serious. The two just didn't cross reference on the system."

DS Carter looked at the two. "Surely now is not the time for a post mortem. We can do that after we have charged him."

"Yes, yes." DI Thorpe added. "So, what other potential evidence have we got against this man?"

"Well Ben and I did make enquiries at Jeremy's former address in Land's Park. The neighbours knew of him but confirmed that he moved some time ago. Indicated that he was very much a loner." DC Bolton looked at his counterpart ADC Hardy. "Anything you want to add, Ben?"

"Just I think that we need to look at both his alias and his real name when investigating deeper."

"Good call," DS Carter said to them both. "We will."

"DI Chandler, would you like to enlighten us with your take on Jeremy?" DI Thorpe asked as though he were chairing the meeting.

"I just had a hunch that things weren't right with this guy. His neighbour 'disappeared' and was reported as missing. I got authorisation for 24-hour surveillance on him." DI Chandler looked at his partner, DS Kent.

DS Kent slipped off the edge of the table that he was resting on, mainly because his rear was going numb. "We have witnessed him going out and returning at all times of the day. Nothing overly suspicious though, apart from last night when Mr Dempsey here turned up."

"I tracked him through the courts as I said. I then waited and followed him. He did try and lose me when he realised that someone was following him. When I finally caught up with him as I was checking the vehicle on his drive which was, I might add, covered with a tarpaulin as if to hide it away, he stared at me." Jack was genuinely concerned as to Jeremy's behaviour. "He didn't admit anything. But the stare he gave me both when I was checking his car, and then when he followed me to the end of the driveway." The room went silent, and Jack could see the brains of all the officers working overtime as to what they were going to do next.

"Do we bring him in for questioning, Guv?" DS Carter asked inquisitively.

"On what grounds?" Thorpe replied. "Buying a book and waiting for the author outside the shop? Speaking to the Police Officer who was later found dead?" He shook his head. "I don't think the DCI would go with it."

"He is very clever, but very deceiving," DI Chandler mentioned whilst running his fingers through his hair. "But we need concrete evidence. If we bring him in for the fraud of using an alias to obtain goods, that is all we can question him on. Any solicitor would notice anything else."

DI Thorpe looked at his team. "We will assist with the surveillance on the suspect. Although he is going to watch his step and cover his tracks if he knows that we are onto him." Thorpe looked over at DS Kent as his mobile rang and he quickly stepped outside of Thorpe's office to take the call in private. "We need evidence people! Let's get this guy before he kills anyone else! Be careful, because if he is our man, he is dangerous and is probably armed!"

ADC Hardy put his hand up as though he were still at school and had to ask the teacher something. "Guv?"

Everyone stopped making a bolt for the door. "Yes, ADC Hardy," the inspector replied knowing that it may be another of the young man's ideas.

"Well, I was just wondering. We are taking it that Byron Maddocks could be his first murder, or even the Horgan's. Should we not be looking at open murder or MISPER's just in case he has killed before?"

"Good thinking," DI Thorpe responded. "There is a job for you and DC Bolton to handle."

DC Johnson perked up after remaining silent during the whole meeting, not because he wasn't interested, he was a thinker, best known when he did the Belbin test on team dynamics as 'The Plant.' "Guv, myself and ADC Gibbons will take up any surveillance on him at his place of work."

"Remember it is the County Court," Jack Dempsey interrupted. "Armada Way."

"Thanks," DC Johnson added as he watched the door and noticed DS Kent coming back in whilst returning his mobile phone to his jacket pocket.

Kent looked at his guvnor, DI Chandler, but raised his voice so everyone could hear. "Guv, Jeremy Cornelius-Johnson is on the move. The relief team are tailing him."

"So, he is not at work?" DI Thorpe questioned.

"Day off?" DC Bolton asked as he tried to put some light into the situation.

"Possibly. DC Johnson make those enquiries when you get down to the court," DI Thorpe said with a frowned forehead and his mind working overtime. Surely he should have been at work?

Jack Dempsey looked at his two Police contacts. "He is going to do a runner, isn't he?"

DS Carter shook his head. "Not yet. He has unfinished business."

"Neil Marsh!" DI Thorpe exclaimed. "Get a uniformed presence down there, Mike," he ordered DS Carter.

"Will do," he said rushing out towards his desk.

Jeremy Cornelius-Johnson knew that he was being followed, if not by the reporter whom he had dealt with on the previous evening, it would be the Police. He was sure inside that they were on to him which could be down to 'that Jack Dempsey' finding him. But he decided that he couldn't stay in just for the sake of it. His Father had told him that he still had a job to do. He needed to finish the mess he had started. Deep inside, he knew that the Police would be safeguarding Neil Marsh because of the suspicious death of his wife and the notes that he had sent Marsh prior to her death.

That morning he had telephoned in to his workplace and said that he was ill. In reality he thought that Dempsey would be watching his every move from now on, but then looking in his rear-view mirror he realised that he had more of a problem than his reporter friend. Two men in an unmarked vehicle who were obviously Police officers.
'Teach them a lesson. Get rid of them!'

Jeremy was hearing his Father's voice once more echoing around the car. He had to do as his Father instructed or he would be deemed a failure again.

'You haven't got the nerve, boy!'

"Shut up! Shut up! I'm doing it!" Jeremy shouted to the entity that was talking to him and filling his head with thoughts that were making him feel useless. He drove out of Wembury and took the turning on the left which took him towards Jennycliff. There were plenty of lanes there in which he could hide. He looked in his mirror. The Vauxhall Astra was still following him, and the passenger was on his mobile telephone. Jeremy checked in his coat pocket for his gun, the car swerving as he took his eyes off the road to do so. Then he put his foot on the accelerator and started speeding down Ford Road. He could now just see his tail in the distance behind him. There was a turning on the right which he wasn't sure where it led to, but at high speed he skidded off the Ford Road and drove down at speed. It was a single lane with just enough room for one car. He stopped about five hundred metres down, out of sight of anything, houses, people, farms and just shy of a corner in the lane. Suddenly he saw the tailing Police car coming down the lane and it skidded to a halt to avoid going into the back of Jeremy's blindsided Nissan. Jeremy didn't hesitate. He got out of his car, took out his handgun and started firing at the windscreen of the Police car.

DC's Dave Kemp and Christian Haynes stood no chance as they didn't expect the suspect to be armed. The bullets ripped through each of the officers chest, the driver slumping forward over the steering wheel and the passenger, still on the mobile, fell sideways with his head leaned over towards the driver's seat. Blood had splattered all over the inside of the windscreen.

Jeremy could see no movement, so he walked up to the driver's window, reloading his chamber on the gun as he did so. He hit the side window with his elbow so hard that it shattered. He could see that both officers were dead but couldn't resist putting a bullet in each of their heads to make sure. Life was extinct. He looked one last time, then calmly and collectively walked back to his car, got in the driver's side and drove away.

'Ha! That's my boy!'

The voice was still speaking to Jeremy, this time congratulating him, and he smiled at the thought that he had made his Father happy. He headed back towards the main road, although he wasn't quite sure where this lane headed. Further down he passed what looked like a farmhouse and continued down noticing that on the horizon he could see the roofs of other cars and what looked like the same petrol station that he had stopped at yesterday on the junction of Wembury Road and Staddiscombe Road. He knew where he was and two minutes later was pleased as he came out onto a familiar road which led to his home one way, and Elburton village the other.

'Marsh is next! Finish the job!'

Jeremy's Father had spoken. He had to get down to Marsh Mills and the best way for him was going to be the back lanes although the Police would suspect him of going that way, so he decided to keep to the usual route of going through Haye Road, past the cats and dogs home and down to the Industrial estate. That's the way he would take, he thought to himself quickly.

Back at the Police Station, DS Kent had been speaking to DC Haynes who was giving him the commentary on the surveillance of Jeremy. DS Kent became concerned as the conversation ended after what appeared like gunshots in the background. "Guv,"

DI Chandler was talking to DI Thorpe, so DS Carter came over to see if it were anything that he could do. "Everything alright?"

"No," he replied as he shook his head. "One minute I was talking to one of my DC's who was in pursuit of our suspect, the next minute, nothing. Listen." He passed the phone to DS Carter who put it to his ear."

"It sounds like the engine is still running," DS Carter said inquisitively. "Nothing else. What was their last location?"

"Ford Road just outside of Wembury. I thought I heard what sounded like gunshots as well."

The word 'gunshots' alerted both DI's. "What was that?" DI Thorpe asked checking that he wasn't hearing things because of his ewe's dropping tactics. "Did I hear something about gunshots?"

"Yes Guv," DS Carter said worriedly. "DS Kent was speaking to one of his DC's."

"There was what sounded like gunshots, and now I can't seem to get in touch with neither DC Haynes nor DC Kemp." DS Kent raised the mobile to his ear again. "The phone is still connected."

"We both think we can hear the sound of the car engine," Carter said worriedly.

"Here, Guv," DS Kent said to DI Chandler. "Have a listen and see what you think."

DI Chandler listened to the sound of the engine roaring on the car, as though they had stopped but the driver had forgotten to take his foot off the accelerator. "I don't like this," he said. "What do you think?" He passed it over to DI Thorpe to listen.

"That's definitely an engine." He decided to try and call for someone to answer. "Hello? Can you hear me? Hello? This is Detective Inspector Thorpe." There was no reply. "Are you sure that you heard gunshots?"

DS Kent nodded. "I'm sure."

DI Chandler became worried. "I don't like this," he said emphatically. "I think we need to get an ARV out there now!"

"Especially under the circumstances," DI Thorpe added with major importance. "We can also get a team out there to search. DS Carter and perhaps your DS could get out there as soon as?"

DI Chandler nodded in agreement. "Yes, that sounds like a good idea."

"Mike, I'll arrange the ARV. See what you can find. Be careful you two. Jeremy could be armed!"

"Guv," DS Carter acknowledged as he disappeared outside closely followed by DS Kent.

Jack Dempsey was listening in closely to everything that was being said, and then picked up his jacket from the back of the chair and went to leave. "Right. There's a story to be told here. I'm off!"

"Just be careful, Jack."

"I will. Don't worry," the reporter replied intensely. "Make sure that you and your officers keep safe. This guy is dangerous."

It was a beautiful area, greenery and ploughed fields all around together with the old-style farmhouses and a direct view of the sea over Wembury, Jennycliff and Bovisand. It was about to be made a crime scene as flashing lights and sirens filled the lanes as DS Carter and DS Kent joined in the search for the missing Police car. Uniform had sealed off the area and two units of armed response were combing the area and trying to get a fix on the location of the mobile telephone.

Jack Dempsey couldn't get past the cordon set up at the Jennycliff end of the area blockade. Well, not in his car in any case. He was considering making the journey on foot but realised that the story he wanted could be anywhere. Then he looked at the bigger picture. Jeremy would not hang around or come back to the area if he had killed two Police Officers in cold blood, especially if they were on an official surveillance of him. Where would he go? Who would be his next victims? It could be anyone, he thought to himself. This guy was unstable. He wouldn't be here. Let the Police find the two missing Officers. Find the culprit, Jack thought to himself. The question was where?

Chapter 18

The voices were going around and around in Jeremy's head. His Father shouting abuse at how useless he was to the world whilst his Mother was telling him not to listen to his Father. It was like the two of them were in the back of his car arguing like two married pensioners who had been together for years.

He drove down towards Marsh Mills, but knowing that the Police would be in the area, continued up towards Leigham and parked in the car park beside the Windmill pub. Then he crossed the road and headed down towards the woodland, and the mud paths that went either way towards Marsh Mills or in the other direction towards Neil Marsh's house.

Jeremy was focussed although not in a good way. His attention was all on his target and the thoughts going through his mind on how he could get rid of the criminal if the Police were there. He had his handgun fully loaded. But using it could be a bit of a problem, especially in the daylight. His escape would be hindered by the possibility that he could be seen by someone. His Father would then instruct him to kill them as well. He chose not to think of what might not be and walked quickly along the path which suddenly split but with the process of elimination he guessed that he would have to take the right-hand split as this appeared to go down towards the road. To get to the Leigham Manor estate would be quite a walk. He was lucky enough not to be seen by any members of the public on the woodland paths or any pedestrians or cars passing when he started walking on the road.

The time went quickly and without realising, he stood at the junction of Parkfield Drive and Woodlands Lane and looked down towards the Marsh's residence. There were two uniformed officers in a Police car parked outside Neil Marsh's house but on the other side of the road.

'Go around the back you fool'

"I know. I know. Leave me alone. I can do it!" Jeremy said out loudly to the voice of his Father. He did as instructed though and went around to the back of the properties, with the small walkway leading to garden gates. Before heading down the back lane, he silently and cautiously checked that no one was there. It could have been that there were Police protecting Marsh at the rear as well as the front of the house. As he managed to get out of sight of the main drive and all the houses on it, he pulled his handgun out of his jacket pocket and stopped to check that it was fully loaded. He knew it was, but from the day he was a young boy, his parents had always made him double check everything. His homework. The times of the bus. His schoolbag. The list was endless. But his Father was just an over-the-top perfectionist. He got to Neil Marsh's back gate and could hear someone talking in the back garden. He didn't waste any more time. Without hesitation Jeremy kicked at the gate and it went crashing inwards. There was little time as Jeremy aimed his gun at Neil Marsh.

"No!" he shouted as the voice on the other end of Neil's mobile tried desperately to find out what was going on. "Please. Don't do this. I have children!"

Jeremy had no conscience. He didn't speak but stared at the frightened man in front of him, enjoying seeing him squirm and noticing that he was far from the cocky little twat that he had seen in court. Jeremy fired three shots in quick succession and the body of Neil Marsh fell to the floor, the blood from his headwound hitting the patio door behind him as the back of his head exploded with the force of the shot. The assassin turned and ran out of the gate and up the lane, this time turning right up Parkfield Drive. He looked around for an escape route but there were no pathways leading off. But there was a man washing his car.

"You are looking lost, young man. Are you looking for anyone in particular?" the man asked politely as he watched the stranger walking along as though he was on a mission.

Jeremy stared at him psychotically and then snapped, "Yes. You!" He then raised his handgun and took the resident out with one gunshot to the centre forehead followed by two in the chest. Without hesitation he jumped into the victim's Renault and started the car, instantly speeding off the driveway and down Parkfield Drive and back out towards Marsh Mills. But about half a mile down the single-track road, he stopped the car right in the middle of the road and switched the engine off. Quickly he got out of the car. Blocking the road would stop any further emergency services getting to the crime scene and delay any search that they may carry out giving him enough time to get back to his car. He closed the car door and used the remote to lock the Renault. Then he threw the keys down in the direction of the football field, immediately turning and running up the mud path towards Leigham.

PC's Jensen and Gregory had heard what sounded like gunshots coming from the rear of the properties but weren't sure although the look that they gave each other said otherwise. PC Dudley Jensen got on his radio as he exited the driver's seat and slammed the door shut.

"438 to Sierra Oscar. We have what sounds like gunshots fired, I repeat, gunshots fired in Woodlands Lane. Please inform DI Thorpe."

"438, await back up. ARV on its way."

PC Chase Gregory looked over at the house and then back at his colleague. "What do we do?" he asked as felt slightly gripped by a situation that he hadn't been in before.

"We could try and get closer," Jensen replied. "There haven't been any more shots fired and the last ones sounded like they were further away than the first." He then started slowly walking towards the Marsh's place with caution ready to run for cover if he had to and detached and extended his baton just in case he had to defend himself, although he realised that unless he was lucky, baton versus gun could be no defence. But then most of the time a gunman would not hang around to admire his handiwork for too long through fear of a shootout with armed Police Officers.

Waiting for the ARV, both officers looked out for any members of the public that may be in the vicinity and who they would have to tell to return to their homes for safety. But there were only two of them and the shots seemed to have come from the rear of the house, but both PC's realised the importance of staying put.

It had been thirty minutes since requesting armed back up and still nothing had attended. The ARV was stuck in Leigham Manor Drive where Jeremy had left the stolen car wedged between the two road edges, one a drop down to the football field and the other side a steep bank to the path. FLO Sergeant Morrison jumped out of the passenger side and banged the side of the van.

"Let's move this bloody thing and fast!" He ordered as he looked around the direct area just in case the abandoned car was left there by any suspected gunmen reported by the two officers at the scene. "Washington.

Murphy. Cover the team. If this belongs to him, he could still be hiding."

"Yes, Serge," replied Washington whilst Murphy nodded in agreement as they immediately aimed their weapons up to the woodland and scanned using their telescopic lenses whilst the rest of the team exited the vehicle and tried their hardest to move it out of the way, but it was the single-track road that made it difficult for them to originally move it enough for the van to get past.

"Okay, the Sergeant shouted. "Let's just ditch it up and over down there." He pointed in the direction of the football field. "Everyone on this side. After three!" He watched as the team all took their positions at the side of the car, and then gave the signal. "One! Two! Three!" He watched the car being lifted by the other six FLO's firstly onto its side and then, after short break for them to catch their breath, they pushed it onto its roof where the decline took the car with a slide in the dampened mud down into the ditch.

SFO Morrison looked down towards the car and checked that for the time being it was safe and wouldn't move. He also realised that it could be a piece of evidence that he had just demolished, but life is more important than a car. He had to protect the public. "Back in the van!" he ordered, watching as Washington and Murphy continued to cover the team and as the sixth man got into the back, the two made their move and joined them, slamming the doors shut once they were in. The Sergeant then got back in the front passenger side and the van sped away whilst he closed the door.

The van driver put the blues and two's on for two reasons, to let the uniformed officers know that they were on the way and also to ensure any cars travelling down Leigham Manor Drive towards them would hopefully get out of the way, but in the end there were no cars and there were no more abandoned vehicles either.

PC Jensen flagged them down in Woodlands Lane, but to the left at the end of Leigham Manor Drive, a woman was waving her hands as well and was screaming hysterically as she heard the sirens, so the van stopped at the junction and the team of eight jumped out of the van.

Sergeant Morrison had seen the civilian waving. "Johnson, May, Lord. Come with me. The rest of you seal the area and liaise with the uniform guys." Morrison headed up towards the screaming woman instantly trying to calm her slightly by raising his hands.

"He shot my husband! Help! Help!"

"Is the gunman still around?" Morrison demanded as he tried to get information from her which was proving difficult. He flicked his hand to indicate for the three-armed officers to check out the crime scene.

"He shot my husband! Then took his car!" The woman looked at the three ALO's rushing towards her house with rifles at the ready to shoot if need be.

"What sort of car does your husband have?" He asked in between cries and screams.

"You have to get an ambulance," she choked. "You have to get an ambulance."

Sergeant Morrison wasn't the most empathetic person in the world. He blamed it on his wife's Mother who used to complain about the least little thing but then suffer the Sergeant's wrath because he had seen worst sights than some of the things she would complain about. He raised his voice. "Madam! What sort of car does your husband drive?"

She shook but felt the importance of what the Sergeant was asking her. "Renault. Green Renault."

Morrison nodded his head knowing that the one they had found in the lane was the same Renault, which means that he escaped on foot and there was still an armed man on the lose somewhere in the vicinity. He waved over to the uniformed officers. PC Gregory saw his hand signal and rushed over towards him.

"Yes, Sergeant."

"This lady needs some care and attention," Morrison exclaimed feeling actually good about passing her onto someone else leaving him to do at what he was good. "Try and get a statement. See if one of the neighbours is in to get her a cup of tea."

FLO Sergeant Morrison then turned around to see several Police cars arriving with blues and two's, and behind them an ambulance. Behind the ambulance was an unmarked Police car. Inside was DI Thorpe. Suddenly the Sergeant's radio clicked into life.

"The area is clear, Serge," AFO Johnson exclaimed. "We have one dead, though. Three fatal shots head and torso."

"Okay, stay there and keep the area secure for when forensics arrive. The gunman could still be in the area," Morrison demanded whilst trying to juggle several tasks at once. He took his attention back to the other team. "AFO Washington. How are we doing down there?"

"Sergeant. Area is secure. Looks like the gunman got his target who we think is Neil Marsh. Fatal shots head and chest."

"Right, Washington. You know the drill. Stay there and secure the area. Forensics will be there soon enough, but the gunman could still be in the area."

"Sergeant Morrison." DI Thorpe approached the scene commander.

"Tony. How are you?"

"Good thanks. Are we all good to go in?" Thorpe asked taking a look at the house from a distance where they were standing.

"Yes. Marsh is a goner. But he shot an old man dead and stole his car to escape. Up around the corner. There is one witness to the old man's shooting. PC Gregory has taken her into a neighbour's house form some TLC."

"Okay. When the rest of my team gets here we will need to interview her. Unfortunately, we have had a day of it. Not sure if you heard about the two officers shot out at Wembury?" DI Thorpe would be sure that he would have heard because they would have had to decide which team to send to which incident.

"Yes, I nearly had to attend that one, but we had someone a bit closer to the scene." He looked over to the movement in the trees and more flashing lights. "Looks like we have more company," he said, nodding his head that way.

Thorpe looked at his mobile. "It's DS Carter and the team. He has just text me."

"Well, I will leave you to it then Tony. I had better go and check my team." FLO Morrison waved his hand and walked off towards the Marsh house as the arriving cars came to a halt at the cordon.

DS Carter jumped out of the car and instantly noticed the nosey neighbours all out of their front doors wondering what all the commotion was about. "Guv. What's the damage?"

"Marsh is dead," DI Thorpe responded. "We can go in," he started walking as DS Carter followed his lead. "We have another dead body further up the road. He escaped in the man's vehicle."

"Let's take a look then," Carter said, increasing the pace towards the house. He saw the uniformed Sergeant PS Bickford instructing his team. "George, how are we doing with the house to house?"

"I'm on it, Mike," the officer responded loudly.

"Thanks," Carter replied as they reached the front door of Neil Marsh's house. He looked at DI Thorpe. "So how did he get in?"

"Well, there were two officers on the front. The body is in the back garden so I guess it might have been through the back gate. From what I remember there is a back lane leading to the rear of the properties." DI Thorpe stepped through the open patio door where the body was laying on the floor about three feet in front of them. The SOCO and forensic officers were just arriving and opening their case.

DS Carter noticed the blood splattered all over the closed patio door. "This guy is dangerous," he said concerningly.

DI Thorpe nodded. "Yes. That's what worries me. We need to catch him before he kills again but he is one step ahead of us every time." He looked around the back garden area and saw that it was pretty enclosed. "Something tell me he isn't that far away. Maybe in the woods."

"Do you want to get a team up there?" Carter asked inquisitively.

"I don't think we have enough armed officers at the moment because of the Wembury murders as well."

"Right. So where is the other dead body?" Carter asked the firearms officer who was guarding the crime scene.

"At the top of Leigham Manor Drive," he replied, pointing the way.

"We had better go and see it, Guv." Carter knew that there was nothing that they could do until forensics had finished and photographs had been taken by SOCO, so he retracted his steps, closely followed by the DI and went back to the front of the house, heading up towards the second murder.

An armed officer stood outside so the pair knew exactly where to head as they walked up the road. Police tape had been set up to cordon off the area and as they approached, the uniformed officer lifted the tape for both CID officers to get to the crime scene.

They saw the blood coming from the victim's head and it had flowed all over the concrete driveway where his car had been parked before Jeremy had driven away in it.

The first bullet had gone right through the head and lodged into the shed door.

"The thing is, if we did have enough armed officers to do a search of the woodland, this guy wouldn't care. He shoots anyone. Police, civilians. You name them he will just shoot." DI Thorpe looked at the victim and his injuries without actually having any contact with the body.

DS Carter joined him in his observations. "We need to get ahead of him then. Decide what he would do next and beat him to the scene."

"Easier said than done sometimes," Thorpe responded as he put his hands on his hips and looked around him. "We don't know who he going to target next."

The killer had reached Leigham and was headed back to the car park where he had stored his car. He had noticed the flashing blue lights and heard the sirens in the distance so knew that the Police were at the scene already. As he went through the subway towards the shops at Leigham, he suddenly noticed that he had some blood splatter on his clothes, so he immediately took off his jacket, looked around for a waste bin and walked over towards it. He checked his pockets and removed a few things before thrusting the jacket into the bin, ensuring that it was buried and covered with other litter. Then he continued through the precinct and headed back to his car.

The landlord of the Windmill pub was out putting up a new banner advertising the live sport when he saw the extremely suspicious character looking around to check if anyone was behind him and watched him take his jacket off and throw it away in the communal bin. Once Jeremy had disappeared around towards the car park, he dropped the banner, stepped down the ladder and walked over to the bin scattering the litter aside that Jeremy had covered his jacket with. All he saw was blood splattered over the item which he chose not to touch. He got his mobile out of his pocket and called the Police whilst standing guard over the bin and wishing that he had used the camera on his mobile to take a picture of the suspicious character.

Jeremy drove away thinking that it was best for him to exit Leigham from the far end over towards Asda because there would be a large Police presence along the other road. They would now be looking for his blue Nissan Duke. It was time to get rid of the car.

'That judge took bribes.'

His Father's voice was once again instructing him what he had to do next. The Judge? Jeremy had thought it himself before his Father had told him because of the number of cases he was glad to abandon at last minute. Everyone has a price, Jeremy thought to himself. He wondered just what Judge Kang Lim Koh's price was. Jeremy knew that up until he suspected the Judge, he looked up to him, even though he could be a bit of a pain in the arse sometimes. The guy knew the law. He knew where to head next. He couldn't do it in court mainly because he was off sick and there were too many people there plus some busty security officers that could easily apprehend and detain him. It would have to be his home, and Jeremy knew where that was because the Judge had held a barbecue and invited most of the staff to it last summer. He knew the layout of the place. He had time to kill because he doubted the Judge would be back much before 17:00 hrs depending on what happened in court that day.

'He must feel the wrath of your justice!'

Jeremy decided to kill a bit of time by looking at the wild animals around the old Yelverton airfield. He bought an ice cream from the van and wandered over slowly to the rock itself. Luckily, it was school time so there were hardly any children there shouting and screaming, and the ones that were there were very few and far between which he was grateful for immensely.

He sat down on the hard surface and ate his whippy ice cream thinking of the times when his Mother and Father would bring him out here when he was a young child. Mum would pack up a picnic and they would lay the blanket down away from the rock because the children played with footballs near it, which would upset his Father when they landed close or sometimes in the middle of the food.

Jeremy loved the wild ponies, and it was foaling season so there were plenty of young ones around. Many people would try and feed them or get close to the foals. The Dartmoor Rangers tried to spread the message that it was wrong for them to have human contact. This could result in them getting rejected by the Mother and therefore they would miss the Motherly goodness in the milk. There was also the problem of the Mother attacking by kicking randomly with a hope it would catch the offender. Jeremy saw them as peaceful animals. Running wild and free. That is how he wanted to be.

Jack Dempsey had sat in court for most of the day, after not being able to get through the Wembury Corden. He was disappointed that Jeremy wasn't there, and a few enquiries and little white reporter lies had given him the information that he was 'sick.' Jack had nearly responded, *'Yes, I know. In the head!'* but bit his tongue to save grace. But he decided to watch the Judge that Jeremy normally worked with. He could get an interview. He must go out for lunch, surely. That's what Judges did. Jack could just imagine them all around a table eating lunch and then dozing off during court proceedings in the afternoon. The thought made him smile.

Suddenly, his mobile telephone rang, luckily in an adjourned court room and so he answered it. "Hello?"

"Jack, it's Mike Carter. Just bringing you up to date on the latest escapades of our friend."

"What was all the commotion at Wembury?" the reporter asked intensely.

"He shot and murdered two CID Officers who were following him."

"Two of DI Chandler's men?" Jack snapped back.

DS Carter nodded as though Jack could see him and then responded, "Yes. His two DC's. After that we think he went down and finished the job on Neil Marsh, and also shot a neighbour."

"Well, I'm at the County Court hoping that he will turn up even though he has called in sick," Jack said remembering his agreement of 'You scratch my back and I'll scratch yours.' "I'm hoping to try and speak to the Judge he normally works with. Judge Kang ...." He hesitated as he forgot the name.

"Kang Lim Koh," Mike Carter reminded him.

"Yes, that's him."

"I can tell you know he is a very private person and probably won't speak to you if you tell him you are a reporter. We have trouble speaking to him as Police officers." DC Carter looked at his watch and saw that time was moving fast. "I'd better go, Jack. Keep in touch."

"Will do," Jack replied as he closed the call and returned his mobile to his pocket. He started talking to himself to decide. He would ask the Court Clerk first, so he walked over to the black-gowned man right away so he wouldn't back down after the doubt DS Carter had put in his mind.

"Can I help you?" The Court Clerk asked as though it were official business.

"I was wondering if I could see the Judge?" Jack asked politely contemplating if he should tell the court clerk he was a reporter. Yes, he would. Be honest.

"And you are?"

"Jack Dempsey," he said as he held up his press badge. "I'm an investigative reporter. I need to speak to the Judge about something important. He is in danger."

The Court Clerk looked at his badge and then looked at him wondering if the person who the Judge was in danger of was him. "I will ask. But you should request an interview with the press office."

Jack nodded and smiled nicely. "If you could." He watched the Court Clerk disappear in through the door behind the bench which closed heavily behind him.

"Your honour," the clerk said to the Judge who was sat at his desk signing paperwork.

He looked up at the clerk. "What is it?" Just the tone of his voice indicated that he didn't want to be disturbed.

"I have a reporter in the court who wanted to know if he could have a word. He says you are in danger."

Kang Lim Koh instantly thought of Stuart Newell's gang who had paid him to throw the case. Did the reporter know about that? Was he about to be headline news? "I will see him quickly," the Judge replied, desperate to know what the press knew or didn't know as the case may be.

The Clerk went back outside and noticed Jack doing things that reporters normally did and being nosey by looking at things that they shouldn't. "Ahem. Judge said that he will see you."

"Oh?" Jack replied with surprise in his voice as he looked up from reading the notes on the court clerks table.

"Yes, please come through." He pointed his arm in as if to show the way which made Jack chuckle inside as there was only one way that he could have gone in any case. "Mr Dempsey, your Honour."

Judge Kang Lim Koh normally had a grumpy voice, but this distraction had made him be that little bit grumpier than normal. "What can I do for you, Mr Dempsey?" He looked up from his desk and peered over the top of his glasses.

"Jeremy Cornelius-Johnson. Your court clerk I believe," Jack exclaimed trying to bring the urgency to his voice and get the Judge's undivided attention.

"One of them," the Judge replied. "Not today though."

"There is a warrant out for his arrest, Judge."

"I beg your pardon?" the Judge snapped. "A warrant? For what? I think you may be wrong, Mr Dempsey."

"I'm not wrong, Judge. Earlier today he shot two plain clothed Detectives dead in cold blood. Then he went on to kill a known criminal and one of his neighbours."

"What, Jeremy?" the Judge questioned with puzzlement filling the frowns on his face. "He is not even capable of tying his own shoelaces sometimes."

"Judge. There are several other murders that he is suspected of having committed and believe me he has links to in most cases."

"So why am I in danger, Mr Dempsey?" The Judge requested to know.

"I'm not saying you are, Judge," Jack answered calmly. "But you may be. This guy kills anyone and anything. Men, Police, women, even children."

"Oh my God. He uses my Logon to the National Computer. He has been able to access names, addresses, telephone numbers. Not only of accused people but their families as well." The Judge fell back into his chair with a bewildered look on his face and shook his head.

"So, he has a reason to target you, your Honour. To keep you quiet." Jack made his way to the door. "He is dangerous, Judge. If you see him, alert the Police."

"Thank you for the warning," the Judge exclaimed as Jack walked out of his room.

Jack waited until he was clear of the court room and then called DS Carter. "Mike?"

"What have you got for me?" DS Carter asked importantly.

"I managed to get to see the Judge," Jack replied. "He said that Jeremy had access to the National computer and the personal details of defendants and their families."

"If he has access to that, he has access to Police staff addresses and Judges, and anyone on the electoral role." Carter shook his head as his boss was stood beside him wondering why his DS was getting so uptight.

"I think at some point he may target Neil Marsh's parents and maybe even his children whom they are looking after," Jack exclaimed seriously. "Or he may try and silence some of the court staff."

"You may well be right, Jack. I'll have a word with the DI. Call you Later." He ended the call.

Chapter 19

Judge Kang Lim Koh arrived home after a hard day's deliberations with the jury on the case being asked to leave the court room on several occasions and at one point for the public gallery to be cleared. The law was just getting too easy to avoid on occasions when the defendant's had clever Barristers and a first-class law firm behind them. The Mother of the baby had changed her plea and was adamant that she had done the crime and her husband Michael had nothing to do with it. The case was adjourned for the third time.

The Judge inserted his key and walked into the bungalow. He was glad to be home at last and dropped his bags onto the chair which was the first piece of clear furniture inside the door.

"Tell me Judge. How much did they pay you?" The killer had broken into the Judge's home and gone through all his personal belongings that were in the sideboard drawers and his bureau. He didn't like what he had found, what he had seen on the Judge's bank statement. Jeremy came straight to the point, no holds barred, as he started questioning the corrupt lawman.

"I beg your pardon?" Judge Kang Lim Koh snapped whilst at the same time tensing his body and looking at Jeremy, feeling instantly threatened after what Jack Dempsey had told him.

"The Newell's gang. The one you let off without even a fight the other day."

"You had better be incredibly careful what you are accusing me of, Jeremy! You break into my home and looking at the state of the place have been rummaging through private details. I can personally say your days as a Court Clerk are over." The Judge became very defensive and wanted to change the subject but knew that this wasn't going to be for the time being.

"You haven't denied it though!" Jeremy snapped. He had been thinking of this since the early hours of the morning, waking up sweating after a nightmare about his neighbour Ken Meadows. "It was totally out of character for you, Sir. Totally. So, I'm saying that there can only be one other reason."

The Judge turned away, in order that Jeremy was looking at his back and therefore he couldn't be caught out with any facial expressions. He looked out of the window over in the direction of his neighbour's farm, hoping that his neighbour would be out with his animals and see that the Judge was home. "You should know that I am totally against corruption in any shape or form, Jeremy," he snapped, turning back around to face his accuser.

"I don't care if you did, Judge. Stuart Newell is dead. Haven't you seen the news?"

Kang Lim turned around and looked at Jeremy. "No, I haven't. How did he die?"

"There was a fire a couple of nights ago in Stonehouse. He was one of the people in the gymnasium where the fire started. It appears according to the news that none of the people in the gym stood any chance. Stuart Newell has been identified, along with his henchman, Mick Walters." Jeremy stared at the Judge, his eyes giving the impression that he knew everything when in reality he was guessing everything and just waiting for the Judge to admit to it. "Mick Walters was renowned for doing Newell's dirty work for him, like frightening witnesses, or bribing Police Officers and, if need be, court staff."

"So, this fire. Did you have anything to do with it?" The Judge asked inquisitively, his mind wondering why Jeremy was so interested in Newell anyway.

"Did you throw the trial?" The two men stared each other out, both waiting for a reply, both not trusting each other at this moment in time.

Kang Lim poured a glass of orange juice but didn't offer one to his unofficial visitor. He took a sip and then put the juice down on his coffee table. "What would you think of me if I said yes?"

"What would you think of me if I said yes?" Jeremy responded, smiling psychotically at the judge.

Judge Kang Lim Koh sat down in his leather chair and cleared his throat. "The night before the trial, someone was in my house. He told me to throw the trial, or I would be killed. He also said that twenty thousand pounds would be paid into my bank account for doing so." There was a short silence as the judge wondered just what Jeremy's next move would be.

"I decided enough was enough," Jeremy commented on his crime spree. "My Dad, who as you know was a Judge like yourself, spent most of his later life trying to put the scum behind bars. The law has changed so much that only the minority of cases come to court, and there has been an increase in the ones that get thrown out and the perpetrator gets to walk away scot free. Sometimes because of people like you." The thoughts in Jeremy's head were going around and around. What was Kang Lim going to do now that he had told him about taking justice into his own hands?

The Judge picked up his drink for another sip of the orange juice. He was thinking the same thoughts as the man opposite him. What was Jeremy going to do now that he knew he had thrown the trial of Stuart Newell? He put the glass back down. "Sometimes justice is blind, Jeremy. I don't condone vigilante tactics, but thinking of it, sometimes it is the only way. But as you know from what I have done, the vigilante tactics come from both sides of the law."

"Justice was served by me where the law failed the people!" Jeremy snapped. "You failed in your position as a trusted law Judge by accepting a bribe and doing as they asked!" Jeremy held the bank statement in his hand whilst with his other hand he reached inside his trouser pocket and pulled out his handgun.

The Judge froze and slowly raised his hands up in front of him. "Jeremy, now wait. I had no choice."

"You had twenty thousand choices, all of them you accepted. Just not the right one."

The potential victim was frightened. He could feel the adrenaline rushing through the blood in his veins and he didn't know how to stop the man in front of him. He didn't know how to get out of this situation. "I'm sure we can come to some agreement son," said the Judge whilst keeping his eyes on his hand and how tight he was holding the trigger. "I can share the money with you. I can give you half." The trigger clicked a bit more and Kang Lim squirmed that little bit more expecting the gun to go off at any moment. He squinted his eyes and turned his head slowly. "Please, Jeremy. I will transfer the lot to you, how does that sound?"

'Kill him, now! Do it! Fucking do it!

"There we go," the gunman replied. "The one person I thought would never break has a price not only to break the law but to save his own skin. You are nothing more than a fucking coward!"

'Kill him! Kill him now!'

Kang Lim looked around the room. Who was speaking to his Court Clerk? It was an older man going by the tone of his voice. But where was it coming from?

'Finish him! He is not fit to be a Judge!'

The Judge still looked around thinking that Jeremy had an accomplice hidden in the shadows somewhere in the room, but he couldn't see anyone. No one else was there. Then his body became cold as he realised where the voice was coming from. He remembered what Jack Dempsey had told him. This man is dangerous and doesn't care who he kills. He stared at his work colleague still wondering what was going to happen even though he could have guessed. But he was speaking to himself in different voices.

'When justice is done it brings joy to the righteous but terror to the evildoers!'

Jeremy pulled the trigger, his trademark assassination trait of one through the centre forehead and two to the torso around the area of the heart. He smiled as the Judges body fell to the floor and then walked over to view his kill, his piercing psychotic look just as still as the Judge's corpse. The blood flowing freely from the wounds and making the cream-coloured carpet a dark shade of red. Jeremy watched more and more of the blood spill out and get engraved in the fibres before coming out of his trance and looking around the room.

'You have done well, Son.'

"Have I," he questioned angrily. "Have I really?" He turned around as though his Father was stood behind him bellowing out the commands that made him commit the crimes.

'The law has no conscience, and neither does justice.'

Jeremy had to get out of there. He had to escape before anyone who may have heard the gunshots in this tight-knit community came around to check on their neighbour and investigate the noise. He threw the damning bank statement onto the coffee table, the same coffee table where the Judge had placed his drink minutes earlier. Hopefully, the Police would see that justice was done, he thought to himself. As he was about to go out of the front door, he noticed the Judge's car keys on the key hook. He needed a different car. His was parked in the Yelverton shopping precinct car park opposite the petrol station. But everyone was looking for the blue Nissan Duke now. They would be stopping every Nissan this side of Exeter just to check if were him in the car. He picked up the car keys to the Mercedes parked on the driveway. It would do him for the time being. He unlocked the car and jumped in, firstly driving over to his car ensuring that he had his bag with his weapons and ammunition inside. Checking that he had locked his Nissan, he got into the Judge's Mercedes and then headed out onto the roundabout and onto the A386 back towards Plymouth.

DCI Tomlinson had given the go ahead for a search of Jeremy Cornelius-Johnson's property now that it was confirmed that he was wanted on suspicion of murder, and DI Thorpe was going to see to it personally with DS Carter and a team of uniformed Police officers.

Flashing lights and sirens filled the normally quiet idyllic street in the Wembury vicinity and the area around the bungalow was sealed off by Police tape, the road closed at both ends just in case Jeremy had returned home somehow and was in there and armed. Thorpe knew that Jeremy was unstable, so arranged for the ARV to be there and to search the property before the team were allowed to enter and search and remain until the team had finished. They had found no one but were shocked by what they had seen.

Police dogs barked viciously, and neighbours had come out of their front doors to see what all the commotion was about, only to be told by uniform that there was a gunman on the loose and he could still be in the area, so they should return to their homes and lock the doors.

DI Thorpe followed the senior firearms officer into the house and immediately looked around making a note that there was nothing out of the ordinary on first impression but knew that first impressions could, and often are, deceiving.

SFO Morrison looked at the DI. "It's the upstairs that is most worrying, Guv. Do you want to come up and see?"

"Yes," DI Thorpe said concerningly as he noticed DS Carter come through the front door. "Mike are forensics here yet?"

"Just arrived, Guv. For some reason they seem to be stretched today," he replied jokingly.

Carter's boss went upstairs following SFO Morrison to the top. "In there," Morrison indicated. "We had to kick the door down because it was locked."

DI Thorpe walked into Jeremy's 'special room' and was instantly shocked. Photographs filled the walls linked by pin-held string which looked like it indicated the order in which he had killed them. But there were more photographs on the board than he expected. "Mike, can you get onto DC Bolton and ADC Hardy to see how they are doing with tracking down any missing persons?"

"Will do, Guv," Carter replied, immediately getting on his mobile to telephone the office. "By the way, forensics have started downstairs and are already concerned."

"I'll be down in a minute tell them."

"Guv," DS Carter said as he disappeared back downstairs to make the telephone call to DC Bolton.

"This guy is a psychopath," DI Thorpe said softly as he shook his head with his hands placed on his hips. "Collecting photographs of his victims when they are alive and then again when he has killed them. Look."

"PC Horgan. He must have taken a photograph of him when stopped in Plymstock Broadway," SFO Morrison commented solemnly.

"Yes, but Horgan's baby. It's like he gets a kick out of looking at his kills afterwards." DI Thorpe followed the pattern that Jeremy had created. "Hold on. This one. I recognise this one. I was a young PC when this guy went missing. He was due in court and never showed. It was about twenty years ago." He looked at the name that Jeremy had scribbled underneath the photograph on the whiteboard. "That's right. Daniel Priestly. But Jeremy would have only been about ten years old when he went missing. So why is Priestly on his trophy board?"

"Well at least you can wipe him off the wanted list," SFO Morrison said jokingly.

"You know me. Body first. They are not dead until I have physical evidence." Thorpe had an unusual frown on his forehead as he was trying to understand the sense of it. Then he looked at some of the other photographs that appeared older than the current kills.

DS Carter reappeared in the doorway. "All done Guv," he said after having a conversation with DC Bolton. "Oh God. What the hell is this?" He walked into the room and joined his boss.

"I think that this is our man's trophy board," the DI replied to him worryingly as he watched DS Carter step closer and start following the connected victims. "What's behind that," the DI asked noticing that there was a small noticeboard of some kind on the back of the special room door, but it had been covered up with cloth.

SFO Morrison was closest so pulled the cloth away displaying the board. "It looks like his to-do list," the firearms officer commented.

DS Carter turned around to look at the board and instantly felt terror. "That is little Max. Horgan's little boy. He is staying with Emma and I. Shit! He wants to finish the job by shooting a kid again! I've got to get home."

"You go, Mike. Let me know what is happening," the DI said as Carter left and ran down the stairs, the DI unsure whether his Sergeant had heard anything that he had said.

The firearms officer then looked at the other pictures. "Do you know any of these people?"

"Yes, I do." He pointed to the photo of the Judge. "This is Judge Kang Lim Koh. Our suspect actually works with him in the crown court. I don't know these two," he continued pointing to a joint photo of a man and a woman together. But this one. This is our friendly neighbourhood investigative reporter Jack Dempsey."

"I think we need to get these people some protection, Guv," Morrison exclaimed. "Pretty quick as well."

DS Ayres looked over the top of the bannister rail. "Guv, Todd needs you to look at something," he said indicating that the forensic team had something quite urgent for the DI to see. "I think you had better come and look."

As the DI followed DS Ayres he could see that the room that he had walked in first was dark, the curtains drawn at both ends of the room and Todd Armstrong waiting for him in the doorway. "What have you got for me Todd?"

The forensic officer switched on a large infrared light that he had set up on a stand in the corner of the room. It lit up the darkened room. Patches splattered all over the walls, ceiling and floor, as though they had been washed intensely.

"Is that what I think it is?" DI Thorpe asked, shocked by the amount of blood that was showing up on the infrared. He watched as Todd Armstrong nodded.

"It certainly is. So much of it that I guess it from more than one person."

"I couldn't believe it either," DS Ayres commented showing that he was just as shocked as the DI.

"Are we sure it is human blood?" Thorpe asked inquisitively. "Could it be animal blood?"

"I won't know until I get back to the lab. I will have to take swabs first," Todd replied officially knowing that he had his work cut out over the next few days. "I am going to ask SFO Watkins for his assistance on this one. Two heads are better than one."

"There was me thinking on retiring," DI Thorpe said jokingly. "It wouldn't be anytime soon," he added as he looked up at the ceiling. "So, what would cause that splatter pattern, Todd?"

Todd looked up as well. "Well, there seems to be quite an array of different directional blood splatters. This one here," he pointed up towards the light in the middle of the room. "This looks like a frenzied attack with a sharp object of some kind. Whereas this one on the wall, looks like what would be left as the result of gunfire which would explain why there is a filled hole in the wall here." He continued to look at the ceiling and the walls. "The blood on the carpet is probably what has just been left behind when the bodies have collapsed. But looking at this, we could be looking at a dozen or so victims."

SFO Armstrong's assistant came through the front door and looked at the staining in the room. "Oh God. Look at that."

"Rachel, how are you getting on with the outbuilding?" Todd asked her, hoping that she was nearly finished.

"The cadaver dog has picked up something," Rachel replied. "It looks like the scene has been washed down, but I have found evidence of human remains albeit small, mainly skin and ligament, behind the shelving."

"Have you bagged it up?" Todd enquired, knowing the answer as Rachel was always so efficient in her job and came out of University with a 1:1 in forensic science.

"Yes," she replied. "It may be worth using this light in there to get a better idea of the scope of things. I am only using the hand held one."

Todd knew she was right. "Good idea. I have a spare one on the van. I'll get one of the guys to bring it in for you."

"Thanks," she replied sharply, but that was her manner, and she didn't mean anything by being that way. Todd used to think it was sign of intelligence and was always thankful that he had her brains on the team. "When you have five minutes, pop over!"

"Will do. Won't be long." Todd always thought that Rachel had a certain way with words, a real Plymouth girl if ever there was. Mentioning for him to 'Pop over' made him wonder if she was inviting him to the family barbecue, but that was her, and it kept him sane sometimes in this stressful demanding job.

"Can you get onto this ASAP, Todd?" DI Thorpe needed a favour because who knows when or if they would catch up with the suspect. Would he try to leave the Country? He wouldn't get far because there was already an all ports warning in place since the warrant was authorised by the DCI.

"I'll give it the utmost urgency," Todd replied, reaching down into his kit bag in order that he could take scrapings from the hidden blood stains and therefore cross reference the findings with the DNA of those persons on the PNC.

Meanwhile stood at the cordon was Jack Dempsey. He had tried to get past, but the young PC wouldn't allow him, but had promised to call for DI Thorpe in order that if his claim were genuine, he could let him through.

"Look. I am working with DI Thorpe and DS Carter on this case," Dempsey exclaimed quite harshly. "Can you please get in contact with them urgently?"

"I've heard it all before. You are just a reporter trying to get a story." The young PC stood firm refusing to let Jack in or contact the officers concerned. Jack decided to do it himself with a hope that one of them would answer their telephones.

DI Thorpe's mobile burst into life and he quickly looked at the display, saw it was Jack Dempsey on his display and answered in order that he could kill two birds with one stone because there was something that he had to tell him. "Jack. Where are you?"

"Just outside at the cordon. The PC won't let me in or contact you."

Thorpe looked out of the front door, saw Jack waving and waved for him to come forward. He tried but was once again stopped by the PC. "Let him past," DI Thorpe shouted loud enough for the PC to turn around.

"There," Jack exclaimed. "That is DI Thorpe requesting you to let me go past the cordon." He bent down and went under the tape and then ignored the PC whilst he went up to the DI.

"Jack, glad you could join us."

"I guess you got your warrant then?" Jack asked knowing that he was having difficulties up until the point that it had been reported that Jeremy had shot two CID Officers.

"Thank God we did. Put this on," he demanded, handing the reporter a white bunny suit and foot coverings. He was thankful that Jack knew the drill and didn't moan about putting it on as some senior Police Officers didn't stop complaining at times. "It's not a pretty sight. There is also something else that you will be interested in because it affects you."

Jack stood still. "Affects me?"

"I'll take you up and show you." He noticed that Jack had finished suiting up and then started walking in the front door. "Come and have a look at this first." They both walked into the living room.

"Wow," Jack acknowledged knowing exactly what he was looking at having reported on such at other crime scenes. "That is a lot of blood." He took out his mobile and took some pictures.

DI Thorpe nodded in agreement. "We don't know just how many people's blood is here. We have to wait for forensics to try and make sense of it." There was a momentarily silence as both men looked around the room in disbelief. "But I need you to see upstairs. Come on."

Dempsey and Thorpe walked up the stairs and into Jeremy's 'Special Room.' Jacks face dropped as he saw the victim's wall. He froze as it suddenly hit him that the suspect was a lot more dangerous than either he or the Police had thought. Taking more photo's with his mobile, he asked, "How many are on here, do you know?"

Thorpe shook his head. "It's confusing. Some of these pictures date back to bodies that were found many years ago whilst Jeremy was just a child. Yet the pictures are on his victim wall."

"Well surely a child wouldn't have been able to kill in the way that he does now?" Jack asked inquisitively as he bit his lip whilst deep in thought.

"You wouldn't think so," Thorpe replied. "But the most worrying is yet to come. Turn around."

Jack followed his lead and spun around to look at the back of the door and stared at the noticeboard but most of all the pictures on it. "Do I take it that these are his next targets?"

"We think so. Mike has gone home because this little guy is Max Horgan, the only survivor of the PC Horgan shootings and he is in foster care with Mike and his wife at the moment. Then there is the Judge, you, and we don't know these two," he said, pointing at the unknown photograph.

"I can tell you who those two are," Jack exclaimed as he instantly recognised the two suspected child killers currently on trial in the Crown Court. "Michael and Kayleigh Stevenson. They are being tried for the murder of their baby as we speak."

DI Thorpe shook his head as he stared at his reporter friend. "This just gets worse. We need to get protection for all these people on here. Including you."

"Me?" Jack replied with a surprised look on his face. "Why me? He knows I am chasing him."

"No," Thorpe responded. "He knows that you are on to him. He is chasing you. No one is safe." Thorpe's cogs in his brain were going around and around at a superb pace as he was thinking about his next move and how many officers he was going to have to assign to protection. Because of the circumstances, it would have to be armed protection, and they must be willing shoot to kill.

"I'm not going back to my Sister's house. If he follows me there, she will be in danger, if she isn't already. I will get a hotel room."

"Right, we can arrange that for you. Just the others. The Judge and now we know who this pair are, we can keep tabs on them. They are probably already on remand on suspicion of child murder."

Senior Forensic Officer Todd Armstrong had joined his colleague Rachel Clarke in the garage and workshop at the back of the driveway. The neon light had been set up. Both forensic officers and the PC that had carried the light in and plugged it into the mains stood back in disbelief as the infrared filled the room and highlighted what could be deemed as a blood bank. Multiple stains on the walls, floor, ceiling and on the back of the garage and workshop door. "Oh my God," Todd said unbelievably. "What the hell is this guy going to do next?" He looked at Rachel knowing that in her short time since leaving University she had seen some crimes, but nothing on this scale, and noticed that she was just flabbergasted at what she could see around her. "Are you alright, Rachel? Do you need to go out and get some fresh air?"

She shook her head. "I thought it was bad. I didn't think it was this bad."

"Thank God you asked for the bigger light," Todd replied back to her. "We have certainly got our work cut out. Can you go and get the DI? He's upstairs in the house."

She nodded, although the realisation hadn't settled in of what he had asked of her. Not as much as the realisation of the crime scene. But she came to and left via the garage door, stood outside and caught her breath, the fresh air filling her lungs and for once she was glad to taste the fresh air.

Chapter 20

The Judge's Mercedes S 500 L sped along the A386 and was about to pass the Roborough Park and Ride terminal, but Jeremy had to stop at the traffic lights. He became impatient and started revving the engine. Most of the other car drivers that were waiting in line with him just thought that it was a 'typical Mercedes driver' showing off. He was mumbling to himself as he was held up and banging the steering wheel in anger. The driver beside him thought he was tapping to the beat of music, but there was no music to tap to.

He looked around the cockpit of the car thinking that it was very stylish compared to his Nissan. Wooden style dashboard and bright LED controlled displays and it had all the gadgets from reversing sensors to assisted braking system. He realised that no one would realise that the Judge was dead and not realise his car had gone for a few days. Just enough time for him to target his last victims.

The lights went green. At last, he thought to himself. He had checked on the addresses of his next kills whilst at the Court and decided to head out to Plymstock and the home of DS Carter where the Horgan's child was being looked after.

His Father suddenly started speaking to him. Jeremy looked in the rear-view mirror thinking the voice was behind him.

'It won't be long, and justice will be done.'

"Justice has already been done," Jeremy screamed back at his Father. "What are you doing to me? Why do I have to keep proving myself to you?"

'You have not lived up to my expectations. Do you think that I want such a weak, pathetic example as a son?'

"I am not weak," Jeremy replied angrily, realising that he had to be careful not to be disrespectful to his Father. "I am not even pathetic. I am your son!"

'I even had to get you the job.'

"And I am good at that. You have never had a good thing to say to me! You always said I had to be the best in everything I do. But my best just wasn't good enough for you!"

'Your best? Your Mother and I gave you everything on a plate.'

"Except love! You didn't know how to love, Father! You were quick enough to punish me for what I did wrong, but never to praise me for what I did right!" He saw the children in the car next to his pointing at him and laughing as they realised that he was shouting for no reason. Taking his eyes of the road for a few moments, he raised his middle finger to them, but then realised that he had to brake hard to avoid hitting the car in front, but luckily the ABS cut in.

'You were just an unlovable child. Just in the way most of the time.'

"You never even tried! When did you ever try? When did you take me to golf or teach me to play tennis? You were too interested in teaching your friends children. Not your own son!"

'You were an embarrassment. You should have been born a girl. Always around your Mother anyway She should have taken you to her sewing class.'

"I was afraid of you, Dad! Your hate qualified more than your love!" Jeremy was getting worked up inside with a mixture of anger and sadness, fear and disgust and finally guilt. The thoughts going through his brain were just too much. Was there anything more that he could have done as a child, teenager or young man? He didn't think so. His face was red, and without hesitation he put his foot down on the accelerator and headed down towards the A38 at Manadon. He could see the traffic lights ahead, but this didn't worry him as he had other things on his mind. He drove through the red light and instantly drivers of all types of vehicles started sounding their horns. One lorry barely missed him, and the lorry driver stopped and give a hand gesture as he shouted abuse at the driver.

Jeremy didn't acknowledge any of the aftermath of him jumping the red light but continued to speed down the slip road heading east on the A38 and sped right out into the dual lane by-pass, again suffering the wrath of those drivers he had angered. "Mum are you listening to this?"

'I am, dear. Very much so. But you know I can't go against your Father's word. He is the man of the house!'

Jeremy put his foot down again on the accelerator but did not realise that the car was now hitting 90 mph in the outside lane, but the other drivers around him did. As he passed the Marsh Mills interchange, he looked in his mirror. There was a Police car behind him with blues and twos on trying to force him to stop. But Jeremy wasn't having any of it. His Father's voice echoed once more.

'They are going to use that child against you. They are going to show him pictures. You have to get rid of the child.'

"Where the fuck do you think I am going now?" Jeremy answered back. He looked out the driver's side window as he noticed the Police car beside him equalling his speed and the officer in the passenger seat making a strong gesture for him to pull over to the side.

Traffic Officer Dan Halliwell looked at the driver of the Mercedes having already completed a PNC check on the vehicle and determining that it belonged to Kang Lim

Koh, an IC5 male. Dan looked at his colleague. "Does he look Chinese to you?"

"No way. Looks like it might be a stolen vehicle. He's not going to stop if that is the case!" The driver of the Police car picked up even more speed to try and get in front of him, but knew that he may need other units to try and slow him by sandwiching him in. At 110 mph, PC Banks managed to get the Police car in front of the speeding Mercedes and then began the standard attempts at slowing the vehicle down.

"You see what you have done now, Father?" Jeremy shouted at the invisible entity. But the Deep Lane interchange came up and Jeremy skidded to Mercedes by turning off at the same speed that he was doing on the by-pass. It happened so fast that the Police car shot past the turning.

"Fuck it!" PC Banks shouted as he watched the target vehicle go up the slip road heading towards the junction.

"He could be going one of two ways! Plympton or Plymstock direction," Dan Halliwell said instantly. "I doubt that he will go back down the A38." He clicked his radio on his lapel. "SO372 to Sierra Oscar. Attention required to a white Mercedes registration KLK 2020 possible stolen vehicle. We have lost him at the Deep Lane interchange. We need units to Plympton and Plymstock." His driver slowed back to national speed limit and continued towards the next turn off where he could return back down towards Plymouth and even turn off safely at Deep Lane coming from the other direction in order that he and his Sergeant could join the pursuit.

Meanwhile Jeremy had sped off at such a speed that if anything had come the other way in the single- track lanes he would have to hope that the ABS worked or there would be one massive accident. But he wasn't thinking straight after what his Father had said to him. He just had to get to the house where Max Horgan was, and he was there.

DS Carter quickly put his wife Emma and son Thomas, together with Max into the car and headed off towards the Police Station at Charles Cross, himself taking all the back roads through Plymstock Road and down to Oreston in order to escape any sighting of the killer. Jack Dempsey had telephoned him to find out what was going on and arranged to sit in his car overlooking the Carter's residence from Underlane with a hope that he wouldn't be spotted. He had parked and was trying to stay out of sight by edging himself down in the seat whilst being able to see through the windscreen. It was more difficult than he thought. Across the road from him were the armed response in an unmarked van ready and eager to get their hands on the man.

Minutes later, Jeremy drove the Mercedes down Underlane towards DS Carter's house. He looked around for anything suspicious, noticing when he stopped at the junction that there was only one car on the driveway which would have been right if DS Carter were still at work. But he predicted that by now they had raided his home and found the special room together with the pictures.

The traffic was busy at the junction. Jeremy looked left and right several times but then in his side mirror he noticed that a car like the one that had followed him home days ago was parked on the hill on the other side of the road. He couldn't see the driver, so pressed the button to lower the driver's side electric window. Without thinking he put his head out of the window and looked backwards towards Jack's hire car. He was right. Was this a set up? Why was Dempsey waiting for him? Vehicles queuing behind the Mercedes started to get impatient as several times they felt he could have edged his way out especially as he was going left.

Jack had seen the head poke out of the window. Then he looked at the number plate on the Mercedes. KLK 2020. It was the Judges personalised number plate. What was he doing here in Plymstock when he lived out at Yelverton? It also didn't look like the Judge's face that quickly looked his way. Suddenly, Jack feared the worst. If it was Jeremy, why did he have the Judges car?

Jeremy realised that he had been seen and abandoned his plan to go left and instead just put his foot on the accelerator and went right. Jack started his car, rolled down the hill to the junction and as he beeped his horn he shot over to the right and in pursuit of the fugitive. He quickly called DS Carter via his Bluetooth connection.

"Jack, tell me you have him?" Mike Carter exclaimed.

"Sorry Mike. He saw it was a set up. Where are you now?"

"The car park at the Police Station," Mike replied urgently as he seemed to be holding two conversations at once trying to get his wife and the two children inside whilst getting the latest information from Jack. "We are just going in now. They will be safe here."

"I'm trying to follow him, but he is driving that dangerously, jumping red lights and driving on the pavements. He is desperate to get away."

"I'll get you some back up."

"He is not in his own car. Looks like he is driving Judge Kang Lim Koh's car, which could mean one thing." Jack tried to see where Jeremy was going. Billacombe Road. Sooner or later at this rate there was going to be an accident. He watched the madman just drive on to Billacombe roundabout again without stopping. Jack didn't manage to get onto the same roundabout so stopped. It was too dangerous to try the same manoeuvre. "I've lost him at Billacombe roundabout. He is heading west. He has a choice of going onto Embankment or on the road that turns off to the City Centre. But he could go anywhere."

"Shit!" DS Carter said, suddenly putting his hand over his mouth as he realised that he had sworn in front of the children and didn't really like doing so.

"I think you should get a unit out to Kang Lim Koh's house. I think he may be a goner." Jack knew that he had warned the judge but also knew that Jeremy Cornelius-Johnson had been one step ahead of them the whole time. He should have told the judge to stay put at the court, but then realised that he wouldn't have been safe there either.

"Will do," DS Carter replied. "Although we are running out of ARV's. I am also going to arrange for ANPR to pick up the Judge's Mercedes anywhere it can. Although I guess he will swap vehicles again now."

Jack put his thinking cap on. "He must have got to Yelverton somehow. If he has swapped cars, then his blue Nissan Duke could still be in the vicinity. It would be every forensic scientist's heaven to have that."

"Good call, Jack. Well, his next victims are either you or the pair in custody. I think you should get to your hotel, and we can get that armed back up for you.

Jack nodded as though Mike Carter could see him. "Yes if he goes to his own plan, the only one he could target tonight is me."

"He won't know where you are. Try and sleep tight." DS Carter sounded as though he were speaking to his six-year-old son and smiled as he thought that he could even arrange to go down and read Jack Dempsey a bedtime story. "I will come around for you first thing tomorrow."

"Cheers Mike," Jack replied before ending the call. He thought for a while and then decided there was something he had to do back at the hotel. It was time to start the story of a lifetime.

He had failed. Jeremy Cornelius-Johnson had failed. Again, and again. He knew that his Father was going to chastise him for this failure as much as he had done for others for most of his life so far. He wasn't looking forward to it. But right now, he had to find somewhere to sleep. He couldn't go home for obvious reasons, but if he were going to sleep in the car he needed to find somewhere out of the way where no one would suspect him. He drove around for ages deciding to get out of the main centre and find somewhere quiet to park on one of the outer locale of the City. Somewhere that didn't have a big Police presence in the first place because of the crime rate in that area. He also needed to ensure that the Mercedes was hidden because once they found the Judge's body, every Police Officer in the area would be looking for it. He knew a place. It came to him. There was more or less an abandoned car park at the bottom of Talbot Gardens in Barne Barton. But then he thought twice about it because chances are someone would try to steal it with him in it or vandalise it because it was a top-class Mercedes parked in a deprived area. He continued to drive around heading further and further out, through Southway and up to Roborough. He knew another place. He crossed right across the Roborough interchange and headed towards Glenholt and then Estover Industrial Estate. The old headquarters of one of the major retailers in Plymouth was still empty and abandoned. He could park up around the back of the warehouse.

'You think they won't find you there?'

"You again?" Jeremy snapped at his Father. "I've had enough of you. It is you that got me into this mess." He continued down the road before turning right and driving into the car park. He looked around to check that no one was around, like a security company checking on the premises which they sometimes did with empty industrial units. But he knew if worse came to the worse and he was disturbed, then he would just make the perpetrator his latest victim. Then he drove around the back as planned and right up to the corner, turned his lights off as he came to a standstill. It wasn't long before he was sleeping after reclining the driver's seat and making the most of the comfort.

The next morning, the sunlight shined on his face waking him up from his deep sleep. As he rubbed his eyes he began thinking that it was the best night's sleep he had experienced in a long time, which didn't say much. At home he had always felt like there were ghosts around, his Mother and Father, looking over him, always there and never leaving him alone.

Jeremy checked the handgun in his pocket and made sure that the cylinder was full of ammunition. It was time. He had to get down to the court ready in time for the arrival of Michael and Kayleigh Stevenson. If he weren't in time he would have to wait until the end of the day when they would be escorted back to the security van to be transported back to the remand centre and he didn't want to do that.

Jack Dempsey had woken earlier than normal and blamed it on a strange bed, the standard type of lodge bed that were as hard as nails. He did think in the middle of the night whether he would be better off sleeping on the floor.

It was time to put his plan into action. Somehow he was convinced that Jeremy would be trying his assassination attempt on the two child killers either today or sometime over the next few days. The only problem was he could be wrong and therefore he would be next after finding out that he was on the list. If it was going to happen to the Stevenson's, then it would have to be externally. Every staff member inside the court now knew about Jeremy's involvement in the multiple murders and were ordered to call the Police if they saw him and not try to apprehend him themselves.

He picked up his mobile and called DS Carter, waiting impatiently for him to answer. "Mike?"

"Hiya Jack. I was just leaving the station to pick you up."

"Meet me at the coffee shack in front of the crown court. I'm nearly there."

Carter looked confused. "I thought that I was going to pick you up?"

"Too late," Dempsey replied much to the annoyance of the detective. "Don't be too long." Jack was going to get there first but not park close. He felt that Jeremy would feel the necessity to do that in order to make a quick escape. In addition, he knew that Jeremy would be looking around to see if he was being followed especially in the place that Jack had parked days earlier. So, he would park up in the Guildhall car park and find a place to view Princess Street where the prison vans drove to the rear of the Court and offloaded all the prisoners. He parked the car and then walked around the front of the court building and over to the coffee shack. All the time he was looking around, this time for a Mercedes and a killer who looked familiar.

He joined the queue to order two coffees ready for when Mike Carter arrived, which, surprisingly, he wasn't too far behind, joining him in the queue and whispering in his ear, "How the hell am I supposed to protect you if you go it alone?"

"Good morning to you as well, Mike." It was his turn to be served, so Jack looked at the young lady and smiled. "Two skinny latte coffees, please, and two croissants. Could I have a receipt as well, please?" He turned his attention back to the Police Officer.

DS Carter hadn't had breakfast so was so pleased that his friend had ordered something to eat, even if it were just a croissant. "You know he has no conscience and would shoot you anywhere, anytime don't you?"

"I will not hide away, Mike," Jack replied forcefully. "I know I'm not safe out here in the streets, but I am not safe in the hotel room either." He took out his debit card and tapped it on the contactless part of the handheld console that the girl was handing him before she passed him the receipt. "Thanks," he said as he grabbed the tray.

"No problem. Enjoy!" The girl replied as she watched the two men walk away over towards some vacant chairs.

"Right, just keep your eyes open whilst we are sat here. I know it's early, but he may be thinking the same as us. Get there early and position yourself." Mike took a sip of his coffee, trying to act as normal as possible which wasn't hard as there were several lawyers and barristers all either drinking or queueing to get refreshment before their hard days began. Mike Carter looked around noticing the large water enclosure in front of them and thinking that the Council no longer looked after their installations. There used to be a waterway that ran down from the North Cross roundabout right down through Armada way. It hadn't worked for years and was deemed too expensive to repair. Typical of this City, he thought to himself.

"Have you let the DI know what you are doing this morning?" Jack asked as though he already knew the answer, but you never know.

Carter laughed and nearly choked on his coffee. "Actually, I told him I was looking after you. I didn't say that we were playing Columbo and chasing our main suspect."

Jack joined his humour with a chuckle and smile. "I love that programme. My Mum and Dad used to make me watch it with them on a Sunday. It used to make me laugh. If Lieutenant Columbo was following you around, you were guilty!"

"If only it were that easy, the DI would get him working for CID." Carter said whilst gulping down the last of his drink. He looked inside the empty cup. "That was gorgeous," he said.

"Hold on Mike," Jack exclaimed, becoming alert to a car that had just passed along outside the court towards the Guildhall car park, the driver seeming to take an interest in the front of the courthouse. "Mercedes. KLK 2020. That's our man!"

DS Carter got his mobile out of his pocket and speed-dialled his boss. "Guv, it's Mike."

"Are you coming in to do any real work this morning?" the DI joked knowing he was baby-sitting Jack Dempsey for most of the day.

"Guv, we are down outside the Combined Court. We have just eyeballed Jeremy Cornelius-Johnson driving past in the Judge's Mercedes. I think we are going to need armed back up!"

DI Thorpe sprang into action. "I'm on my way. I'll get an ARV down there." He ended the call.

DS Carter looked at the reporter. "He's getting an ARV and coming down here himself."

"So, what do we do, Mike? We know why he is here." Jack kept his eye on the Mercedes which was disappearing out of sight around to the car park.

"We wait for back up. But I'm going to have to go over and inform the court security staff that there is a problem." With that, DS Carter checked both ways on the road and headed over to the main entrance. He showed his warrant card and then started talking to the big burly guard on the front desk.

Jack waited patiently but kept his eyes open just in case either the Mercedes drove around again, or the suspect appeared somewhere. If anything, he would be waiting around the back of the court because that is where they transferred prisoners from van to custody. Jack quickly crossed the road and headed over to the side of the Guildhall. There was a path that led to an emergency exit down the side of the Guildhall which overlooked the rear of the court car park. He quickly text DS Carter and DI Thorpe to let them know that he had moved. But he kept low in order that Jeremy would find it hard to see him if he came around that way.

Inside the court, DS Carter had asked to speak to the head of security Jon Barnes, indicating that it had to be with the utmost urgency that he had to be disturbed.

"Detective Sergeant Carter?" the tall, muscly man asked coming into reception.

"That's me," Mike replied. "You must be Jon Barnes."

"Yes that's right. So, what's so urgent?" he asked getting right to the point in order that he could get back to his work which was piling up on his desk.

"There is going to be an assassination attempt this morning on two prisoners."

"Which two?" Jon asked now appreciating the urgency that he was pulled out, although he did wonder how the Detective knew about this.

"Michael and Kayleigh Stevenson. They are both on remand for the murder of their son." Mike Carter looked at him seriously as though he wanted immediate action.

Jon Barnes looked worried. "I think that van has just arrived outside." He got on his radio to try and find out if his suspicions were right.

"Tell them not to offload the prisoners but turn around and get out of there." Mike ordered.

Back outside, Jack Dempsey had seen a security van arrive but wasn't sure if it were the one with the Stevenson's on. His attention was then distracted by the sight of DI Thorpe running behind a team of armed officers who were coming his way. The took position aiming towards the van.

DI Thorpe joined the reporter and ducked down with him behind the metal fence. "What's the situation?" he asked worriedly.

"No sign of Jeremy as yet apart from the sighting at the front in the Mercedes. It may be worth some of the ARV team making a sweep around the court in case he is lying in wait somewhere. They can't miss the car. It has a personal registration KLK 2020." Jack continued to look over at the security van. But there was a problem. There was another security van coming through the barrier, and no one knew which of the two would be targeted. "Shit," Jack exclaimed to the DI.

"What's wrong?" Thorpe asked quickly.

"There are now two security vans," Jack answered worriedly. "We don't know which one the targets have been transported in."

"Think of it sensibly, Jack. If we don't know, then chances are our gunman doesn't know either." DI Thorpe hoped more than he knew that this was the case. Unless he had prior knowledge then Jeremy would be in the dark just like them. He waved his hand to the armed response senior officer, Sergeant Morrison, who saw the gesture and, keeping low, edged his way over to the Inspector.

"DI Thorpe. Any intelligence on the situation?" Morrison asked authoritatively.

"No sign of the suspect apart from what DS Carter saw at the front of the court. But we have two security vans, and we don't know which one the targets are in." DI Thorpe was searching his brain to try and decide what to do next. He took his mobile out and called DS Carter. "Mike, where are you?"

"The security guys and I are just inside looking at the back of the vans," Carter replied. "The head of security thinks the Stevenson's are in the left-hand van as you look at them from the front. So currently the one farthest away from you."

"I heard," SFO Morrison commented to the DI. "I'm going to put an armed perimeter around both vans." With that he waved his arm in the air in a circular action and pointed towards the security vans. Within seconds, armed officers ran the short distance over the car park and took kneeling positions around both security vans. Telescopic sights scanned the area around the rear of the court. "What next, Guv?"

"Do you think it is safe to get the prisoners out of the vans? Or should we tell them to leave and go back to their respective remand centres?" DI Carter had to decide but didn't have the answer.

SFO Morrison didn't help by replying, "Wherever they are the occupants are in danger. Going back to the remand centres makes them sitting ducks in the open."

"Buggered if we do and buggered if we don't," Jack Dempsey commented sarcastically.

"It looks that way," DI Thorpe responded in agreement. "Unless we get them into the building. Can we do that?"

"It is the easiest and safest option under the circumstances," SFO Morrison exclaimed, happy that the DI had thought about that option.

"Do it then, Sergeant," the DI Ordered. His mobile telephone rang. "DI Thorpe."

"It's ADC Hardy, Sir. Three things. We have twenty-seven cases of missing persons with either criminal records or had never made it to court within the last thirty years. All of them were either tried or were going to be tried in a court headed by Rufus Cornelius-Johnson as the Judge."

"Good work, Ben," The DI responded. "We will look at that when I get back." He knew that Ben Hardy had just confirmed his suspicions on Jeremy's family life. Something wasn't right even before Jeremy took over the reins of being Judge and Jury. "What's next on your list young man?"

"Bad news, Sir. Judge Kang Lim Koh's body was found this morning. The report's indicate that he was murdered in his home. The good news is that a blue Nissan Duke was found close to the Judge's home, and it belongs to our suspect. Forensics have it now."

"You certainly have been busy," the DI exclaimed, wishing that all of his team were as proactive.

"Lastly, DC Bolton and I attended Chelson Meadow first thing this morning. Looks like we have found the body of Jeremy's next-door neighbour. Or what's left of it." Ben went silent whilst waiting for a response from his boss.

DI Thorpe just sat there, silent for a few moments before looking at Jack Dempsey. "I just want to retire peacefully," he said with a tired look in his eyes that told the reporter that the DI was exhausted with life. "Thank you, ADC Hardy. We will meet when I get back. Which won't be any time soon by the looks of it."
The call was ended.

Chapter 21

The psychopathic Jeremy Cornelius-Johnson wasn't on the outside of the Crown Court, he was inside. Amongst all the commotion he had ditched his stolen Mercedes parking it partly on the pavement at the side of the court building, knowing that this in itself would soon cause a security scare and the building would be evacuated. But he didn't care. He was inside. He had said good morning to someone having a cigarette who was holding one of the fire exit doors open that led to the offices in order that they didn't have to go through security to get in. The word had not spread about Jeremy as yet, so not everyone was aware.

He just looked like another member of staff, and when he arrived on the first floor after climbing the stairs only used by staff and officials at the rear of the building he walked quite unannounced into the court waiting area and straight down towards Court two. Walking in whilst trying to avoid prying eyes he headed directly to the public seating area. The new Court Clerk was busy at his desk speaking to the Court Usher and took no notice of who was coming in and who was going to realise that he was there. There were five others sat down, albeit in the front row.

Jeremy waited, not making it obvious that he wasn't really supposed to be there and that outside armed Police were waiting for him to appear and were covering all angles of the car park.

At the back of the Court, SFO Morrison had ordered his team to form a perimeter around the back of the vans that had reversed as close as they could to the prisoners entrance doors which led directly down to the holding rooms. DI Thorpe and reporter Jack Dempsey watched from the side lines over on the Guildhall path and also kept a lookout for any suspicious characters.

The armed officers all looked through their sights to scan the top of each building and the direct area. "Right," SFO Morrison shouted. "Let's get the first one inside. Open the door," he said to the private security guard in charge of the detention of prisoners who nodded an acceptance to the Sergeant. The doors opened and SFO Morrison looked inside. "Move inside as quickly as you can! Go! Go!"

There were eight prisoners who were all rushed down the steps and into the secure area where they were immediately locked in their temporary cells.

"Next van!" Morrison shouted. "Open the doors!" He noted only three prisoners in this one but rushed them just the same with each prisoner looking at the armed officers and wondering what was going on. Two of them had been in court on the previous day and had never had this protection before. Something must be going on. But within seconds, they were secure and the thick metal protective door that led to the cell block was locked behind them.

DI Thorpe looked at Jack. "Well, that went easier than I thought it would," he said as his forehead held a frown of puzzlement due to the inactivity of what they were expecting.

"But don't you always feel in these circumstances that something isn't quite right?" Jack responded with a similar look of confusion and puzzlement on his face as he bit his lower lip slightly and started to think what he would do if he were the killer. "I've got a bad feeling."

The Inspector nodded at him. "This seems all to set up. He is around here somewhere. Carter and you saw him. But where is he? Has he abandoned his plan after seeing all the armed response in the area?"

SFO Morrison and one of his team walked over towards the Inspector. "No problems so far," he said authoritatively. "There are three options now."

"I can guess those," Dempsey responded.

SFO Morrison nodded. "Either he has gone, he is going to attempt the assassination after the case on leaving the court, or he is already in the court."

"That is exactly what I was thinking," DI Thorpe said looking at an equally deep-thinking reporter. "I think we had better get in there. I'll see where Carter is." He grabbed his mobile and clicked the speed dial for his DS.

"Guv. What's up?" Mike Carter asked wanting an update either way.

"Believe it or not," Thorpe exclaimed, "Nothing happened outside. Prisoners are down in the detention rooms. Anything your end?"

"No. Jon and I are doing a room to room search just in case."

"SFO Morrison has given the option of him already being inside. Jack Dempsey and I are just walking around the front now, so I'll let you know when we are clear." Thorpe waved his hand to Jack and started walking around to the front of the court quite quickly.

"Ok, Guv," Carter replied intensely.

It was time for the Courts to be in session. The court was getting busy and there were only a couple of seats left in the public gallery. The security guards rattled the door that led from the cells to the dock. The jury had been seated and ready for the trial. The defendants heads appeared at the top of the stairs from the cell block, and they were ushered into their respective seats a little apart from each other with one of the security guards stood between them indicating that there had been some disagreement between the two.

Then the Court Clerk who had replaced Jeremy stood and shouted, "All rise," as the new Judge Magnus Willoughby came from his chambers, sat at his desk, and nodded to his clerk. All persons in the court sat down again.

"Michael Stevenson you are charged with murder in that on October 26th, 2020, you did murder one Kieron Stevenson aged eight months causing him severe injuries prior to his death. How do you plead?"

The defendant smirked sarcastically whilst looking at his wife's parents who were sat close to Jeremy in the public area of the court. He was about to answer when suddenly Jeremy stood up and took out his handgun. "He's fucking guilty. They both are!"

There were screams around the court as the realisation of a gunman being present in the room hit home to those who were there. Jeremy pushed his way past the people who were next to him in the row of seats and headed over towards the dock.

"There! You know what it is like to be frightened now, don't you?" He asked the two defendants who were trying to shield themselves with their hands. The security guard stood in the middle of them quickly leaned over and tried to grab the handgun from the madman. Jeremy shot him without even realising, the bullet catching the guards grabbing hand and continuing into his stomach. He fell to the ground and the Judge tried to make a move over to him to give him first aid.

"Fucking leave him!" Jeremy said, aiming the gun the Judge's way.

"But ..."

"Do you want to be next, Judge?" Jeremy asked nastily as he peered with his psychotic eyes at the lawman who returned to his seat with his hands up.

Michael Stevenson also held his hands up as the volume of the screams increased. "Listen. It was her, Not me! She has already said she is guilty!"

Jeremy looked around and the people in the public gallery were screeching and trying their hardest to leave. He aimed a shot at the doorway. "Sit the fuck down!" He shouted loudly as the court clerk came towards him.

"Jeremy, it is Jeremy isn't it? I'm sure we can work something out. Put the gun down. Let's talk about this."

Two more shots, one piercing the court clerks centre forehead and his body fell over his desk and onto the floor leaving a trail of deep red blood sprayed across the dock behind him and his desk.

Kayleigh Stevenson froze, certain that both of them were going to be executed at any time. Jeremy saw her panic and frightened emotion.

Jeremy looked at her. "Kayleigh Stevenson you are charged with murder in that on October 26th, 2020, you did murder one Kieron Stevenson aged eight months causing him severe injuries prior to his death. How do you plead?" She was still shaking as though she didn't know what to do or say and looking like she was in shock. Jeremy raised his voice. "I said how do you fucking plead?" She was still silent. "Guilty!" he shouted as he pulled the trigger in his trademark fashion and her head exploded as the bullet went through her forehead. There were more screams.

Michael Stevenson looked in horror. He knew that his time was limited. "Please, sir I beg you. I am innocent!" He squealed before looking down and noticing that his bladder had given him an involuntary action as the urine made a wet patch in his trousers.

Jeremy shot one more time in the air this time as he tried to quell the noise of the screams and shouting from the crowd. "For fuck sake shut up!"

'Kill them all. They are all useless!'

His Father ordered him to complete the task, so he pulled out another handgun from his trousers realising that the chamber on the first was empty. The people all heard the strange voice, the Judge looking at him and horrified that the voice was coming from Jeremy's lips.

"If you lot don't fucking be quiet I'll shoot the fucking lot of you! Just like this!" He aimed at Michael Stevenson. "Guilty!" Then he fired through the head and two in the chest. The body joined Kayleigh and the security guard, who was still alive, on the floor.

"Oh my God," the Judge whispered as he crouched down behind his bench. Jeremy overheard him.

"God? What has he got to do with this? He never defended or saved the kid that they murdered! I have done God a favour!" He looked psychotically at the congregation of the courtroom. "I have done you all a favour! So be fucking grateful!" He walked behind the bench, paused and looked down at the Judge. Jeremy stared at him, his eyes widening. He didn't see Judge Magnus Willoughby, but he saw the vision of Judge Rufus Cornelius-Johnson. His Father. The screaming continued as Jeremy escaped the courtroom through the door leading to the Judge's chambers.

'Well done Son. I never thought that you had it in you!'

"You never gave me the chance," Jeremy replied to his Father.

DI Thorpe and Jack Dempsey had just met up with DS Carter and the Court's Head of Security Jon Barnes. All four of them froze in order to listen closely to the noise from upstairs in the court area.

"Was that gunfire?" DS Carter asked worriedly.

"It certainly sounded like it," Thorpe replied looking cautiously up the stairs just in case the gunman came their way. He took out his mobile. "SFO Morrison. We have gunfire in the court building!"

298

"We are on our way," the Firearms Officer replied as within seconds they rushed the front desk not bothering with any security checks due to the urgency of getting in and securing the area. The SFO stopped beside the two detectives. "We need to get everyone out of the building safely," he ordered. "I'll leave that to you."

"Mike," DI Thorpe said, looking at his second in command and nodding for him to move.

"I'm on it," DS Carter replied before turning to Jon Barnes and asking, "You okay to help?" The bigger man nodded to show his support, and they both walked towards the offices on the ground floor.

Outside, the Uniformed officers had started cordoning off the area around the front of the court and stopping people from coming to the area from the both the City Centre and Plymouth Hoe. The commotion had started to make crowds gather at each cordon and the uniformed officers were finding it hard to move the people on until their Sergeant started walking around and threatening any person who refused with arrest for breach of the peace. PS Payton knew that a threat of arrest usually worked, but you would always get the one or two individuals who still wouldn't listen.

In the court building, SFO Morrison led a team of armed officers with their weapons live and in the firing position, up the stairs, slowly accounting for the fact that they didn't know what was around the corner. They soon found out as a crowd of people came rushing towards them trying to escape from Court two and the waiting area where the receptionist had heard the commotion and tried to evacuate everyone safely. One of the firearms officers directed the crowd from court two down the stairs as the court usher still dressed in his black gown, approached him.

"He has escaped out through the Judge's chambers at the back of the court," the usher commented frantically, his body, like most of the others who were in the court, shaking with fright, fear and worry.

"Thank you. Down the stairs," AFO Washington said to him before looking at his Sergeant and softly commenting "Guv. The usher has just said that the suspect has exited through the Judge's chamber at the back of the court."

SFO Morrison gave AFO Washington the thumbs up and then indicated for some of the team to take position outside the door of Court two, ready to storm the courtroom. He then counted down with his fingers in the air, three, two, one. "Go! Go! Go!" he shouted as the first of the officers burst through the court door.

"Police! Stay where you are!" AFO May secured his position ready to give cover for his fellow team members who were right behind him and already taking their positions just in case the shooter was still in the room. They each edged their way forward.

"I need an ambulance!" the voice shouted from the dock.

"Down on the ground!" AFO Johnson ordered the man who he guessed was either a judge or barrister due to the wig, but he knew that he couldn't make assumptions. This might be Jeremy.

"No, no. Don't shoot!" The Judge replied from his uncomfortable restricted position in the dock. "It's the security guard! He needs an ambulance. He's been shot!" AFO Johnson used his common sense and still with his weapon cocked, looked over at the casualty.

"Serge. We have a live one. Ambulance needed," AFO Johnson shouted urgently across the room. He leaned over and checked for a pulse on the other two bodies.

"They are both gone," said the judge, still shook up from the ordeal. "The defendants." He shook his head. "Innocent until proven guilty."

"I think you had better get out of there, Judge," Johnson commented. "We can take over. You aren't in the right frame of mind at the moment." He helped the Judge up whilst watching the rest of the team gather around the chamber door to make a further entry. The door of the chambers was forced open, and the armed officers stormed the room one by one, shouting their commands even though they weren't sure if anyone was in there.

SFO Morrison walked in behind the team and watched them search the various hidden points of the room and then the echoes of 'Clear' came from the same areas. He was about to lower his weapon when suddenly an alarm started sounding around them. At first he thought it was because they had stormed a Judge's chambers and it could be the warning alarm for that purpose. But then he thought that it must be the fire alarm and instantly associated it with an escape plan by the suspect. If that was the case, Jeremy was still in the building. But to top it all, the sprinkler system operated automatically. Morrison thought quickly. It means that there must be a fire and it wasn't a false alarm. Either that or someone has placed a burning item under the sensor. "Murphy?"

"Yes, Guv," AFO Murphy responded becoming alert to his Sergeant's request.

"Get down and check the alarm out. See if it is false or otherwise," SFO Morrison ordered. "Quickly if you can." He then thought that the best way forward was to get the Judge and the injured Security Guard out of the building as fast as possible.

Downstairs, DI Thorpe and Jack Dempsey were waiting patiently for the go ahead to view the crime scene when the alarm sounded and seconds later they found themselves being covered in water from the sprinkler above their heads. DS Carter and Jon Barnes had started clearing the offices and side rooms ordering an immediate evacuation. Jon Barnes team were overseeing it to ensure that there was minimal panic and therefore minimal potential casualties. Members of staff guided the few members of the public out towards the front door.

DS Carter was happy that the ground had been cleared. But then he realised just why the fire alarm and sprinklers were operating as he looked at the security door which led downstairs to the detention cells. There was smoke coming out from underneath the door. This was no false alarm. "We need help, Jon!"

"The fire brigade are automatically despatched when the alarm goes off. They should be here any minute," Jon replied cautiously whilst looking at the same hazard. "I think we should get out as well."

"I think you are right," Carter replied as he joined the Security Chief and headed for the front of the building. As they reached the reception area, the fire engines started to arrive at the front and Carter noticed the Fire Chief waving one of the engines around the rear of the building. He looked at Jon Barnes who was busy on his radio.

"Shit!"

"What's up, Jon?" Carter demanded to know.

"There is a suspect vehicle parked around the side of the building. I am going to have to call the bomb squad. Standard procedure."

The Fire Chief came into the reception just as Jon was talking to DS Carter. "What was that?" He asked inquisitively. "Bomb Squad?"

"Suspect vehicle at the side of the Court Building," DS Carter replied. "It has to be treated as suspicious, especially under the circumstances."

AFO Murphy was talking to DI Thorpe to get an update on the fire alarm but was interrupted when the DI broke away and instantly walked over to see what all the commotion was about overhearing the conversation. "Right, we need everyone out, now." He knew that this would give Jeremy the perfect opportunity to escape in some way what with all the confusion and the various emergency services coming and going.

The Fire Chief looked at DI Thorpe and DS Carter. "I can't let my men in until given the all-clear by the Bomb Disposal Unit."

"I thought you were going to say that Chief," DI Thorpe retorted.

"The smoke is coming from the cell block underneath the building. What are we going to do about the prisoners?" DS Carter snapped as he realised that they could have several dead if they couldn't be rescued almost immediately.

"The sprinkler system should help stop any flames. But the smoke inhalation could be fatal." The Fire Chief looked like his hands were tied. "We could open the back door, but it could be more dangerous than the smoke. There could be a backdraft and then a massive explosion which would kill them in any case.

The DI shook his head. "Fuck!"

The ambulance arrived and pulled up in front of the fire engine. Two paramedics jumped out and headed for the reception but were stopped at the outer doors by two fire officers. "We can't let you in due to a possible IED," one of the firemen snapped quickly.

"We have been told that there is a gunshot victim in one of the courtrooms," the senior paramedic responded with urgency in his voice.

DI Thorpe rattled his mobile and typed in SFO Morrison's number whilst forgetting that he was on his speed dial list. "It's the DI. You all need to evacuate now. There is a suspect vehicle at the side of the building which could have an explosive device inside."

"Shit," SFO Morrison exclaimed. "We have several dead and one barely alive. We need that ambulance!"

"No can do," the DI responded as though he were giving an order to the firearms Sergeant. "Everyone out, now!" He ended the call.

"Fuck it," SFO Morrison exclaimed before turning to the injured man. "This is going to hurt, but it is the only chance you have of survival." He looked around to AFO Johnson. "Lift. After three. One, two, three!"

The security guard screamed in agony as he was lifted upwards and without hesitation rushed towards the exit door. AFO Washington grabbed the Judge's arm. "Come on. Let's get you out of here!"

Jack Dempsey didn't hang around. He knew that this was more or less an escape plan. Smoke, sprinklers, fire alarm, car parked at the side which could have a bomb inside. He was certain that this was Jeremy's way of escaping. He walked around the side of the Court building and noticed Judge Kang Lim Koh's Mercedes parked half on and half off of the pavement but at an odd angle. Surely he wouldn't leave the vehicle that he was going to escape in such a prominent position. This was just a smokescreen Jack was sure of it. Then he thought of the fire alarm which was still sounding and walked quickly over towards the rear car park where he could see the fire doors on the back of the building. They were alarmed but right now if one were opened, who would hear the alarm apart from the security guard who would normally be covering the control desk viewing the CCTV and alarms but had vacated his post due to the fire. This was the perfect opportunity for Jeremy to escape. He knew the building. He knew the exits.

Jack waited and stared at the rear of the Court building with shear anticipation but knew he would have to be careful because the assailant was so unstable and would shoot anyone or anything that moved at this moment in time. Suddenly his mobile rang. It was DS Carter.

"Jack, where are you?" DS Carter asked concerningly because both he and DI Thorpe had noticed that he wasn't with them anymore.

"Working on a hunch," Jack replied whilst still checking out the car park area.

"What hunch?" Carter asked inquisitively.

"The kind that says get your arse around the back of the court! It's him!" He cut the call as he noticed someone in a black gown and a wig leaving through the fire exit carrying a large bag on his back. He was next to the cell block entrance and heading over towards a posh black Bentley Flying Spur. Jack watched the man struggle with the key fob to unlock the car and become pleased as he finally achieved the task. The man was obviously too young to be a Judge and Jack could see that. He was the build of Jeremy Cornelius-Johnson. Turn around! Jack mumbled to himself. Turn around! Confirmed!

"Jeremy!" Jack shouted over to the serial killer who instantly turned to look at the reporter and panicked slightly as he realised that he had been clocked. He threw the bag onto the passenger seat and then jumped into the driver's seat, slamming the door shut. Jack started making his way over towards the car dodging the parked cars which were so close together that he found himself zigzagging at times which hampered his progress slightly. The car reversed at some speed and rammed some of the cars parked in the row behind. The tyres screeched as the driver did not realise the power of the Bentley, but he managed to turn in order that front of the car was aimed at the exit barrier. There was one problem for Jeremy. Jack was stood in the middle of the lane potentially blocking his exit. But this didn't bother Jeremy. He was going to escape at any cost. He revved the engine and headed directly at the reporter.

Jack realised he wasn't going to stop and at the last minute threw himself sideways landing on the bonnet of one of the parked cars whilst watching the Bentley crash through the exit barrier. Jack felt pain in his shoulder and took a few moments to catch his breath before he moved. He rested his back on the bonnet of the car and tried to stretch but there was a stabbing pain in his right shoulder where he had forcefully landed. He heard loud voices.

The Bentley has screeched to a halt. DI Thorpe, DS Carter and a handful of armed officers were now stood in front of the Bentley blocking it's required exit leading to Notte Street. Jack looked at them and once again mumbled to himself, MOVE! He knew that the officers were in complete danger stood where they were.

"Armed Police! Get out of the vehicle!" AFO Lord commanded as two other officers joined him one on each side. "NOW!"

Jeremy wasn't going to wait. He put his foot on the accelerator and headed towards the three Officers in his way at excessive speed, ducking sideways in the driver's seat as there were gunshots heading his way from them momentarily until there was a loud THUD! He had hit AFO Lord with some force and his body had flown upwards hitting the windscreen and rolling over the roof of the car. AFO's Washington and May had escaped injury by throwing themselves sideways just as Jack Dempsey had done minutes before and both tried to stop the vehicle by firing at the wheels. It was too late. The Bentley had gone.

DI Thorpe and DS Carter looked and saw that the car had gone so rushed over to the body lying on the floor, that of AFO Lord. Carter shook his head. "I'll get an ambulance," he stated importantly towards his boss before moving away and grabbing his mobile.

The Inspector proceeded to start CPR on the downed officer as he realised that there was no sign of life. "Come on!" He shouted. If there was one thing he hated it was the loss of a Police Officer who was only doing his job. DS Carter finished his call and headed over towards the DI.

"It's on its way," Carter exclaimed noticing that Thorpe was trying his hardest to save the life of AFO Lord.

"I think they will be too late," he replied whilst continuing to try and get some sign of life in the Officer.

Jack Dempsey appeared at the exit barrier of the court holding his shoulder. "Where is he?" He shouted over to Carter who looked back to see where the voice was echoing from.

He looked at Jack. "He's gone. Notte Street," he replied suddenly seeing the younger man start to run down towards the Unitarian Church and the pathway beside the Church that led to Notte Street. "Jack! Wait!"

It was too late. Jack had started making his way over to the Notte Street/Hoe Approach junction with a hope that the lights were controlling the delay in escape of the fiend. He looked distressed as he searched for the Bentley, knowing that it was an unmistakable car and would stand out in any City but particularly in Plymouth.

Meanwhile DS Carter told himself that he didn't want another dead body that day. He stood up. There wasn't a lot that he could do to save AFO Lord, so he started running in the same direction that Jack had gone moments ago. As he reached Notte Street he looked to the left and saw the reporter running in the direction of the car driven by Jeremy which had been stopped by a car turning right into the Barbican. He started running after Jack Dempsey whilst keeping a close eye on his movements, not knowing what he was going to do nor the lengths that reporters would go to get a story.

Jeremy was waiting to continue his escape but the car in front of him was having trouble turning right what with the busy traffic. He sounded his horn several times in anger telling himself that if he didn't move soon he would ram him out of the way. For all he knew the Police could have sealed off the area by now and if not would be pretty close in doing so. Then he had a thought. Another escape route. The Mountbatten ferry. He put his foot on the accelerator and pushed the obstructive car out of the way and turned right into the Barbican himself, with oncoming cars having to brake to avoid collision and each sounding their horns in anger and disbelief. Jeremy sped off down through the Barbican hoping that there were no more obstructions.

Jack Dempsey stopped to catch his breath as he noticed the Bentley disappear into the barbican. "Fuck!" he commented as DS Carter caught up with him and joined him in recovering from their run.

"Where did he go?" Carter asked whilst bending down slightly and leaning his arm on the reporter.

Jack managed to catch his breath. "Down there," he replied, pointing down Southside Street.

"Well, he is limited there. Only so many roads you can take in and out. I'll get the area surrounded." Carter got on his phone to his DI but then realised that he may not answer if he still performing CPR on AFO Lord, so rang SFO Harrison instead.

"Harrison," was the snappy reply.

"The fugitive has gone into the Barbican area. We need the place surrounded."

"Okay," SFO Harrison said in reply. "Leave it with me."

"Thanks," Carter said before ending the call. He looked at Dempsey. "All done. You ready for round two?"

Jack nodded as they both crossed the road and headed in the same direction as the wanted man.

Chapter 22

The Bentley stopped at the Mayflower steps and Jeremy got out leaving the driver's door open and then reached inside for his bag. He walked over to the wall and the small balcony that overlooked Plymouth Sound and the dock for the various boat trips and pedestrian ferries that left from there. He wasn't going to get far. There were two officers, although unarmed, on the jetty checking anyone who was queueing for the next ferry to Mountbatten. They had obviously been given the task of trying to locate the fugitive.

Plan B, Jeremy thought to himself. Over the footbridge towards the National Marine Aquarium. He quickly placed the bag over his shoulder and much to the amusement of those around him left the car and headed to the footbridge. He was lucky. Just as he got to the other side, the alarm went off and the lights flashed indicating that the footbridge was about to be closed for any boats to either exit or enter the marina. He also knew that the Police could not follow him that way for the next few minutes if they saw him.

He quickly headed up towards the aquarium. At the top of the path, it split into two, one going towards the car park and the other over to the housing estate, so he followed the right fork to the Teats Hill residential housing estate.

'You will need a car quick. The Police are on to you!'

"State the fucking obvious, Father," Jeremy replied to the voice. "I'm going to get away. Don't worry." He headed up to the flats on the right-hand side. There was a delivery driver getting some parcels out of the back of his van. Jeremy took advantage of the door being open to the driver's seat, jumped in and started the van and without hesitation driving away. The delivery driver was still in the back of the van and the back doors were still open. He didn't last long as Jeremy's erratic driving threw him out of the van and onto the hard tarmac. All the driver could do was look at his van disappearing into the Cattedown area.

Jeremy knew that he had to escape the area. He couldn't go home. He knew that the Police would be all over his home, searching every nook and cranny. Investigating the blood in the garage and workshop areas. Even digging up the garden and ripping up the floorboards in the house. His time there was done. But he had to escape quickly because at any time that delivery driver would be calling the Police to tell them that someone had stolen his van. Deciding to try and keep off the main roads where the Police cars and ANPR would be desperately looking for him, he headed out towards Elburton and the back lanes that would take him to Plympton. He knew exactly what his destination would be. He knew the area and it was so vast that it would be hard for the Police to find him.

DS Carter and Jack Dempsey arrived at the abandoned Bentley on the waterfront of the Barbican. He looked around to see if Jeremy were still around knowing that it would be the sort of thing that he would do, looking at them from somewhere he couldn't be seen.

"The ferry," Jack said, heading over to the Mayflower Steps and looking down to the jetty just as the killer had done earlier. DS Carter joined him, hoping that they would find him there. "The Mountbatten ferry has just left."

"Hold on," DS Carter exclaimed. "There are officers down there. Chances are he wouldn't have risked it. The DI has ordered that the area be secured." Carter looked around thinking that he could be anywhere what with the Sutton Harbour, the Hoe and the old Barbican with its cobbled back lanes and ancient hiding places from the days of pirates and the Pilgrim Fathers. "What about there?" He asked pointing over towards the Aquarium.

"There's only one way to find out. There should be plenty of witnesses."

Carter nodded. "Police!" he shouted holding up his warrant card. "Did anybody see where the driver of this car went?" Suddenly he was rushed by half a dozen concerned members of the public who each wanted to give their information. Multiple voices each drowning out each other were suddenly silenced.

"One at a time!" Dempsey shouted trying his hardest to support the DS. He noted a larger man who looked like he was the sort of guy that you wouldn't want to meet down a dark alley and dare not pick a fight with. "Sir, did you see him?"

"Yes, he looked over the wall there and then ran over the footbridge," the man said.

"Thank you," DS Carter exclaimed instantly making tracks towards the footbridge closely followed by Jack. They reached the fork in the path. "Which way? Hold on," Carter said as his telephone started to ring.

"Mike. Where are you?" DI Thorpe asked worryingly concerned for the two of them who had left the court area in pursuit of the suspect.

"We are down at the Barbican. He dumped the car and crossed the pedestrian footbridge," Carter replied whilst glad that he could catch his breath momentarily.

"We have had reports of a stolen van over at Teats Hill. It may be related." The DI waited for a reply as he overheard DS Carter talking to Jack in the background.

"Stolen van. We will go that way," he said, nodding towards the right fork.

"Guv, got to go." He ended the call and started running with Jack up towards Teats Hill looking for anyone that resembled a person who had just had their vehicle stolen. "Bingo!" He announced as he say a frantic man cursing in the middle of the road.

"If he has taken a vehicle, we have lost him," Jack said, bending over to catch his breath and wiping the sweat from his forehead. Then he followed the DS to the victim.

"Hello Sir," DS Carter said again flashing his warrant card. "Are you the gentleman that has had his van stolen?"

"Yes. He just jumped in and drove off. I was in the back and as he pulled away I was thrown out onto the road. Bastard." He was holding his right arm as though something was wrong with it.

Jack noticed him grimacing as he talked to Mike Carter. "You probably should get that seen to," he commented.

Carter was more interested in getting the lowdown on the van. "Did you see which way he went at the end of the road?"

The man nodded. "He turned right up towards the crossroads," he said.

Reaching for his mobile, Carter dialled his boss who answered almost immediately. "Yes, Mike?"

"We have spoken to the man who has had his van stolen. If it was Jeremy, he is headed in the direction of the crossroads at Macadam Road in a white van, registration," he stopped and turned to the victim whilst putting his other hand over the mouthpiece.

The man semi-whispered back, "BZ16 HFD".

"Bravo Zulu one six, Hotel Foxtrot Delta."

"Okay Mike, I'll get that circulated. I'll get someone over to pick you up." DI Thorpe felt annoyed that they still hadn't caught the wanted man yet knowing that he was going to get it in the neck from the DCI at some point.

"I'm glad that you offered," Carter replied. "I don't think I could run anymore."

Back at the court scene, DI Thorpe was overseeing what was now a clean-up operation. Most of the prisoners unable to escape the detention block were overcome with smoke inhalation problems as the fire was controlled by the sprinkler system but the smoke had nowhere to escape very easily. All the staff had made it out and at last the ambulance staff were able to get in for the casualties of the shooting. Michael and Kayleigh Stevenson were both pronounced dead whilst the paramedics tried desperately to save the life of the security guard who was in the dock with them. It was a mess, the DI thought to himself. But he didn't want to end his time in the Police on a bad note so was determined to get this madman. He looked over to the cordon and saw that there were TV cameras gathering and newspaper reporters all waiting for an official statement on what had happened and why there were armed Police in attendance. He placed both hands on his face and rubbed it as though he were wetting it with water. His mobile rang once more. "Oh God, what now?"

"DI Thorpe?" the voice asked on the other end of the phone. "It's Todd, still up at the Cornelius-Johnson house. Forensics has dug up the garden. So far we have the skeletons of about twenty corpses. Most of them look like they have been here for some time.

"How long would you estimate?" The DI asked, shaking his head at the extent of the number of dead.

"Anything from twenty to forty years."

"Okay, Todd. Thanks. I will get up there as soon as I can."

"That's alright. I think we are going to be here for some time yet," Todd replied. "Bye."

DI Thorpe's hunch was right. This didn't only stem from Jeremy Cornelius-Johnson because he wouldn't have been able to kill so many at a young age, and some of the corpses may have been killed before he was even born. Was it a family trait? They would have to get forensic tests done on all and cross reference any results with the information that ADC Hardy had put together. The next decision that they had to make was whether or not to give Jeremy's name to the press. If they didn't, no doubt one of Jeremy's neighbours would let it slip. So, the decision was inevitable. Now was the time. He would call the DCI and let him come down and handle the panache of speaking to the press. He was good at that side of it.

"DI Thorpe. How is it all going?"

"You don't want to know, Guv," DI Thorpe replied genuinely seeming stressed. Down but not out. "We have the press on our backs. This is quite a major story. I think now might be the time to name our suspect and warn people to stay away."

"And you want me to come down and handle the press?"

"Well Guv, you are better than me at all that PR stuff," the DI replied to his senior. "It might sound better coming from someone higher in rank given the circumstances." Underneath, he was thinking, 'please, please say yes you will come down.'

"Okay. Give them the usual verbal rubbish and tell them an official statement will be at," DCI Tomlinson looked at his watch. "Two PM. That gives me just enough time to write something and get down there."

"Great. I'll meet you outside the front entrance."

"Good. You can also give me an update then," the DCI said sarcastically knowing that they were no closer to catching the suspect now than they were yesterday.

The line went dead as DI Thorpe continued his walk towards the media who were all standing two or three deep behind the cordon which was guarded by two uniformed PC's. The questions came thick and fast as DI Thorpe announced, "Ladies and Gentlemen, there will be an official press conference at the front of the courthouse at 2pm. Until then no questions will be answered. Thank you." He walked away. He just wanted today to end.

1400 hrs. DCI Tomlinson appeared from his car which he had parked inside the Guildhall car park due to the attendance of the emergency vehicles in front of the court. He was immediately met by DI Thorpe who acknowledged him and headed over to the press who were all gathered at the side of the coffee shack.

"Ladies and Gentlemen. Thank you for holding off until now. For those of you that don't know me, I am Detective Chief Inspector Tomlinson. Please leave your questions until after my statement. There was a shooting incident at the Combined Court building this morning resulting in the deaths of three persons and the serious injury of one other. Further to this there was a fire which was started by an unknown person in the detention block and in pursuit of the suspect, one firearms officer was knocked down by the getaway vehicle and unfortunately did not regain consciousness. Everyone else managed to escape although most of the prisoners have been taken to hospital as a precaution due to the smoke inhalation."

"Do you have a suspect?" one of the reporters shouted out but was ignored by the DCI because it happened to be part of his next statement.

"The suspect is called Jeremy Cornelius-Johnson, male around 5'10", medium although strong build. He was last seen in the Teats Hill and Cattedown districts where he stole a van. He is wanted for questioning as a suspect for multiple deaths that have occurred in the City and outskirts over a course of several years. The man is armed and extremely unstable and dangerous, so we urge members of the public not to approach him but if seen, dial 999 immediately. My Officers will give each of you a photofit of the suspect.

DI Thorpe edged himself forward realising that the DCI hadn't had any direct intervention in the case so far and therefore may struggle with any answers to questions put to him. "Right, we will be taking a limited number of questions."

"Is it true that the suspect works at the Courts?" asked the reporter from the Daily Mail.

"I can tell you that the suspect was a Court Clerk here at the combined courts." DI Thorpe pointed to one of the reporters from one of the TV channels.

"Exactly how many deaths have been confirmed as committed by the suspect?"

The DCI intervened. "We are still waiting on forensic evidence to be returned at this moment in time so we cannot confirm anything at the moment."

The Sky News reporter reacted to the DCI's answer. "Well, you must have some idea, Detective Chief Inspector. What two, three, ten, twenty?"

"I cannot answer you at this time," the DCI repeated.

"So, do we have a serial killer on the loose in the City?" the BBC intervened, not wanting to be outdone by their rival TV company.

DI Thorpe jumped in once more. "We cannot confirm the number of deaths attributed to Jeremy Cornelius-Johnson at the moment, so we are unable to clarify him as a serial killer."

"Why haven't the Police managed to catch the suspect so far?"

DI Thorpe thought he would answer this question as diplomatically as possible so did so before the DCI could put his spin on the answer. "He had access to various resources that kept him one step ahead of us."

"Is it true that your team is working with the Sun reporter Jack Dempsey?" asked the rival reporter from the Daily Mirror, who was annoyed that the Police were going against all protocols by allowing a reporter inside their domain with access to investigatory information.

As the DCI cleared his throat to answer, DI Thorpe cut in quickly as if to justify his reason for allowing the reporter access to confidential information. "Mr Dempsey has been helping us due to the fact that he was friends with one of the possible victims and therefore could give us information that we didn't know."

"Thank you. That will be all the questions," the DCI shouted as he ruffled his papers and headed back to his car quickly followed by DI Thorpe as more unanswered questions were shouted from the media crowd.

Jeremy was fleeing and had travelled through the lanes to Deep Lane and headed over towards Sparkwell and then turning up towards Lee Moor where the clay pits rose either side of him at times and were huge like silver-grey mountains. But he didn't take notice as his mind was set on getting somewhere elsewhere no one would suspect that he would return to. The scene of a murder. Burrator. He could ditch the van and hide there because there was so much woodland around that he could more or less disappear. The Police would be looking for him in the City, he thought to himself. He was always going to justify his thinking more than any of them. He was taking in the beauty of the moorland. His Mum and Dad used to take him to Cadover Bridge when he was a child and let him swim in the river. He remembered hiding under the bridge and his Father getting really upset with him for doing so. He looked back on it now and wondered if his parents truly were worried and actually loved him. He stopped momentarily in the deserted car park which was usually full of kids and an ice cream van especially for the purpose of the children pestering their parents for lollies and cornets. He drove on.

The turning for Sheepstor village on the right and the land started to get filled with wild ponies. They calmed him, although he remembered getting bit by one as he had fed them and ran out of apples and carrots that he had given them. Vicious bastard, he thought to himself as he drove down the hill towards the village.

It was noticeably quiet with not a soul in sight as he headed over through the lanes going through the village and over towards the dam itself with its stone construction built when things were constructed to last. He would get rid of the van and then walk around the dam on the mixture of footpaths and roads, trying to stay hidden from the outside world. He turned right to head up to the other end of the reservoir and after a few minutes saw the smaller narrow humped bridge which went over a stream. But he didn't want to go that way. He turned left and headed up to Drakes Moat. As he reached the top of the hill, he headed right on the dirt track and took the van to a parking space which was hidden in a recess from the mud track. Somewhere that the van couldn't be seen from the road.

Grabbing his bag, he stepped out, locked the van and started to walk up the path which ran adjacent to the moat. It was rumoured that the moat came from a spring and Sir Francis Drake had ordered the moat to be built in order that it could go to Drake's reservoir near the Plymouth University to supply parts of Plymouth with fresh water. That was what his Father had told him some years ago anyway.

'Are you doubting me, boy?'

He was still around, Jeremy thought to himself as he tried his hardest to dismiss and ignore his Fathers voice. As he exited the forest, he turned downwards on the right to the path that would take him to the car park at the far end of the reservoir and the entrance to the footpath beside it which was well hidden by the trees and undergrowth. Ten minutes and he would be there, although he felt safe walking along the path this side of the road. He had been there before, and it was only used by hikers and there wouldn't be many of those out now.

Back at the combined courts, DS Carter and Jack Dempsey had joined the DI who was angry that the DCI had left the team at the crime scene after the press conference as soon as he finished without a word of praise for their hard work so far. They were so close. He was on the run.

The DI saw his DS stood next to the reporter and walked over towards him. "From now on, anywhere we go to try and find him, we go in force. There is safety in numbers."

"I've got a hunch," Jack said, his mind working that little bit faster all the time. He had been right so far, so there should be no problem with the two detectives listening to him.

"Go on," DI Thorpe said importantly as he felt now willing to listen to any ideas.

"There were a couple of people who could give evidence if this case ever went to court. The Manageress of the book store Jenny Baker and the Priest at Burrator Father Reed." Jack was hoping that he was right with his latest hunch just as he had been before, well with the help of his sister.

"But they weren't on his picture board," DS Carter added confusingly.

"They could have been if the Police hadn't raided his home preventing him from returning there," Jack stated with a hint that he was right, and it was worth investigating. If they didn't, he would do it himself. "We know that he was headed in the wrong direction to remain in the town. I tell you. He is on his way back to Burrator."

The DI thought silently for a few moments whilst staring Jack in the eye and wondering what was going through his head.

"If he was the photographer up on the hill when myself and Father Reed were looking at the crime scene where Byron Maddocks was killed, he would not only have my photograph but that of the Priest as well."

"Well, I think Jack could be right, Guv," snapped DS Carter whilst looking at him and nodding his head at the reporter's common sense. "But it is also a good place to hide."

The DI looked at them both then looked at the floor as if he were searching for inspiration but also the right answer. He didn't want to get a bad report on his retirement and finish on a dull note. But they had nothing else. Jack's hunch did make sense. "Okay," he said. "Let's get these two people protected. Two ARV's, one to Burrator with us and the other to take Jenny Baker to a safe location until it is all clear."

"Good call, Guv," DS Carter replied feeling nothing but respect for his senior officer.

"We need every available officer on this. Get Bolton and Hardy, DS Ayres and ADC Gibbons down here. Ayres and Gibbons can arrange the protection for Jenny Baker as there is less of a risk for her under the circumstances." DI Thorpe looked around for the Sergeant in charge of the Armed Response. "Any idea where SFO Morrison is located at this moment?"

"Yes, Guv. He is over handling the situation with AFO Lord who was killed earlier.

"We need him and his team even though they have had a tragedy today. Can you ask him to come over, Mike?"

"Yes, Guv," DS Carter replied as he headed over to the side of the court building.

DI Thorpe looked at Jack Dempsey with some seriousness now that DS Carter had gone. "I do hope you are right Jack."

Chapter 23

The convoy of Police vehicles fronted by the ARV headed towards Burrator as fast as they could with blues and two's echoing in the early evening sky. Traffic stood aside as the drivers realised there must be something going on due to the number of Police vehicles passing them. The ARV van and several unmarked and marked Police cars raced towards the dam.

DS Carter had telephoned Father Reed who for his own safety had locked him and his family inside the church. God will look after them, he exclaimed.

Residents came out to see what the commotion was about as the convoy turned left into the last road before they would hit Burrator dam and reservoir. Jack Dempsey was in the back of the unmarked vehicle being driven by DS Carter. "That's a beautiful sky," he said as he looked over the horizon at Sheepstor. "A deep shade of red and not a cloud or hint of blue anywhere."

"Let's hope tomorrow is a good day for everyone," DS Carter replied. "This has to end if your theory is right." The cavalcade began to slow ad instantly the detectives noticed that the armed officers decamped and provided cover with a perimeter around the arriving vehicles. SFO Morrison waved at the arriving Police vehicles to give them the all-clear and they all decamped from their respective vehicles.

"He hid up there in the rocks when he was taking photographs of us," Jack commented staring up to the left.

DI Thorpe walked over to them both. "I have India nine-nine on its way to scope the area from the sky. If he is here, we need to pin point him. It's a big area. There are going to be two armed officers each side of the dam just in case he is near and wants a gunfight."

"Has anyone gone over to the Church, Guv?" DS Carter asked in a serious tone because he was concerned for Father Reed.

The DI nodded. Then he looked at the water in the reservoir glimmering under the blood red sky and making it seem like the water was red. He only wished he had the time to take a photograph of the phenomenon. "There's the helicopter now." He took his radio in his hand. "DI Thorpe to India nine-nine."

"India nine-nine," came the reply.

"We are looking for a white transit van. It should be somewhere in the area. Any movement from a lone male in the area as we need to target a smaller location."

"Will do," came the reply. "India nine-nine out." The pilot decided to follow the edge of the reservoir in a clockwise direction at a safe height just in case the gunman was going to fire at them.

"He could be anywhere around here," DS Carter exclaimed whilst quickly scanning the area and making a gesture with both hands.

"I think he will stay close to the dam. Don't they always say that a killer returns to the scene of a crime?" Jack joined DS Carter in looking around, trying to notice any strange glare of reflection that may occur, but it was difficult under the blood red sky.

"India nine-nine to DI Thorpe. We have sighting of a white van parked north-west of the reservoir close to Drakes Moat. Looks like he has tried to hide the van on a dirt track. There are no signs of any movement."

DI Thorpe walked over to SFO Morrison to tell him the news. "India nine-nine has found what they think to be the white van. I'm going to send DC Bolton and ADC Hardy up to check it out. Can we have some armed response as well?" He looked over in the direction of the hovering helicopter that looked the size of a toy in the distant sky. "It's over by Drake's Moat where the helicopter is currently hovering."

"Washington. Murphy." SFO Morrison shouted over to two of his team. "We need to provide cover. The van has been sighted over by the helicopter."

"DC Bolton," the DI ordered knowing that ADC Hardy would just follow his mentor's lead.

"Guv."

"You and ADC Hardy go with these armed officers and check out a white van that has been sighted by India nine-nine," the DI ordered. They will make sure it is safe and then we need transportation back to the forensics lab for any evidence."

"We will see to that Guv," DC Bolton replied, nodding to his young trainee whom he took to have heard the order. "Come on Ben."

Jack Dempsey's thoughts were deep as he overheard the DI mention about the van. "Don't you think that the van parked in that direction is just a decoy?" he asked DS Carter. "If he is after the priest, the church is in the village on the other side of the dam."

"You could be right," DS Carter replied as he saw the sense in the reporter's madness."

DC Bolton looked at his trainee. "I know where it is. I take the kids up there on my days off in the summer and we race their toy boats from one end to the other of the moat. There is a big parking recess that digs into the hill. There, turn left here, he said to the armed officer driving the car. It's up the top of the hill on the right."

The helicopter saw the car approaching and headed off to continue its search for the suspect around the reservoir hovering over several places where their body heat scanner picked up something, which turned out to be an animal of some kind. But they didn't need to use the scanner for much longer. A silhouette appeared on the dry bank of the reservoir looking up at the helicopter. The pilots were unsure whether this was their man, but it was soon confirmed as he raised his hands and pointed at the chopper with a handgun and then began to fire. The pilot took evasive action banking to the right over the water. If the gunman had hit the chopper and they had to crash land for any reason, it would be easier and safer in water.

"India nine-nine to DI Thorpe."

There was a momentary pause before the DI answered. "We have a sighting of a possible suspect on your right-hand side as you look from the dam. Suspect is firing at the helicopter. We do not appear to have sustained any damage, but we will be finding a place to land to check things out before we return to base."

"Okay, thank you India nine-nine. Out." He turned to look at the search team and shouted whilst pointing in the direction of the mud bank, "Listen up! We have a sighting on the right-hand side on the mud bank of the reservoir. We have to move fast but armed officers will be leading. Let's go get this son of a bitch!"

SFO Morrison quickly gathered members of his team placing two at the rear of the search party and five in the front, weapons cocked and ready to use. They hopped over the fence and slowly walked up the at the side of the water spreading themselves out as the green woodland widened to the road on the far right, checking every potential hiding place along the way. The dog handler joined them, and barking filled the area as 'Torpedo' the German Shepherd became ready for action. He started sniffing everywhere and trying to pick up some sort of scent.

DS Carter and Jack Dempsey went side by side on the end of the search party looking desperately around. "Mike, I think we should head over towards the church. So far he has organised a decoy with the van. What if this is just another decoy and he has crossed the road?"

The two men looked at each other as DS Carter said, "I think you could be right." He looked over to the DI who was busy directing the search team and indicating points where he could be hiding. "Guv?"

The DI nodded his head upwards in a silent response. "Mike," he replied whilst still checking that every nook and cranny was being searched efficiently.

"Jack and I are going to head over to the church. We both have a suspicious feeling about this."

"Okay," the DI replied. "Stay safe and don't be heroes!" The last thing the DI needed was another dead Police Officer even if the last one wasn't on his team but killed in the course of duty for an operation that the DI was controlling. He watched as Carter and Dempsey walked over towards the road which led to Sheepstor village.

"I hope you are right about this," DS Carter said to his friend. "We are taking a terrible risk."

"I know," Dempsey replied walking as fast as he could up over the brow of the hill and thankful that the rest was downhill, although the downhill bit seemed to go on forever. "I've been right about most things so far," he said as they saw light at the end of the tunnel and the end of the road came into their sight.

"Which way is the Church?" DS Carter asked as he slowed in his tracks.

"Left. We go left."

"Are you sure?" Carter asked as he tried to get his bearings in the little village. It was different in a car because you didn't take in the sights as you passed through a small little village to get to the other side.

"Yes," Dempsey replied. "I was over there remember looking at Byron's rented property." The church came into sight as they walked around the corner, but they just froze in their tracks. There was a man at the entrance gate with a gun in his hand. Carter and Dempsey quickly put their backs into the hedgerow in order that they wouldn't be seen.

DS Carter grabbed his mobile phone and dialled the DI. Softly and quietly, he whispered, "Guv, he is here. At the entrance to the church graveyard. He is looking at the two officers guarding the church."

"Okay Mike. I will get the team diverted over there immediately," the DI said with some urgency as he ended the call. "Okay, listen up. We have a sighting of our man. He is over in Sheepstor village at the entrance to the church. He is armed and dangerous so let the armed officers take him. I want radio and mobile silence. Let's go get him!"

The team stopped their search and changed direction heading over to the route that Dempsey and Carter had taken minutes earlier, the rush reminding the DI of the Boxing Day sales where everyone rushed to get in the shops for the bargains.

ADC Hardy was next on the telephone to the DI. "Sir, DC Bolton and I have found evidence of explosive substance in the van."

"Shit," the DI replied. "Any idea what it is?"

"No," Hardy replied cautiously. "But there is an empty box for some type of timing device. It could be armed and ready to explode."

The DI closed the call. Jeremy was going out with a bang. He continued walking and his mobile rang again. He looked at the display. Todd Armstrong from forensics. "Hello Todd. What have you got for me?"

"Problems, Guv," Todd replied with concern and urgency in his voice. "None of the DNA matches those of the kills."

"What?" snapped the DI. "That's impossible surely?"

"Both myself and Rachel have taken samples at most of the crime scenes, so we can't be wrong. We took a sample of DNA in Jeremy's special room from the computer keyboard and the printer. We also took fingerprints from the photographs on the pin boards. There are two different types of DNA evidence."

"So, are you telling me that there could be two killers Todd?" The DI had a worrying feeling that all this time they had been played because the killer, or killers as the case may be, were always one step ahead.

"Yes, there could be. But one could be innocent. They could be twin brothers. I'm getting Rachel to check out the records now."

"Okay. Let me know as soon as you have any further information." After ending the call to Todd, he dialled DS Carter. "Mike, we have a problem."

"I don't like the sound of that," Carter replied concerningly.

"Todd Armstrong has just called me. The DNA points towards the fact that there could be two of them. Possibly twin brothers."

"You are kidding, right?" Carter snapped negatively.

"No. The DNA profiles just do not match to one person according to Forensics. Todd has been doing all the tests on the dead bodies including the ones found buried in the garden."

"This could be bigger than we originally thought, Guv," Carter said. "How do we know if we have Jeremy here or his twin brother?"

"I have met the one who is the Court Clerk," Jack interrupted inquisitively by listening in on the call between the two Detectives.

"All we know is one has spent most of his latter life in a secure psychiatric unit and is mentally challenged, diagnosed with schizophrenia. The other is Jeremy who has obviously gotten away with it." The DI checked his watch. "Anyway, I'm nearly there."

Suddenly the armed response officers came behind the pair who were still hiding in the bushes hanging over the wall of the church. "AFO's May, Johnson, Tyler and France. "Where is the suspect?"

"Around there at the church gate," Carter replied with some importance in his voice. "He has a weapon in his hands, although he doesn't appear to be using it at the moment."

AFO May held up his hand with three fingers upright and counted down by lowering each one. Then the four officers stormed around the corner. "Armed Police. Stay where you are!" He ran as close as he could towards the suspect whilst raising his telescopic sight to his eye and placing his finger ready on the trigger. "Throw the weapon to the side and get down on the ground! I said Get down on the ground!" The suspect wasn't complying with his orders. "We will shoot if you do not get on the ground and spread your legs and arms!"

The fugitive looked totally confused as though he wasn't understanding a word of what was being said. He tilted his head and he smiled psychotically at the armed officers, his eyes looking right through them as though they weren't there, or they were his friends.

"Get down on the floor! Lose the gun!"

The gunman didn't comply. He saw the rifles aimed at him and started to panic. With speed he raised his hand which was holding his handgun.

The four officers didn't take any chances but immediately reacted, each firing at the gunman several times. His body fell backwards, his eyes giving one final stare at his executioners. AFO May looked at the body on the floor, with zero movement and with his rifle still ready to shoot moved forward slowly to check for a pulse in case he needed to radio for an ambulance. But he guessed the outcome before he moved forward. No movement, so he knelt down and checked his carotid artery in his neck, no sign of life. Jeremy was dead. AFO May clicked his radio. "Target suspect is down. No sign of life!"

DI Thorpe finally made it to the scene. He was cut short as Rachel Clarke from forensics rang.

"Guv. I went through the electoral role from the past ten years and also checked the medical records. Jeremy Cornelius-Johnson is one of twins. His brother is called Tristram. He is schizophrenic and was in a secure unit until his escape whilst attending his parents funeral two years ago. He has never been found."

"Thank you Rachel," The DI said sorrowfully shaking his head and closing the call. He then looked at his sergeant. "What's going on Mike?"

"Jeremy, if it is Jeremy, has been fatally shot by the armed response team." SFO Morrison and the three firearms officers who arrived with the DI provided the cover for all the Police and civilians present, scanning the area for any further criminals. Just when they thought it was safe, the DI remembered what ADC Hardy had told him.

"Explosives," he said now realising the urgency of the situation and wondering why Jeremy didn't go in the church to finish the job with his handgun but just stood at the gate two hundred metres away. "Shit! Get down!" he ordered. Too late. The church exploded with some force as the powerful explosive device that Jeremy had made forced the heavy stone from the church sideways and up in the air with most landing and sometimes rolling further on the ground. The flames instantly burnt high, and the black smoke rose quickly into the air as the wooden pillars and roof supports took the brunt of the explosion and started to burn.

The two officers guarding the church ran around, their bodies burning and each one finally fell to the ground, burnt to smithereens. The priest and his family gone. Their God had decided it was their time to leave the earth. They had no chance of survival in the inferno.

DI Carter shook his head. He looked at Jack Dempsey. "Well at least you have got your story, Jack."

DI Thorpe stood beside them and looked at the dead body of the suspect. It could be either of the twins.

Jack Dempsey shook his head. "I can tell you now, that is not the Jeremy that I met in the court."

"If you are right Jack, then he is still on the loose," DS Carter mentioned as he worried about their safety. The Church had gone up in flames. Just what was he possible of next?"

The DI didn't care. Now was the time to retire.

Epilogue

The lonely figure stood on the edge of the reservoir looking into the water and then up to the beautiful sky, it's redness reminding him of the blood of his kills. Over the trees he could see the flames burning high after hearing the explosion, the orangey-red heat adding to the glory of the early evening sky. Tomorrow was going to be a good day, he told himself.

Jeremy Cornelius-Johnson had put his brother out of his misery. The man had the IQ of a ten-year-old and was severely mentally challenged. His father had made him that way. It could have made Jeremy the same with all the ridicule and lack of love that came their way.

It placed right him at the church gates, give him a toy pistol and tell him to shoot any birds that came into the graveyard. Tristram Cornelius-Johnson could about manage that.

Did Jeremy worry about his brother's death? No. He had no conscience.

'At last, you are a man, son.' His father said.

Also available from Stephen Knight

Available in eBook and Paperback from Amazon
ISBN : 979-8664192926

Available in eBook and Paperback from Amazon
ISBN : 979-8553122140

www.stephensamuelknight.co.uk

Printed in Great Britain
by Amazon